My Wicked Marquess

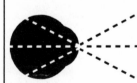

This Large Print Book carries the
Seal of Approval of N.A.V.H.

MY WICKED MARQUESS

GAELEN FOLEY

THORNDIKE PRESS

A part of Gale, Cengage Learning

GALE
CENGAGE Learning

Detroit • New York • San Francisco • New Haven, Conn • Waterville, Maine • London

GALE
CENGAGE Learning

Copyright © 2009 by Gaelen Foley.
Thorndike Press, a part of Gale, Cengage Learning.

ALL RIGHTS RESERVED
This is a work of fiction. Names, characters, places, and incidents are products of the author's imagination or are used fictitiously, and are not construed as real. Any resemblance to actual events, locales, organizations, or persons, living or dead, is entirely coincidental.
Thorndike Press® Large Print Romance.
The text of this Large Print edition is unabridged.
Other aspects of the book may vary from the original edition.
Set in 16 pt. Plantin.
Printed on permanent paper.

LIBRARY OF CONGRESS CATALOGING-IN-PUBLICATION DATA

Foley, Gaelen.
   My wicked marquess / by Gaelen Foley.
     p. cm. — (Thorndike Press large print romance)
   ISBN-13: 978-1-4104-2182-1 (alk. paper)
   ISBN-10: 1-4104-2182-1 (alk. paper)
    1. Aristocracy (Social class)—England—Fiction. 2. England—Social life and customs—19th century—Fiction. 3. Large type books. I. Title.
   PS3556.O3913M9 2009
   813'.54—dc22   2009034551

Published in 2009 by arrangement with Avon Books, an imprint of HarperCollins Publishers.

Printed in the United States of America
1 2 3 4 5 6 7 13 12 11 10 09

Any fool can tell the truth, but it requires a man of some sense to know how to lie well.
— Samuel Butler

September 1, 1815
Dear Lord Rotherstone,

If you are reading this, then I must welcome you gladly back to London after your long and perilous journeys. You charged me with no small task in your absence, but I have forged on without ceasing and now am pleased to present you with the fruits of my labor. After months of making all the inquiries you requested, also using the unusual research methods that you imparted to my understanding, I have assembled the list you desired — five of London's most sought-after aristocratic brides for your consideration.

Rest assured that all five excellent young ladies meet Your Lordship's exacting criteria of health, youth, breeding, beauty, pleasant temperament, good family, and above all, a stainless reputation. Your prospective brides' names are as follows:

1. Miss Zoe Simms — age nineteen, excellent singing voice, highly accomplished. Niece of the Duke of Rowland.

2. Miss Anna Bright — age eighteen, daughter of the Bishop of Norwell; a budding essayist, first published work titled "Virtues for a Young Lady."

3. Lady Hypatia Glendale — age twenty-one, known as a spirited sportswoman and huntress, rides to the hounds.

4. Miss Adora Walker — age sixteen. Though barely out of the schoolroom, considered the greatest beauty Society has seen in many years, thus a coveted prize.

5. The Honorable Miss Daphne Starling — age twenty, a leading belle of the ton, known for her kindness to strangers — but problematical, my lord. Beware! (See Post Script.)

I am at your service to discuss my findings in greater detail, though I surmise Your Lordship will wish to continue the investigation in person from this point onward. All my files on this matter are available as soon as you wish me to send them. (As you directed, I assembled a file on each young lady containing more detailed biographical information, as well as upcoming social calendars and typical weekly schedules. This should more easily allow Your Lordship to observe each girl at your own convenience.)

Awaiting your further instructions — and again, my lord, with all the joy of England's great victory at the end of this dreadful war — welcome home.

Your servant respectfully,
Oliver Smith, Esquire.
Solicitor & Gentleman-of-Business

Post Script: About Lady Number Five, sir — You may wish to cross Daphne Starling off your list straightaway, for over the past few weeks, there has been an unfortunate whiff of scandal concerning this young lady.

Due to her recent refusal of a suitor, a leading dandy by the name of Lord Albert Carew, I fear Miss Starling has begun to gain a reputation as a jilt.

CHAPTER 1

She entered the realm of lost souls in a single horse gig with her footman and maid. Leaving the safety of the well-traveled Strand, she crossed into the shadowy labyrinth.

Her horse tossed its head in protest, but obeyed William's urging, walking nervously into the narrow lane between the crowded buildings. Above them, half obscured by the thick morning fog, the great blocks of tenement houses loomed, as forbidding as medieval towers.

The clip-clopping of her trusty gelding's hooves echoed everywhere off grimy brick and stone, but little else stirred at this hour. The rookery came alive only at night. To be sure, they were far from the green, sculpted grounds of her father's elegant villa now.

This was no place for a lady.

But these days, however, what the world thought of Daphne Starling mattered to her less and less.

Losing her reputation was proving to be

oddly liberating. It had given her a new perspective on things, and refocused her attention on what mattered most.

Like getting the children out of this nightmare world.

Wraiths of mist floated past her small, open carriage, which was loaded with sacks of supplies that she had collected for the orphanage since last week's visit. Though she had been coming here for some time, the conditions of the rookery still shocked her.

A stray dog with protruding ribs scavenged for a meal in a pile of refuse in the alley. An unhealthy odor fouled the air; neither fresh breeze nor sun could penetrate the tight, crooked alleys. People here dwelled in constant twilight due to the closeness of the buildings, their broken windows like the broken lives of all those who had simply given up. Here and there the homeless slept: inert, shapeless bundles strewn by the gutter.

A dark spell of despair hung over this place. Daphne shuddered, drawing her pelisse a bit closer around her shoulders. Perhaps she should not be here — sometimes she felt as though she was living a double life.

But she knew how it felt to be orphaned young. At least she still had a loving father, a safe home, enough to eat. It was Mama, anyway, who had early ingrained in her the duties of a gentlewoman toward the less fortunate.

More importantly, she knew deep in her heart that if *someone* did not go into the dark places of the world and give a little love to those who had no one, then life was truly meaningless. Especially the pampered life that she had always known as the only child of a viscount with a large fortune and an ancient title.

Still, however privileged she was by birth, she did not ever want to become one of those selfish, artificial creatures like some of those in the ton who had been turning against her so easily of late.

A fleeting thought of Lord Albert Carew's smirking face flashed through her mind, but every time she thought of his oh-so-"romantic" proposal, she wanted to scream. *The leading dandy and the leading belle — a perfect match! What do you say?* Albert's arrogance made him blissfully unaware of just how obnoxious he generally was. There was only one true love in Lord Albert Carew's life: himself. Daphne gritted her teeth and kicked her jilted suitor out of her mind as William made the turn into Bucket Lane, where the dreary orphanage sat amid the squalor.

Bucket Lane, or "Slops Bucket" Lane, as the rough locals jokingly called it, was a street where sin vied openly with virtue. Unfortunately, darkness seemed to be winning the battle here.

Though a small city church still made a stand at the end of the lane, one last crumbling stone angel looking on in dismay, there was a large raucous brothel on the corner, a pub across the street, and a gaming house a few doors down from that.

Last month there had been a murder in the alley.

Two Bow Street officers had come by asking questions, but no one could be found who would cooperate, and the lawmen had not been back.

Life in Bucket Lane had gone on as usual.

"Tell me again what we're doing here, miss?" her maid, Wilhelmina, peeped as they proceeded down the lane.

"Hunting adventure, I reckon," Wilhelmina's twin brother, William grumbled.

Though there might be a grain of truth to the charge, Daphne looked askance at him. The country-bred pair were known in the Starling residence as the "the two Willies." They were good-hearted and exceedingly loyal, as their accompanying her each week to the orphanage proved.

"Look to the window, William." Daphne nodded upward as she waved a gloved hand in greeting. "They're why we're here."

Little faces full of excitement were peering down through all the grimy windows; little hands waved back.

He harrumphed. "I suppose you're right, miss."

Daphne sent her footman a bolstering smile. "Don't worry, Will. We won't be long. Perhaps an hour."

"Half an hour?" he pleaded as the gig rolled up to the orphanage. "We don't have Davis today, miss."

"True." She usually brought two footmen with her, but today — quite deliberately, no doubt — her stepmother had insisted that burly footman Davis stay at home to help re-arrange the furniture in the parlor.

Again.

Busybody Penelope was the queen of the meaningless chore, as well as the queen of the meddlers.

The whole Albert debacle had been her stepmother's scheme from the start, a brazen bit of matchmaking in her eagerness to get Daphne out of the house.

"Very well," she conceded reluctantly. "I will do my best to keep to half an hour."

William gave her a grateful look and set the brake.

"Miss Starling! Miss Starling!" a high-pitched voice cried as Daphne stepped down from the gig. She looked over and saw running toward her one of the older boys who had left the orphanage last year.

"Jemmy!" He was thin and threadbare, but still capable of a sunny grin. She greeted him

15

with a motherly hug. "Oh, I've been wondering about you! Where have you been?"

"Here and there, miss!"

She grasped his shoulders and saw that he was nearly as tall as she was. "You've grown so big since I last saw you! How old are you these days?"

"Just turned thirteen!" he said proudly.

She smiled at him. "Any chance you've changed your mind about an apprenticeship? I know of a wheelwright's shop that's looking for an honest boy."

He scoffed; she frowned sternly, and he instantly remembered what few manners he possessed. "Sorry, miss." He lowered his head. "I'll think about it."

"You do that." She was not yet ready to call Jemmy one of her failures, but he was heading down a bad road. He had run away from two posts she had found him already, enamored with the "easy life" of the criminals he looked up to. "Don't break my heart, Jem. If the law catches you making mischief, they'll show you small pity. They don't care if you're just a boy. They'll still send you off to Australia."

"I ain't done nothin' wrong!" he cried with the sparkle of a born charmer, nor was he a bad actor, either.

"I almost believe you." She eyed him archly, then she noticed the man posted across the street as the local gang's lookout. The scruffy thug was smoking a cigar and leaning in the doorway of the pub, staring at her.

He tipped his hat when she looked over, and sent her a broad, leering grin that was more threatening than friendly. Tensing at his stare, she realized she had better get inside. She nodded back primly, however, not daring to show disrespect in this place.

They generally did not bother her because they knew she was not here to cause trouble, but to help their own cast-off children. The small residents of the Foundling House were classed as orphans, but while some of their parents actually *were* dead, most of them had merely been abandoned. Daphne did not know which was worse.

The only thing she knew for certain was that she had to get these children out of here as soon as possible.

She had been working on finding better accommodations for the orphanage for the past year and a half, lobbying all her erstwhile friends to contribute to the charity.

She had even found an ideal property for sale, an old boarding school, that could have housed the orphanage, but despite her best efforts, the sum still fell far short.

Well, I had better come up with something soon, she thought as she and Wilhelmina each lifted a sack off the back of the gig. The youngsters grew up so fast around here, and if no one intervened, the boys, like Jemmy, were almost destined to become members of the brutish local gang.

An even worse fate, too horrible to contemplate, lay in store for the precious little girls. Daphne sent a look of hatred over her shoulder toward the brothel on the corner. In her view, it was worse than the gin house, for what went on in there made a mockery of love.

Love was the only hope these children had — or anyone else, for that matter.

Well, by God, none of *her* little girls was going to end up in that house of flesh. She would just have to work harder. She must find a way.

Above all, she could not permit Albert to do any more damage to her reputation, for she understood full well that if he succeeded in turning high society against her, then her fund-raising efforts to move the orphanage to a safer location would all be for naught.

The children were depending on her. In a word, they had no one else. With that, she heaved the sack over her shoulder, summoned up a carefree smile for the little ones' sake, and went in to a loud greeting of high-pitched cheers that warmed the very cockles of her heart.

What in the hell is she doing in there? Bride Choice Number Five continued to puzzle him. *Half an hour.* He checked his fob to confirm the time, then snapped it shut again.

Shaking his head slightly to himself, Max St. Albans, the Marquess of Rotherstone, slid his watch back into the breast pocket of his black waistcoat and resumed surveillance.

In the interests of careful research, he had tracked her to this godforsaken hellhole in the very armpit of London, and had taken up a position across the street from her destination.

With his small pocket spyglass nosing through the tawdry curtains of the brothel's third-floor window, he ignored the harlot nibbling on his ear.

"You've got the room for the hour, love, and all that comes with it. Are you sure you don't want to play?"

"Positive," he murmured, studying Miss Starling's waiting carriage and the brawny hayseed of a footman that she had left holding her horses.

Before going in, strangely, Miss Starling had turned and looked straight up at the brothel, as if she could feel him watching her. An electrifying thrill had run the length of Max's body in response. The deep brim of her bonnet had hidden her face from his view; of course, she was wise not to put her charms on display in this place. The plain, beige walking dress and the deep poke bonnet both served that purpose, no doubt. But the brief moment had left him all the more hungry for a look at her famed golden beauty.

For now, he deemed it wise to keep an eye on her solitary footman. God, that overgrown farm boy was out of his element here. *This* was supposed to be her protection? Even Max, who was trained in combat skills both exotic and mundane, did not come into a place like this lightly.

In the compact circle of his telescope, he could see the young manservant glancing uneasily around the cramped, dirty street. The sturdy country lad stood his ground faithfully, but he looked slightly terrified, as well he bloody might.

Fortunately, the more streetwise ragged boy whom Miss Starling had embraced remained on hand, perhaps for moral support, ready to speak up on the do-gooders' behalf, Max hoped, if any of his fellow ruffians bothered the trio.

The boy not only looked tougher than the footman, but also, Max thought with a twinge of sadness, rather reminded him of himself at that age. All threadbare clothes and attitude, empty pockets and a swagger full of bravado.

He, too, had grown up poor, but it had been genteel poverty, more a matter of shame than the kind of daily hunger that street boy was probably used to.

Still, studying the youngster, he could hardly believe he had been no older than that boy when the Order had first recruited him.

When his father had handed him over to be molded into . . . what he had become.

He thrust the past out of his mind. The damned thing was done; his medieval ancestor's blood oath was fulfilled; the Order's secret, savage war was won; at last it was time to get on with his own bloody life.

His first order of business as a private citizen, as he had long planned, was to clean up his family's tainted reputation, after a few generations of declining fortunes and wild Rotherstone ne'er-do-wells.

It wasn't going to be easy, especially after his longstanding charade as the decadent Grand Tourist. Thanks, moreover, to his involvement in the notorious Inferno Club, he was at a particular disadvantage in his new quest.

But, no matter. He knew how to woo human nature. He would soon have Society eating out of his hand, for he knew exactly what line of attack would deliver him to his desired destination with swiftest efficiency.

In a word: marriage.

The right sort of bride was the perfect instrument to help him begin reversing the dark fame of the Rotherstone lords. And so, a new hunt was on — this time, not for an enemy agent. His new mission was to find a wife.

Which did not at all explain what he was doing here.

From a strictly logical standpoint, he was just wasting his time. Obviously, he could not choose Daphne Starling, the last name on his handy list.

And yet, after reading her file, he had been unable to resist the temptation. He'd been compelled to come here today, merely to have a quick look at the girl.

There could be no harm in that, surely.

Once he had satisfied his curiosity, Max was sure he would go back home and make the right choice, probably the bishop's excessively virtuous daughter. Or, perhaps, the "spirited" horsewoman — he could not abide a shrinking violet. He would not pick the little sixteen-year-old, of course, since he was nearly old enough to be her father, but any of the others would do, as long as they weren't Daphne Starling.

One scandalous soul in the family would be quite enough, and that distinction already belonged to him. He needed a wife with a gleaming *good* reputation to counteract his own wicked one.

Personally, Max did not give a damn what anyone thought about him, but he was adamant that his future children not be semi-outcasts in the world as he had been. Repairing his clan's reputation meant giving his heirs every advantage in life. The great fortune that he had painstakingly built over the past decade was only half the equation:

Money alone could buy neither respect nor true belonging in London society. The great merchant families could attest to that.

No, it was key that he choose a wife, and a mother for his little future Rotherstones, who sprang from impeccable bloodlines and was a certified darling of the ton.

Until quite recently, Miss Starling had fit the bill. But now with her present troubles, Max mused, Oliver had been quite right in suggesting that he cross her off his bride list straightaway.

Max's initial interest in her was naught but a lark, anyway. At least that's what he kept telling himself. It had been sparked when he had turned over the bride list and had read his solicitor's postscript.

Max had been astonished, and then had laughed aloud to discover that her jilted suitor was none other than his boyhood arch-enemy.

Albert bloody Carew.

He shook his head in sardonic amusement, still staring out the window, waiting for her to come out of the orphanage, and ignoring the harlot, who was now massaging his shoulders and stroking his hair and doing everything in her power to try to get herself bedded.

Dear old Alby! *Ah, God.* Max would've liked to say that after twenty years, now a grown man, he would've forgotten all about his boyhood nemesis and their ferocious rivalry, but, unfortunately, he remembered him all too well.

The Carew brothers were the sons of the previous Duke of Holyfield; his obscenely wealthy neighbors had lived on the next estate out in the country where he had grown up in Worcestershire. Except for Hayden, the timid eldest, now the current duke, they had been a pack of little horrors growing up, and beating up on Max had been their favorite pastime.

It was a convenient sport for them, as well, since their palatial home had sat not far from his own father's crumbling country manor. Max had had to walk past the duke's land each day on his way to his old tutor's cottage.

Most days, he'd been ambushed near the cow pasture or by the old pine grove.

Albert, the second-born and leader of the younger ones, had been his particular nemesis. He shook his head wryly to recall their mighty battles — and his own stubborn pride. Though he was always outnumbered, Max had refused to take any alternative path to his tutor's house.

No wonder he had drawn the attention of the Order, with the warrior instinct of his Norman ancestors so obvious in him even as a boy.

Well, lucky for dear old Alby, vendettas

went against the Order's code. Obviously, he had long since parted with any hopes of juvenile revenge.

On the other hand, with all the serious weight of the war finally behind him, it was a luxury to indulge in trivial amusements. He couldn't help taking pleasure in hearing how the Starling girl had trounced the haughty Albert Carew. Oh, to have been a fly on the wall for that interview . . .

Competitive creature that he was, Max had instantly wondered if *he* might fare any better with this apparently choosy young lady.

But of course I would, he had thought at once. Youthful self-doubt was far behind him now.

Lord, it was tempting! The whole thing struck him as hilarious.

He had known at once he had to meet this girl. He had, at least, to dance with her in front of dear old Alby.

The Order might forbid revenge, but the code said nothing about giving a small twist to the knife that somebody else had plunged in.

So he had written back to his solicitor at once, requesting the file on Lady Number Five. Oliver had sent it over quickly, but when Max had poured himself a brandy and sat down to read it, he got so much more than he had bargained for.

Indeed, from the moment he had finished

reading her file, a strange breed of hope had taken hold of him.

He had read it through several times last night, familiarizing himself with every detail. One particular point that stood out in his mind was Miss Starling's nickname in Society as "the patron saint of newcomers."

She was known for befriending outsiders and those arriving in the frigid ton with few acquaintances. She took them under her wing, introduced them around, and made sure that they were included.

As a longtime outcast in the eyes of many, Max knew the value of such kindnesses.

Admittedly, he was intrigued. He had come today in part because he wanted to see her for himself. To find out firsthand who she was when she thought no one was looking.

There was still the trouble with her reputation, of course, but now that he knew Albert was involved, Max severely doubted that any of it was her fault. Knowing Albert's sneaky ways, Max saw at once that, failing to get what he wanted, that spoiled knave would not hesitate to stoop to slander to soothe his wounded vanity.

It was then that the fatal thought had struck. If Miss Starling was being unfairly attacked . . . *perhaps she needed help.*

Ah, damn, Max had thought with a sinking feeling and the irresistible pull of his innate need to help any damsel in distress. Especially when he, too, knew how it felt to be the target of Carew's malice.

From that moment, he could not get Daphne Starling out of his mind. The injustice of an innocent, kindhearted lady having her sacred honor maligned by the likes of Albert Carew gnawed at every chivalrous inch of his body, and had kept him awake last night for some time, staring at the ceiling, and rather wanting to hit someone.

So, here he was. Despite the fact that he knew full well the choice of a wife was too serious a matter to base on mere emotion.

It just went to show that Miss Daphne Starling had a worrisome effect on his brain. He had not even met her yet and somehow she already showed a talent for clouding his cool calculation.

No wonder he had chosen to observe her today from a safe, detached distance, so he could leave like a shadow. She'd never know he was there.

Of course, seeing this lawless rookery, he was doubly glad he had come. *Somebody* ought to be keeping an eye on the chit.

Honestly, didn't Lord Starling *know* the true condition of this place where his daughter conducted her charity work? Max did not at all approve.

Right on schedule, just as it said in her file, she had appeared for her weekly orphanage visit at her usual time — Friday morning at nine on the nose. Apparently Daphne Starling was the kind of person who liked her same routine.

Max liked a prompt woman. Then again, her reliable routine made it awfully easy for others around here to anticipate her arrival, and he did not like that at all.

Myriad questions about her revolved in his mind like the spheres on an astrolabe, but his painted hostess in the brothel's upper room was growing petulant at his lack of attention.

"Why are you watching that lady?" she demanded.

"Because," Max said slowly, sardonically, keeping his telescope aimed out the window, "I am considering marrying her."

The harlot let out a laugh of surprise, then twitched her skirts at him. "You're havin' me on!"

"No, no," he denied in an idle tone, though he was still not sure himself how seriously he meant it.

"Well, you've got a strange way of wooing, don't ye?"

"Old habits die hard," he said under his breath.

She gave him a teasing poke in the arm, not knowing what to make of him.

Few did.

"Come, sir, no woman likes a husband who spies on her!"

"I really don't care what she likes at this point."

"Cold," she chided.

"Practical," he countered, glancing over with a cynical smile. "One wants to know what one is getting into."

She snorted, eyeing him. "You can say that again."

"Relax. You'll get your money."

"By the look of you, I'd rather earn it, love." She sidled closer, hooking her hand over his shoulder. "Men like you don't come in here too often."

He looked askance at her, wondering if she meant trained killers for an organization that did not officially exist, or dressed-down marquesses with a centuries-old title. "Perhaps you should be glad of that," he said.

She fell silent, scanning his closed expression with a troubled look. "Who are you, anyway?"

Depends who you ask. He sent her a softly chiding glance. "Ah, you know better than to ask your clients that." He nodded toward the window. "Do you know her?"

"Miss Starling? Everyone 'round here knows her. Tryin' to save souls, I reckon. Waste o' time." Her short, disdainful laugh spoke volumes. "She don't approve o' the likes o' me."

"I don't suppose she does." Damn, how long did it take to pass out a few cheap toys?

29

Hardening himself against an echo from the distant past with a painful sense of kinship to the penniless, unloved children behind those dingy walls, he noted his growing restlessness while he waited for Daphne Starling to come out again.

Normally he had the patience of a spider, but he had already lost so much time . . . Twenty years of his life sacrificed to the Order.

He drummed his fingers on the window ledge, suppressing a growl. "How long does she usually stay?"

"How should I know?" the prostitute exclaimed, then bravely, she reached out and touched his arm. "I could entertain you while you wait."

Max paused; warily, he watched her make her move. It was the third-floor corner room of the brothel with its vantage point overlooking the street that he had wanted, not the woman that came with it. Nevertheless, he permitted himself a moment's fleeting enjoyment at her caress.

This, God help him, was what he was used to when it came to bed sport. From bored highborn adulteresses, to expensive courtesans, to the prettiest wenches in some low house of pleasure, it all boiled down to harlotry. For so long, he had had to content himself with anonymous liaisons of this sort, or for his work, seductions of a strictly calculated nature. Those usually left him wondering who exactly was the whore.

Now that the war was over, he was forced to face the fact that he was so painfully lonely. The bleak years had worn at his soul, the moving from place to place, always alone. He hungered to find something different. Something that didn't make him feel filthy afterward.

At the moment, however, that delicious filthy feeling was welcome and familiar, and as the harlot's hand traveled admiringly down his chest, Max was silent, tempted by vice, while his possible future wife polished up her diamond virtue at the orphanage across the street.

It was not, perhaps, the most auspicious start to any marriage.

In the next moment, a flicker of motion outside pulled his attention back to the window. Daphne Starling was coming out of the orphanage.

He brushed the harlot's hand away and leaned forward, staring more intensely past the drapes.

Walking out from between the heavy doors of the orphanage, Miss Starling was carrying her hat, and as she crossed to her carriage, followed by her maid, he caught a brief, dazzling glimpse of an angelic countenance.

Neither the dingy street nor the flat gray light of the overcast mid-morning could dim the incandescent gleam of her golden hair, as though she were a source of light unto herself.

Then she put on her bonnet again, hastening to cover up her beauty, before it drew unwanted attention in this place. Max did not even blink.

The harlot was watching her over his shoulder, as well. "Pretty," she conceded.

"Mm," he agreed in a noncommittal tone, but he continued staring out the window, mesmerized, his years of hungry isolation homing in on her.

Every motion brisk and businesslike, no idea she was under such close observation, Daphne Starling paused to confer with her servants, when suddenly they all heard a low shout from farther down the street.

Both the lady and her footman turned to look, as did Max.

" 'Hoy!"

Trouble.

Max narrowed his eyes as five criminal-looking types drifted out of the pub and approached her carriage.

The men of Bucket Lane were grinning broadly at her.

"Here's our angel o' mercy, ain't ye, love?"

"All them sacks o' goodies for the babes! Didn't ye bring any presents for us? I thinks I'm gonna cry!"

Max knit his brow, a scowl gathering. There was no sign of a constable, if they ever dared patrol here. He could practically hear her young footman's frightened gulp from where he sat, could almost feel Miss Starling's heartbeat pounding.

The men swaggered closer. "Come, lovey, ye must 'ave a little somethin' sweet left over for us."

"Like a kiss!"

"Aye!"

With a sharp glance over the entire area, Max assessed the situation. The men were coming toward her carriage from the front, blocking her way forward; the street was too narrow to turn the gig around fast enough for her to escape unmolested.

A distraction. If he pulled them away from her, she could race away from here and slip out past the church.

It could easily be accomplished, of course, but, damn, he had only intended to observe from a distance today. Now he was getting pulled in. Logic said he should not even be here, working at cross purposes with himself in considering a lady who was not in his best interest. But at the moment, he did not give a damn. She needed help, and after all, this sort of mischief was his specialty.

"Excuse me." Nudging the harlot aside, he rose and smoothed his black coat as he marched toward the door.

"Sir, wait!"

"What is it?" He paused, glancing back at

the harlot.

"Be careful with them! This street is their turf! Every shop here pays them protection money."

"Hm," Max answered. He nodded to her and walked on. On his way out, he tossed a few extra gold guineas on the ratty bed.

A moment later, striding down the shadowed hallway, he heard the woman's exclamation of delight from her room as she counted his donation.

With a hard gleam in his eyes, Max smoothly descended the brothel stairs. As he crossed the foyer, however, the mirror caught his eye. He paused.

Chameleon time.

Yes. An old, familiar game.

In the blink of an eye, he had transformed his demeanor, untying his cravat to dangle around his neck, unbuttoning his waistcoat, messing up his clothes, and rumpling his hair with a quick run of his fingers through it. He picked up an empty bottle of wine left behind on the window ledge after someone's drunken revelries the night before.

Damn, he thought, eyeing his changed reflection, now he surely looked the part of the debauched, pleasure-seeking Grand Tourist known to the world as the ne'er-do-well Marquess of Rotherstone.

Not the introduction to Daphne Starling that he would have liked. First impressions could be lasting. But it did not signify. She was in danger, and he had no choice but to intervene.

Taking out his coin purse, he loosened the strings with a slight grimace of regret. It would serve admirably as bait.

Without further delay, he strode toward the exit, and, bringing up his arms, blasted out through the double front doors, ready and willing as ever to raise hell.

CHAPTER 2

With catcalls and wolf whistles, rude leers and laughing invitations, the Bucket Street gang had begun surrounding her carriage. It did not take long for Daphne to realize they were still drunk on last night's gin.

She tried negotiating with them, but her voice was beginning to tremble. "Come now, pl-please! Step aside," she cajoled them. "We really must be going —"

When one of them grabbed her horse's bridle, William barked at him, "Clear off!"

"What are you going to do about it?" The miscreant stepped toward him, but at that moment, a roar erupted from some distance down the street.

"Bring me my bloody carriage — now!"

The thunderous bellow brought all motion to a halt.

The rough fellows surrounding her gig turned to look; Daphne and her servants did the same.

A man — tall, handsome, and well-dressed

all in black, and above all, quite intoxicated, judging by his weaving gait and the bottle still dangling from his hand — had just come staggering out of the brothel, squinting and shading his eyes against the daylight.

"Ow." His mutter of pain could be heard as he visored his eyes with his hand, scanning the street. "You!" He suddenly pointed with his bottle hand at the gang member holding her horse's bridle.

"You, there!" he clipped out again in a loud, slurred, but still lordly command. "Bring me my carriage. I am through here," he added with a wicked little laugh that betrayed the fact that he, too, was still three sheets to the wind, and also seemed to insinuate that he had not deigned to leave the house of ill-repute until he had sampled every blasted woman on the premises.

Good God.

Daphne stared, utterly taken aback by this obviously high-born libertine's shocking behavior and, worse, by her instant awareness of the raw masculinity that radiated from him.

His magnetism was unmistakable, despite the fact that he was a mess with his shirt hanging open and his dark hair tousled every which way, as though he had just stepped off the windy deck of a ship. He wore a short, neat goatee that surrounded his hard mouth, defined his square chin, and made him look, she feared, just a tad satanic.

Staring at him, Daphne found him something more than handsome. Compelling. Dangerous. A lawless sensation raced through her veins; she dropped her gaze in shock as he took a step closer, challenging the low ruffian who still held on to her horse's bridle.

"Are you deaf, man?" he insisted, unwittingly risking his neck in abusing these locals.

The gang member he'd been addressing laughed aloud and cast a stunned, indignant glance around at his fellows. "Who the hell is this fool?"

"Do you refuse an order from your betters?" the drunk lord challenged him, his aristocratic accent dripping with disdain.

"Oh, no," Daphne whispered, risking another glance at the handsome, drunken hellion.

At the same time, Wilhelmina gripped her arm, sharing her fright. The two women exchanged a glance. *Is he trying to get himself killed?*

This was not the place for safely inaccurate pistols at twenty paces, like a rakehell was used to. This was a place where men would cut your throat if you looked at them wrong.

"Are you talking to me?" the gang member barked back, letting go of her horse's bridle and taking a few steps toward the man.

"Of course I'm talking to you, you piece of excrement," he slurred with grand drunken dignity. "I'm talking to all of you! Somebody bring me my — bloody hell!"

Clumsy with drink, he suddenly spilled his coin purse onto the ground. A cascade of bright gold guineas tumbled all over the ground at his feet, rolling this way and that, all around his gleaming black boots.

The man cursed rather elegantly in several foreign languages in succession as he bent down, inch by unsteady inch, to retrieve his lost fortune.

The members of the Bucket Street gang homed in on the money with a visceral, white-hot intensity.

Promptly forgetting all about their game of harassing Daphne, they were drawn magnetically toward the gold.

Evil smiles spread over their faces to find such an easy target in their grasp. Moving in unison like a pack of wolves, they began walking cautiously toward the man.

He seemed oblivious to their approach.

"Sir!" Daphne shouted abruptly.

Wilhelmina grabbed her arm again. "Are you mad? Let's get out of here!"

"Aye," her brother answered, still ashen-faced from the confrontation as he swung up into the driver's seat.

"But we can't just leave him there!" Daphne blurted out, turning to them in alarm. "They'll kill the poor fool! He's too foxed to defend himself!"

"Not our problem," William muttered. "Let's get out of here before they come back for us!"

Daphne's heart was pounding. "It's his gold they want," she reasoned. "Let them have it. We can still save his life if we take him with us in our carriage. Sir!" she started to call to him again.

"No, miss! Don't be daft!" her maid whispered, pulling her down into the seat. "Even if we could get him into the gig, you can't be seen driving around with a man like that! You'll be ruined instantly!"

"She's right!" William agreed. "He just came out of a-a —"

"An unmentionable establishment," Wilhelmina quickly filled in, shooting her brother a prim glance.

"But we have to help him!"

"We came to help the *children,* mistress! You know you can't help everybody. Please don't get us killed!"

Daphne looked at her terrified maid and realized she had no right to risk her servants' necks along with her own.

"He'll be fine," William declared, not too convincingly. "They're not goin' to kill him, miss. Maybe give him a bit of a thrashing, but he's so foxed, he won't feel a thing."

"Perhaps it'll teach him a lesson about frequenting such places," his sister muttered.

"Oh, look at him." Daphne glanced back

with a worried frown and saw the gang members closing in on him. "For heaven's sake, what's he doing now?"

The drunken lord was backing up slowly toward the brothel wall, but he wore such a sly and sinister half smile that she feared he was too foxed even to grasp the danger he was in. Indeed, he looked like he was having fun.

She jumped when he suddenly smashed his wine bottle against the brick wall, instantly turning it into a jagged weapon. He brandished it at the approaching gang with a daring smile that Daphne knew she would never forget.

"Looks to me like he can take care of 'imself," William said flatly. "Besides, 'rank' is written all over him. Not even these blackguards would dare taunt the hangman, murderin' a peer."

William was right about that, she thought. Only an aristocratic rake of the first order would come staggering out of a brothel midmorning, bellowing his demands at passersby. Clearly, he was insane.

"Come, miss, we have to go while they're distracted. Your father would never forgive me if anything were to happen to you."

"Very well." Daphne gave William a taut nod, her heart in her throat. "We'll go and fetch the constable at once. Let's go."

"No need to tell me twice." William applied

41

the whip to the agitated horse's rump, and instantly the gig shot forward, the horse as happy as they to be gone.

Daphne's bonnet flew off her head with the sudden jostle, but the ribbon tied around her neck stopped it from blowing away. Her hat hung down her back as her carriage went careening toward the dilapidated little church ahead.

Behind them, however, shouts and a general ruckus could be heard; holding on to the seat's low side rail for dear life, Daphne turned to see what was happening.

She expected to find the gang members piling on the drunken rakehell, but an anxious glance over her shoulder revealed just the opposite: The man from the brothel was beating the blazes out of the gang!

He punched one fellow square in the jaw, and turning, all in one motion, jumped high to kick another in the chest. When he landed, he rammed his elbow into the throat of one who attempted to sneak up behind him, then brought up his fist with clockwork precision, felling the man with a neat blow. Coolly and methodically, he was mowing them down, one by one, with no sign of drunkenness whatsoever.

The most astonishing thought popped out up in her mind like a jack-in-the-box.

A ruse!

Why, he wasn't foxed at all! He had only

pretended it . . . *to lure those brutes away from her.*

She stared in amazement.

The last thing she saw before the church blocked her view was the crowd of *all* the other gang members swarming out of the pub, en masse, unleashing a collective roar as they rushed to their embattled mates' aid.

She turned white at the sudden reversal of fortune, looking forward again with a gulp. "Faster, William! Oh, never mind — move over!"

She snatched the reins from her startled footman, driving at top speed until she turned onto the busy Strand and spotted the nearest watchman's box ahead.

"You want me to go where?" the old constable echoed apprehensively after she had frantically gasped out her situation a few minutes later.

"Bucket Lane, I already told you!"

"Well, I'm going to have to call for more men."

"Whatever it takes, just hurry! His life is in danger, I tell you!"

"Whose life?"

"I have no idea who he is! Just — some lunatic!"

"Oh, bloody hell," Max whispered when he saw the rest of the Bucket Street gang come pouring out of the pub, forty of them at least.

There was a time and place for valor, but a gentleman knew when to make a graceful exit. He had thrown away a small fortune in that alley, and the gold had done the trick. But with Miss Starling out of harm's way, he had nothing left to prove.

Time to bow out.

Impressive how fast a man could run with a whole angry rookery on his tail. Lucky for Max — damned lucky — he was as well-trained in the wily art of escape as he was in fisticuffs. A bit of hiding, a bit of climbing, a bit of jumping from roof to roof, and then swinging back down to street level, and all he had left to do was to stroll back out onto the street and hail a hackney, the same manner of transportation by which he had arrived.

One stopped and he got in, but as it rolled away, Max spotted a cluster of uniformed lawmen rushing past in the direction of Bucket Lane.

He furrowed his brow, turning around to watch them out the grimy back window of the old coach. The fracas had only just happened. How could they have known — ?

Unless *she* had told them.

He stopped, struck with sudden astonishment.

She had gone for help. *Well, hang me.* Miss Starling must have gone straight to the constable to fetch some officers in to assist him. She . . . cared?

Max stared blankly at nothing for a moment, not even feeling the bumps and jolts of the ill-made coach rumbling over the cobbled street. The sudden woozy feeling in his brain had nothing to do with having been punched in the face. He shook his head as he realized uncomfortably that, a very long time ago, he had stopped expecting anybody to care what happened to him.

A strange, sweet, melting feeling softened his innermost core without warning, the place in him that he usually kept so steely.

But truly, it had never even occurred to him that Miss Starling might have given one thought for *his* safety.

My God, he thought in wonder, *perhaps I really have found something here . . .*

When he walked into his Town mansion on Hyde Park a short while later, a bit banged up but none the worse for wear, his old butler Dodsley greeted him with a dry glance that took note of his dishevelment. "Good afternoon, sir. Shall I fetch the medical kit?"

"Ah, no thanks, old boy. Bit of a row. Do me a favor, if the constable comes knocking, tell him I was here all morning, will you?"

"Killed someone again, did we?"

"Never before luncheon, Dodsley. It's still early yet."

"Indubitably, my lord."

Max gave him a sardonic look, but headed at once for his study. He went straight for the file on Daphne Starling, still sitting out on his desk.

Obviously, he had to see her again, and soon.

He flipped the file open and turned to the social schedule that Oliver had so carefully researched and recorded, trailing his finger down the page.

There.

The Edgecombe ball. Tomorrow night.

Max's eyes gleamed with speculation.

Maybe he had been looking at this all wrong. This was a bride search, after all, not a hunt for an enemy agent. Wasn't a woman more than just a tool for one of his strategies? Perhaps, for once, he could let himself be a bit more of a human being and less of a spy.

He had served in the Order's secret war against the Prometheans for too many years, obviously; but did every choice he made still have to be so perfectly cold-blooded?

Miss Starling might be "problematical," but why should that bother him? So Society was the obstacle? Well, he was trained in manipulation, in deception, in making people see what he wanted them to perceive, and only revealing the truth at the precise moment of his choosing.

If it turned out that he *really* wanted her, Max mused, he supposed he could probably have her. He would just have to work for it harder than he had ever intended to, would have to get a little more deeply involved than he had ever planned on doing . . . or was quite comfortable with.

On the contrary, he was accustomed to the rule of secrecy imposed on him by his vow. Holding others at arm's length had become second nature, until only his brother warriors — and perhaps his old butler — truly knew him at all.

That secrecy, that isolation, was a basic fact of his life, and after reading her file and seeing a glimpse of her mettle, he was not sure that a woman like Daphne Starling could be easily kept in the dark about his past and his true activities for the rest of her days. It could get messy.

He still wasn't convinced it was worth it. But all the same, he had to see her again.

Dodsley appeared by his side just then, silently, as if by magic. He offered Max a draught of whisky on a tray.

Max glanced at him in surprise and saw that Dodsley had brought the whole bottle. "Do I look that bad?"

"You look like you could use it, sir," his sphinxlike butler observed.

"Cheers," he murmured to himself as he tossed back the whisky to take the edge off after his brawl. He savored it, impressed by the quality. "That's good."

"That Highlander master-at-arms of yours

sent it over while you were out, sir."

"Virgil sent it? Excellent!" Last night, Max had sent word to his handler, Virgil, as soon as he had arrived home. "Was there a note?"

"Here it is, sir." Dodsley handed him the small sealed card that had arrived with the bottle of Scotch whisky. Max quickly opened it and read.

A proper malt in honor of your victory. Welcome home, my lad. Received your note from Belgium. Fine work on the Wellington matter. Well done. The others are not back yet, though I expect them soon. Come to the club at your leisure. We've made a few improvements that you may find intriguing.

V

Max couldn't help smiling as he read his old mentor's note. Improvements, eh? Lord, what new devices had Virgil come up with this time? Resourceful as any Scot, the grizzled old warrior was ever tinkering with his gears and machines and inventing strange new bits of machinery for Dante House, the Order's London headquarters, Max could only wonder about the latest modifications to the place.

For now, the more intriguing news was that he had made it back to Town before the other members of his team. He could barely wait to see his brother warriors.

On the other hand, the fact that Warrington and Falconridge were not yet back in Town gave him a distinct advantage in his bride hunt, one that he did not intend to squander. After all, he thought as a roguish grin tugged at his lips, they *were* his only serious competition when it came to women.

Like him, the fellow wolves in his pack had been putting off marriage due to their involvement in the Order, but their titles, like his, would require them to choose a wife and start begetting heirs. Like it or not, all three of them would have to go in for the old leg-shackle.

Max couldn't help laughing up his sleeve a bit in genial rivalry to know that he had got a head start on them.

Given the calculating side of his nature, he had obviously started preparing for this well in advance, just as he would for any other mission. Now, out of all the best brides to be had on London's marriage mart, he would have the pick of the litter — and with that, his thoughts returned directly to Daphne Starling.

"Anything else I can get for you, sir?" Dodsley asked, watching him intently.

"An invitation to the Edgecombe ball." Max took another swallow and winced at the whisky's brief burn while Dodsley's snowy eyebrows shot straight up. "What is it, Dodsley?"

"You, sir? Attend a ball?" the old fellow uttered in stately astonishment.

"I know," Max said dryly. "Wonder if anyone will faint this time when I walk in."

Dodsley dropped his gaze, pondering his master's rare foray into Society. As the supreme commander of the household staff, he had been kept apprised of His Lordship's bride hunt; he had never needed words to express his feelings on any subject to the brave, eccentric marquess whom he had so long served.

But now he could barely suppress his exultation upon correctly deducing that His Lordship must have taken a more serious interest in some eligible young miss.

He adopted a delicate tone, nearly holding his breath: "Might we hope there may soon be a lady of the house, my lord?"

"A certain viscount's daughter seems intriguing," Max admitted, "but all is not smooth sailing, I'm afraid. Especially now." As far as Daphne Starling knew, he was a wastrel, a drunkard, and a whoremonger.

No doubt, the sight of him stumbling out of that brothel would only seem to confirm what she would soon hear about him in Society if she learned his name and started asking questions.

Unfortunately, it wasn't as though he could just sit her down and tell her the truth. *No, not at all, Miss Starling, I wasn't there rogering harlots. I was only there to spy on you.*

That was not exactly going to help his cause.

What cause? He was not choosing her for his wife. He was *not.*

He frowned in irritation at himself. "At least I want to go to this ball for a little while and make sure she's all right," he grumbled. "Also let her see I'm quite unscathed so she won't blame herself."

Dodsley looked at him with no idea of what he was talking about. "Naturally, sir."

"You know how women are. The way they worry."

"If they have a heart," his butler said with a sage stare.

"She does. By God, she does," he murmured barely audibly, staring at nothing as his thoughts returned to her reluctance to leave the scene of the fight. *"Sir!"* she had called to him.

Twice. Risking her own safety to try to save him, even in the midst of *his* attempt to rescue her.

"Well, then." Dodsley took the empty shot glass back from him and lifted his chin. "I shall inform Lady Edgecombe to expect Your Lordship at the ball tomorrow night. Being so recently returned from abroad, it is only fitting that my lord should wish to pay his respects to his noble kinsmen."

"Ah, my kinsmen . . . I like that angle,

51

Dodsley! I had almost forgotten. They *are* my distant cousins, aren't they?"

"On your mother's side, my lord. Second cousins, twice removed."

Max smiled at his longtime servant in amused appreciation. "Good, then. For Lord knows, I shall have my work cut out for me."

"With the Edgecombes, sir?"

"With the girl," he said with a wince. "Afraid I've got some repair work to do."

"Already?" Dodsley asked indignantly.

Max just sighed.

Daphne did not leave the Strand for another half an hour. With her worried servants looking on, she paced anxiously, waiting for the magistrate's men to return with word of her mysterious rescuer — at least to find out if the gang had murdered him.

She was eager to learn his identity, but when the old watchman returned, he told her they had found no such person on the scene, just a dozen low thugs nursing bloody noses, bruised ribs, and a couple of nasty gashes.

The other officers had made a few arrests for disorderly conduct, and had gone to haul their prisoners off before the magistrate; but in typical Bucket Lane style, no one admitted seeing anything.

Nobody had anything to say.

This news left Daphne even more distressed. While it might mean the lunatic lord had escaped, it could just as easily suggest that they had already killed him and stashed his body someplace. He had been so badly outnumbered.

The officers had made a cursory search of the pub and the brothel's first floor, but they could not scour the other buildings on that dark and dingy lane until they came back with a warrant. Even the Bucket Street gang had their rights.

"I'm sure he must have got away, whoever he was," William said with a worried glance from the driver's seat of the gig as the three of them finally headed back to South Kensington on the green and pleasant outskirts of London.

"The main point is, we did the right thing," Wilhelmina chimed in.

"Oh, what if he was killed?"

"I should think, miss, that when a gentleman goes to a place like that, he must know what he's in for, surely. He had no cause to provoke them like he did."

"I think he was trying to help us." She turned to her maid in distress. "You know, to lure them off!"

"I think so, too," William admitted with a grim look. "Even foxed like that, a gentleman knows what he must do to help a lady."

"God!" Daphne whispered, sickened to think she might have got a man murdered today. Equally disturbing was the thought of what might have happened to *them* if he had not come stumbling out of that brothel when he did.

"Now, miss, ye must have faith," her footman offered stoutly when he saw her stricken face. "I know what our old mum would say — the angels looks after fools and drunks and children."

She gave him a look of gratitude, then she shook her head. "Still, I cannot help wondering who he was."

"Maybe he'll be at the Edgecombe ball," Wilhelmina spoke up with a simple shrug.

Daphne suddenly stared at her.

"Aye, if he is highborn, why not?" her brother agreed.

Daphne absorbed this in wonder, but even as the notion filled her with wild thrill, she had no idea how she would react if she spotted that handsome maniac in the ballroom.

The thought was so unsettling that she put it aside. "I implore you both to forgive me," she said with a chastened glance from one twin to the other. "I had no right to risk your safety, no matter how noble the cause."

"Ah, 'tis no matter, miss. All's well that ends well," William said as the gig glided to a halt before the Starlings' large stone villa.

"Thank you. You both are so good to me. Um . . ." Daphne hesitated, turning back to them with a sudden afterthought. "There is no need to mention this, er, unfortunate incident to Lord or Lady Starling, is there?"

The twins exchanged a firm but uneasy glance.

"No, miss," her maid replied. "But we will not go back there." The stubborn looks on both their faces told her they meant business.

Not overly surprised at this rebellion considering all she had asked of them already, Daphne dropped her gaze. "Fair enough." She'd have to figure something out for next week.

They all went inside, and were immediately engulfed in all the usual clamor of home: the pounding of the pianoforte as Sarah banged away dutifully at the keys, while Anna went romping down the corridor amid raucous laughter, tormenting the cat.

Daphne's stepsisters, the two young, coddled, boisterous Amazons, ages fourteen and twelve, were the products of the once-widowed Penelope's previous marriage to a navy captain.

"Anna, where's Papa?" she called after the younger girl, now dangling poor Whiskers.

"Upstairs!"

Daphne nodded, then paused, glanced in the parlor on her way, where footman Davis's labors were evident in the newly rearranged furniture. Her eyes widened suddenly as she saw Mama's old pianoforte now positioned on the wrong wall. Sarah stopped playing and looked over. "I hate this song! It's too hard!

What are you staring at?"

"Your mother moved the piano," she said softly.

"What do you care? You never play it anymore." Sarah huffed and changed to an easier piece, then resumed her banging.

Daphne shook her head and moved on. Maybe she'd have been better off marrying Albert, if it meant getting out of this madhouse. She parted ways with the Willies in the entrance hall as they all went about their business.

Still shaken up by their brush with danger, Daphne longed for a moment of her father's company. He always made her feel calmer, and she wanted to let him know she was back. He was not in his cluttered library, so she sought him upstairs, moving lightly as she took off her bonnet and gloves.

As she neared the master chamber on the upper floor, however, she slowed her pace with a sinking feeling, already hearing Penelope browbeating Papa again through their cracked bedroom door.

Once more, it seemed Daphne's refusal of Albert was the cause of their marital strife. She winced, knowing she had made her peaceable father's life more difficult.

"Honestly, George, you are too sentimental by half! When is she going to grow up? All little birdies have to leave the nest eventually!"

"My dear woman, why do you work yourself into these tizzies? You know that I require a tranquil household."

"Oh, George, you've got to *do something* about her!"

"Do what, dear?" he countered wearily.

"Find the girl a husband! If you don't, I will!"

"You already tried that, Pen. I don't think it warrants a repeat," he said archly.

"Well, it will take a fearless gentleman indeed to brave her scorn after her latest refusal! That's three suitors now she's rejected!"

Oh, you can't even count those other two, Daphne thought with a scowl as she leaned quietly against the wall outside their bedroom — not eavesdropping, mind you, just waiting for the right moment to make her presence known.

"George, you've heard the talk. People are beginning to say she is a jilt."

"You mustn't listen to gossip, my dear. When the right fellow comes along, she'll know. We all will know."

"I hope you're right, or she is going to end up a spinster."

"Nonsense. She is far too beautiful for that."

Oh, Papa. Daphne fought a smile and leaned her head against the wall, still grateful to him from the depths of her soul for not

57

forcing her to marry Albert in spite of Penelope's pressure.

Penelope had all but accepted Albert's offer on her behalf, but thankfully, Daphne's frantic arguments over the match had roused her vague and distant papa from his waking slumber for once. At last, he had heard her plea not to be handed over to that spoiled cad.

Good old George, Lord Starling, had ambled over to White's, his club and second home whenever he needed to escape the drama of an all-female residence, and had quietly taken Lord Albert Carew's measure for himself.

Papa had returned promptly with his judgment. It was rare for him to make a show of strength, but when he did, he was as immovable as Gibraltar: "No. I will not have my daughter tied to that shallow, empty-headed coxcomb. I am sorry, Penelope. He will not do. Not for my little girl."

Daphne had been overjoyed, and had hugged her father tearfully. Having spoken, Papa retreated once more into his pleasant, unassailable fog.

As for Penelope, losing her little game had sharpened her spite. To be sure, she had made her husband pay for it every day since then.

"Try not to show so much favoritism, George," she said in withering reproach. "My daughters might not be as pretty yet as your golden girl, but they will blossom in due course. Lud, you're lucky you married me before you had spoiled Daphne entirely," she added. "You already indulge her far too much as it is."

He does not. Glancing discreetly through the angle of the open door, she caught a glimpse of her stepmother pacing. Penelope Higgins Peckworth Starling was a woman of formidable energies, capable of doing many things at once.

She was small and dark-haired, in her early fifties, but the strain of her existence as a navy wife before she had married Papa was written in the lines on her tense face, pursed mouth, and the excitable temper reflected in her always worried, darting eyes.

Daphne often wondered if part of Captain Peckworth's fighting spirit had remained behind in his widow, for she certainly ran a tight ship and loved giving orders, but one wrong word could flare up a war.

Sometimes Daphne felt sorry for her, because it was plain that Penelope had never really settled into her new, vastly raised station as a viscountess. Some in Society might make her feel unworthy, but her lower birth had never mattered to Papa.

As a couple, the two could not have been more opposite. Papa was as easygoing as Penelope was high-strung.

An English gentleman down to his fingertips, Viscount Starling was so secure in his well-aged title and considerable fortune that he had never been particularly impressed by others' rank or wealth, or put off by the lack of either. He took people as they came, and had taught Daphne to do likewise.

"Truly, George, I shall never understand why you did not insist that she marry Lord Albert! Think of the advantage he could have brought to our family! He is a second son — if the elder brother dies, she might have had a chance to be a duchess!"

"Penelope, for heaven's sake! Young Holyfield may not look much of a duke, but certainly, he is alive and well."

"Alive, yes, but I'd hardly call him well. Poor, frail, pasty little poppet. I swear he is consumptive! I'm sure Lord Albert would have made a far more splendid duke than his elder brother, in any case. Oh, but it's past worrying over now. The chance is lost!"

"The chance to have my daughter profit by some poor fellow's death?" Lord Starling asked dryly at his second wife's dramatics. "Come, Penelope. Daphne saw through that arrogant buffoon from the start, and now that Lord Albert has shown his true colors, spreading these rumors about her, I applaud my daughter's wisdom all the more."

"The rumors — oh, George! — you aren't thinking of calling him out?" Penelope declared with a sudden gasp.

Daphne's eyes widened.

"Woman, don't be daft!" he said dismissively. "I'm much too old for that. Besides, no Starling lord has ever engaged in silly duels."

"Good! I just hope you will not rue the way you have let her run wild."

"Wild?" he echoed in a quizzical tone. "My Daphne? The girl does not have a wild bone in her body. Daphne is a lady, through and through."

"What is that supposed to mean?" Penelope snapped. "You reproach me because I never went to a finishing school!"

"No, no —"

"Just because *I* am not as highborn as your first wife does not make me or my daughters count for less —"

"My dear, I meant nothing of the kind!"

"Well, if by 'a lady' you are referring to your daughter's expensive mode of life, I cannot disagree with you on that point. We cannot afford her, George! We have to find the girl a rich husband who can pay for all these ball gowns and party dresses, theater gowns and fripperies and modistes! And then there is her charity! She gives half of our money away to the poor!"

"Now, now, there you go, exaggerating again. It's only gold, anyway."

"Only gold?" she cried, aghast. "Oh, but *you* have never known poverty, George." She let out a sudden sob, and it sounded surprisingly genuine. "I know that we will end up in the poorhouse!"

"Tut, tut, my dear, there is no need for tears." Through the doorway, Daphne saw her gray-haired papa go over to his wife and embrace her fondly. "I know you suffered much after Captain Peckworth died, but those days are long behind you now. I promise, you and the girls are quite safe. Come, now. I told you not to worry. Markets go down, but they always go back up again. We will be just fine."

"Yes, I know, but — oh, my nerves cannot take it, George! Truly, they cannot!"

"Let me send for one of the servants to bring you some tea."

"They're all useless." Penelope sniffled. "Very well."

Realizing her father was about to come out of the room, Daphne swiftly withdrew into her own chamber a few doors down the hallway. Embarrassed by their discussion of her, she waited there until he had passed. After all, she did not wish to be accused of spying.

After a moment, she leaned her forehead against the closed door, not knowing what to think about Penelope's claims that they were running short of funds.

She knew her father had lost money in the great stock market plunge that had caught all London off guard right after the Battle of

Waterloo, but he kept saying everything was fine, so why was she left feeling guilty?

If Papa wasn't going to come out and be honest with the family about their situation, then what was she to do? Read his mind? He was her father, and she had been raised to accept his word as law. If Papa said everything was fine, then she would take him at his word.

If it was not — if there was a problem — then he had better speak up in plain English. *He knows that I don't play these sorts of games.*

In any case, it was no great mystery whom she intended to marry, anyway — Jonathon White, her dearest friend — when she was good and ready, and not one minute sooner.

Jono and she had been as inseparable as the two Willies were since they both were knee-high to a bumblebee.

Now that they were grown, it was true that Jonathon cared a bit too much for fashion and could not arrive on time at an event to save his life, but he was always droll and agreeable, a nice-looking fellow with beautiful manners and a dashing sense of style. Like Papa, he would never duel.

Above all, he was much too smart ever to try to tell Daphne Starling what to do. On the contrary, he had been content to follow her lead and to obey her wiser-headed orders since they were five years old.

Most importantly of all, unlike Albert, Jono knew she was a human being. He treated her with respect, and in turn, she trusted him implicitly. They were two peas in a pod.

She had been keeping a little distance from Jonathon lately, however, merely to keep him out of the line of fire of the Carew brothers.

With a sigh, she turned and leaned her back against the door. At once, across the bedchamber, she saw her delicious new white ball gown hanging on the door peg of her closet in anticipation of the Edgecombe ball.

She gazed at it for a long moment.

It had just returned from the modiste's shop with the final alterations. The sight of it reminded her afresh of the coming confrontation with Albert.

The Edgecombe ball tomorrow night would be the first time since she had refused his offer of marriage that they would have to face each other publicly.

She had it on good information that he was going to be there. Daphne intended to have a word with the cad and hopefully put a stop for once and for all to his petty carping against her good name. She was not looking forward to this.

It was not her way to become embroiled in ugly public fights with anyone, but enough was enough.

He was making a fool of himself in all this, and really, what did he want her to do?

For heaven's sake, she had tried to make the disappointment easier on him. Out of courtesy to him, and for modesty's sake, she had stayed out of Society for a whole fortnight after his frankly embarrassing proposal.

The horrid fop had barely looked at her throughout the ordeal, watching himself coyly in the mirror behind the sofa where she had sat, smiling at himself in the reflection, that golden-haired beau of the ton.

Daphne had nearly gagged on his attempt to kiss her, but somehow she had found the words to decline so great an honor. He had not taken it well. In fact, he had promised that she would be sorry before storming out.

After that, she had been careful to avoid running into him in Town. But no longer would she stand by and let him keep working to turn people against her.

But if tomorrow night was, indeed, to be battle, she had chosen her armor well. The exquisite, simple gown was made of the most tender crepe silk that she had ever touched, and it fit perfectly.

With all eyes on her — and not for the reasons a girl might hope — she knew that she would need to look impeccable. Appearances were all that mattered to Society, anyway, and in this gown, she could be confident that at least she'd look her best.

Beyond the perfect dress, she had no real strategy in mind but to be her usual easygoing self and show the ton that she was fine and everything was normal.

If Albert gave her any trouble, she knew she need not even make a scene. A few subtle comments delivered with a smile should be enough, she trusted, to cast his backbiting in a whole new, foolish light.

All was not lost. She was confident she could still turn her situation around. Admittedly, it was ironic to find herself in this position after she had been so conscientious about her behavior all her life.

In honor of her mother's memory, she had tried at all times to conduct herself like the perfect lady.

Fortunately, she had faith that some good always came from even the most difficult challenges. For example, this whole episode was a valuable lesson in finding out who her real friends were.

Some had turned away, and she intended to remember their names; but many others, like Carissa and Jonathon, had remained steadfastly loyal.

Thankfully, above all, she still had the blessing of the powerful ladies who ultimately controlled opinion in the ton. This was due, in part, to the support of her formidable great-aunt, the Dowager Duchess of Anselm.

If it came to it, Daphne knew she could always summon her old dragon aunt to come and breathe fire on the ton on her behalf. But unless it became a true emergency, she preferred to handle it herself.

In all, having Albert Carew for an enemy was no easy burden to bear, but having him for a suitor had been even more annoying. At least she no longer had to sit through his artificial paeans to her beauty.

Pushing idly away from the door, she went to set her bonnet on the head form atop her chest of drawers, but her thoughts returned to the row in Bucket Lane. She still could not stop wondering what had become of her unexpected rescuer. She had so many questions about him.

He was quite a mystery. Had his whole performance been indeed a ruse designed to lure the criminals away from her? Surely he had been as foxed as the gang members were to have attempted such a thing. His verbal abuses of them, his demands for his carriage, dropping his coin purse on purpose? She shook her head in amusement. If so, the man deserved a round of applause for his acting skills.

It was difficult to know what had been real with him and what had been illusion. She just hoped he had escaped the mob alive.

Wouldn't that be something if her maid was right and he *did* show up at the Edgecombe ball?

He did not look like the sort of man who would be received there. And even if he was invited, perhaps he had a prior engagement at the *brothel.*

Daphne snorted. The dark stranger might have saved her life, for which, of course, she owed him her thanks. But beyond that, obviously, she could have nothing to do with any fiend who ever set foot in that place.

If the gang had beaten him up, perhaps he had learned his lesson. Really, a gentleman ought to know better.

With a soft, prim humph, she put the enigmatic stranger out of her mind and glanced in the mirror, cynically wondering which beauty potions to put on her face tonight in preparation for tomorrow. With the ton's worst gossips sure to be watching, waiting eagerly to see the little drama unfold between her and Albert, she did not want to look one jot haggard or careworn over his nonsense.

Who could say? She shrugged to herself. Perhaps her jilted suitor was finally over his tantrum. Albert might even surprise her, and greet her like a gentleman.

It pleased her to think there was that chance.

Then again, she rated the likelihood of it about as highly as that debauched, magnificent wild man showing up in the Edgecombes' ballroom.

Whoever he was.

CHAPTER 3

The night of the Edgecombe ball arrived and brought with it a late summer thunderstorm, but Max was undeterred.

His long, onyx town coach plunged on through the inky night, the four horses fierce and black, tossing their heads at the thunder, snorting steam.

Glowing spheres from the lampposts flickered over the gilt trim of the ebony coach as the team cantered through another puddle, hooves splashing. The high, whirring carriage wheels flung out silver scythes of rain.

Hell of a night to be out.

Inside the coach, the downpour drummed the wooden roof, an incessant droning music broken only by the crack of the lightning bolts that seemed to be following him.

Max took another drag off his cheroot, a rare indulgence, and slowly blew the smoke out the open crack of the carriage window. The rain coursing over the glass distorted the dark world beyond as he stared out.

He was in a rather strange mood. Subtle doubts tugged at him tonight. On the Continent, the goal was usually plain. He always knew exactly how to operate. But here in London, it felt like a different world, his own place in it unclear.

It was not that he was nervous about meeting Miss Starling face-to-face. For God's sake, he had dined with royalty. Nor was he overly concerned about going back into the ton; no matter what they might say about him, he knew more of *their* secrets than they'd ever know about his.

It was just that Virgil had set up the ruse of the Inferno Club long ago. Max had gone along with it faithfully, playing his diabolical role, never counting the cost: He had given his word and he knew his duty.

But tonight was the first time, perhaps, that he might learn the full price of his involvement in the Order. Perhaps it was too late ever to bridge this isolation . . .

He brushed off his dark musings as the carriage slowed, reaching its destination. Max glanced out the window at the broad dimensions of Edgecombe House.

His soaked footman hurried forward and opened the carriage door for him, umbrella at the ready.

Max stepped down, flicked away his spent cheroot, and smoothed his velvet coat. Tugging his sleeves about his wrists, he gave his dripping servant a nod of studied indifference. "See that you get some shelter," he commanded. "I don't want my horses catching cold."

"Yes, my lord." Holding the umbrella high to shield his taller master, the footman hurried to keep up with Max's longer paces, escorting him under the portico, and then backing off with a bow.

From the inky blackness of the September night, Max strode into the brilliance of the mansion's interior.

A thousand beeswax candles in countless chandeliers and crystal sconces sparkled on the gilded ceilings of Edgecombe House and made its marble columns gleam.

Still, perhaps it was just his jaundiced view of the world, but he couldn't help noticing how the dampness of the stormy night had permeated the house. Wet footprints marred the shining floor, traces of mud carried in on guests' shoes. A heavy humidity hung on the air, pulling a faint, musty smell out of the rugs and causing the feathers on the ladies' toques to droop. Declining to draw too much attention to himself, Max brushed off the butler, going in without the formal announcement of his arrival.

Thanks to his work, he was no stranger to dropping into other people's parties uninvited, or going wherever the devil he pleased. The trick was to carry oneself as though one

71

had every right to be there.

He proceeded to do so, making his way at a casual saunter through the fairly crowded first floor. A few people here and there glanced curiously at him as he passed by, but Max avoided eye contact, knowing it wouldn't be long before they realized who he was.

Sure enough, word began to spread after a few people recognized him; he could feel the stares and whispers as he proceeded slowly, relentlessly, toward the ballroom. He got a few shocked looks, but at least nobody fainted. The distant music steadily grew louder.

He lifted a glass of red wine off the tray of a liveried footman. He passed two large reception rooms where tables were set up for the customary light supper served at midnight, which was almost at hand.

Ahead, he could now hear the pounding steps of a country dance in progress. Passing under some columns at the end of the corridor, he came out onto a landing that overlooked the ballroom.

Rather than going down the elaborate marble staircase to join the party at once, he drifted over to the gilded railing, where he paused and scanned the crowd as intently as if he were still on the Continent, hunting one of his targets.

As he scrutinized the weaving lines of dancers, he suddenly spotted a flash of golden hair. His eyes narrowed, pulse surged.

His gaze homed in on Daphne Starling.

He took only the slightest note of her tall, lanky partner — just enough to remind himself later to find out who that young fop was, with his gregarious smile and his reddish-gold hair.

Then Max indulged himself in staring openly at Lady Number Five, savoring her supple grace in the movements of the dance, and perhaps undressing her with his eyes. He liked the low cut of her airy white gown exceedingly.

It was obvious to him now why she had been careful to keep herself primly covered up going into Bucket Lane. If those men had realized just how beautiful she was, she might have caused a riot — like the one that she inspired in his blood now.

Max took her all in with a sweeping gaze, from her white satin slippers to the pale pink rose in her hair; the glorious whole of this splendid young woman so ripe for a lover's awakening.

The drumbeat of his pulse thundered in his ears. He wanted to touch the curve of her cheek, feel her silken skin beneath his fingertips. Explore her lush young body with his hands, his lips; set her pulse to pounding. No man could behold the likes of her without the stirring of desire. But there was something more in his hunger, something unfamiliar. A deeper need . . .

As she turned smoothly in the set, her arm outstretched, her high-gloved hand joined with that of her partner, he noticed her preoccupied expression, subdued and faraway. She sent her flamboyant male partner a polite but distant smile, circling around him as did the rest of the ladies with their beaux, in the figures of the dance.

But as her restless glance skimmed the ballroom, she suddenly spotted Max watching her. Their gazes locked; she stopped in her tracks without warning.

Her partner released her hand and retreated back to the male line, but Miss Starling stood motionless in the middle of the dance floor, staring back at Max as though she had seen a ghost.

He did not react, holding her stunned gaze in dark, serene patience. He tried to reassure her with his stare and his slight smile that he was quite unharmed.

Meanwhile, her sudden halt had caused a degree of confusion in the set, to which Miss Starling still remained oblivious.

The other dancers were milling around her, bumping into each other while her partner tried to get her attention. Her big, blue eyes stayed fixed on him, full of overwhelming emotion that he actually found difficult to read, for all his training.

But it was then that he knew with an

electric certainty deep in the core of him that the rest of Oliver's bride list was irrelevant.

He knew he had found the one. And as he held her gaze, a single, searing thought filled his mind, body, and soul, and whispered to her soundlessly: *You're mine.*

You . . .

Perhaps some wizened sorcerer had summoned the dark, wild storm that raged outside tonight and conjured it into the form of a man, for he stood on the landing looking as though he had just blown in astride a thunderbolt.

Unfortunately, Daphne had always found storms irresistibly exciting. She couldn't take her eyes off him — her rescuer from yesterday!

Relief flooded her to see him alive and well, though she could not imagine how he had gotten away with the whole Bucket Street gang out for his blood. As she held his gaze with a jubilant sensation tingling through her body, she had the strangest sensation that he had come here tonight expressly to find her.

After all, she had never seen him in Society before — and he was not the sort of man a girl could fail to notice.

Her gaze trailed admiringly over his tall, muscular form. He was no dandy like Albert, but something far more dangerous.

The way he carried himself reminded her

of Continental royalty, with his short devil's beard and the hint of extravagance in his jeweled perfection. He was tall and lean, wide-shouldered, elegantly powerful, with an Italian flair in his mode of dress: a bold splash of color in the scarlet waistcoat beneath his black velvet coat, a slightly more artful twist to his cravat, perhaps, a flourish to the ruffle at his sleeve.

He took a sip of bloodred wine, still watching her, his pale eyes gleaming by the candlelight.

Daphne managed to tear her gaze away at last, feeling slightly faint, half bowled over anew by that same dark, delicious magnetism she remembered vividly from her first glimpse of him in Bucket Lane.

A bit disoriented, she only then realized she had stopped dancing and made a muck of the set for the others.

"Hullo, Star? Wake up! Anybody home?" Jonathon was calling to her from across the row, using his particular nickname for her, short for Starling.

"Oh — sorry!" Heart pounding, she cast a flustered look around, trying to find her place, but Jonathon merely laughed at her, as he was wont to do.

Life was all a lark to Jonathon White, which sometimes annoyed her intensely, but he was loyal. Her childhood friend had remained chivalrously by her side for most of the night for moral support in her coming confrontation with her rejected suitor.

Jonathon's job was to keep an eye out for Albert, since his lanky frame was taller than average. With his bright, short-cropped, strawberry-blond hair gleaming like a beacon, Jonathon was always easy to find in a crowd, and if you couldn't see him, you could usually hear his laughter.

Daphne sent him a harmless scowl in exchange for his amusement at her expense. Of course, just when she found her place again, the music ended.

The dancers bowed and curtsied to their partners, and then applauded noisily for the musicians. She stole another glance back up at the landing where the dark-haired stranger had stood, but he had disappeared into the crowd.

Jonathon came bopping over to her. "You all right, my lamb? You're looking rather odd."

"I'm fine," she said vaguely. "I just got a little — distracted."

"Well, you had better snap out of it," her childhood friend warned in a wry tone. "The moment you've been waiting for, I think, has just arrived. Carew's headed this way."

"Oh, God." She turned, following his nod, and saw, sure enough, there was Albert marching toward her, two of his arrogant younger brothers flanking him.

Daphne bristled at the sight of them.

Lord Albert Carew had perfect, sculpted features, and hair in sandy waves. Beau Brummell himself had once complimented him as the second-best dressed dandy in London, and he owned a slightly scratchy voice that gave him a rakish aura and drove the other girls in the ton quite wild. On Daphne, alas, none of his charms had the slightest effect. She was fairly sure it was her indifference to him that had first attracted his attention.

He must have thought it incredible that any female could resist him, but all she could see when she looked at him were his cold eyes and the haughty tilt of his handsome nose. Still several yards away through the dispersing ranks of dancers, he sent her a superior smile with a cold sneer beneath it.

She squared her shoulders, putting the black-haired stranger out her mind for the moment. The time had come for their long-awaited confrontation.

Still a few yards off through the crowd, Albert narrowed his eyes threateningly at the sunny-tempered Jonathon, looking him over in disdain.

"I say!" Jono murmured, but to Daphne, the menacing look at her best friend only ignited her ire.

"Jonathon, dear, would you mind fetching me a cup of punch?" she ground out, staring at her jilted suitor.

"Star, I'm not afraid of —"

"Go. I don't want you getting drawn into this."

"I'll not leave you —"

"I can handle him. He can't challenge *me* to a duel."

"Duel?" Jonathon echoed with a gulp, turning to her, wide-eyed. "Do you really think —"

"I'd *really* like some punch. *Now.*"

He hesitated. "Well, as much as I adore you, old girl, I-I do rather value my life."

"Just go!"

He bobbed his head in a sheepish nod and disappeared without further insistence. Daphne was glad.

The last thing she needed was Albert and his brothers making a target out of innocent, harmless Jonathon. Her fashionable friend was no warrior, and besides, he had had nothing to do with all this.

Her gloved fists clenched by her sides, the sharp words she had prepared for Albert sizzling on the tip of her tongue, she waited for him to reach her, eager to give the cad a piece of her mind at last.

But then, all of a sudden, just a few feet ahead, her rescuer from yesterday stepped between them, heading crosswise into the Carew brothers' path.

Without warning, and seemingly by accident, he rammed Albert hard with his shoulder, causing his drink to slosh. "Oh, pardon, frightfully sorry," he apologized at once in a lavish, velvet tone.

"Watch where you're going!"

Daphne sucked in her breath and stared. *Zounds, he's at it again!*

Albert turned on him in outrage, flicking wine off his hand. "Are you blind, you fool?"

"No harm intended, my good fellow, do forgive me," the man soothed, his voice low-pitched and urbane.

She detected a hint of treachery in his silken words.

"I was just on my way to meet a friend," he said. "But — wait." The stranger halted, studying him with a keen stare. "Don't I know you?"

"What?" Albert muttered, giving him a contemptuous glance. "No. I don't believe so."

Daphne watched in fascination, though impatient for her turn to vent her wrath on her former suitor.

"Yes, of course," the stranger said all of a sudden. "You are Lord Albert Carew, are you not?"

"Yes. Why, yes, I am." Albert drew himself up, looking exceedingly proud of this fact, though he was not quite tall enough to meet the stranger eye to eye.

"You all three are sons of the late Duke of Holyfield if I am not mistaken?" He glanced around at the Carew brothers.

Daphne sensed trouble.

"Indeed, we are," Richard, the youngest, declared.

"And *you* are?" Albert prompted with a haughty air.

"Come, don't you recognize me?" the stranger countered with a knowing smile. "Look into my eyes. It was a long time ago . . . Think. It will come back to you, I'm very sure."

Daphne barely realized she had been holding her breath. She had no idea what all this was about, but she felt more going on here than met the eye. In any case, their meeting right in front of her gave her the furtive chance to study her rescuer at closer range.

The overall expression of his very masculine, rectangular face was one of intensity and precision. His chiseled features were well-formed, his nose and chin both large and definite, balanced by his knife-hilt cheekbones, angular jaw, and thick, dark, feathery eyebrows.

His black lashes, short and thick, rimmed his gray-green eyes. Albert stared for a second into those piercing eyes and seemed to forget all about his indignation, as though falling under the stranger's unfathomable spell, much as Daphne had experienced a few moments earlier.

"Come, think back," the stranger intoned

in silken menace, as though his brooding eyes and soft voice and his slight, dark smile could mesmerize any unsuspecting victim. "We were only boys then."

"It can't be," Albert whispered. "Max . . . Rotherstone? Is it you?"

The stranger nodded slowly while Daphne committed his name to memory.

Perhaps it was due to drink, but Albert now appeared quite entranced. He shook his head vaguely. "I don't believe it," he uttered while "Max Rotherstone" continued to control him, rather like a snake charmer. "You have been gone for as many years as I can remember, you just . . . vanished."

"Yes," he said. "But now I have returned."

"Why?" Albert demanded at once, suspiciously.

"I have done and seen all that I wished to do or see." He tilted his head intently. "And what have you been doing, Albert, with *your* life all this time?"

Albert's sculpted countenance went blank.

Nothing. The sorry truth was written all over his face. Daphne almost pitied him when he could not find an answer, but the pointed reminder of his lack of purpose in life seemed to jar the leading dandy from the spell.

Albert changed the subject, suddenly eager to be rid of his old acquaintance, it seemed, this long-lost friend who had posed such an uncomfortable question. "Well, Max, you said you were off to meet someone. Don't let us keep you."

"Ah, yes. The Grand Duchess of Mecklenburg." The handsome smile he flashed made Daphne catch her breath.

"Grand Duchess?" Albert echoed in a dubious tone.

"Mm, yes, charming lady. I met her in the course of my travels on the Continent."

"I say!" Richard Carew mumbled with reluctant admiration.

Max Rotherstone folded his hands politely behind his back. "Shall I introduce you?"

Albert seemed to remember himself then. He shot Daphne a gloating look past the stranger's shoulder. "Meet a Grand Duchess? I'm sure any man would fancy that."

"Indeed." Rotherstone sent Daphne the merest, dismissive glance over his shoulder, barely paying her any mind. "Of course, I don't wish to interrupt —"

"Not at all," Albert cut him off, sending an icy look her way. "We were finished here, believe me."

"Good, then! Come with me," he commanded, clapping Albert on the shoulder. "Her Highness is seated this way. After you, old boy." With his other hand, he gestured toward the far end of the room; his brawny arm rose like a turnpike before Daphne's face. None of the men paid her any further attention. She might as well have been invisible.

"I am a frequent guest among the highest circles myself, you know," Albert remarked to Rotherstone, unable to resist one last, self-congratulating look in Daphne's direction. "I hear I'm quite a favorite with the Regent."

"Fascinating. You must tell me all about it."

"Well, His Royal Highness first complimented the cut of my coat one day . . ." As Albert eagerly obliged his utterly insincere inquiry, he walked ahead of the stranger, as obediently as you please.

Daphne stared after them in amazement, not quite sure what in blazes had just transpired.

But as "Max Rotherstone" deftly steered the Carew brothers away, all three neatly under his control, he glanced back oh-so-casually over his shoulder at her, a discreet glimmer of deviltry in his eyes.

Daphne shook her head at him in bewilderment.

His wicked smile in answer and his slight, private nod merely seemed to say to her, *You're welcome . . . again.*

CHAPTER 4

"Well, I never," Daphne breathed. She could not decide if she was delighted, intrigued, or irked that he had spirited Albert away and stolen her thunder before she could give the cad the tongue-lashing he deserved.

But one thing was clear: This Rotherstone man was as bold as brass and as slick as they came. He had interfered twice now in her affairs, and though she had overheard his name, she still had no idea who in blazes he actually was.

Strange, for she usually knew everyone. She stood on her tiptoes in riveted curiosity, trying to peer over the crowd to keep him in view.

When she spied him across the ballroom introducing the Carew brothers to the Grand Duchess of Mecklenberg, as promised, she couldn't help grinning. The look on Albert's face was priceless as Rotherstone presented him to a very stern-looking old lady with a sour frown. Her Highness eyed the Carew brothers in thorough disapproval.

Well, he is full of tricks, isn't he? Daphne's mind was still awhirl with questions about him when she heard her father's voice.

"Ah, daughter, there you are!" She turned as Lord Starling ambled over to her, his gray eyes beaming with fondness. "Did you hear the announcement? They're serving the supper now. Would you like to come and eat with us?"

She smiled at him. "I would never turn down your company, Papa." Doing her best to shake off her distraction, she hooked her wrist through the crook of his offered arm. "Do you mind if Jonathon joins us? He went to fetch me some punch."

"If he must." Her father harrumphed. It was no secret that Papa considered Jono a very silly young man.

"Papa?" As they made their way, arm in arm, toward the grand dining room where the light repast was being served, she leaned closer to murmur in his ear so they would not be overheard. "There is a gentleman, Papa — he is most mysterious. I wonder if you know him."

"Hm. Where?"

Daphne glanced around, then scowled. "Oh, dash, I do not see him anymore! He seems to have a talent for vanishing into thin air . . . I heard someone address him as Max Rotherstone."

"*Lord* Rotherstone?" Her father stopped and turned to her in surprise. "The Demon Marquess?"

Daphne furrowed her brow at his answer, then burst out laughing. "*Demon* Marquess?"

"My, you're brave, aren't you?" Papa teased. "Dance with him, my sweet Persephone, and he'll whisk you off to Hades, and I only shall see you but half the year."

"Oh, Papa!" she chided, laughing, still holding on to his arm. "Why do they call him that, I wonder?"

"I know not, but he probably deserves it." He winked at her. "Maybe you should ask the rogue."

"George!" They were interrupted as Penelope blasted into their presence, whirling out from amid the crowd, and waving her fan at top speed. "George, George! Oh, George, for heaven's sake, there you are! I've been looking for you here, there, and everywhere! Where on earth did you wander off to?"

"I am right here, darling," he said in a soothing tone, retreating back into his amiable fog.

"It was very wrong of you to leave me, George!" Penelope bustled over to Lord Starling and claimed his other arm, fully prepared to play a hard game of tug-of-war with Daphne over the poor man, or indeed, to break him in two as though he were a wishbone.

"I only went to fetch Daphne to dine with us, as you can see, my dear."

"But George, it's quite impossible! I've already secured two places for us at Lord and Lady Edgecombe's table — only two!"

"Can we not make room for the girl?"

"Demand a *third* chair at the hosts' table? I could never be so rude! Lord and Lady Edgecombe would think us thoroughgoing barbarians!"

Daphne suppressed a polite cough. "I'm sure they could never think that, ma'am," she murmured.

Her father gave her a stern look askance.

"It's enough of an honor, surely, that they have invited us at all, George!"

Daphne had no doubt that her stepmother had invited herself. "It's all right," she spoke up. "I will just sit with my friends."

"Yes, let her sit with the young people, George. That is as it should be. Come, we must not keep the Edgecombes waiting!" Without further discussion, Penelope dragged him away.

Daphne was left standing there, but thankfully, Jono returned just then with the punch.

"Your father's a saint," he remarked as he handed her the goblet, apparently having overheard their exchange.

"I'm not sure that's what you call it," she said in a wry, philosophical tone. "Why does he let her run roughshod over him like that, do you suppose?"

Jono shrugged. "She is a woman of mighty will."

"Well, fortunately, so am I. Otherwise, right now, I'd be engaged to Albert Carew." She shuddered. "If that domestic tyranny is marriage, I want no truck with it."

"Nor I." Jonathon raised his glass. "To the single state, my dear."

Daphne nodded at him, clinked her glass against his, and they drank to that, in perfect amiable harmony with each other, as usual.

When her female best friend, Carissa Portland, joined them, they all three went into the long, rectangular dining hall, which was filled with damask-covered tables for the guests.

They made their way over to a table ringed by more of their friends, a colorfully garbed array of belles and bucks of the ton. She had noticed a few judgmental looks here and there tonight and had received a few terse, chilly greetings, but here was a fine group of friends that Albert had still failed to turn against her.

They made up a gay and fashionable company, while various chaperones kept an eye on their female charges from nearby. As the others engaged in brisk repartee, Daphne kept furtively scanning the dining hall for the mysterious Lord Rotherstone. *Why did they call him the Demon Marquess?* Then again, did she really have to ask, after all that she had seen of him so far? She was actually a little put off to find that he was friends with Albert.

Just then, she spotted the four of them, Lord Rotherstone, Lord Albert, and the two younger Carew brothers. They were congregating on the threshold of the dining hall, standing in one of the many arched doorways of the adjoining colonnade. They appeared to be catching up on old times while the other guests kept ambling in past them, finding seats at all the various tables.

Daphne's expression darkened with worry as she furtively watched their exchange. She froze when she saw Lord Rotherstone point her out discreetly to Albert.

When they put their heads together, obviously discussing her, she suddenly couldn't breathe. Lord Rotherstone folded his arms slowly across his chest.

As he lowered his head, listening intently to Albert's gossip about her, Daphne felt her heart sink. *No!* she thought in helpless anger. *Don't believe his lies about me!* She looked away, her heart pounding, but that was the moment she had to face up to the fact that she *liked* this Rotherstone man.

For the life of her, she could not say why. He visited horrid brothels. He brawled like a wild barbarian. He possessed strange, slippery skill in managing other people, as he had just demonstrated with Albert. And he had looked at her in the ballroom as if he was imagining her naked.

But she had never before in her life seen anyone like him — the brash, bold grandeur of the man, his quick mind, his unhesitating courage and smooth style.

He made her quite breathless.

But now, before they had even been introduced, Albert was going to ruin it for her. Because *he* couldn't have her, he spitefully wanted to see her end up alone.

Her friends chatted on at the table, but Daphne was no longer listening. What could she do? Run over there and tell Albert to shut his big mouth?

Oh, what did she even care what he told Lord Rotherstone, anyway? If the "Demon Marquess" believed Albert's lies without hearing her side of the story, then he was a fool.

Still, it was upsetting, after she had spent the past twenty-four hours thinking of him as her hero.

Rough-and-tumble he might be, but the man had risked his neck for her. But now, hearing whatever lies his old friend Albert was speaking about her, the intriguing marquess would not want anything to do with her.

She knew the men were still talking about her, and she felt naked sitting there, an easy target for their mockery.

In dire need of a moment to compose herself, she excused herself abruptly from her friends' table. She walked stiffly to a door on the far end of the room in order to avoid going past him.

She could swear she felt his eyes on her as she walked out of the dining hall. Holding her head high, she was determined to make at least a show of dignity, but as soon as she escaped his line of sight, she picked up her crepe silk skirts and fled the rest of the way to the safety of the ladies' lounge.

Hm, Max thought, watching Daphne Starling.

She had looked a little upset just then. Her sensitive face had paled, almost as if she could hear her former suitor's unflattering words.

Carew's rant continued, but Max had concealed his true sentiments about the blackguard's words long enough.

He had wanted to hear firsthand exactly what complaints Carew had been leveling against her so that he could deal with the man appropriately.

To be sure, the slightest encouragement on this topic had repaid Max with an earful.

"Top-lofty she is, fickle, narcissistic little tease. She lures men close just to knock them down again. She thinks she's too good for everyone —"

"You know, Carew," Max cut him off in a mild tone, willing self-control. "If you keep talking about her that way, people are going to think it's just sour grapes."

"What do you mean?" Albert retorted, taken aback.

"It looks bad, man. Petty," Max said idly, exerting all his rigid discipline to keep his anger in check. "I don't know, it rather makes it sound as if you merely want to damage her in others' eyes, just because you couldn't manage to win her for yourself."

"That's not the case!" Albert snorted. "My only interest is in finally letting the truth be known about everyone's *precious* Miss Starling. Maybe then the next man won't get burned!"

"Oh, so you are only acting from benevolence. I see."

"Of course!"

"Well," Max said slowly, meaningfully, staring into his eyes, "all the same, I'd shut my mouth if I were you."

Albert paused, registering the menace behind Max's low-toned words and cool, polite stare.

The other two Carew brothers exchanged a startled glance. They seemed to remember that this was how it always used to start.

Albert scoffed and looked away, shaking his head with a mocking smile. "Well, you're not me, are you, Rotherstone? You only wish you were."

"You listen to me, you preening piece of mediocrity." Max stepped closer, staring more fiercely into Albert's eyes. "Leave Daphne Starling to someone better suited to manage a lady of her quality."

"And who might that be? Jonathon White? He's a bigger pansy than my brother Hayden. Wait — *you?*" Albert suddenly narrowed his eyes. "*You're* interested in her?"

"Utter one more word against her, if you care to find out."

Albert let out a short bark of laughter. "Are you threatening me, Max?" he challenged, not quite realizing the danger he was in.

Max leaned closer with an icy look and whispered, "I'm merely giving you fair warning — Alby."

Finally, the message seemed to sink in.

Albert stiffened, easing back a step, but still, he clung to his trademark arrogance. "You think you can win her where I failed? Good luck, Max," he said in disgust, giving him a dismissive, once-over glance. "I'll be cheering for you."

"Well, well, isn't this just like old times? You boys are at it again already, I see."

They both glanced over as Albert's frail elder brother, Hayden, joined them. The easygoing young Duke of Holyfield had the delicate look of a poet. He glanced from Max

94

to Albert with a rueful smile. "Come now, gentlemen, we're all grown up here, aren't we?"

Albert rolled his eyes, but Max knew he was right. They had begun reverting into churlish juveniles.

It did not at all surprise him that Albert had openly thrown down the gauntlet, challenging Max to prove himself the better man if he thought he could succeed where Albert had failed. What surprised Max was that it would work. Now that he had an inkling of Daphne Starling's goodness and compassion, he was unhappy with the stirrings of his own competitive nature, that would almost rise to the bait of making her some sort of trophy between them. Max knew full well it was wrong and idiotic to make a contest of it, but, damn, the Carew bastards had always brought out the worst in him.

Albert snorted in contempt and then turned to his two younger siblings. "Let's get out of here." He eyed Max and Hayden with renewed hauteur. "This is a very dull company. The Edgecombes must be lowering their standards."

Max smiled menacingly at him, but was hardly sorry to see the bastard go. Now perhaps Miss Starling could enjoy the ball. Quietly exhaling his churning irritation, he turned to greet the eldest Carew brother with a more adult smile. "Holyfield."

"Rotherstone. Nice to see you again! I thought I recognized you. God, it has been years! I was sorry to hear about your father," Hayden added, jarring Max from his seething distraction.

"What? Oh. Yes, of course. Thank you. Same to you."

"Say, Max — all that traveling you've done, any tips on what to see in Paris? My wife wants to go before she enters her confinement."

"Confinement? Hayden!" Max stared at him in shock. "You're going to be a father?"

The young duke beamed. "Our first."

"Congratulations!"

"Scared to death of it, actually."

"Ah, it's all the mother's worry," he said with a cheeky grin, as if he would know. "So, you're taking her to Paris?"

"Mariah wants to see the place while she's still able to travel. Once the babe comes, I don't suppose we'll have many holidays for a while."

"Well, you must see the Tuileries, and the Louvre, of course, and Versailles, and Notre Dame Cathedral." They had a brief discussion of the great Parisian landmarks, but Max was eager to go find Daphne Starling.

He congratulated Hayden again, then extricated himself from the conversation. But as he went in search of his golden-haired quarry, he still couldn't believe that that pasty little fellow had managed to wed and bed a wife before *he* did.

Blazes, he would've never thought it possible. Rather depressing, actually.

Hunting for Daphne Starling, he had not seen her come back into the dining hall, so he went and looked in the ballroom, but that was all but empty now. Casually, he went and checked a few of the reception rooms, but seeing her nowhere, he grimly concluded that she was hiding from him.

Damn, he thought. Maybe that was enough for tonight. They were not off to the best start. Perhaps it was better to try again later, when there weren't prying eyes everywhere. Max decided to go. At least he had accomplished what he had set out to do tonight — he had let her see him, so at least she need not worry that some harm had come to him on her behalf.

On second thought, it might be slightly vain of him to think she even cared. His face hardened at the dark drift of his thoughts. He withdrew from the deserted ballroom and headed for the nearest exit.

He did not belong here, anyway.

Safely ensconced in the ladies' lounge, Daphne gave her reflection a firm look in the mirror. Having had a few moments to steady herself, she knew what she had to do, and it did not include one more moment of hiding

97

in here like a coward.

She had to go out there and talk to him.

Talk . . . to the Demon Marquess.

She swallowed hard at the prospect, faltering for a moment. Her ladylike sensibilities protested at the notion of approaching a man to whom she had not been properly introduced. But if Albert had told him lies about her, her pride insisted on defending her reputation.

Somehow this mattered more to her at the moment than the confrontation with Albert that she had planned. Why she cared so much what this stranger thought of her, she dared not examine. She preferred to tell herself it was simply a matter of etiquette. The man had saved her life. The least that she could do was go and say thank you.

Gliding back out to the party, she moved with a graceful but alert stride, glancing around for him watchfully from behind her open fan.

He was no longer standing in the doorway of the crowded dining hall, nor did she see him in the ballroom. Daphne frowned. Where had he gone? Just when she was starting to fear she had missed her chance, she spotted him striding down a lonely marble hallway toward a side door of Edgecombe House.

He's leaving?

Oh — dash! She picked up her skirts and hastened after him, her heartbeat quickening in time with the soft pattering rhythm of her satin-slippered footfalls. Her stare was glued to the broad V of his back.

Say something! she ordered herself. *He's getting away!*

He was almost to the few stairs at the end of the corridor. These led up into a small foyer before a rarely used door. She knew she had to stop him, but Daphne now found herself ridiculously tongue-tied.

Oh, this was so unlike her.

"Um — excuse me." Her voice came out as barely a whisper, too soft for him to hear. She rushed after him, determined to try again — not that she had any idea of what she'd do with such a dangerous beast once she had caught him.

Watching him, she could not help admiring his bold, confident walk ahead, as if he could march through fire and not get burned. "Excuse me!" she called in a louder tone. She faltered — rallied quickly. "Er, don't I know you?"

He stopped in his tracks.

Daphne winced at her decidedly unoriginal greeting, then bit her lower lip. At least this time it seemed that he had heard her call to him.

She waited, wide-eyed, for his reaction, not knowing what to expect. But she decided on the spot to hide the fact that she already knew his name.

Just in case he *had* been making fun of her with Albert, why give him the satisfaction of knowing she had cared enough to note that information?

Ahead of her, he stood very still; he had not yet turned around.

If he had, she might have seen the startled flicker of victory in his eyes, and then the sly satisfaction that curved his lips.

"I beg your pardon, sir." Her heart thumping, Daphne bolstered up her courage and took another uncertain step in his direction. "You are leaving — so soon?"

Finally, his motions wary and deliberate, the darkly handsome marquess pivoted to face her. His guarded stare traveled over her. "I'm not sure," he said slowly, "there is any reason for me to stay." He lifted one eyebrow slightly after his words, as though challenging her to tell him otherwise.

Daphne's knees knocked beneath her petticoat, threatening to give out as she faced the Demon Marquess in all his raw, male magnetism.

She swallowed hard. "I can think of one."

"Oh?"

She fiddled with her fan, but was determined to have her say. "I-I wanted to thank you for yesterday," she asserted. "It was — noble of you to come to my aid."

"Noble?" he echoed, both raven eyebrows arching high now.

"Yes." She nodded fervently. Something in his stare made her fingertips tingle. The tingle crept up her arms with sweet warmth, into her chest, and straight into her bosoms. She ignored the odd sensation with a will. "It was a clever ruse — oh, but it was risky!" she chided. "It could have gone quite badly, you know. I'm not sure you should have done it." She swallowed hard. "But, fortunately," she continued, "since you appear unharmed, do please accept my gratitude."

When he just stared at her in mild bemusement, his eyes slightly narrowed, as though examining some strange species of prey animal, Daphne, not knowing what else to do, sketched a modest, formal curtsy to punctuate her thanks.

Her acknowledgment of his heroics appeared to entertain him; his chiseled face softened considerably as he held her gaze.

"I am happy to be of service, Miss Starling, and am humbled by your concern. The honor was mine." He offered her a gallant bow in answer.

They stared at each other for a second, with several yards of marble hallway still between them.

Daphne barely realized she was holding her breath, as though she were in the presence of some magical creature, a unicorn in a moonlit grove.

Belatedly, she noted Lord Rotherstone's use

of her name. "I take it Lord Albert informed you who I am."

"No, actually," he said in a casual tone, "I already knew."

"You did?"

"No light as bright as yours, Miss Starling, can easily escape notice."

Well, that was prettily said, she thought. Maybe he was not as quick as some people to believe Albert's lies. She watched him in fascination as he walked back down the few steps from the landing ahead, approaching her at a leisurely saunter.

"The patron saint of newcomers, I presume?" he greeted her with an enigmatic smile.

"Oh — right." With a quick, modest smile at the nickname, Daphne lowered her gaze. "I take it that would include you? I have not seen you in Society before. Are you new to Town, sir?"

"I have been traveling abroad for some time."

As he closed the distance between them, she had to lift her chin to keep holding his gaze, for he was quite tall.

"Traveling abroad? During a war?"

"What is life without a little danger?" he countered, flashing a very dangerous smile, indeed.

"Oh." She dropped her gaze, cursing herself for the blush she could feel stealing into her cheeks. "I have never been beyond the, um, Home Counties myself."

"Oh, I would bet you have been to a dangerous place or two in your day, Miss Starling." He smiled faintly, a knowing look in his light-tricked eyes; their outer corners crinkled with a hint of amusement. He was referring, of course, to yesterday, she realized, and her little trip to Bucket Lane.

He stopped just in front of her, and stood gazing into her eyes with that same thoughtful expression she'd noticed before. He seemed to peer down into her very soul. "You looked upset when you left the dining hall a little while ago."

His frank observation took her off guard. "Oh — yes, well — it's nothing. I-I just thought . . ."

"I think I know what you thought," he murmured when her stammering trailed off into awkward silence.

Daphne lowered her head, but Lord Rotherstone shocked her when he touched her gently under her chin. She caught her breath sharply as he tilted her face upward again and looked into her eyes.

"I know what you thought," he repeated, "but, I can assure you, you were mistaken."

"Was I?" Her heart pounded at the light but sure pressure of his warm fingertips against her skin.

"Very. I should never wish to be the cause

103

of your distress, Miss Starling."

"What did Albert say to you about me?" she blurted out in a hushed tone, struggling to form a clear thought against the magic of his touch.

He smiled and lowered his hand to his side once more. "Better you should ask what *I* said to *him* about you."

She shot him a wary look of question.

He shrugged with a nonchalant smile. "I simply let him know that he can either mind his tongue or lose it."

Her eyes widened. "You *threatened* him?"

He sighed regretfully, folding his hands behind his back. "I'm fairly sure that's why he left the party. Pity, no?"

Daphne stared at him, her astonishment bordering on laughter. *Well! I was right from the outset. He is a lunatic.*

"You look surprised."

"I thought you were his friend!"

He looked away with a low laugh. "Not exactly."

She shook her head in wonder, trying to make sense of it all. "How do you know him?"

"He grew up near me when we were boys in Worcestershire."

"I see . . ." It was hard to imagine the tall, formidable man before her as a boy.

"Miss Starling, I could never let any man insult you in my presence. Rest assured of that."

"Oh," she whispered, trembling at his chivalrous vow.

It dawned on her that she was making a cake of herself, but she couldn't seem to help it. Her wits were somewhat routed by their exchange so far. Oh, but she was relieved to hear he had not been making sport of her, or even tolerating Albert's rudeness. On the contrary, the magnificent hellion had defended her.

She beamed. Daphne suddenly found herself growing desperate for a proper introduction. He was a positively thrilling man!

Eager to get that formal step out of the way, she cast about for some means to nudge the marquess into telling her his name. Yes, of course, she already knew it, but just now it seemed too forward, rude, and gossipy to admit that she had heard it while eavesdropping on his conversation with Albert.

"Well, I barely know what to say!" she exclaimed, trying to sound like the blithe Society coquette she could be when the need arose. "Two rescues in twenty-four hours, and I don't even know your name!"

Again, the eyebrow lifted. Perhaps she should have read it as a warning. "Shall I reveal it to you, or do you prefer the mystery to continue?" he asked dryly.

Oh, dear. The cynical tone of his voice instantly made her wonder if he could somehow tell that she was lying.

"Why, that's an odd question," she evaded with a quick, uneasy smile, opting to be vague.

He sighed and gazed toward the ceiling. "Yes, it's just that once you realize who I am," he mused aloud, "you may run from me. And that would make me sad." He looked at her again, intently, his pale green eyes keen and searching beneath the coal-black fringe of his short lashes.

Trapped in his stare with the strange sense that he could almost read her mind, Daphne was still unsure if he saw through her amateur deception.

Unfortunately, having started down this path, she saw no choice but to carry it through. She waved her fan faster, and kept smiling, though her cheeks were beginning to hurt. "Well, you can do as you please, I'm sure! I think you've earned that right. On the other hand," she countered with a coy flutter of her lashes, "I can't dance with you if I don't know your name, now, can I?"

"But my dear Miss Starling, I haven't asked you yet."

Her fan stopped. "You were going to, weren't you?" she exclaimed in indignation.

He flashed a smile. "Maybe."

"Well!" She tossed her head. "I had planned a dance as your reward for rescuing me, but now I'm not so sure."

"My dear young lady, if I had done it for

the reward," he murmured, moving closer still, "I promise you, I would be asking for more than a dance."

Daphne stared at him, wide-eyed.

The sheer wickedness of the slow, lazy smile he gave her made her catch her breath against the squeeze of her tight stays. All of a sudden, she longed to be rid of them, rid of most of her clothing, actually, when he looked at her that way. Her own little game was completely overwhelmed by his palpable expertise, and she thought again of the brothel. *What would he be like to . . . ?*

She warded off the naughty thought before she could complete it. Feeling slightly faint, shocked at the extremely unladylike drift of her imaginings, she looked away, waving her fan again very fast, indeed.

Having left her speechless with his silken innuendo, Lord Rotherstone now paused, as though he had all the time in the world to play with her and steer the conversation wherever he willed.

"You see, my dear, even more than a dance, what I really want from you is a promise."

Her eyes flared as she sent him another swift glance. "What kind of — promise?" she asked hoarsely, barely daring wonder what a demon marquess might want from a girl.

To her surprise, however, he leaned down to glower into her eyes and pointed his finger in her face. "Do not *ever* go back to that treacherous alley again," he ordered her matter-of-factly. "Next time, I may not be there to rescue you. Do you understand me?"

His command and his domineering stare took her aback.

She looked at him in astonishment. Who exactly did he think he was?

"I beg your pardon." Not about to be told what to do by a man she had only just met, she lifted her index finger and pushed his aside with a dainty strike, as if in a miniature duel.

"You heard me," he murmured in a husky tone, hooking his finger and effectively capturing hers. He held on to it, and locked stares with her at close range. "Promise," he whispered, with a dark, irresistible charm that seemed to engulf her.

Daphne studied his lips for a second, then shook off the shiver of awareness that ran through her body. "No," she informed him in crisp tones. "I cannot promise that, I'm afraid."

"You can," he told her sweetly, "and you shall."

"No," she repeated, just as kindly, and as firmly. "I'm afraid you do not understand, my lord. The children at the orphanage, they need me."

"Alive, one presumes," he said with an equally unflappable smile, though his eyes were flinty. "You are no use to them dead, now, are you, sweet Miss Starling?"

Losing patience with his highhandedness, she tugged her finger free of his light hold and scowled at him. "You don't understand, I *have* to go back there whether I like it or not — at least until the orphanage is moved! I can't let those poor children think I've abandoned them, like their own parents have. Besides, I didn't question *your* business in Bucket Lane, now, did I? I hardly think it fitting that you question mine."

She relished his startled look at her polite reminder of his visit to that disgusting brothel, but he recovered quickly. "Young lady, you listen to me —"

"Pish-posh," she said with an idle wave of her hand. "All's well that ends well."

He looked at her in amazement. "Did you just say pish-posh to me?"

"Why, yes, I believe I did." She folded her arms across her chest, giving him a serenely stubborn smile.

"Lord Rotherstone?" a voice intruded.

They both looked over.

"Yes? What is it?" The marquess frowned at Daphne, while a harried-looking footman came rushing down the hallway with a folded piece of paper on a silver tray.

"A message arrived for you, sir. I was afraid I'd missed you! Forgive the interruption. The courier said it was urgent."

"Here, I will take it." He beckoned the man

forward with an impatient flick of his fingers.

"Lord Rotherstone," Daphne echoed softly, sending him a twinkling smile. "Are you sure it's not made out to the Demon Marquess?"

He narrowed his eyes at her. "So, I was right. You already knew my name, you saucy thing."

She grinned, feeling better to come clean. "I could not let you have the advantage of me, now, could I?"

He snorted and shook his head, turning away with a low laugh to read his note. "If you'll excuse me for a moment?"

"Of course, Lord Rotherstone."

He gave her another sardonic look at her arch repetition of his name and unfolded the letter, swiftly scanning it.

Daphne kept a polite distance, but she watched his chiseled countenance with avid curiosity. She was not one to read over anyone's shoulder, but she could not resist teasing him in the hopes that she might pry a little intelligence out of him as to its contents. "Do I detect a whiff of brimstone in the air?"

"Quite," he said dryly, then folded the note again and slid it into the pocket of his waistcoat. With a wave of his hand, Lord Rotherstone dismissed the footman, who had stood waiting for any reply he might wish to send. He glanced at her. "Regretfully, Miss Starling, I must go."

"Oh, but we were only just getting acquainted," she said with a playful little pout.

"Trust me," he murmured with a roguish look, "we will pick up soon where we left off."

"But what of our dance?"

"You'll owe me one."

She frowned in sudden concern. "It's not bad news, I hope?"

"No, no, it's excellent news, but the sort I must attend to at once. An arrival, actually, that I have long awaited."

"Arrival?" A sudden horrible thought flashed across her mind out of nowhere. "Is your wife having a baby?" she cried as he began to turn away. In the next second, she was even more aghast at what she had just blurted out; she clapped a hand over her mouth and stared at him.

"My wife?" He stopped and turned back to her, frowning in surprise. "What do you know of my wife?"

She lowered her hand slightly from her mouth, longing to hide under the nearest rock. "Nothing! Oh, God — I beg your pardon. I didn't mean, that is, I'm sure it's none of my —"

His soft, tickled laughter put a halt to her mortified stammering. His pale eyes danced. "My dear Miss Starling," he teased, laughing warmly at her flustered attempt to find out if he was a married man. "If I had a wife about to give birth, I would hardly be here, letting a charming young beauty enchant me. Though,

I must admit, I can't help but feel a little flattered that your thoughts turn so easily to breeding in my presence."

She gasped, rendered speechless. Still chuckling as she turned rosy, he captured her hand and bowed over it, pressing the briefest of kisses to her knuckles. "*Au revoir, cherie.* Until we meet again."

"Oh, will we?" she retorted, yanking back her hand as he released it, barely recovered from her embarrassment at his ribald teasing.

"Count on it," he whispered, and took leave of her with a wink.

Oh, that man!

For the longest moment, she stood just where he'd left her, watching him stride away, and then staring dazedly at the empty hallway even after he'd slipped out the door.

Vaguely, she lifted the hand he had kissed to her heart. She could feel her whole chest pounding with the crazed reaction he inspired, a potent mix of thrill and joy, uncertainty and complete exasperation.

Well! she thought in belated, still rather mortified humor. At least now she knew he wasn't married.

She was so caught up in her thoughts of him that Daphne did not even notice her friend Carissa rushing up the hallway toward her until a feminine hand gripped her arm, turning her around, and a familiar whisper exclaimed by her ear, "Are you *mad?*"

"Oh — Carissa." Blinking like a woman waking from a dream, she smiled dazedly at her friend. "I've hardly seen you all night."

"Well, luckily, I saw you! Better me than anyone else, to be sure! What do you think you are doing, talking to *him* — unchaperoned, no less? Have you lost your mind?"

With auburn hair and emerald eyes, the fey-featured Carissa Portland waited for her explanation like an angry fairy queen.

Daphne shook her head, still feeling the aftereffects of his spell. "Whatever do you mean?"

"Daphne! He is a scoundrel!"

"Nooo!" she protested in lavish denial, waving away this objection. "He is perfectly amiable, believe me."

Well, except for that whole brothel business, came a niggling thought.

"Do you even know who that *is?*" Carissa demanded.

"Of course I do! The Marquess of Rotherstone."

Carissa dropped her voice to an emphatic whisper: "The Demon Marquess!"

"Oh, that's just silly —"

"No, it's not!"

"Pish-posh. Let's go get some sweets!"

"Daphne, listen to me." Carissa gripped her arm. "I don't know what's got into you, but you must not go near that wicked fellow again. Haven't you heard?"

113

"What?"

"He is one of the leading members of the Inferno Club!"

"The what?"

"The Inferno Club!" The redhead beckoned her a little closer and glanced around with a conspiratorial air, then endeavored to explain. "They meet in Dante House, not far from the other gentlemen's clubs in St. James's. But they are altogether wicked, so I've heard."

"Why? What do they do?" she asked eagerly.

"Things decent girls like us ought never contemplate!"

Daphne furrowed her brow. Carissa was not normally a prude. "What else do you know?"

"Only that they are a scandalous society of decadent, highborn libertines, infamous for pursuing all manner of debauchery. That is why you must not speak to him. If you thought stupid Albert Carew and his jealous rumors could harm your reputation, that's *nothing* compared to the damage you could suffer if you're seen overmuch in the company of Lord Hellfire there." Carissa nodded toward the door by which Lord Rotherstone had left.

Daphne thought again of his charming smile and gave her friend a crestfallen look. "There must be some mistake. He's new to Town. He told me he's been traveling abroad."

"Well, yes, but when he does stop in London, those Inferno Club hellions are the sort of company he prefers. Half of Society doesn't receive him," Carissa added. "I warrant the only reason he was invited tonight is because he is related to Lord Edgecombe."

Daphne's heart began to sink.

An image of him stumbling out of the brothel yesterday came easily to mind, but even so, she did not want to believe what Carissa was reporting.

"You know the gossip is always exaggerated."

Carissa shook her head stubbornly. "I was just talking to some of my officer friends, and you would not believe what they said. According to them, Lord Rotherstone showed up at Waterloo. *Not* to fight Napoleon. Just to watch the battle, as if it was the latest circus spectacle at Astley's!"

"Really? Not to fight? You're sure?"

Carissa nodded. "They referred to him as the Grand Tourist, for he lives only for pleasure. They said he did nothing useful for the cause, but spent the hours before the battle getting drunk, chasing the tavern wenches around, and making a spectacle of himself laying wagers against Boney. He even made himself comfortable right inside General Wellington's headquarters. Can you imagine? A complete libertine — but he is so rich and powerful that none of the officers could naysay him."

"Why didn't Wellington throw him out if he was such a nuisance?"

She shrugged. "Probably Lord Wellington was too much of a gentleman — or was simply too busy to care, on the eve before battle."

"Hm." Daphne wrinkled her brow in complete befuddlement and glanced toward the door by which Lord Rotherstone had gone.

Obviously, Carissa believed what she had heard from the officers, but having met the man in question, Daphne felt that this did not add up. She remembered all too vividly the look of gusto on his face when he had broken that bottle in Bucket Lane and invited half the rookery to try him.

Of course, she admitted skeptically, he had been foxed then — or at least still feeling the effects of the previous night's indulgence.

"Whatever you do, just be careful with him," Carissa warned. "Such a man's intentions are not likely to be honorable, and I saw how he was looking at you," she added with mixed humor and disapproval. "I don't want to be the bearer of bad news, but I do hope you'll heed my advice, as one who adores you and will be forever in your debt."

"Stuff and nonsense, Miss Portland, you are not in my debt," Daphne said with a smile. "You are my friend."

"And *you* were the only person who was kind to me when I first arrived in London.

116

Not even my dreadful cousins treated me humanely. You championed me, and now I must protect you. And for your sake, my dear Daphne, I should be like a-a mother bear minding her cub!"

"You? A bear?" she asked in amusement, glancing at her friend's slim, petite frame. She started laughing. "A good breeze could blow you away."

"I am a bear in spirit!" Carissa hooked her arm through Daphne's elbow and smiled fondly at her. "Don't let your generous nature lead you into a snare with this man, promise? I fear it would be a great mistake for you to try taking up Lord Rotherstone's cause as you did mine, however tempted you may be. Lost souls are hopeless cases, even for you."

Lost soul? Demon Marquess? Daphne didn't know what to think. "Honestly, he seemed all right to me," she defended him as they strolled back toward the ballroom, arm in arm.

Carissa shrugged, still dubious. "To be sure, he is beautiful to look at. Not to mention rich and powerful. And probably a brilliant catch — if he could ever be brought to heel. But that is extremely unlikely. His ancestors were all bad, too, I hear. Don't make me worry for you," she complained, nudging her with her shoulder. "We both know you're already on shaky ground with this whole Albert debacle. Promise me you'll stay away

117

from him, for your own good."

She glanced abashedly at her friend. "I can't."

"Daphne!"

"I can't help it!" she exclaimed, shrugging and blushing again like some foolish cake head. "I owe him a dance, I already promised!"

"You don't owe anything to any man!" the elfin lady thundered in righteous indignation.

Daphne bit her lip as her blush deepened.

"Oh . . . wait one moment! I see what is going on here!" Carissa propped a hand on her hip and looked at Daphne matter-of-factly. "You *like* him."

Daphne winced at the accusation. She pursed her lips, refusing to admit it aloud.

"Daphne! Oh, leave it to the perfect lady to take an interest in a bad, wicked scoundrel!"

"It's not like I'm going to marry the man!" she retorted in a whisper. "What harm can there be in one dance?"

"Famous last words," Carissa said archly. "Come, you little henwit, I will save you from yourself!"

Taking Daphne's wrist with sudden laughter, Carissa dragged her back to the ballroom and cheerfully shoved her off to dance with someone safe and boring.

But all throughout the dance, Daphne kept glancing at the door, hoping against her bet-

ter sense that Lord Hellfire might return.
Fortunately for her reputation, he did not.

CHAPTER 5

Pish-posh? Inside his lightless carriage, Max shook his head, the lingering trace of a smile on his lips. It was not easy to leave her. *Delightful creature.* She was even more alluring up close. The light scent of her floral perfume still clung to him as his coach traveled through the midnight streets of London.

The earlier storm had tapered off into a thick cloak of mist; the moon shimmered in the watery sky like a silver coin at the bottom of a garden fountain.

Though his first encounter with the enchanting Miss Starling had left him hungry for more, Virgil had summoned Max to the club with the news that Warrington and Falconridge had just arrived in Town.

It was turning into a very good night.

The Inferno Club lay only half a mile from the brilliance of the Edgecombe ball, but in the darkness, it seemed a world away.

As his carriage rolled into the shadow of Dante House, a place of mystery, he glanced out the window at the sinister-looking building, dubbed by locals "the Town residence of Satan."

Between its black, twisty spires, a glass-domed observatory bulged atop the roof. At the street level, a high spiked fence and misshapen mounds of overgrown thorns warded off the uninvited.

Warped shutters and roof shingles creaked when the wind blew off the river like a tribe of moaning ghosts, but the diabolical aspect of Dante House was only a façade. What appeared a haunted mansion to the outside world was in fact a compact, efficient fortress in disguise.

The paradox of it pleased him.

While the evil members of the Promethean Council contrived to present themselves as upstanding pillars of European society, it seemed only fitting, in turn, for good to hide behind a mask of wickedness, the better to wage their shadow war.

Max got out of his carriage and told his coachman to drive home without him. There was no point in making the man wait around till dawn. With his friends back at last, Max had no idea how late he might stay out. This night called for celebration. They had not seen one another in about two years, and there had been moments during the war when he'd wondered if they would ever get through it alive.

He walked through the front gates of Dante House and closed them behind him. Ahead, the entrance portico loomed.

In a wry tribute to the poet for whom the house was named, the front door had a brass knocker in the shape of a medieval scholar's head, his expression inscrutable under his flat-topped cap.

Above the door hung a placard with a word of advice to visitors, echoing the famed inscription over the poet Dante's gateway to Hell: *Abandon hope all ye, etc.*

With the worldly, irreverent ennui for which most Inferno Club members were famous, the placard did not even bother finishing the quote. Which was just as well, for few would enter here. Entrée was strictly guarded, by invitation only, possibly on pain of death.

Occasional wild revelries were held here for the sake of keeping up the appearance of dissipation, but these were actually highly choreographed events overseen by Virgil himself.

Security was intensive, all possible measures taken to assure that none of the painted ladies who were brought in for the fun had any idea what was really going on.

The door swung open ahead with a mournful creak, and there stood Mr. Gray, who had been the butler at Dante House for time immemorial.

The tall, gaunt butler — who looked like

something the resurrection men had dug up — had always possessed uncanny timing. Standing aside, he bowed gravely as Max strode in.

"Good evening, Marquess."

"Evening, Gray." He stepped into the foyer. "I understand we have cause tonight for celebration."

"Indubitably, sir." Gray closed the door behind Max just as a few of the Order's hell-hounds came bounding forth to greet him.

Great black-and-tan dogs of German origin, tamed demons, all gleaming fangs, sleek speed, and rangy motion, they danced around Max, tails wagging, their big canine grins at odds with their fierce looks and spiked collars. "Sit!" Max held up his hand to silence their raucous greeting.

The guard dogs immediately dropped to their haunches. One large pup-in-training licked its nose nervously and stared at him with a small whine. "Good boy." Max gave the dog a pat on the head just as Virgil joined them.

To this day, Max was not sure if that was really his handler's name.

The gruff, giant Highlander had always filled Max with a certain degree of awe, ever since that day so long ago when Virgil had arrived at the Rotherstones' dilapidated country house in his role as Seeker.

The first time Max had met him, himself

only a boy, Virgil had been wearing the kilt of his clan. Though he wore ordinary clothes in Town, he still had the air of a mighty laird. In his fifties now, he had a good deal of gray mixed in with the reddish-gold of his wild hair. His impressive orange mustache, which Max had so envied as a lad, was shot through with salt-and-pepper grays. But he was still formidable, a grizzled warrior of a man, with all the scars to prove his lifelong loyalty to the Order.

Rather than mellowing him, the years had only seemed to harden the Scot. After thirty-five years spent in the Order's struggle against their Promethean enemies — slightly more time than Max had even been alive — Virgil was now the head of the Order in London. Who Virgil's superiors in the government were, that was information Max was not privy to.

As the Link for his team, however, he knew of other cells in great cities throughout the Continent, wherever the Promethean Council had been gaining too much sway.

To be sure, the Promethean Council had had tentacles in every court in Europe. They planned not in years, but in decades, in centuries, driven by their endless lust for power over mankind. From time to time, they rose to threaten humanity, but never before in all their history had the Prometheans come so close to their aims as they had in the past twenty years, by infiltrating the structure of empire Napoleon had built.

Parasites that they were, it was their way to creep in unobtrusively, gaining the trust of the powerful by degrees, extending their own dark influence ever deeper in the guise of trusted advisors, seasoned generals, longtime friends; patiently, quietly, always deniably, they spread their corruption, taking over slowly from the inside like a cancerous disease.

This time, they might have succeeded. But when Napoleon was finally vanquished at Waterloo about three months ago, the Promethean overlords' fondest dreams of destiny had also come crashing down.

If Napoleon had won that battle, Max mused, the future of the world would have looked very different. But Bonaparte had been defeated, and now the nations of the earth might know another fifty years of rest before the Promethean enemy rose again in some new, ruthless incarnation.

Of course, the Council had succeeded in delivering one last, cruel parting blow before going down in defeat.

A Promethean spy had delivered false news to London about the outcome of the Battle of Waterloo. In the early morning hours, someone had spread the word that Wellington had lost — that Napoleon had crushed the British army in Belgium, and the long-dreaded nightmare of "the Monster" landing on England's shores was imminent.

The terrible rumors had ignited London, causing a panic that day in the financial markets. The London stock exchange had crashed violently, but the soulless Prometheans had been ready, buying up solid British companies for pennies on the pound.

Every stockholder in London had wanted out of their investments immediately, believing they'd need their money in hand to survive, perhaps to flee, if necessary, to save their families from the soon-to-be-invading Grande Armée. Panic had run wild. In their desperation, people had been willing to take whatever pittance they could get for their stock, but the only ones buying were the shell companies the Promethean overlords had set up in anticipation of this deception.

Great companies had changed hands overnight. Countless reputable merchants had been ruined, the life savings of countless innocent people wiped out, and no one, not even the Order, had seen the thing coming.

Max's own holdings had taken a thrashing, but fortunately, most of his investments were in land. The market panic had been halted when the truth of Wellington's victory at Waterloo had arrived, but by then, much of the damage was already done.

The Prometheans had walked away with a fortune of many millions. No doubt it would help to fund their next attempt to impose their tyranny on the world, which was why the next generation of warriors for the Order of St. Michael were already being trained at the same remote castle in Scotland that Max had been brought to as a boy.

"Good. You got my note," Virgil said gruffly as he joined Max in the foyer.

"So, where are the bastards?" Max asked with a grin as he shook his old mentor's offered hand, that grasp that had once seemed to him as big as a bear's paw.

Now his own was equal to it, and as for the Scot's towering height at which he had marveled endlessly as a youngster, Max now met him eye to eye.

"Below," the Seeker answered. "They've both finished giving their reports."

God, he had missed those lads. "Virgil?" Max stared into his sharp blue eyes with a trace of worry. "Are they all right?" Max immediately saw that he should have expected the testy scowl he got in answer.

"Of course they're all right! I didn't raise you lads for a stroll in the daisies, did I?"

"Er — no, sir." He dropped his gaze in amusement, the memories of those brutal years of training at the Order's secret castle up in Scotland seared into his mind.

The punishing regimes, the steely discipline, the "games" that involved the youths beating the blazes out of each other so they'd all be toughened up for the hell that lay ahead for every one of them. The endless rounds of lessons in so many diverse disciplines, turning them into gentlemen as well as killers, "worthy companions of kings," like the ones they'd go on to protect from time to time.

The countless tests of body, mind, and soul had finally forged Virgil's young recruits into a brotherhood bound by loyalty, and sealed by the Order's blood oath.

While other boys their age had been shirking their books, taunting girls, and playing pranks on their headmasters, Virgil and the rest of their trainers had been molding them into cold-blooded assassins as the occasion called — trained liars, survivors, spies.

The Highlander had known, of course, that they would inevitably suffer in body and mind during the course of their missions, so he had prepared them to be able to take it, to keep moving forward relentlessly in their various quests. All that mattered was the Order's ancient guiding mission to keep the Prometheans' evil under their heel, and to guard the security of their secret web with their lives.

"You head on down," Virgil grumbled. "You lads will want to catch up, and God knows ye've earned your rest. Ring if ye need me, Gray," he added over his shoulder as he headed back about his own business. "We've all got to stay on our toes until we're certain no one's been followed."

"Yes, master." The sepulchral butler bowed once more, then spoke a sharp order in German to the dogs to resume their duties guarding the premises.

Max suddenly snapped his fingers. "Virgil, before I forget, have you found anything yet on those fake companies that raked in all those profits from the market crash? Whenever you've got a lead for me to follow, I can start looking into it."

"Not necessary. I put another team on it."

"Are you sure? I have the time."

"Beauchamp's team is still across the Channel tying up loose ends on the Continent, and since the only lead I've got concerns a man by the name of Rupert Tavistock, who apparently left England months ago, I put them on the matter. Beauchamp and his men are to track this Tavistock down before they come home."

"Rupert Tavistock," Max echoed. The name was not familiar. "Very well. Let me know if you need anything."

Virgil looked askance at him, well aware of his bride hunt. "You've got more important things to worry about at present, don't you?"

Max smiled.

"Get to breeding, my boy!" Virgil said as he turned and began walking away. "This fight is never really done, you know."

Max frowned at his ominous words, but

called after him. "Virgil, one more thing." The memories of the old days at the castle had triggered a thought of another friend he had not seen in far too long. "When do you expect Drake's team back from the Continent?"

Virgil went still, then lowered his gaze to the floor, as though he had hoped to escape before Max asked that question.

Max sensed his hesitation. "Virgil?"

"They're not coming back, Max." The Highlander turned around slowly. "Drake's team was killed in Munich."

Max stared at him in shock. "When?"

"Six months ago, far as I can reckon."

Turning away as he tried to absorb it, Max ran his hand slowly through his hair.

"Go and see your friends, lad," Virgil muttered.

"The few I've got left," he breathed.

"At least all three of you came back alive."

"Who killed them — Drake and his team? Do we know?" Max asked tautly.

Virgil shrugged. "They were tracking Septimus Glasse when we lost contact."

"Septimus Glasse . . . ?" Max echoed. He knew the name. Septimus Glasse was the head of the Council's operations in Germany.

Virgil nodded, then fell silent for a moment. "I'm sorry, Max," he said at length, retreating into his usual gruff demeanor. "Go on below, now. I'll let you know as soon as I learn anything. The boys are waitin' for you."

"Yes, sir," he answered barely audibly, but he still could not believe that Drake had fallen. The man had been one of the best fighters they had.

He watched Virgil walk away into the dark corridor that led off deeper into Dante House.

Left standing alone, his mood darkened by the news, Max shut his eyes and offered up a reverential silence for his friend. When he opened them again, Virgil's advice to start producing sons returned to his mind. *Why?* he wondered bitterly. *So they can get killed, too?*

For God's sake, he had only just discovered what might well be the woman of his dreams, but he was far from married yet, and already Virgil seemed to be counting on his unborn sons as future knights for the Order.

No, he was not the first Rotherstone to have served in the Order, and would probably not be the last. But he could not fathom how he could ever knowingly hand over any child of his to be subjected to the same kind of life he'd had to endure. It was a hell of a thing to contemplate on the night he meant to celebrate the *end* of battle with his brother warriors. *Virgil's right. It never really ends.*

A curse arrowed through his mind.

Damn it, it had ended at Waterloo. He had to believe that. Had he not witnessed those bloodred fields with his own eyes? It *had* to be over. He couldn't take any more. After twenty years of this, his very soul was starved for some new kind of life. Whatever that might be, at least he'd have the opportunity to try to find it, unlike Drake.

Suddenly, he could not shake off the shadow that had fallen across his heart. He walked restlessly into the club's vast feasting hall, where the walls were painted with a large, eerie, fantastical mural portraying Dante's trek through the various circles of Hell.

The dining room's massive Renaissance chimneypiece was worthy of any grand chateau. Ornately carved of alabaster, it had thick brass candelabras affixed to both ends of the mantel. Max walked over to the right side of the white mantel, glanced warily over his shoulder out of habit, then reached up and twisted the brass base of the middle candleholder, until he heard a low mechanical click.

At once, hidden gears beneath the floorboards rumbled faintly and there was a scraping *whoosh;* a rectangular section of brick in the back of the fireplace slowly rotated open, revealing a low doorway beyond which there was only darkness.

He ducked his head and stepped over the empty coal basket, going into the secret passageway. It was only one of many entrances into the labyrinth of hidden passages that ran through Dante House.

Once through the opening, he straightened up in the darkness, giving the hand lever on the wall a hard pull. Again, the heavy gears churned; the mechanical slate rotated back into place, and the fireplace hid its secrets once again.

Turning to his right, Max began moving confidently behind the wall toward his destination. The pitch-darkness and claustrophobic narrowness of the secret corridors were designed to confound anyone trying to navigate them, but he had memorized the maze years ago and did not need the benefit of light to find his way to the dank limestone cellars underneath the house.

Through several corridors, up a ladder, a left-hand turn, up another ladder, and then a right turn, all the way through the labyrinth, he thought about Drake and all the others who had died, and when the darkness seemed like it would overwhelm him, he reached like a drowning man for the memory of Daphne Starling.

Her golden hair, her radiant eyes, her luminous skin.

In his mind's eye, she glowed like a light.

Ahead, the faint flicker of a single torch led him out into the antechamber of the Pit, where a hole about eight feet wide gaped in the center of the stone floor. A single, thick rope hung down from the ceiling and disappeared through the hole into the darkness below. It was one of only three entrances to the Pit.

It had been a while since Max had indulged in these acrobatics, but he removed the velvet coat he had worn to the ball, threw it aside, then unbuttoned the wrists of his white shirtsleeves and rolled them up a cuff or two.

With three quick running steps, he leaped and grabbed onto the rope. He steadied himself, and in the next moment, was sliding down the line at a controlled glide.

His face was as grim as his thoughts as he landed square on his feet at the bottom of the dark shaft.

Releasing the rope, he dusted off his hands, then gazed ahead into the hollowed chamber they called the Pit. The old stone cellars beneath the three-hundred-year-old house had long served as the headquarters of the Order.

Max stepped out of the shaft toward the dark stone chamber ahead. It was dimly lit by flickering torches affixed to the walls. Immediately to his right, there was another arched doorway carved in the limestone.

Through there, he knew, a pitch-black corridor led down on a slight incline to the river gate and the small boats' landing area beneath Dante House. Agents could be ferried in from larger vessels arriving on the Thames or spirited away unnoticed as required, but when not in use, the arched entrance to their private docking area was barred by a jagged portcullis, like that which guarded the river gate inside the Tower of London.

Max's footfalls reverberated in the cavelike hollow of the Pit as he walked slowly into that familiar chamber.

To his left, he passed a small door in the stone-block foundation wall at waist-level. This was the secret dumbwaiter by which supplies could be sent down to the men below. Beside it sat a weapons case, which always held a few guns and swords in case anyone needed extras.

Heading for the rugged wooden table and two plain benches on the other side of the room, he walked across the round floor medallion that bore the likeness of the Order's patron saint, the Archangel Michael.

The Byzantine mosaic had been taken from a church sacked by Saracens and rescued by the group of Crusaders who had been the first members of their clandestine Order.

Set into the center of the floor, it showed the heroic archangel with a flaming sword in his hand, trampling upon Satan.

A thick and weighty Maltese cross hung from the subterranean rock, suspended on a rusted chain.

A glass-doored cabinet with a few shelves held useful books, an array of poisons and their antidotes, a clock, and other sundries. A wooden coat rack stood by the wall, with one dripping greatcoat hanging on it. There was a small bank of bells on the wall like those used in servants' quarters; these allowed the men to receive signals, warnings, and alerts, from Mr. Gray upstairs.

As Max approached the table, the lantern there illuminated a large bottle of port with a few glasses waiting for the three friends' reunion. It was already opened, left to breathe.

He heard voices coming from the direction of the landing dock and turned, just as Jordan Lennox, the Earl of Falconridge, appeared under the arched doorway.

"Max!"

The instant Max saw him, some of the pain of Drake's death lifted. Thank God his closest mates had come home safe.

Jordan's short-cropped sandy hair was wet, and rain still dampened the clean, sharp angles of his face — Max gathered the travelers had been buffeted by the storm on their way up the river — but their expert codebreaker's ice-blue eyes glowed with his usual foxlike cunning, and with his pleasure at finally arriving home again.

"Jordan." The two old friends strode toward each other and met at the edge of the floor medallion, where they clasped arms, laughing. "You made it."

"Do you believe it? We finally got rid of those bastards!" Jordan exclaimed. "It's over! We did it."

"We did, thanks be to God — and to Virgil."

"And to us!" Jordan agreed heartily. "You got my message?"

"Damned right I did."

The coded message from Jordan was what had put Max on the trail of the traitor lurking deep undercover right there in Wellington's headquarters.

In the guise of a British officer, a Promethean agent called Major Kyle Bradley had been under orders from the Council to assassinate Wellington there on the battlefield if things went badly for Napoleon.

Stopping him was the mission that Max had been sent to carry out at Waterloo.

Jordan's eyes gleamed with cunning wit. "I trust my information proved useful."

"Very much so." His polite tone belied the savagery of the private fight he and Bradley had waged in the forest not far from the raging battlefield.

The only witnesses to their brutal combat had been the local peasant families hiding in the forests while the armies clashed, waiting for it all to be over to see if there would be anything left of their farms.

"I trust you dealt with it handily."

Max gave him a dry look and shrugged.

"Wellington's still alive."

Jordan shook his head, marveling. "Ah, you cannot imagine my envy of your witnessing that day. Waterloo!"

"You'd have been welcome company, believe me."

"You must tell me all about it."

"Gladly. You'd have appreciated the noble officers' haughty reaction to the Grand Tourist. It was rather amusing. So, where's Rohan?"

"He's getting his things off the boat," Jordan said.

"Shall we go and give him a hand?" Max asked. They did not use servants in their secret lair.

"You can try. He might bite your head off, though."

"Ah, the Beast is in a mood?" Max inquired.

"Don't discuss me behind my back or I'll smite you," a gruff voice echoed to them from the corridor a moment before the massive outline of Rohan Kilburn, the Duke of Warrington, appeared, with one of the vicious black dogs trotting tamely by his heels.

Max grinned. "Welcome home, Your Grace."

Rohan growled and advanced into the room. The dog's chain ran out, so it retreated to its post guarding the docks, but Max watched in amusement as his other boyhood friend, now a towering warrior, swung the prodigious sack of his supplies off his mighty shoulder and let it clomp down onto the floor.

Max folded his arms across his chest with a sardonic look. "Pleasant journey, old boy?"

"It has fucking rained," the duke declared, "the entire time since we left bloody Ostend." He dragged a hand through his long, damp hair.

Jordan sent Max a wry glance. "I fear the weather has ruined his jovial nature."

"I hate traveling," Rohan muttered.

"Good news, then. Have you heard? Your wandering days are at an end. You can lock yourself up in that haunted castle of yours until you are old and gray, my friend. The whole damned business is done."

"I'll believe that when I see it," he said.

"Oh, come, this is no time for your superstitious nature," Max chided. "We accomplished what we set out to do all those years ago, and now, God willing, we may be private men."

"Whatever that means," he replied.

"You're such a killjoy, Warrington," Jordan remarked, but when Max offered Rohan a hand, the duke clasped it, then pulled him in for a quick, crushing bear hug.

The big knight clapped him once on the back, nearly breaking a rib, then released him with a sudden rugged laugh. "Midas Max! Everything he touches turns to gold! Man, it's been too bleedin' long."

"Two years."

Max noticed the new, star-shaped scar above the outer corner of Rohan's left eyebrow. He nodded at it. "Like the new addition."

"Oh, yes," Rohan said with a snort. "I just keep getting better-looking, don't I? God, where can a man get a drink around here?" Rohan stepped around Max and headed for the bottle of port.

Before long, they were all seated at the coarse, sturdy table, laughing by the glow of the single lantern as they recounted various misadventures and close calls.

But when the second round of port had been drained from their cups, they drifted into silence as each began to ponder the realization that their battle days were truly at an end.

"So, here we are," Jordan murmured at length. "Alive."

"More or less," Max said wryly.

"What of the others?" Rohan asked. "There's bound to be losses." The question was directed at Max, since he was the Link, or leader of their team.

To protect the Order's overall security in case any agent was captured, only the Links were authorized to communicate with other team leaders.

The exception would be for some larger, special mission for which Virgil would summon as many trios as were needed to assemble and work together temporarily. But on those occasions, the talk was all business, and names were generally not used.

If an agent recognized a fellow knight of the Order in Society or elsewhere, he was to show no sign.

Max lowered his gaze. Drake, too, had been the Link for his trio of men. "One of our teams was completely wiped out."

"God," Jordan whispered. "Anyone we'd know?"

With the war over and the men dead, Max didn't think it mattered anymore if he revealed it to them. "I didn't know his fellows, but the leader was Drake Parry, the Earl of Westwood."

"Westwood," Jordan echoed. "I think I met him once. Black-haired. Welsh?"

"Yes." Max stared into his cup. "Hell of a fighter. Good as Rohan, almost." He nodded toward the duke, who slid Max a grim look in turn as he opened a second waiting bottle.

"We're sure they're dead?" Rohan asked bluntly.

"They'd better be," Jordan murmured. "Better that than captured." Then he noticed Max's silence. "You knew him well?"

"Fairly."

After a long silence, Jordan lifted his glass. "To Lord Westwood."

Max followed suit, nodding, trying to ignore the tight feeling in his throat. "To

Drake and his men."

"Better them than us," Rohan muttered under his breath and tossed back a swallow of port in their honor.

A lugubrious silence descended as each man privately wondered how it was that he had managed to survive when equally worthy colleagues had fallen.

Max's thoughts turned to Daphne Starling once more, like a sailor searching clouded skies for Polaris, one distant light to guide him in the blackness.

What if it were me instead of Drake? What if I was the one who didn't get to come home? He lingered over his drink. Tomorrow was promised to no man. All he had been through had certainly taught him that.

Hunger for life throbbed in his veins, especially now that his time was his own, to live as he liked, to do as he pleased, to be who he really was — if that was still possible after all he'd seen.

They were still young men, though seasoned. They still had so much life ahead of them, things Drake would never get to experience.

Like love.

Max had never experienced that, either.

Yet who could say when the darkness would come for him? Drake's death was a reminder that he did not have forever.

Get to breeding, Max, Virgil had said. Maybe

the Highlander's wisdom was exactly right once more.

"So, what do we do now?" Jordan murmured as they sat around staring at each other uneasily. "Retire to our estates? Take up fox hunting and become country gentlemen?"

"Bugger that," Rohan said with a dark, rough laugh. "Rogering every whore in Covent Garden sounds to me like an excellent start."

"Good God, man, don't they have women in Naples?"

"I already had all of those —"

"You are such a braggart, Rohan —"

Ignoring their raillery, Max still stared unseeingly at his drink, but all of a sudden, he spoke up in a steely tone. "I know what I mean to do," he announced.

They both looked at him in surprise. The other two exchanged a glance.

"Of course you do, my calculating friend," Jordan said in amusement. "No doubt you've had your plans lined up for years."

Max's heart was pounding. The sound of it rang like thunder in his head.

"Well?" Rohan prompted. "What are you going to do?"

Max paused, bracing himself for their shocked reaction: "I am getting married."

"What?"

"Good God!"

"Already? But we just got back!"

"Are you mad? You're finally free! The old Highlander's got no more claim on us!" Rohan protested. "Why so quick to pledge yourself into some new bondage?"

"Max, you are not serious?"

"Of course I am." He smiled coolly, but sat in silence as they continued trying to dissuade him, until at length, he shook his head. "My mind is made up."

At these words, Jordan stared at him. "Well, then. Knowing you, that's the end of it."

Max shrugged, trying to seem nonchalant about it all, but in a moment, his course was decided.

Over the years, he had learned not to question his instincts. Too many times they had saved his life. Too many times his survival had depended on being able to spot a possible ally in a room full of enemies, and everything in him knew it was Daphne Starling.

He just shrugged. "The damage to my family line isn't going to fix itself, obviously."

"Very well, so who is the lucky chit? Have you got someone picked out?" Rohan asked.

He nodded, his decision made irrevocably. "In fact, I do." He shared the basic facts about Daphne Starling, and they laughed when he told them about the bride list he'd had his solicitor research for him in advance. "You're welcome to my castoffs," he added with a sardonic smile.

"That's very generous of you, you bastard."

"I can just picture your little gentleman-of-affairs running around Town collecting all this information," Jordan said, laughing harder.

"He happens to be quite efficient."

"What did you do, instruct him in field craft?"

"More or less."

"Why didn't you just have Virgil do your spying for you? He's got a bit more experience in these matters."

"He was busy," Max replied. "Besides —" His smile faded, a vague pulsation of suppressed resentment rippling under the surface of his easy tone. "I daresay the old Scot has had enough control over my life for the past twenty years. I don't need him choosing my wife for me, as well."

He took a drink without another word.

They fell silent.

"He does seem rather keen to have us all wedded and bedded," Jordan murmured.

"Did he mention it to you, too?" Max asked.

Jordan nodded, and Rohan glanced grimly at them both. "To me, as well. The Order's ranks will have to be replenished soon enough."

"Haven't we given enough of our own blood?" Max asked softly.

Jordan lowered his gaze. "Apparently not."

"So, Max, what is she like, this lady of yours?" Rohan murmured with a trace of wistfulness in his wary eyes.

"She's perfect." Max shrugged, a rueful half smile brightening his brooding countenance slightly. "Beautiful. Witty. Kind."

"And she agreed to marry you?"

Max lifted his eyebrows. "Oh, I wouldn't say she's exactly agreed to it yet."

"Oho!" the duke exclaimed. "A little co-quette? Playing hard to get?"

"No, it's just that I haven't asked her yet."

"When do you intend to?"

"As soon as I make the arrangements with her father."

Jordan turned to Rohan in astonishment. "He's going to the father first! How terribly quaint."

"Very old-fashioned of you, Max," Rohan agreed. "Didn't know you had it in you."

"Well, I would hardly leave the decision up to a known jilt, now, would I?" He gave them a lordly frown, refusing to worry about her answer. "A good aristocratic girl will do as she is told."

"Yes, but you told us she already jilted one man."

"I am not Albert Carew," he replied in a prickly tone.

"Well, of course." The earl studied him for a long moment, needing no words to express his skepticism — or his utter amusement.

Max looked at both of their dubious faces and scowled.

"When have you ever known *me* to take no for an answer when it comes to something I want?" he demanded.

"The lad's got a point," Rohan said, grinning.

Jordan smiled wryly. "Right. Then I suppose that's that." He poured them another round and lifted his glass in a toast. "To Max! The soon-to-be-married man."

"Poor lass," Rohan said. "She's got no bloody idea what she's in for."

"Trust me," Max replied. "She will soon find out."

All three laughed. Then they clanked their glasses together and drank.

Across the Channel, the night's rain still persisted. Low clouds like dark fleece raked the slate-blue turrets of a grand Baroque chateau in the Loire Valley, drizzling on its ornate gardens, soaking its vineyard acres.

The damp, dark night blotted out the stars, but a few lights glowed in the castle's upper windows despite the late hour.

In the inner sanctum of the Promethean Council, with its chessboard floors, and the gold veins of its black marble columns glittering in the torchlight, defeat lay heavy on the air.

The Grand Masters of the Ten Regions and the three Revered Wanderers sat at a round table with a hollowed center, fashioned like the eight-spoked Wheel of Time.

One chair was raised, thronelike, above the rest. The man planted firmly in this elevated position had spiky, white-blond hair receding at the temples, and cruel blue eyes that swept the gathered company in cold superiority. His name was Malcolm Banks, and as head of the Council, he was about to make an example of Rupert Tavistock.

Indeed, he was looking forward to it.

But first he had a few grim facts to lay bare for the Promethean elite.

"Bonaparte is finished," he confirmed. "Even if we helped him escape again, he would receive no further support from any quarter, so for us, it is not worth the effort. With Napoleon's ruin at Waterloo, we are bound to face the bitter fact that our ambitions with the French empire have come to naught. Fortunately, however" — he leaned back in his chair, steepling his fingers — "I allotted for this possibility years ago by cultivating our influence in King Louis's court throughout the Bourbon exile." He shrugged. "When Louis returns to the throne of France, at least that will bring us back to familiar territory."

The others were silent, none too impressed with his foresight, it seemed. Malcolm looked around at all their stony faces and grimly understood that this defeat had made some of them begin to doubt his abilities as their leader.

Which was why the coming show of force was necessary. He knew he had to rally them before they started turning against him. After all, if they attempted to overthrow him, then it would complicate his desire to make his son his successor. The thirty-year-old Niall sat beside him, never mind the fact that many of the men present thought he did not yet deserve a place on the Council, that he was too young.

Malcolm, however, was grooming him for the headship.

This, too, was controversial, for by their tradition, new leaders had to be voted into power by the Council, chosen from among themselves based on who had the most experience and the proper temperament for the role. Unlike other types of power, it was not passed down from father to son.

But Malcolm had his own plans. Having finally grasped the supreme post through his own machinations, he did not intend to part with it. The others had not yet realized that.

"We are greatly set back, my friends, but we are not undone," he continued calmly. "Our eventual triumph is only postponed. Though we require a period of recovery to shore up our losses, we will do as we have always done: Take the world as we find it. Adapt to new conditions. Regroup, and watch for the next opportunity. And when it presents itself," he added in icy resolve, "we will be poised to strike."

A murmur of agreement rippled through their company.

"Now then, before moving on, we have one final order of business that needs to be addressed." He nodded to Niall, who rose slowly from his chair.

Watching him, Malcolm could not help taking pride in the fearsome man his boy had become. Niall had inherited his towering height from their ancient Highlander clan, along with his thick red hair.

"Rupert," Malcolm said mildly, glancing across the table at one of their comrades, "I am afraid there is a price to be paid for your incompetence."

"I beg your pardon?" the portly, balding Englishman blurted out.

"Did you honestly think your failure would go unpunished?" Malcolm asked in a mild voice.

"My failure?" Rupert Tavistock echoed with a gulp. He glanced over nervously as Niall moved away from his seat and began walking slowly, inexorably toward him.

"Oh, yes, indeed. You were the one responsible for getting rid of Wellington in case Napoleon faltered on the day of battle. If your men had succeeded, the messenger Wellington sent to Blücher would never have gotten through; Napoleon would have won the battle, as he was poised to do, and *six hundred years of our hopes might have been fulfilled!*" he finished in thunderous rage.

"Now, wait one minute!" Sweating profusely now, Rupert shot up from his seat, but Niall was behind him, and with one huge hand on his shoulder, pushed him back down into his chair.

"Instead of our vision coming to pass, the agents you got into Wellington's headquarters are dead," Malcolm said. "And you will soon be joining them."

"But it is not my fault!" Tavistock pleaded. "I did everything you said! The market crash — I directed millions into our accounts."

"But Waterloo."

"It is all the Order's doing! They sent someone in without my knowing. Whoever he was, he got to my agents before they could act. I am not responsible!" Tavistock insisted, his voice climbing. "It is the Order's fault. We are never going to win until the Order of St. Michael is destroyed, and you promised us all that they would be, if we voted you into power!"

"What would you have me do?" Malcolm snarled. "They are ghosts."

"They are men! They can bleed! Septimus killed three of them in Munich!" He pointed

151

wildly to the dark-haired, taciturn German who was in charge of operations throughout the many principalities along the Rhine.

"Yes, but that is the problem, isn't it, my dear Rupert?" Malcolm eyed Septimus with wary displeasure. "Our Bavarian friend was not able to restrain himself and did not take them alive. As a result, we still have no idea where in all of Europe the Order is based these days, nor even how many agents they currently have."

"So, what do you suggest, Malcolm?" a cool voice spoke up from the other end of the room. "That we give up? Surrender to our foes?"

They all looked over at James Falkirk, the lean and stately gray-haired Yorkshireman who had asked the question.

As the chief of the three Wanderers, he was the only real rival to counterbalance Malcolm's growing power.

His normal role was to travel endlessly among all ten regions, keeping an eye on everyone, gathering information, guiding the overall strategy of the Prometheans, while the Grand Masters ran operations within their individual territories. But his travels over the past year had taught him many things, especially clues to the mischief that Malcolm was up to behind their backs.

Gazing in unshakable patience at their incompetent leader, James masked his knowledge of Malcolm's scheming, along with his anger. A cool-nerved Englishman to the core, he knew enough to treat these two Highland barbarians with kid gloves. But he saw through them, to be sure.

Malcolm was not a true believer in the ideals their movement stood for, and James had come to despise him for it. To Malcolm, the sacred Promethean philosophy was naught but a secret means to untold wealth and worldly power.

No wonder they had lost everything they had worked for through Napoleon, James mused. They deserved to taste defeat, for they had entrusted their shining dream of one world united under a benevolent Council into the hands of a man without vision. A monstrous Cyclops whose single eye was fixed on mere self-interest.

Unfortunately, what Malcolm offered seemed to have become enough for some of the others lately.

"Oh, don't be tedious, James," Malcolm said in annoyance. "Of course I am not suggesting surrender to the Order of St. Michael. But we must use common sense until we have regained our strength. Pragmatism, James, that is all. Ever heard of it? Not all of life is dreams and visions, you know. Niall, do proceed," he added with an impatient wave of his hand. "There is no point in dragging this out."

Niall nodded, winding the garrote wire around his hands. Rupert tried to get away, but took only three steps across the room, screaming as Niall took hold of him.

"James — help me!"

"Yes, James, are you going to save him?" Malcolm glanced at him inquiringly, well aware that he, James, was the greatest threat to his power.

James leaned back politely in his chair. Rupert Tavistock was a pampered idiot, not worth saving. He had lost his principles years ago, indulging himself swinishly in London when he should have been working to advance the Council's aims. Power corrupted, and these men had it.

James often wondered if he was the only one untouched. "Sorry, Tavistock," he said. "You betrayed our faith in you. You were entrusted with profound responsibilities, and you failed."

Rupert whimpered, Malcolm snickered, and Niall got to work. James held his tongue. As he looked away, leaving Rupert to his fate, his glance happened to meet that of Septimus Glasse across the round table.

The fiery, black-bearded German gave him a grim look that warned him to keep silent. No doubt, young red-haired Junior there had enough garrote wire left over for anyone foolish enough to point the finger at his sire.

Don't worry, my friend, James thought wryly,

grateful that at least Septimus could be trusted.

They both knew that the ultimate responsibility for the Promethean failure lay with the leader, but neither man was fool enough to say it, at least not here and now, like this. Planning would be needed first . . .

Moments passed, and the last surviving embers of James's humanity made him flinch ever so slightly as Niall finished the unpleasant business with great gusto. Rupert's gagging sounds and the odd bump of his flailing limbs stopped.

A stillness followed.

Niall straightened up, his back to them, the wide, young shoulders heaving as he caught his breath.

Looking over his shoulder with an evil glance, Niall sent them all a look that warned them not to mistake him for the typical idiot son who had gained high place by mere nepotism. He seemed quite ready to prove himself to any who might doubt.

Try me, his narrowed eyes seemed to taunt them. His work done, the large Scot wiped the sweat off his brow with a pass of his forearm, and nonchalantly returned to his seat.

"Get rid of it," Malcolm called to his bodyguard by the door, gesturing distastefully at the corpse. "And send in his replacement."

"Replacement?" James echoed immediately as others also burst out with angry responses. "What about the vote?"

"We don't have time for that!" Malcolm snapped. "Settle down! I have merely simplified matters by choosing a man who can at least fill in while the Council undertakes all its usual squabbling about successors."

Shocked but low-toned protests still passed through the chamber while Malcolm's hulking, silent bodyguard opened the door and beckoned to someone outside the room.

The others turned angrily to see whom Malcolm had invited into their midst in this flouting of all precedent. The brighter light in the corridor outside the chamber briefly illuminated a tall, sinewy silhouette.

As the newcomer stepped into the room and sauntered toward the table, they all got a better look at him — a man in his early forties, with dark, wavy hair, aquiline features, and pitiless eyes.

Great Lucifer. James stared in stunned recognition, a chill running down his spine. Had Malcolm lost his mind?

It was Dresden Bloodwell, the most feared assassin in the whole Promethean underworld.

"Welcome, my friend!" Malcolm greeted him, gesturing toward Rupert's empty chair. "Join us."

"Thank you." The renowned assassin

flashed a cold smile at Malcolm, glancing down indifferently at the corpse of his predecessor, merely stepping over it on his way to the table.

James sat in stunned silence while Malcolm's bodyguard grabbed Rupert Tavistock by an ankle and began unceremoniously dragging the dead man away.

"Gentlemen," Malcolm announced, "allow me to present Dresden Bloodwell, one of our most accomplished agents. Few in our organization have proved as worthy as he. He is going to mind our London post for us until a formal successor can be chosen by the usual methods."

Dresden slid into the chair as if he belonged there, and bowed his head politely. "It's an honor, my lords."

Nobody said a word.

James exchanged another guarded look with Septimus, but neither his German friend nor any of the others dared protest, now that they had heard the name.

James felt slightly sickened. It was plain to him now that Malcolm was taking steps to strengthen his faction within the Council. But how he intended to keep control of this monster, especially once Bloodwell had been put in power across the Channel, James had no idea.

With that, Malcolm simply picked up with the meeting where he had left off. Keeping the tone banal, it was back to business as usual. But a deep uneasiness had descended on their gathering.

Well before the meeting had adjourned with Malcolm's invitation to take refreshments in the dining room, James decided that something had to be done, and soon.

Their leader could not be allowed to persist in his quest for ever greater power. Having Niall murder Rupert right there at the table had clearly been intended as a warning to them all. In addition, choosing Dresden Bloodwell to fill Tavistock's post was a plain unspoken threat, that Malcolm was fully prepared to have his assassin friend eliminate any man on the Council whom he could not coerce into obedience.

Something had to be done, and James knew it would be up to him to lead the others against Malcolm.

As the meeting adjourned, the members of the Council withdrew from the chamber, conversing among themselves in low tones. James went apart from the others to tell Talon, his bodyguard and assistant, that they would be leaving tonight. Talon bowed to him and went to make preparations for their departure.

Taking a moment to collect his thoughts before going in for refreshments, James leaned on the marble banister at the top of the stairwell outside the meeting chamber.

He glanced over grimly as Septimus joined him. Despite their friendly acquaintance, James did not intend to breathe a word of his true thoughts so long as he was under Malcolm's roof. The very walls had ears — and now there was also Dresden Bloodwell to contend with.

"Falkirk," Septimus greeted him, offering his hand.

"Glasse." James shook it. "Congratulations on your victory over those three members of the Order. That is quite an accomplishment."

"Ah, I cannot take full credit," the German replied casually, turning forward and leaning his elbows on the railing beside him. "The task required ten of my best men against their two."

"Two?" James countered. "I thought that you killed three."

Septimus looked askance at him and did not say a word.

James froze, furrowing his brow.

Septimus smiled ever so slightly. "Why don't you come and visit me in Bavaria, my friend? I have made the most intriguing new acquaintance. I'm sure you would like to meet him. I find him difficult to understand. The man is English, so perhaps you will have better luck with him than I. I would, of course, be glad to introduce you."

James's heart was pounding. He glanced around to make sure they were alone, dropping his voice to a whisper. "You captured one of the Order's agents? Alive?"

His friend's nod was barely perceptible. "He was their team leader. He got away when we killed the other two, but then, fancy that — he came back to get revenge on me."

"Then he broke protocol." James stared at him in amazement. "Revenge is against their code."

Septimus shrugged. "It would have been better for him if he had heeded that. In any case, he did not escape."

"Extraordinary!" James uttered under his breath. "Did you tell Malcolm?"

"Of course not. I thought I would talk to you first." Septimus paused. "Do not delay, James. I do not think it likely that my, ah, guest will last much longer."

"Was he hurt in the fray?" James asked quickly.

He smirked. "I've had my finest torturers at work on him for months."

"Septimus!" James whispered, horrified. "Torturers? If he's what you say, then he is too valuable to risk!"

"James, you do not understand this man's recalcitrance," Septimus answered, shaking his head with an indifferent look. "The blackguard was at death's door, and still, all my men were able to learn was his name — and even at that, we are not sure if it is his surname, his Christian name, a title he holds, or merely an alias."

"What name did he give you?" James asked at once.

Septimus looked askance at him. "Drake."

CHAPTER 6

Two weeks later, Daphne was upstairs in her sunny bedchamber, diligently writing letters to some of the ton's known philanthropists about the plight of the Bucket Lane orphans, and the available building she wished to secure as their new home.

She was toying with the idea of including Lord Rotherstone on her list of possible donors, for everyone said he was as rich as Croesus, and besides, he had personally seen the dangers of the orphanage's current location.

At least, that was the reason that she told herself she wanted to write to him. If she was strictly honest, however, she had come to mistrust her own motives where *that man* was involved.

Surely her urge to write to Lord Rotherstone could have nothing to do with her desire to jar him into remembering she existed!

The marquess had haunted her mind constantly since the ball, but to her growing frustration, "Lord Hellfire" had been absent from Society ever since.

Why she should care, she did not know.

She had only just met the man, and had mixed feelings about seeing him again: part thrill at the prospect, part fearful eagerness to see what the unpredictable marquess might do next.

She felt rather foolish, though, to recall his apparently idle promise of a dance, for by now, to her dismay, he seemed to have forgotten about her entirely.

Botheration. She did her best to keep putting him out of her mind, but it did not help knowing he had not left London, which would have made his neglect more understandable.

Carissa, who always knew the latest on-dits, had reported that Lord Rotherstone had been seen about Town with two of his unspeakable Inferno Club friends.

This, Daphne gathered, was the long-awaited arrival of which he had received tidings on the night of the Edgecombe ball. According to the gossip mill, the three had been seen laying wagers at a prizefight, practicing at swordplay with frightful skill at Angelo's, and perusing the horses on auction at Tatt's. But they could not be bothered, it seemed, to rejoin polite Society.

Well! Daphne had to admit she was a trifle

miffed. After the way they had flirted together at Edgecombe House, she was sure he would've been as eager as she to collect on that dance they had promised each other. But now, in light of his continued absence, she could only conclude that the worldly Demon Marquess had merely been toying with her, probably thinking her a naïve young miss.

Maybe Carissa had been right about him from the start.

Just then, thankfully, her maid's light knock on the door interrupted Daphne's fretful ruminations. "Yes?"

Wilhelmina poked her head in the door. "Lord Starling wants to see you, miss."

She nodded. "I'll be right there." Happy to flee the chaotic emotions that thoughts of the marquess aroused in her, she left her room at once to obey her father's summons.

It was on her way downstairs that she was suddenly struck by the ominous quiet filling the house. No banging pianoforte. No whiny bickering.

She paused on the wooden staircase, taking it in with an eyebrow raised in immediate suspicion.

Instead of clomping footfalls and boisterous laughter, she could hear the tame drone of her stepsisters practicing their French.

Leaning forward, Daphne could see through the arched doorway of the parlor. The chubby youngsters flanked their governess on the sofa, obediently poring over their French grammar. Penelope sat in her armchair near them, attentive but not hovering for once, minding her needlework. For once in their lives, they looked like a nice, respectable family.

Daphne furrowed her brow with an odd tingle of premonition. She got the strangest feeling trouble was afoot.

Oh, no, she thought all of a sudden. What if Papa had found out about that violent row in Bucket Lane? Maybe one of the Willies had let slip a careless word.

A knot of apprehension promptly formed in her stomach, but she forced herself onward, trying to hope it was nothing at all. Sometimes Papa would send for her when he could not recall the punch line of a joke . . .

But as she reached the bottom of the stairs and passed the parlor on her way to the study, Penelope glanced up from her sewing and met her gaze with a sharp look.

That piercing glance told her plainly that, yes, some kind of storm was brewing. In sudden alarm, Daphne rushed the rest of the way to her father's study to find out what was going on.

When she stepped into the doorway of Lord Starling's cluttered office, she found him gazing out the bay window, his hands loosely clasped behind his back.

"You wished to see me, Papa?" she forced

out at once.

Interrupted from his musings, Viscount Starling turned to face her. "Ah! There you are, my dear. Do come in. Sit down." He gestured to the chair across from his desk. "Oh, and do shut the door, would you?"

Well, he did not look angry. With a wary glance, Daphne did as he asked, pulling the door closed behind her before advancing into the room. "Is something wrong, Papa?"

"No, no," he replied with a distracted smile as she lowered herself into the chair across from his desk, as ordered. "My dear daughter." He strolled around to the front of his desk and perched on the corner of it across from her.

Folding his arms across his chest, he gave her a thoughtful smile and said quietly, "I've had another offer for your hand."

What? The blood drained from her face. "From whom?"

"Can you not guess?" he asked mildly.

"I have no . . . Who was it, Father?" she cried, alarmed by his knowing smile. "Don't tell me Albert's tried again —"

"The Marquess of Rotherstone."

She stared at him in utter disbelief, her mouth agape.

A wreath of smiles broke out from her father's face, but a wave of dizziness had rushed over Daphne. She gripped the wooden arms of the chair, and for a long moment, she could not speak at all.

Her father, meanwhile, was experiencing no such difficulty. "Congratulations, darling! This time you've made a superlative conquest! I always knew you'd make a brilliant match . . ." Her doting papa kept talking proudly, praising her for her beauty, charm, and cleverness to have snared such a mighty peer of the realm, but in her state of shock, Daphne barely heard a word.

His voice seemed muffled to her, deafened as she was by the thunderous pounding of her heart.

The Demon Marquess wanted her for his bride?

How could this be?

She was utterly stunned. The room was spinning, crazed confusion charging through her veins.

There must be some mistake!

Two weeks of dreamy wondering about him turned into panicked confusion. Of *course* she wanted to see him again, but this was considerably more than she had bargained for! How could he think to marry her after one short conversation?

Yes, yes, of course, she knew that every Season, marriages were often arranged on less — but that happened to other girls, not to her! Never to Daphne Starling!

She had always been in charge of her *own* life!

"Father!" she burst out at last, interrupting his soothing monologue on what a wonderful life she was going to have as the Marchioness of Rotherstone, how she was going to be the envy of the ton.

"Yes, my dear?" He frowned as he studied her. "I say, you look a trifle peaked. Do you want some tea? The smelling salts?"

"No!" she cried, then she threw up her hands in bewilderment. "How — ?"

"Well, it was very simple, my dear." He gave her a quizzical look. "Lord Rotherstone came up to me at White's, introduced himself in a very gallant fashion, and asked for a meeting. I agreed — of course, I remembered you had asked about him at the Edgecombe ball, so I suspected instantly." He smiled. "You seemed to have some affinity for him, and the admiration he expressed for you, in turn, was certainly genuine. The reasons he gave for his choice of you were respectful, logical, and appropriate."

"What did he say about me?" she asked swiftly, leaning forward in her chair.

"You see? I knew you were not indifferent to him," her father teased.

Daphne stared at him, unable to speak.

She suddenly found her heart at war with itself. Half of her was besieged by wild joy at the thought that this man who had obsessed her thoughts since she had first laid eyes on him was not just *interested* in her, but deemed her worthy of sharing his title and his name.

The other half, however — quite the more sensible part of her — felt a huge indignation on behalf of all womankind at being left out of all discussion on the matter.

Men!

Oh, but he was a sly one. By going straight to her father, Lord Rotherstone had leapfrogged over all her self-determination, and had already taken control of her life without her even being aware of it.

What immediately came to mind was the memory of how he had so smoothly taken the Carew brothers in hand, steering them as he willed, thanks to his superior charisma, his dominating intellect. Now it appeared he had worked the same dark magic over Papa, causing her father to go along with this match without so much as a by-your-leave.

"Well? What have you to say in answer to this grand news?" he asked.

"I-I barely know where to begin, Papa. I was not thinking of marriage . . ."

"Which is why I had to think of it for you," he countered dryly.

"But Papa —" Her head was whirling as she cast about for words. "I am happy as I am! I *like* my life just the way it is, don't you see? I have a *very nice* life," she cried, "and I-I don't see why everyone is pushing me to change it! Yes! I have my home here, and my work with the children, and my books, and my friends, a-and I don't need a man to make me happy!" she declared with a sudden, impassioned flourish.

He looked at her in amusement.

"Well, what about his awful reputation?" she exclaimed, finally beginning to rally from her shock.

"We discussed it," he clipped out. "I am satisfied with Lord Rotherstone's explanations." A hint of secrecy appeared in the lines of age around her father's eyes, but if the marquess had confided certain things in his future father-in-law, male affairs that Daphne was not to be privy to, the viscount gave no sign.

"After several lengthy interviews and a thorough study of all his documentation, I find Rotherstone to be a man of sound character. Otherwise, I never would have agreed to this match."

"Well, I don't agree to it!" she declared. "I find this all completely underhanded — on both your parts! Why didn't he come and speak to me about it first before going to you?"

"Oh, your silly modern notions of romance," he said with a dismissive wave of his hand. "Lord Rotherstone proceeded in quite the proper way, as honor demands. Indeed, this is the *correct* way that a gentleman proposes, Daphne. Do not reproach him for adhering to the dignified traditions of our class. Now then," he continued. "We hope to conclude the match before the year is out —"

She gasped. "So soon?"

"Why wait? You've already refused three suitors. Yes, I know — the first was too old for you, the second drank too much, and the third, well, Albert Carew was never worthy of you. But you can find no such faults with the Marquess of Rotherstone. He is young, handsome, wealthy, honorable, intelligent, a chap that any father would be proud to call his son-in-law. Not even you, darling, need wait for any finer offer than this. I daresay you will be the envy of all your female friends once it's announced."

"But, sir!"

"Tut, tut, child. As your father, I have a duty to see my daughter well settled in life, and you will live like a princess under Lord Rotherstone's roof. Just think of all the good you'll be able to do in your lofty new position," he added shrewdly. "This is an extraordinary opportunity for you to advance your work among the needy."

"Oh!" She narrowed her eyes at him. The blackguard knew just what to say to her.

The room seemed to pirouette, and Daphne felt herself beginning to panic. She felt powerless, completely overwhelmed.

She cast about for some sort of answer, though the match already seemed a fait accompli, especially when she saw that immovable, Rock of Gibraltar look on her father's face.

"Papa, you know I mean to marry Jonathon someday!"

"Oh, stuff and nonsense," he said with a scowl. "Jonathon White is a boy, not a man. He is not a serious person. With all due respect, my love, you need a strong hand. Lord Rotherstone, by contrast, is a man of sharp wits and experience —"

"Experience!" she exclaimed, nodding emphatically. "You've got that right! The first time I saw him, he was —"

"Yes?"

She suddenly stopped herself from making her intended point, for it dawned on her in the nick of time that if she told her father that she had first seen the marquess stumbling out of a brothel, then she'd have to confess the whole violent row in Bucket Lane, and the true danger she had risked each week by going there.

He had no idea what it was really like.

She huffed and shook her head, thwarted again. "Never mind. Father, you speak as though the whole matter's already concluded. Considering *I'm* the one who'll have to spend the rest of my life with this person, don't I have any say in this at all?"

He stared at her with a frown. "Daphne, listen to me. I know you are aware of Albert

172

Carew's attempts to smear your reputation. Of course, his every word is false and Carew is no gentleman, but the longer you go unwed after that debacle, the worse it all looks. Lord Rotherstone desires to protect you. When you share in his title, no one will dare disrespect you. That is one of the chief reasons that I have agreed."

"But it isn't the main reason, is it?" she shot back, rising from her chair as the finality of it all turned her disbelief to anger. "Penelope put you up to this, didn't she?" she flung out in brazen, angry accusation, feeling cornered. "She just wants to be rid of me, and I know you're tired of hearing it. You'd throw me out of my own home just to stop her nagging! You'd rather sell me to some wealthy peer than put your foot down and tell her —"

"*Enough!*" he roared. "I am your father! How dare you speak to me in such a barbarous fashion?" He stared at her, positively fuming.

Daphne snapped her mouth shut, shocked by his bellow.

"Maybe Penelope's right, and I have indulged you overmuch. Good God, if you are too thick to see what a boon has just fallen into your hands, then you are too *silly* a chit to choose your own husband. My decision stands! Furthermore, Penelope is my wife," the placid viscount forged on in quite unprecedented fury. "You owe her your respect. For

173

shame, Daphne Starling! You cannot always think of yourself! You have a duty to our family, just as Lord Rotherstone has a duty to his!"

Duty?

As lenient as Papa was, it was rare for him to invoke family duty.

Might Lord Rotherstone's famous riches be part of the real reason behind this sudden match? she thought suddenly.

Could it all stem back to her father's market losses? And dear God, if so, then what choice did she have?

"Think of your young sisters," her red-faced sire charged on. "Anyone with eyes can see they are not as well-favored as you — I'm sorry, but it is the truth. By marrying the marquess, you'll be in a position to sponsor them when it's their turn to come out in Society, just as the Dowager Duchess sponsored you. We both know Penelope is not equipped for the task. Oh, I'm not going to explain myself to you!" he said with an angry wave of his hand. "I've found you a husband and you will marry him. If I waited for you to take charge, you would end up alone! I'm not going to let that happen to you, Daphne. *I* know what it's like to be alone for years and years — God's bones, your mother would haunt me to the end of my days if I were to let you end up a spinster! I don't care if you're angry at me," he concluded. "You are marrying the Marquess of Rotherstone, and that is my final decision. Now I suggest you compose yourself, for he has just arrived."

"What?" she breathed.

"To give you your engagement ring, I warrant."

"He is here?"

Papa nodded toward the window. "There is his carriage now. I will go and greet him." Her father eyed her none too happily. "Prepare yourself to meet your future husband."

The word "husband" nearly knocked the breath out of her lungs. Her father walked out, leaving the door to the study ajar. Jolting herself out of her shock, but still feeling the sting of her father's tongue-lashing, Daphne rushed to the bay window and looked out.

Sure enough, an ornate black coach-and-four was just now rolling into the cobbled courtyard. Heart pounding, she held her breath as it glided to a halt in front of the villa, the fine ebony horses stamping the ground and tossing their heads, as if they had borne the Devil himself to his destination right on time to collect some poor fool's soul.

Hers.

Her disbelieving dread climbed as a liveried groom in a tricorn hat jumped off the back and went forward to open the door for his master.

She held her breath as Lord Rotherstone emerged from the coach, every bit as gorgeous and imposing in his dark, brooding way as she recalled from their one meeting.

Dressed in a dark blue morning coat with a plum waistcoat and brown pantaloons, he held an ivory-handled walking stick in one hand and a pretty little box tied up with a ribbon bow in the other.

Oh, God.

He paused, passing a glance over the Starling villa from beneath the shadowed brim of his smart top hat; Daphne ducked behind the curtain, afraid she might be seen.

A moment later, her heart in her throat, she peeked out again, just as he strode out of view on his way to the front door. Her heart pounded like a timpani drum as she heard him being admitted into the house. *Hide!*

No. Brushing off the futile impulse to flee, she forced herself to focus, trying to figure out what to do or say before he came into the room.

She could hear the low, cultured tones of his voice from the nearby entrance hall, though she could not make out the words.

The deep, velvet rumble of his cultured baritone made her stomach flutter, curse him.

Leaning furtively into the doorway, she observed him with her family. Her father was standing near him with a smile, but a trace of worry about his eyes.

As the two shook hands, apparently great friends already, Daphne remembered with a pang her father's one regret in life — that he had never had a son.

Penelope, meanwhile, was positively fawning on him, and as far as Daphne could tell, she was savoring the moment of her victory, and eating up Lord Rotherstone's attention.

Sweeping off his smart black top hat, he bowed next to Sarah and Anna, reducing them to bashful giggling. "What lovely girls," he told Penelope, charming them all like some sort of evil magician.

Penelope thanked him in profusion, falling all over herself to offer him refreshments while both youngsters began prattling at once about their day's adventures, as if he cared one jot.

"Oh, help," Daphne whispered, slightly mortified.

The crisis was almost at hand. Any moment now, they would call for her. She ducked back into the study and leaned against the wall, pressing her palm to her forehead.

Her stomach was full of butterflies, and she still had no idea what to do. *This is tyranny!*

She keenly recalled his bossiness on the night of the Edgecombe ball, ordering her never to return to Bucket Lane. She hadn't liked it then, and she did not appreciate it now.

On the other hand, trying to deny her attraction to him would only give him a weakness in her that he could easily exploit. Very well, she admitted impatiently, she found him rather maddeningly desirable, and, yes, she was intrigued.

But that in no way meant she intended to marry the devil, no matter what Papa might've promised on her behalf.

Then, before she was anywhere near ready to confront him, they started calling for her.

"Daphne! Lord Rotherstone is here!"

Blast. There was nowhere to hide as she heard her father say in a delicate tone, "My daughter is feeling rather shy today, I fear. Let me take you in to her."

"Oh, George, not in the study! It always looks like a whirlwind in there —"

"I'm sure it is quite acceptable," Lord Rotherstone said soothingly to her step-mother. Daphne could hear their voices in the hallway, coming closer. "Whatever makes Miss Starling feel most comfortable," he was saying.

"Oh, so considerate! You really are too kind, Your Lordship!"

"Nonsense."

"Right through there," Papa directed.

Daphne wanted to run, but she knew she was trapped. The mullioned windows were too narrow for a person to climb out of. Standing stiffly in the center of the room, she had no choice but to hold her ground. Her pulse pounded. Suddenly, he appeared — his tall, powerful frame nigh filling the open

178

doorway. Their gazes locked; a tremble ran the entire length of her body.

"There she is!" Penelope said sweetly, slipping in behind him to insert herself into matters, as usual.

Daphne held her breath, her eyes wide as he advanced into the room, hat in hand, like some humble suitor. Well, he might have fooled her family with that smooth charm of his, but she saw through this cunning autocrat, this wicked puppet master. Did he take her for a fool?

"Miss Starling," he greeted her, his pale eyes aglow, a beguiling little smile on his lips.

Oh, he looked so pleased with himself as he bowed to her, she thought. Lifting her chin a notch, Daphne refused to shrink from the intensity in his stare. What did he expect, that she would swoon at his feet like some eager patsy?

"George, look what a beautiful couple they make!"

"Thank you, Lady Starling," the marquess said, not looking away from Daphne.

Penelope beamed a short distance away, already counting the minutes, no doubt, until her irksome stepdaughter would be gone from the house. "We'll leave you two young people alone — but only briefly!" she added with a chiding wave of her finger and a knowing little laugh.

"Of course, madam." Lord Rotherstone

nodded politely to Penelope, who then forgot to leave.

"Come, wife," Papa insisted. "Let them be for a moment."

"Of course I'm coming, George! I should never wish to intrude, I'm sure!" Still simpering at their guest, Penelope finally managed to tear herself out of the room — probably to listen in the hallway.

As the door closed, Daphne decided on the spot that the only way to decipher Lord Rotherstone's game was to hear the slyboots out. Considering his two rescues of her, this only seemed fair. It signified nothing that the raw, male magnetism that emanated from him probably made compasses malfunction in his presence.

God knew he made her needle swing wildly, as though he had swallowed true north — as if all signs pointed straight to him as her final destination.

Max took one look at Miss Starling and saw he had some persuading to do. The young beauty was not the expert that he was at hiding her feelings, and what he read in her face at the news of their betrothal was a mixture of fury and dread.

Very well, so he would have to calm her down and help her see the wisdom of this match. He had had more time than she to get used to the idea.

Indeed, negotiations with her father having been concluded, the thing was so settled in Max's mind that he had already begun to think of her as *his.*

Strangely, any objection on her part merely strengthened his resolve, for it meant that this rare lady would not be won over merely by his title and his gold.

As he crossed the room to her, he could not help taking a moment's softheaded delight in her natural beauty. Indeed, she was a prize.

The last time he had seen her, she had been a shining star in a pure white ball gown, almost untouchable in her pristine elegance, but today, she was warm country sunshine. He found her in an enchanting state of unpretentious loveliness, her long golden hair hanging free about her shoulders, held back from her face with a simple ribbon bandeau.

Her light, floral-printed day dress had a demure white fichu tucked into the neckline, and concealed her slender arms in three-quarter sleeves. Max stared at the delicate wrists, enchanted by the ink stains on her fingers. At the ball, she had worn gloves, but now her naked hands made him long to know her touch on his bare skin.

Keeping a firm check on his desire, he stepped closer with a respectful glance, bent, and pressed a chaste kiss to her smooth cheek.

Her lashes flicked downward, but she did not pull away: He counted this as his first victory. Leaning near, he could feel the heat between them. Without a word, he presented her next with the gift that he had brought.

She looked at the whimsical box, then eyed him dubiously, making no move whatsoever to accept his admittedly extravagant offering.

Though he was fleetingly arrested by the beauty of the sunlight streaming in through the bay window behind her, illuminating her hair and shoulders in a subtle halo, the look she gave him made it clear that he was in for a delicate round of diplomacy.

No matter. He had gone a round with Metternich once. He trusted he could handle one pretty young lady.

He smiled at her and backed off a bit, turning to set the jewelry box aside.

She folded her arms across her chest and watched his every move. "I hear you've been busy, my lord," she remarked with an edge to her soft murmur.

Max turned back to her with a confident half smile. "Didn't I promise you that we would meet again?"

Her cheeks flushed suddenly. "Hardly like this!"

"My dear Miss Starling." Max stepped closer and took charge, collecting both of her sweet hands between his own. He gazed soberly into her eyes. "Would you do me the honor of being my wife?"

She stared at him in shock, looking rather lost.

He waited in staunch silence. Not that she really had a choice.

"Lord Rotherstone," she forced out, "you quite astonish me." She seemed to grasp for words. "I am honored, naturally. But — we barely know each other!"

"Well, that is soon amended," he reassured her softly with a calm and even smile.

"But how can you wish to marry me after one conversation? I don't even know your name — your full name — only your title!"

"It's Max," he said abruptly. "Max St. Albans. Well, there is a good deal more to it than that. I have so many middle names and lesser titles, I barely can keep track of them myself. But 'Max' will do for you and me. What else would you like to know?"

"Everything!" She yanked her hands out of his.

He eyed her guardedly. "Well, that's a tall order," he replied evasively. Though he was highly trained in controlling the flow of information, he was happy to parcel out some basic facts for his future bride.

He'd be the first to agree that she deserved it. After all, not even a secret agent ought to lie to the mother of his future children. Insofar as he could help it.

Fortunately, a young Society bride was not

expected to ask a great many questions of her lord and master.

Especially not when said husband was going to provide her with a mode of life akin to royalty. Only a very foolish chit would jeopardize such gains by prying into the mouth of the proverbial gift horse.

Daphne would be cherished and well taken care of, and that jolly well ought to be enough, Max thought, for any intelligent young lady. As she stared at him expectantly, Max saw it was time to deliver his main points.

"I am from Worcestershire," he began. "I believe I told you that. My parents are dead. I have a sister a few years younger than myself. We don't see each other much — due to my traveling over the past few years." He paused, not sure where to go next. "I am thirty-three years old. And I need a wife." He shrugged. "You seem delightful," he forged on. "Really everything a man could desire in a woman. From your work at the orphanage, I deduce that you like children, and obviously, that is my main concern. I have a great deal to offer you, and in all, Miss Starling," he concluded, "I believe that you and I could have a very pleasant life together."

He lifted his chin and awaited her jubilation.

Her cobalt eyes had grown huge while he talked, but her face had paled. He waited another long moment for her response.

She brought her hand weakly to her brow. "I think I'm going to faint."

Max frowned and stepped into action, determined to prove he was indeed husband material. "Come, sit down, my dear," he ordered gently, taking her elbow and leading her over to the leather couch before the bookshelves.

Once he had safely placed his prize there, he crouched down before her and scanned her face in worry. "Is there anything that I can do for you?"

"No — it's just — forgive me, but — I fear I'm at a loss. I don't even understand how all this came about!"

"Surely you were aware that I noticed you, Miss Starling."

"Yes, but after the Edgecombe ball, you never returned to Society — and now this! I thought you had forgotten all about me."

He shook his head with a lusty look. "Hardly."

She gave him a doe-eyed blink.

"My dear lady, within twenty-four hours of speaking to you, I was in negotiations with your father."

"Really?" she breathed.

"Yes."

"Oh. But, my lord, I do not understand. Why didn't you come to me before going to my father? That is what has me so confused.

Did you not think it prudent to consult my feelings first?"

"How, now, Miss Starling?" he countered, feigning perfect innocence. "I went out of my way to show the proper respect for your father and for you. I proceeded by the book, according to tradition. Besides," he admitted in a more delicate tone, "with the state of my reputation and the recent damage to yours, thanks to Carew, can you imagine the talk if I had begun by pursuing you first, without going through the proper channels, or making it crystal clear that my intentions were fully honorable?"

"Oh . . . I suppose you have a point."

Max gazed into her eyes, intrigued. "Am I to understand that you are not at all pleased by my offer?"

"It isn't that." She stared at him with a torn expression, then dropped her gaze, blushing slightly. "Of course, I am extremely flattered, my lord. It's just, it's very sudden. And I-I can't help feeling that I have been chosen almost at random!"

"Nothing could be further from the truth."

"But . . . you don't even know me."

"I know more about you than you think."

She absorbed this with only a small ripple of uncomfortable suspicion passing behind her eyes. Then she seemed to recall that, of course, any peer of his standing in the world would make sure that all prospective brides for him had been fully vetted.

She lowered her head. "Doesn't the gossip about me bother you?"

He laughed. "Not one jot, especially considering the source. Believe me, I know all about Carew's kind of malice. I am not about to stand by and watch him attempt to destroy an innocent person. If you marry me," he continued, "you will share in my rank, and believe me, the gossips won't trifle with the reputation of a marchioness."

"So, you feel sorry for me and that's why you're offering marriage?"

"It's not that. To be honest, Miss Starling, this alliance is to both our advantage."

"Is that right? How does it benefit you?"

For a long moment, he studied her with wary interest. Some parts of his explanation were not going to be easy to say. "The reputation of the Rotherstone family has been darkened by the bad behavior of a few in recent generations, I'm afraid. My father, you see, was a gambler, just like his father before him." He eyed her, searching for signs of contempt. But he read none. "Personally, I detest the cards and will not touch the dice," he said. "I saw what these games did to my father, and what that, in turn, did to my mother, my sister, and me. We were the ones who paid the price."

More than she'd ever know.

He turned away and forged on. "By the

time I was born, our proud lineage had sunk into a state of . . . lack." He paused, not at all accustomed to being so open with anyone. "I hated it," he admitted in low-toned vehemence. "The humiliation of it. And I swore I would not make *my* children live that way when I grew up. So, when the title came to me, I made it my mission to restore our family's fortunes. That was the goal of my travels abroad," he added, having readied this half truth for his case. "I won't bore you with the details, but the war brought many rich prospects for investment throughout Europe."

That much was true. At the Order's castle in Scotland, Max had applied himself zealously to his studies on the art and science of spotting opportunities others had missed, turning them into gold like a modern-day alchemist.

By his twenties, he had proved his particular talents in this area so well that he had been put in charge of managing great sums for the Order to keep their coffers full for their operations. In exchange for his services, he had been permitted to keep a certain percent for himself.

"Over a decade or so, I succeeded in restoring my family's wealth. I paid off my father's gambling debts. Tore down the old manor at home and built a new one in its place. I also bought my London house, among my other holdings, and now that all that's done, the next step, naturally, is to settle down and start a family. There is no point in fortune, after all, if one has got no one to share it with." He offered her a cautious smile.

She answered with a small nod, perhaps warming up to him by one degree or two.

"But, you see, Miss Starling, here is where I run into more difficulty that my cursed father left me, as yet another charming part of my inheritance."

"What's that?"

"Society's disapproval." He looked at her again. "You are the patron saint of newcomers. I told you at the Edgecombe ball that I might throw myself on your mercy, and now, here I am. I need your help, as much as you need mine. You *belong* in Society. People listen to you, respect you —"

"Oh, I'm not so sure of that at all anymore."

"It's true. That's why Carew went after you so hard, first as a conquest, and then, when he could not have you, as his victim. I need a marchioness who can help me to ensure that whatever sons and daughters I am blessed with won't be treated as outsiders, the way I was. You and I are perfectly suited to help each other."

"Pardon me, but that doesn't make any sense." She was shaking her head in confusion, her brow furrowed. "To me, it sounds like we are both in the same boat, though admittedly, your case is a good deal more

189

severe than mine. How, then, can we help each other?"

"Consider human nature, Miss Starling. What is the source of our common problem? Ton gossip. The very weapon that Albert and your stepmother both have used against you. And what do the gossips hunger for? A drama. So, let's give them one. I assure you, they'll be so intrigued, they'll forget all about Carew's accusations."

"How do we do that?" she asked with a fascinated stare.

"Why, we change the story."

"To what?"

"A romance," he murmured wickedly. "They will not be able to resist. The lost soul Rotherstone returns to rescue the leading belle from Carew. You reform me from my wild ways. They'll fall in love with the both of us. Then we both get what we want — for all this to go away. Once they're satisfied, then we can get on with our lives."

She stared into his eyes with a look of half-scandalized astonishment. "You actually think you can manipulate the entire ton?"

"Of course. Why not?"

"You are rather an expert at creating ruses . . ."

"Well?"

"I barely know what to say!"

"You doubt it could work?"

"It isn't that."

"What, then? You have to admit it sounds like fun."

"Fun, yes, and somehow slightly repulsive at the same time."

He frowned. "I beg your pardon?"

"This is your proposal? A charade? We're talking about marriage here, Lord Rotherstone!"

"Well, obviously. I'm trying to help you. As I said, the alliance would be to both of our advantage."

"Indeed, but what makes you think I ever intended to marry for advantage?" she demanded.

Max gazed at her intently. "What *did* you want to marry for, Miss Starling?"

She tensed, blushed, and looked away abruptly without answering the question.

She did not have to. It was written all over her face.

Oh, dear, Max thought.

"My lord," she ground out after a moment, carefully avoiding his gaze, "you say you want to improve your reputation, but the first time I saw you, you were staggering out of a brothel."

She shot him a look of reproach over her shoulder.

"That kind of behavior does not accord with your plan. Nor would I ever accept it as your wife. A gentleman does not partake in the exploitation of women."

Max's eyes widened slightly at her stern tone, though he had rather known he had this coming. *Hm.* He lowered his head with a show of contrition, also to hide his amusement. Perfect lady that she was, he understood this brothel business could prove a real obstacle between them. The disapproval in her stare made that clear.

Telling her the real reason he had been there that day, however, would surely make it worse. What was normal field craft for him would no doubt sound bizarre in the extreme to a civilian. Besides, if he had not been there doing surveillance on her, then the Bucket Street gang would've got her. Max had no regrets. Instead, he sighed and chose the lesser of two evils. "Well, you know, my dear, I'm afraid I never said I was a saint. I admit, I enjoyed my bachelorhood to the full, with its appropriate pursuits. Likewise, I intend to enjoy my married life in the correct manner."

"So, you mean to change?"

"I do. And I think you could be a wonderful influence on me," he said with winning earnestness.

"Really," she replied.

"I swear to you, once we are wed, I will never visit such places again. You have my word."

"Dashed right you won't," she muttered. "And what about that wicked club that you belong to — what is it called, the Inferno

Club? Would you give that up if I were to marry you?"

He stared at her, taken off guard. But then he shook his head and set his jaw with all the stubbornness in his lineage. "I cannot."

"Why?"

"Daphne — those men are like brothers to me. They're the only true friends I have." He warded off a stab of guilt, but he was not about to drop his cover.

Not even his own sister knew the truth. Max realized he was asking a lot of Daphne, but telling her about the Order was out of the question. She was just going to have to accept his dealings at Dante House and leave it at that.

"I ask you to trust me." He chose his words with care, his conscience smarting with the irony of the request in the midst of the lies he had no choice but to tell. "Things are not always . . . what they seem to be, Miss Starling."

Something in his eyes must have warned her not to press, or perhaps she remembered that he had passed her father's interviews.

Max had told Lord Starling only the barest sketch of the truth, that his travels involved secret work for the good of England.

He had also forbidden the viscount to tell any living soul, including Daphne, for the girl's own safety.

She gazed at him for a long moment, reading him as best she could, but at length, she shook her head and looked away. "I do not know."

"Daphne." He longed to touch her, just to caress her cheek and let her know that though he could not make all the promises in the world to her, his desire for her was genuine. But he kept his hand by his side, restrained from reaching toward her. He must not scare her away.

Her head was down; she twisted her fingers in her lap, as though carefully pondering each word before she spoke. "I grant you, my lord, you have been much in my thoughts since you first saved my life in Bucket Lane. But I cannot like the way you've gone about this."

"Why?" he asked softly.

"It all feels a little — underhanded." She looked at him in distress. "I saw how you got Albert and his brothers under control at the ball, and now, apparently, you've also worked your influence over my father. If you have the ability to manipulate the whole ton, it only makes me wonder what you'd do to me if I were yours!"

"Miss Starling, I never use my powers for evil," he said in gentle irony.

"So you claim, and yet they call you the Demon Marquess! I want to be happy in my marriage, my lord, with someone who respects me, someone I can trust. If this is how you undertake the mere proposal, arranging

194

things without giving me any say, then I can only surmise that you'll run roughshod over me for the rest of our lives."

"That is not so. I hold you in the highest regard, Miss Starling."

"Well, it feels like you are determined to take over control of my life, and I don't appreciate that."

Max said nothing, mulling her words. Why was control so important to her? he began to wonder. Was the need for it the real reason she had refused every suitor before him?

Didn't she dare entrust herself and future into any man's hands?

He began slowly scanning the room, assessing the place, as though he were analyzing the home of some Promethean target. What might it reveal about her?

"What are you holding out for, Daphne? Perfection?" he asked in a musing tone.

"Of course not!" she said defensively.

"Good. Otherwise you'd end up very lonely if that were the case." His gaze homed in on a piece of embroidery work preserved in a small picture frame on the wall across from him.

Sewn in a messy, childish hand, it had an awkward pink flower in the middle, with an inscription above, and a painstaking needlework signature below. A simple gift, costing nothing, but ever-so-lovingly crafted.

To Mother.
Love Always, Daphne.

As soon as he saw it, Max knew what it meant. He experienced a pang of comprehension. So, while he had been a lad far away in a Scottish castle having the rule of secrecy beaten into him as part of his brutal training regimen, away down here in England, her little world had also been falling apart. *My poor, sweet girl.*

He lowered his gaze, fighting the urge to gather her into his arms and hold her close. At least now he had an inkling of what lay behind her fear.

He spoke up barely audibly, wanting with all his soul to reach her all of a sudden. "I'll bet I can guess the first time you felt like everything was out of your control," he whispered.

"What?" she asked faintly, staring at him. He registered an uneasy note in her soft tone.

"Your father told me you were ten years old when your mother first got sick. You were powerless to help her. There was nothing you could do. You were just a little girl. You must've dreaded to wonder what was going to happen to you without her there."

He turned with a gentle gaze, and saw her staring at him with a stricken look. "Daphne," he said quietly, "I will always keep you safe."

She bristled as though he had given her

some great insult. "No." She shook her head, looking accusingly at him. "No one can promise that."

"Oh, I can be very determined," he whispered, but with a tender half smile, as he saw he shouldn't push. It was obvious he'd already touched a nerve. "As I said, my dear, I am not perfect. Far from it, in fact. But this is not a world where anyone should have to be alone, and when you're mine," he added softly, "I will do all in my power to make you happy."

"How?" she demanded, her blue eyes glittering with remembered pain and, he thought, her resentment that he had uncovered her secret hurt. "How can you claim you'll make me happy? You don't even know me."

"I know more about you than you think."

"Like what?" she challenged him.

"I know you are kind to strangers. You're witty. Wise enough to know a fool when you see one." He reached out and very gently tucked a stray lock of her hair behind her ear.

He was encouraged that she did not pull away.

"Your confidence pleases me. Your sense of humor delights me. And your heart . . . your compassion for those poor children compels my admiration and respect."

She trembled, staring at him.

"You are brave," he continued as she turned away abruptly. "The fact that you lingered in Bucket Lane at your own risk just to make sure I'd be all right — and then had the presence of mind to send for the constable during that row — it all bespeaks your courage and good sense."

She sat very still, listening like a doe in the woods, but poised to run from him. Just as she had run from all the others.

"It makes me feel that I can trust you, Daphne Starling. Trust in your integrity. Which is a miracle. Because I never trust anyone. But besides all that," he added with a simple shrug, speaking utterly from the heart, "I just rather like you."

Slowly, she looked over at him in dismay; she found herself rendered briefly helpless by his words.

It was difficult to argue with a man who praised her not for superficial things, as Albert had, but for the very qualities that she most valued in herself.

Perhaps he *did* understand her a little better than she wanted to give him credit for.

He was gazing at her with an air of surprising openness as he sat beside her on the couch in a casual, manly pose, his arm draped along the back of the leather sofa behind her, one ankle resting atop his opposite knee.

He waited patiently for her reply, but her efforts to find an answer flagged when she got distracted by the fascinating blend of sea blues, smoky grays, and crystal greens that made up the pale color of his eyes.

He raised that damnable eyebrow at her, waiting, so knowingly, so thoroughly in control.

She let out a small sound of frustration, rose from the couch, and walked to the other end of the room.

"I am serious about this offer, Daphne," he said matter-of-factly. "I want you."

She turned to him with an impassioned air. "Doesn't it matter what I want?"

"Of course it does." The intensity receding slightly from his stare, he smiled fondly, rose, and joined her in front of the bay window.

She found it daunting to meet his determined gaze, but when he touched her chin, tilting her face upward as he had at the ball, alas, she became entranced again.

He stared for a long moment into her eyes. "It matters a great deal what you want," he told her softly. "Just don't ask me to believe that you don't feel the attraction between us."

She turned her face away in blushing frustration.

"Or that you're indifferent to me, after you sought me out and stopped me from leaving the ball. Or when you so smoothly inquired if I already had a wife," he added with a faint half smile. "Did you think I had forgotten that?"

She looked at him from the corner of her eye, noted the teasing sparkle in his eyes, but huffed all the same at the reminder of her awkward gaffe on the night of the ball.

She turned her back on him and stared for a moment out the window, trying to gather her thoughts; but her heart skipped a beat when he touched her.

Standing behind her, he gently fingered a lock of her hair. "You're very beautiful, you know. I suppose you don't want to hear it, but all the same, it is true."

She stood rooted in place, unable to pull herself away as he then trailed his fingertips slowly down her spine.

"Yes." He leaned down to murmur at her ear while his hand came to rest on her waist, his touch fraught with subtle possessiveness. "Quite irresistible," he whispered. "When you are mine, I will treat you like the rare jewel you are."

She wanted to deny that that was ever going to happen, but her tongue refused to fashion what might well be a lie. The rest of her body was already quite in favor of the match; her pulse raced at the warm tickle of his breath on her earlobe, and the feel of his hard body behind her, ready to support her as the delicious nearness of him made her dizzy.

"You say we barely know each other, so I say we must remedy that," his silken baritone cajoled her, his lips skimming her ear with maddening softness. "I will come by tomorrow in my cabriolet and take you out for a drive."

She bit her lip, pained to think she must decline. This scoundrel made her body ache in the most confusing fashion. "I am not sure that's such a good idea."

"Of course it is. Come, my dear," he cajoled her, his deep and worldly voice beguiling her. "Be fair — to both of us. You said yourself that you don't know me, so how can you refuse me out of hand? You haven't even learned yet what you might be giving up. You might find you like me if you'll give it half a chance. Come, I saved your neck, didn't I?" She let out the tiniest of moans as his warm lips skimmed her neck to emphasize his words. "That must be worth a little of your time, at least."

"Very well," she forced out breathlessly, attempting to sound dignified as his hands glided up and down her arms with maddening pleasure. "For the sake of fairness, then. You may — take me driving in the park."

"There, now." She could hear the smile in his voice. "That wasn't so hard, was it?"

Finally gathering her wits, she turned her head a little to meet his mischievous gaze askance over her shoulder. "Best not to push your luck," she advised in a voice gone soft and scratchy with desire.

His smile widened. "I shall count the hours, *cherie.*" Removing himself from their lovely close proximity, he made his bow and headed for the door.

"Lord Rotherstone?"

"Call me Max, please." With one hand on the doorknob, he paused, glancing back at her. "What is it?"

She ignored his invitation to the dangerous familiarity of first names, and nodded toward the fancy little present he had brought. "What's in the box?"

He leaned against the doorframe, the sketch of manly elegance. "Why don't you open it and find out?"

"Is it a ring?" she asked with wary bluntness.

"Er, no." When he took in her skeptical look, he laughed, a roguish sparkle in his eyes. "I didn't know your ring size yet. What is it, by the way?"

"I'm not telling you!" she exclaimed, refusing to give in to the temptation of a smile.

But she was relieved to hear it. A ring would have seemed too distressingly final.

Perhaps he understood that she was nowhere near ready for that so soon.

"Suit yourself," he replied as he opened the door again to leave. "Four-thirty, then, tomorrow. Don't be late."

Another order from him? she thought, but she could not help smiling guardedly after he had gone.

She was nowhere near agreeing to this, but all things considered, she had to admit, a woman could do worse.

CHAPTER 7

"His mind is gone, poor bastard. He is a hollow shell." Septimus Glasse nodded toward the captured Order agent who sat slumped nearby in the invalid chair. "His body should heal quickly. He is young and strong. But his wits are scrambled, James. He just sits there, staring into space. He barely speaks."

"And whose fault is that?" James bit back in seething anger as they stood out on the rooftop battlements of his friend's ancient castle tucked among the Bavarian Alps. "Look what your torturers have done to him! They have all but driven him mad! The one man who can unlock the Order's secrets for us, and now he barely remembers his own name!"

"So he claims," Talon remarked with a doubtful look.

"You think he's faking? You try surviving months of torture and see if your own mind does not shut down!" James rebuked his assistant, then he looked again at the blankly staring man, the once-mighty physique half wasted away after months in his dungeon cell.

James had demanded that Septimus remove this "Drake" from the bowels of the castle immediately. They'd had the surgeon examine him and cut off all his thick black hair to get rid of the lice. But even with his head shorn, the prisoner still had an aristocratic bearing.

James had no idea who the agent really was. But in spite of the fact that they should have been mortal enemies, he was moved to pity for their silent captive.

"Well," Septimus said resignedly, "I doubt he will be of any use to us now. He is a broken man."

"I could get rid of him," Talon murmured.

"No!" James ordered, turning to them in exasperation. "Nobody touches him, do you understand me? Somewhere in his brain lurks the names of all his fellow agents. We must treat him gently, give him time to heal."

"And when he's strong again, what if he turns against us?" Talon asked, keeping his voice down. "Given all we know about the Order's knights, I say best to kill him now, while he's still weak."

"Talon, you will obey me in this," James warned. "Why do the two of you fail to see my vision? Imagine what a boon he will be to us when we have helped him see the light. Don't you understand? I will change him. Teach him to understand that where he really belongs is on *our* side."

"How do you intend to do that, James?" Septimus shook his head. "It sounds extremely risky."

"He's been torn down. I will build him up again. Obviously, I mean to gain his trust." James glanced grimly from their captive back to them. "I do not know for certain if the damage to his mind can be undone, but we must try. When I have turned him, then we can destroy the Order of St. Michael for once and for all. As long as they survive, we will never succeed in advancing our vision. Every time we come close, they ruin it in the final hour."

Motionless a few yards away, Drake caught only snatches of their low-toned conversation, but he did not sense any danger in this moment, so he made no effort to try to hear their words. He was too exhausted in mind and body to care, anyway. All he wanted was to be left alone, breathing in the chilly alpine air.

It helped to clear his muddled head — and to keep the panic at bay. Losing himself in the sweeping view before him, he watched the sunlight play over the orchards and the high meadows filled with goats and wildflowers; the bright glitter of the distant snowy peaks stung his eyes with unshed tears.

His captors found it strange that he always wanted to be out on the roof now, beneath the open sky. But they might have felt the same if they had spent the past few months in the castle's lowest dungeons, in the dark. He blinked away the pain that haunted him like a wraith.

As his heart began to pound with remembered terrors, he strove to make himself empty again, empty, and pushed the fractured memories down again in a silent wave of desperation. He scrabbled for the words of his new creed, finding calm once more by saying them slowly, over and over again, in his mind. *We . . . are beyond good and evil . . . the elite . . .*

They had forced this litany down his throat, and made him learn it and recite it until his mind had screamed never to hear it again. But he must have broken through the pain, for speaking the words as his captors ordered in that cell had somehow, finally, reduced his agony.

Strangely, now the same words he had hated so bitterly began to bring him comfort.

He groped into the black void of his mind for the next phrase. *The elite . . . made of pure will . . .*

Was it not pure, savage will that had kept him alive all those months? Maybe they were right. Maybe he belonged here. Maybe as his savior, James, had said, some new destiny awaited him.

Forever reborn, new-kindled like the flame . . .

Drake, too, had been reborn.

He, too, had survived his daily torment like the god Prometheus, enduring the horrible talons and tearing beak of the eagle. The mere echo in his mind of the torturers' footsteps approaching down the hallway toward his cell made him break out in a cold sweat.

But the worst part was the fact that his time in hell was the only part of his life he could remember now — caged, forced to play the intolerable role of victim.

They had interrogated him endlessly, and it seemed to him he must have known the answers to their questions once, but if at first he had refused to tell them of his own free will, the day had come after a particularly bad beating when the answers were simply no longer there.

Vanished into the recesses of his mind — as though someone had erased them in between those blows to the head. His knowledge had been swallowed up as if by a vortex in the sea that sucked down ships.

His name was Drake. He was fairly sure of that much, but most of the life he had lived before was gone.

They had beaten it out of him, out of his body, out of his mind until he was hanging by a thread over this emptiness.

He was no longer sure who he was, could

not remember where he had come from or why. The simple facts of his existence had shattered and dissolved, and were as much a puzzle to him now as they were to his captors.

If he dwelled on it, the panic rose. He had almost wished that they would kill him. But then James had come.

The kind old man had rescued him and assured him this wild fear, this profound confusion all would pass. Such sweet promises. James had vowed gently to help him rediscover all he'd lost. For Drake's part, he now loved the old man with a blind, instinctive faith as his only hope for survival in this place.

The others feared James, respected him. They did as he ordered. For the first time, Drake had hope that the agony might truly be behind him now, as long as he did exactly what James said.

When the distress rose again from the slow-moving whirlwind of his confusion, Drake took comfort anew in the reassuring presence of his aged savior not far away. He knew he owed the kind old man his life. He longed with all his heart to please him, for he understood perfectly that, whenever he wished, James could send him back down into the depths of Hell.

"Drake?"

The deep, patrician voice seemed to reach him from a million miles away.

"Drake?" James appeared beside him, resting a bony hand on the back of his wheelchair. "Good morning, Drake." He bent down, peering into his face with solicitous concern. "How are you today? Feeling a bit better?"

Through a thick fog, Drake turned his head and gazed at him. "Better . . . yes." Injury and despair had made him docile, but though he couldn't quite remember, he did not think he had always been this way.

He saw a trace of pity in the deep-set gray eyes. James Falkirk was slight of build, with a shock of pewter hair, gaunt features, and a prominent nose. "Good," he murmured, the timeworn lines etched around his mouth and eyes deepening as he gave Drake a reassuring smile.

Behind him, the dark-eyed, bearded German, lord of this castle, regarded Drake with a wary mix of pity and contempt. The third man stood farthest away, but even from his distance, Drake saw the animosity in his cold hazel eye. The other eye was covered with a patch.

The youngest of the three, called Talon, was tall and rather husky, with rugged features and dirty blond hair. That one-eyed stare frightened Drake. He sensed an unspoken threat from the eye-patch man, but knew he was too weak right now to defend himself adequately if he was attacked.

He could feel the distress building up in his chest, but did not even realize how he had sunk down in his chair, cringing from Talon, until James spoke up again.

"It's all right, Drake. No one is going to hurt you. Drake, now, listen to me. There you are. Good lad," James soothed as Drake obediently gave James his attention. "I have exciting news for you, Drake. Talon and I are going to take you to England."

"England?" he echoed barely audibly, tasting the dimly familiar word.

"We believe that was your home. In another week or so, you should be strong enough to travel." James paused. "You know I promised to help you regain your memories, didn't I? When you see the places you once knew, I believe your memories will start to come back."

Drake's first thought was that he didn't want his memories to come back. It was best if they were hidden. He was certain of this, though he didn't know why. His mind must have swallowed them into the void for a reason.

Unfortunately, he realized that was not the answer James desired. "Yes. Thank you, sir," he whispered, trembling a bit. He lowered his head.

"You will get well in time," James encouraged him. "We must both be patient. And when you are well, Drake, when you're strong again —" The old man's voice deepened and turned slightly sinister. "I will help you get revenge on the so-called friends who left you here for dead."

The next day, Max arrived at the Starling villa at the agreed-upon hour to collect his intended for their courtship drive — a quaint and proper tradition, he thought in amusement. He was eager to see what Daphne's manner would be now that she'd had a full twenty-four hours to get used to the idea of marrying him.

He wasn't sure what to expect, but when he arrived, she received him with an attitude of subdued grace, alluringly dressed for their outing in a delicate pink carriage dress with long transparent sleeves.

His gaze trailed over the V-neck of her gown, festooned with frothy lace, but he forbade himself to stare too much. He spent a few moments dutifully conversing with her family — he really liked her father — but at last, she put on her matching pink hat, and he whisked her away for their outing, with a promise to have her back soon.

With her little sisters spying out the window, they walked out to his ridiculously expensive cabriolet, a light two-wheeled vehicle drawn by a single black gelding. Max opened the little low door and handed her in.

In truth, the late summer day was too hot

for this time-honored courtship ritual, but he raised the nautilus-shaped leather hood of the cabriolet to provide his lady with shade. He also suggested a stop at Gunter's for their famed ice cream, but they had not yet decided on that.

He was merely glad she did not attempt to back out of their appointment using the strong sun for an excuse.

Then they were under way.

They set out at a sedate pace, but when her shyness persisted, and the conversation flagged as a result, Max quickly decided to break the stilted tension with a heady dose of speed.

Nothing like a brush with danger to bring two people together. He drove his horse on faster while Daphne shrieked with half-terrified delight.

"Slow down! You are a lunatic!" she cried as they went thundering down a long, flat stretch of finely graveled road in a less-peopled region of Hyde Park.

Max laughed. He would have listened to her pleas if he believed her protests, but her exuberant laughter and her beaming smile told another story.

He slapped the reins again over his galloping horse's rump, half standing in the driver's seat, his leg braced against the footboard.

His coattails flew out behind him as they barreled on; likewise, the white ostrich plume on her bonnet waved like a pennant in the breeze formed by their velocity. He liked the way she reached for him, clinging onto his arm to steady herself.

She was responding to the excitement exactly as he had calculated — of course, he was too skilled a driver to put her in any actual danger. The illusion of it was enough.

They raced on down the dusty road, through patches of shadow cast across their path by the late day sun, angling over the tall, dry trees.

"Max!" she cried.

He thrilled to her use of his first name. At least they had cut through that irritating tension.

"Yes, Daphne?" he replied with a breezy glance.

She pointed ahead. "Look out!"

"Whoa!"

As they thundered up over a rise, both carriage wheels left the earth. Daphne let out a small scream and gripped him for all she was worth as, indeed, they went a little more airborne than Max had quite intended.

He laughed heartily as the cabriolet bounced back to earth, bumping them back down onto the seat.

"Oh!" she exclaimed after a moment, pressing a hand to her heaving chest. "We were — flying!"

He flashed a grin. "Want to do it again?"

"You *are* mad!" she burst out, but her shaky smile admitted that she at least realized he was joking.

"Only mad for you, Miss Starling. Only mad for you."

Her eyes sparkled at his soothing flattery, but he slowed the black gelding to a swift, cooling walk. The animal's glossy coat had begun to lather in the heat, and in any case, they were coming upon a more crowded region of the park.

She let go of his arm and put a small distance back between them. Max forced his attention to the road again, but his fierce awareness of her beside him roused his most elemental instincts, and took his imagination where it ought not go.

At least, not yet.

The hour of the promenade had now descended on Hyde Park. Elegant riders trotted and cantered to and fro; fancy equipages rumbled by on full display; fashionable walkers sauntered along in pairs or in small groups along the Serpentine.

Daphne returned a polite wave from someone in a passing carriage as they turned onto the Ring.

Max was well aware of the startled looks they drew as Society took note of them together.

This was exactly what he had wanted, and she would have certainly anticipated it, too. If she had had reservations, she would not have agreed to go out with him today.

Nevertheless, a fresh current of tension rippled beneath the surface between them as they debuted as a couple before Society. He could only imagine how the rumor mill would soon begin to churn. He was an old hand at dabbling in scandal, but he hoped she could withstand the pressure. The beating summer heat did not help.

A trickle of sweat on the back of his neck soaked into his cravat. "The park seems more crowded than usual for this time of year," he spoke up, hoping to chase away the awkward silence that had returned ever since she had noticed that they were being watched. He glanced at her.

"Yes. Society is off its schedule this year with the war's end." She nodded gracefully to another acquaintance as they rolled along. The friend stared back in amazement to see them together. "You were lucky you weren't here in July, when the casualty lists from Waterloo began appearing in the newspapers." She glanced at him suddenly. "By the way, I have a friend who told me you were there. That you saw the battle."

"What kind of friend?" he replied with a dubious frown, immediately recalling all the glory-hound officers at Waterloo who had referred to him as the Grand Tourist, never realizing he was only there to save Wellington from an assassin. Cringing to think what she might have heard, he felt a fleeting wish that he could've told her of his own heroics that day. But of course, she'd never know.

Futile vanity.

"One of those insufferable officers, no doubt," he grumbled. "I'll bet they all go fawning over you."

"Why, Lord Rotherstone, are you jealous?" she asked with a coquettish glance.

"Occasionally, as warranted."

"Well, you needn't worry." She gave him a sly little smile. "It was not an officer who told me. It was a young lady, one of my closest friends, actually. And if I decide to marry you, you're going to have to be nice to her."

"Am I?"

"She is very dear to me. Miss Carissa Portland."

"Hm, be nice to a chit who gossips about me. That's a fine thing. How did your Miss Portland know I was there? Was she at the Duchess of Richmond's ball in Brussels?"

"No, Carissa was here, and she knew, my dear Lord Rotherstone, because actually, between you and me — Carissa is a spy."

"A what?" He looked at her in utter surprise, but she merely laughed at him.

"Carissa always knows the gossip. I've no idea how! I fear she has nefarious ways of finding out these things, but I never question it. Her information often comes in handy —

just as it did regarding you."

"Aha." He was quite taken aback, however amused to hear her mischievous explanation. With a soft laugh, he looked at the road again. "Well, you must introduce me to this lady spy of yours. Perhaps she can teach me something."

"I don't think I will," she said. "She is afraid of you. And you didn't answer my question. Was she right? Did you really witness the battle that day at Waterloo?"

He shifted in his seat a bit. "Some of it, yes."

"What was it like?"

"Not a sight I will forget anytime soon." He slapped the reins lightly over his horse's back, urging the animal into a jaunty trot.

"You needn't protect my feminine sensibilities," she said. "I am English, too. I have a right to know."

He shrugged at her desire to know more. "Picture your worst nightmare, and multiply it by ten thousand. That was Waterloo."

She stared at him, absorbing this. "They say it was England's greatest victory, but . . . fifty thousand dead on both sides after just a couple days of fighting? Who can fathom that?"

Max said nothing.

She was silent for a moment in her thoughts. "I'm sorry. I don't mean to turn our outing morbid. The important thing is that people have pulled together to help each other through these difficult times."

"As they should."

"I imagine there will be all sorts of celebrations when all the troops are withdrawn from France and the ships start arriving, bringing them home. The autumn should be very merry. I'll be glad of the cooler weather. London is just ghastly in the summer. But now it shouldn't be too long before someone is giving a hunt ball."

"Good," he replied. "Because you still owe me a dance."

She glanced at him in surprise, and they exchanged a smile.

Max feared he held her gaze a bit too long. "Does your family have plans to remove to the country for the autumn? Your father seems the sort for all the good old country sports."

"No," she answered with a pert smile. "He does enjoy a bit of fishing and shooting now and then, but only if he's invited to someone else's country box. We Starlings are unusual in that we reside in London all the year round."

"Why? Is he active in the Lords?"

She shrugged. "Moderately so."

"Tory?"

"Of course. You?"

"Independent," he replied.

"Interesting," she answered, eyeing him

with a nod.

"I can't say it's won me many friends," he answered dryly. "The party leaders so love being able to predict one's vote. But if not for politics' sake, why does your father keep you in Town year-round?"

She let out a wistful sigh, gazing down the road. "He sold our country house after my mother died. The memories were too painful for him there. We moved into our present home when I was fifteen, and I have been a Town girl ever since."

"A Town girl, eh?" he teased her softly, determined to chase the note of sadness out of her voice. "Everyone knows about *them.* Sophisticated, fashionable, and fast —"

"I am not fast!"

"No? I don't mind, truly, if you ever want to act fast with me, I'm perfectly willing to let you —"

"You are bad!"

They exchanged mutual smiles of cautious delight.

"It's my turn for a question," he said.

"All right."

He glanced over at her. "How soon after your mother's death did your father marry the present Lady Starling?"

"Ugh. A few years." She watched an impressive coach-and-four go thundering by. "The ironic thing is sometimes I think Papa married her more for *my* sake than his own. He was convinced I needed some sort of mother in my life. I do have a slightly terrifying great-aunt who was my sponsor in Society. The Dowager Duchess of Anselm. But she's more like a grandmother to me."

"A duchess? Well, indeed."

"And Penelope had her own two girls to think of. She was newly widowed, and my stepsisters only babies at the time." She let out a sigh. "Frankly, I think Papa felt sorry for them."

"Maybe he loves her. Ever think of that?"

"He loved my mother," she replied in a prickly tone. "She never henpecked him or bossed him around like a shrew."

"I meant no offense." Determined to keep the mood genial, he changed direction slightly, not just with the conversation, but also with the cabriolet. "Did you enjoy living in the countryside before you moved to Town?"

"I hardly remember it."

"What about now?" he asked. Still bristling over this obviously sensitive subject, she did not seem to notice they had turned out of Hyde Park. His horse had perked up, however, recognizing the familiar way home. "Do you like spending time in the country?"

"Visiting is all right, as long as it's not too remote." She shrugged. "I enjoy visiting my friends at their country houses, but when you're with friends, it doesn't necessarily give a true picture. Most of the other young ladies assure me the rustic world is a dead bore when there are no amusing houseguests to keep one entertained."

"I see."

"Perhaps it's just my nature. Too much solitude depresses me. I require agreeable conversation and pleasant people on hand to associate with."

Max realized she was taking care to explain her preferences because when they were married, he would be in charge of where they lived. But she needn't have worried.

He was determined that she should be happy, above all, as his wife. "I see," he mused aloud. "A social butterfly. You do seem to know everyone," he added as she waved at a group of ladies going by in a barouche.

"I don't know if I'd go that far. I just enjoy being around people."

"God knows why," Max drawled. "They are miserable creatures."

"Lord Rotherstone!" she exclaimed. "For heaven's sake, I'm beginning to think you are either a dedicated cynic or a misanthrope."

"Right on both counts, actually."

"And you wonder why they call you the Demon Marquess?"

"Honestly," Max said with a laugh, "I think it's just the beard."

"Then you should shave it," she declared.

"Don't you like it?"

"No," she answered, to his vast amusement. "Frankly, my lord, it makes you look like Lucifer."

"Maybe I want to look like Lucifer," he replied.

"To scare everybody away, no doubt! Yes, that is my point exactly," she chided with an arch smile. "You say you want to improve the Rotherstone reputation, but I am getting the feeling you actually enjoy making people uneasy. You deliberately provoke them into steering clear of you."

"Me? Miss Starling! I am an innocent lamb."

"Ha. More like a wolf who barely bothers with sheep's clothing. You hardly ever come into Society, and when you do, you get into fights."

"I didn't get into a fight," he protested in a droll tone.

"You threatened Albert, didn't you? You told me so yourself."

"But that was different, Daphne, sweet. I did it for you. Nor do I regret it. If the blackguard says one more word about you, by the way, I have promised to put him through a window — just so you know."

"You see?" she exclaimed. "You are not helping yourself. You just can't do that sort of thing."

"I can't *not* do it," he answered amiably, "being me. Oh, very well! Tell me how you want me to make nice to all the lovely people in the ton."

She gave him a vexed look in exchange for his sarcasm. "They're not that bad. Not all of them."

"You fascinate me. Defending the fools who would gossip about you."

"They don't mean any harm. All I am trying to say is that if others interpret your demeanor as hostile — or dangerous — it's only natural they'll steer clear of you, however undeservedly. I mean, I've been spending time with you, and I can see you're a good person —"

"I beg your pardon!" he retorted in mock indignation.

"Oh, never mind! You are impossible," she scolded lightly. "So, there. You've had my advice on Society, and now I need your expertise in investment matters, if you would oblige me."

"Certainly." He looked at her in surprise.

"It's about the orphanage."

"Bucket Lane? Tell me you have not been back there."

"No, unlike certain marquesses, I do not have a death wish."

He looked askance at her.

"I've been seeking contributions to buy a new building for the orphanage. The children clearly need a more suitable location. Well, I've found the perfect place — a boarding

school for sale in Islington. I have been trying to raise money to secure the property
before somebody else buys it. But after the
market chaos, nobody wants to give just now.
I understand people are worried about their
own affairs, but I cannot let those poor
children stay in such a place. You've seen the
conditions —"

"Of course," he agreed at once. "Don't
worry. I'll take care of it."

"What? Oh!" Her eyes widened. She began
to blush. "No, it's all right. I didn't mean
that you should have to —"

"Not at all. Consider it done."

"Done? What, you're going to buy it?"

He almost said, *Consider it a wedding
present.* But then he saw the sudden alarm
written all over her face, and he stopped
himself abruptly.

It dawned on him that with her need for
control, such a gesture might only make her
feel pressured and torn, as if he would hold
the children's welfare over her head to coerce
into going along with the marriage. *Well,
damn.*

He was not about to hold her hostage.

"My friends and I were less affected by the
market drop, since many of our holdings are
abroad. I will talk to them," he said as he
turned the cabriolet into his street and
headed for the mews. "We'll make sure you

get the contributions needed."

"Your friends?" She stared at him dubiously. "From the Inferno Club?"

"Yes. If it's all right with you, I will go and see the new location you have found. Make sure everything's structurally sound, or if any repairs will be needed before the children can move in."

"That would be . . . lovely of you." She stared forward for a moment, as though in stunned disbelief at his words.

Max stole a sideways glance at her and saw the relief that crept back into her demeanor.

She looked at him suddenly. "Maybe we could go and look at it together."

His heart leaped at her suggestion of an outing, but he hid his jubilation behind his usual cool insouciance. "As you wish." He gave her a casual nod. "I'll have my man set up an appointment with the agent."

He could feel her staring at his profile; when Max glanced over at her, she gazed into his eyes and gave him, slowly, the most beautiful, beaming, beatific smile that he had ever seen.

He was entranced. The light that shone from her was like the dawn. He stared back.

No one had ever looked at him that way in his life. So tenderly, with so much hope in him. As if he was a hero, not a fiend.

God, he thought in a sudden wave of bewildered desperation, *I have got to win her. She has to say yes.*

In that moment, he could not imagine having to go back to his life the way it was. Back to the darkness, to the cold, to the endless isolation. He'd had no idea till now just how deep his hunger was. He had successfully ignored it for so long, pledged to his duty.

But to be with her now, this angelic creature, to receive that shining smile — and then, to have her refuse him, that would reduce him to the state of some poor prisoner who had crossed the czar, sentenced to a life of hard labor in the northern reaches of Siberia.

Whatever it took. He knew then he would do anything to bring her into his life, permanently. He was shaken by the intensity of his desire; his very soul flamed with a whole new motivation to complete what had been, until now, essentially a marriage of convenience.

Whatever it took, this woman would be his.

Having turned into the mews behind his house, he now brought the carriage to a halt.

At once, a groom in dark red livery rushed out to take the horse's bridle.

"Where are we?" she asked all of a sudden, glancing past him at the large brick building in whose cool shadow they now lingered.

He set the brake, then turned to her, gazing deeply into her eyes. "I call it home."

"This is your house?" she exclaimed, glancing from it to him in startled apprehension.

He nodded stoically, holding her stare. "Would you like to come in?"

CHAPTER 8

"Lord Rotherstone!" Daphne said breathlessly, dropping her gaze. She floundered. "I'm sure you know that would not be proper. We have no chaperone!"

"It is no matter," he murmured softly, staring at her with an intimate half smile. She could feel the sheer force of his willpower surrounding her, tempting her to do what she should not. "We are already engaged."

She looked up again in alarm. "That has not been settled!"

His smile widened knowingly; his pale eyes had darkened several shades. They mesmerized her. "Aren't you just a little curious to see what I am offering you?"

"Is that why you brought me here, for a bribe?" she demanded in rattled defiance.

"Oh, come in, just for a moment," he cajoled her with consummate skill. His voice had deepened to a husky timbre that plucked at her senses like clever fingers unlacing her stays. "I would so like to show you the art that I collected in my travels, Miss Starling. Allow me to offer you some light refreshments, as well. Perhaps a drink?"

Daphne quivered. She knew what he was doing, casting that spell of his again, with his dark-velvet voice and beguiling little smile.

"You *know* you want to see where we would live."

She could feel her strength to resist him draining away. He did not wait for her answer, but stood up in the driver's seat, then jumped down from the carriage, coming round to her side.

Daphne racked her brain, trying to rally a protest before he arrived to hand her down. But their talk about Penelope a few moments ago had reminded her of the reason she had greeted the marquess today in a more co-operative mood, and had decided to let herself be more open to his persuasion on the question of their match.

Her stepmother had made it clear that she was not particularly welcome in her own home; therefore, Daphne had to ask herself why she was fighting so hard to stay in a place where she was not entirely wanted.

Would it not be better to accept this admittedly brilliant match, this outstanding man for her husband, and create a home and family of her own?

Maybe it really *was* time to move on in life. She could not live like a child forever under her father's roof, after all. There came a time when a grown girl had to take a man and become, truly, a woman.

But was Lord Rotherstone the right man for her?

There was no point denying that she was attracted to him. She had changed her gown three times today before he had arrived. She had never gone to such silly lengths to impress a suitor before. Indeed, after twenty-four hours to think it over, she *was* seriously considering his proposal. She was not a fool. And dash it all, she *wanted* to go in and see his house. Their house, maybe. Someday.

But, God, if they were seen, if Society caught wind of this reckless act of daring, there would be no turning back. *Might that be his ploy?*

"Oh, such intense concentration," he observed in affectionate amusement as he sauntered up to her side of the carriage. He rested his elbow on the edge of the door. "My dear lady, do not hurt yourself."

"Rogue," she answered.

He flashed a smile that made her heart rebel against all the strictures placed on nice young ladies.

"I think you're beginning to like me in spite of yourself."

"Delusion."

He knew better, said his smile. "Are you just going to sit here arguing with yourself?"

"Can you read minds?"

"Faces, and do you know what's written all over yours? Confusion. Rather adorable, really. Very well, what is the argument? What says the prosecution, what claims the defense? Shall I get my parliamentary wig and debate the bill at hand?"

She shook her head. "You are too much."

"It's just a visit, darling. Something cool to drink. A stroll through the long gallery to see my nude Italian paintings."

"Nude!"

"Shocking," he drawled.

She fought back laughter as she held his twinkling gaze. "You're sure you're not going to ravish me?"

"Not unless you want me to," he replied in a husky murmur, staring at her with a look that turned her bones to jelly. He offered her his hand to help her down from the cabriolet.

With a small groan, Daphne looked at his waiting hand and then at his handsome face, so calmly assured. "Oh, botheration!" she burst out, sweeping to her feet and grasping his offered hand, powerless to resist. "You are going to drag me over the cliff with you, aren't you, Rotherstone?"

"Max," he corrected her for the umpteenth time that day.

"Lord Rotherstone!" she repeated with a warning look.

"As you wish," he murmured, taking her gloved hand to his lips after he had helped her step down from the carriage.

She gave him an uncertain look, but he smiled reassuringly at her again, tucked her hand into the crook of his arm, and escorted her toward the back entrance of his house.

"You still haven't opened my gift from yesterday, have you?" he remarked.

She sent him a quick, guilty glance. "How did you know?"

"Obviously, if you had, you would be raving." He eyed her with interest as he opened the door for her. "Aren't you the slightest bit curious to find out what it is?"

Her only answer was a troubled frown.

He dismissed his question with an idle wave of his hand. "Never mind, then. But I do hope you open it soon. I don't like being deprived of the pleasure of spoiling you."

With that, he opened the door before her, and ushered her into a world of opulence.

Marble floors stretched ahead of her as Daphne stepped inside. They had entered what appeared to be a narrow back foyer. He shut the door and led her toward the entrance hall proper, through a richly pedimented doorway flanked by a pair of little topiary trees in Grecian urns.

She followed, staring at a gorgeous demilune table by the wall as she passed by. Delicate French chairs were arranged on either side of it, with curved legs and pale damask upholstery.

Behind the furniture, white-framed panels adorned pastel walls, along with graceful paintings — landscapes, portraits, equestrian scenes — all in thick, carved frames.

Her gaze traveled up beyond the artwork, to the elaborate, gilded friezes around the room, and the intricately painted ceilings. From these, in turn, hung three stunning chandeliers at regular intervals all down the wide central hall. Their scores of beeswax candles were not lit, of course, but their countless crystals shimmered in the daylight.

A gentle cross-breeze from open windows around the first floor made the crystals tinkle faintly and stirred the gauzy sheers. Otherwise, the grand house was still.

Daphne was agog, even more so to think she could become the lady of all this.

He turned to her with a casual air. "Much cooler in here, isn't it?"

"Yes," she answered faintly.

"Ah, Dodsley! There you are."

A sweet-faced, snowy-haired butler had appeared without a sound. He clasped his hands behind him and gave them both a deferential bow. "My lord. Ma'am. How may I be of service?"

"Miss Starling, this is Dodsley — the most efficient butler on earth. Couldn't do without him. Anything you need around here, old

Dodsley is your man."

She smiled and nodded shyly to the butler. "How do you do."

"Dodsley, we would like refreshments. Something cool? I trust you have the Champagne chilling somewhere in the house?"

"The dining room, my lord."

"Champagne, in the middle of the day?" Daphne interjected.

Her handsome host turned to her in question. "I trust you don't object?"

She thought for a moment, but why quit now? In for a penny, in for a pound. She shrugged.

"I'll get it, Dodsley, if you can scrounge us up a bite to eat. Have we got that cold sorbet stuff? What's its name . . ."

"The lemon cream?" The butler nodded gravely as though discussing matters of state. "We do. Miss Starling, may I take your hat?"

"Why, thank you — yes." Carefully, Daphne removed her pink hat with its frothy, curved ostrich plume. Since there was talk of a snack as well, she took off her white gloves.

Lord Rotherstone was doing the same, drawing off his driving gloves. "Miss Starling, given the weather, I wonder if you'd think me quite beyond the pale if I were to shed my coat."

"Considering it must be nearly eighty degrees, I think we may safely ease up on decorum just a bit."

"Bless you." He peeled off his tailored indigo coat and handed it to his waiting butler. "That's better."

"I daresay," Daphne uttered faintly. His snugly fitted waistcoat beautifully revealed the hard, carved architecture of his torso, the sweeping angle from his powerful shoulders and sculpted chest, down to his lean, tapered waist.

His loose white shirtsleeves were slightly clingy in the heat, hinting at the rugged arms beneath that paper-thin layer of elegant white lawn.

"Come, I'll give you a tour while we wait for Dodsley to bring us that lemon cream."

"Yes — of course."

As he turned away and walked ahead of her to begin showing her the house, Daphne couldn't believe that she was ogling his compactly muscled bottom — she was quite shocked at herself — but, after all, such regions on a gentleman were usually covered by tailcoats, and besides, his was too lovely not to look at. His fawn-colored trousers fit him to perfection.

"Here we have the anteroom, where my business visitors wait until I am able to see them."

She dropped her gaze instantly when he turned around.

"Is something wrong?"

"No, nothing," she said guiltily.

236

"Right. Over here is my study." He went to the second doorway.

She joined him, peering into the dark, handsomely appointed room. "Beautiful stained-glass window." She nodded toward it, in the wall above the desk.

The late day sun glowed through the Gothic-era glass, giving the wood-paneled room a monastic atmosphere.

"Thank you, yes. It came from the family chapel at my seat in Worcestershire. One of the previous structures on the site burned down hundreds of years ago, but this was saved."

"It is St. Michael?"

"Mm." He nodded as he glanced at her, then turned away and ambled on down the corridor. "Back here is the morning room. Across the hall is a warming room, where the kitchen staff assemble their final preparations before serving meals here, in the dining room." As she followed him, he pointed himself toward the round wine cooler on a stand in the far corner. "Champagne."

"My," Daphne murmured, staring with awe all around the sumptuous chamber. In most grand houses, the dining room was where no expense was spared to impress guests with the owner's fortune and taste. The Marquess of Rotherstone had certainly complied with this tradition.

Here his luxurious mode of life was on full

display, from the richly patterned carpet, to the carved mahogany furniture, all the way up to the artful white plasterwork that wrapped around the tops of all four walls in an energetic design of garlands and flowers and urns.

She thought at once of what Papa would have called it: ostentatious. Again, she thought of her father's whispered losses in the stock exchange.

Now that she had firsthand evidence of just how wealthy the Marquess of Rotherstone was, an uncomfortable question was starting to gnaw at the back of her mind . . .

"What do you think?" he asked as he lifted a bottle of French Champagne out of the ice-filled cooler.

She did her best to shrug off her misgivings that her beloved papa could have sold her to him for financial reasons, sending him a smile. "It's simply gorgeous. Everything is."

"I am glad you like it." He returned her smile and carried the bottle over to the sideboard. "I do think it rather handsome myself, especially by an evening's candle-light."

"I can imagine."

The central chandelier was exuberant with crystals like a fountain. Straight beneath it, on the long dining table, which was polished to a mirrorlike sheen, sat a glorious floral arrangement — a profusion of roses in several

shades, summer lilies, and simple white daisies.

One small intruder, a honeybee, must have
found its way in through an open window,
and was hovering about the bouquet, alighting here and there to sip the nectar from the
blooms.

Resting her hands on the back of a chair,
Daphne stared at the insect while Max
poured some water from a white pitcher into
a porcelain hand bowl. She joined him as he
washed his hands in preparation for their
snack. She followed suit, glad of the chance
after their dusty drive.

As he dried his hands on a small towel, he
nodded toward the waiting bottle of Champagne. "I'll do the honors here if you'll get us
two goblets from the cabinet over there."

"Fair enough." She smiled at him and nodded, then went to the mahogany china cabinet
across the room and opened one of the glass-
paned doors. As she took out two glasses of
the sparkling crystal, she noticed the gilt-
edged china dinner plates on display. They
were hand-painted with his family crest and
a monogrammed R.

The pop of the Champagne bottle echoed
through the room. When he let out a wordless exclamation at the foaming fizz, she
laughed and rushed back to help him catch it
in the glasses.

"Cheers," he said a moment later, when he

had poured them each a glass. "To you, Miss Starling."

She blushed a bit at his toast, but shrugged and flashed a smile. "If you insist — to me!"

They both laughed. They touched their goblets together and then each took a sip, staring at each other.

"Mm," she murmured in appreciation after a heartbeat. His eyes took on a silvery luster as he watched her enjoying the excellent vintage.

Just then, a light knock sounded on the open door down at the far end of the room.

Max glanced past her. "Come in, Dodsley."

Daphne turned around as the butler took the tray from the liveried footman who had been holding it for him.

Max pulled out the nearest chair for her with a gallant smile, while Dodsley and the footman made a dignified procession into the dining room.

Daphne sat down, and Max took a seat beside her; Dodsley placed the silver tray on the table between them. When the servants withdrew, they exchanged a smile and helped themselves to the light repast that was the very picture of elegant simplicity.

The chilled lemon cream awaited in petite china cups with silver spoons. A crystal bowl tempted them with a fresh fruit salad: apricots and plums, raspberries and blueberries, all generously sprinkled with sugar.

Perfectly balanced with the tart zing and smooth texture of the lemon cream were the crisp, pale, wafer-thin biscuits universally known and loved as ratafia drops. The sweet sophistication of their understated almond flavor paired with the creamy sorbet to perfection.

Though Dodsley had also brought them a pitcher of chilled tea with a sprig of mint and a slice of lemon floating in it, they both opted for a second glass of the Champagne instead.

"There's something I've been meaning to ask you," Daphne spoke up as they sat together.

"What's that?"

"The night of the Edgecombe ball — well, I wasn't trying to eavesdrop — but I heard Albert say you 'vanished' when you both were boys. He seemed quite mystified by it, and frankly, so was I. What did it signify?"

"Oh, I was sent away to school when I was thirteen. Albert and his brothers went to Eton, but . . . my father could not manage that for me at the time. So I attended a small academy in Scotland."

"Oh." She smiled at him, not wishing to remind him of his family's earlier lack. "That makes sense."

Looking around at this house, she saw he had certainly come a long way.

"Shall we?" he asked a bit later when they finished their snack, much refreshed. "I'll

241

take you up to see the long gallery now."

"Yes." Daphne joined him eagerly, and they continued the tour. The time was flying, and she dared not stay much longer.

Max showed her out of the dining room and up a grand staircase with marble steps and a flowery wrought-iron banister. She had an increasingly surreal feeling to find herself on such intimate terms with a man she had seen on only three occasions in the past — a man who even now considered himself her betrothed.

Strangest of all was how naturally they both seemed to fall into this easy companionship with each other. He was almost as easy to talk to as Jonathon, but the two could not have been more different.

Perhaps he really did know what he was doing, she thought, stealing another sidelong glance at him. He was older and much more experienced than she was, after all.

At the top of the stairs, the white marble floors gave way to light oak parquetry. Though the staircase continued on to upper regions where, presumably, the bedchambers were situated, their destination was the main floor, with its elegant reception rooms.

He showed her the pale blue drawing room at the front of the house and the music room behind it, the two adjoined by sliding pocket doors. The music room boasted not only a large, graceful harp, but a fine black pianoforte, as well.

Daphne glanced at her host. "Do you play?"

"No, but I am an avid listener. Sometimes I hire a trio to come in and play for me. Do you play, Miss Starling?"

Long-lost days of playing the pianoforte beside her mother came to mind at once, but that was long ago.

She shook her head. "So, where is this grand art collection that you keep bragging about?"

"Across the corridor. After you." He swept a gesture toward the doorway of the music room.

With a teasing glance, Daphne exited as he bade her and crossed the wide, graceful hallway, but when she peeked ahead of him into the long gallery across the way, the room was dark.

He brushed past her, going in first. "We keep the shutters closed to protect the paintings."

He crossed the gallery, approaching the row of nearly floor-to-ceiling windows along the opposite wall. The click and creak reverberated through the long, narrow room as he opened each tall shutter, and folded it back into place.

Light slowly permeated the splendor of a classic picture gallery with golden parquet floors and red walls, a traditional background for his collection.

Daphne stepped into the room, staring all around her in wonder. To be sure, it was a treasure trove. Some paintings were huge; others, lovingly framed miniatures. All different eras were represented: courtly lovers in the Baroque style, awash with lace, in towering wigs and Watteau gowns. Glowing Venetian landscapes. A stone slab with Egyptian hieroglyphs was displayed on the opposite wall. There were numerous statues, both bronze and marble. Dutch portraits, dark and moody. A pair of two-handled Roman amphorae as tall as herself.

She cooed over a brilliant illuminated manuscript on a stand, and then became entranced by a glittering Byzantine mosaic to her right.

He watched her in mysterious silence.

Drawing in her breath, she approached a modest sepia sketch of a portly naked female, ever so sensitively rendered. Then she turned to him, wide-eyed. "Is that — ?"

He nodded, rich satisfaction in his eyes. "Leonardo."

"God," she breathed, pressing her hand to her heart. It was the closest she had ever stood to the genius of Leonardo da Vinci.

"My tastes are eclectic, as you can see. This one is a particular favorite of mine," he added, turning to a tall alabaster statue of a female water bearer a few feet from where he stood. He walked over to it. Daphne also approached. "She's Roman, circa A.D. 56. Isn't she splendid? The skill this must have required — and the fellow never even signed his name. One of history's unsung heroes."

"She is exquisite."

"Hm. Solid stone, and yet," he added in a thoughtful murmur, grazing his fingertips along the water bearer's thigh, "you almost expect to feel the diaphanous cloth of her robe."

Something about his idle caress made her full attention home in on his strong, graceful hand. She shivered a little, but fought off the dart of desire that came out of nowhere.

"What robe?" she answered archly.

He flashed a rueful half smile. "She isn't wearing much, is she?"

Daphne returned his smile, rather mystified. Then she shook her head, turning to look all around her again. "I can't believe you have these things."

"Well, you know, Europe's been a battleground these many years. I was privileged to save many of these beautiful pieces from destruction. Shall we?" With a courteous gesture, he invited her to join him on a stroll around the gallery.

He folded his hands behind his back as she fell into step beside him. Some of the pictures he explained to her; others he merely stood back and let her enjoy. But when they came to a portrait of a man with pale eyes and dark hair, she was riveted.

"Who is this?" she murmured, half impressed, half intimidated by the way the lordly figure stared out from the canvas with a face full of arrogant intensity.

"That," Max answered dryly, "is my father."

Daphne looked at him in surprise. "Oh — I should have known. You have his eyes. Indeed, you are a copy of him."

"No, I'm not," he answered airily, avoiding her gaze with a broody little smile.

Taken aback by the steely undertone in his quiet reply, she turned to him in question, but when he blithely ignored her, she decided not to press him. "Are these your ancestors, too?" She nodded toward the next few portraits.

"Aye, there's a whole row of the blackguards."

His apparent ambivalence about his forebears puzzled her. Intrigued, Daphne spent a few minutes studying the various Rotherstone lords. Their clothing reflected different periods, but that same guarded intensity had obviously been passed down through the bloodlines over time. Some of the marquesses were shown in court robes for their official portraits. Others wore military uniforms, while a few were portrayed in gentlemanly country clothes with a horse and an estate behind them.

But one small detail in some of the portraits

caught her eye: a white Maltese cross adorned with some obscure insignia. "What is that?" she asked, her curiosity piqued.

"What is what?"

She pointed to the symbol, sometimes shown on the clothing, sometimes obscurely tucked away into a corner of the painting. *"That."*

"Oh — that's just one of their honorifics. Different members of my line have been inducted into several noble orders. Many of them are hereditary. Basically meaningless, but you know, funny robes and whatnot. The occasional odd ceremony once a decade or whenever the ruling monarch takes the whim."

"I see." They had come to the end of the room, where a rectangular Persian carpet defined a small seating area arranged in front of the plain white fireplace.

The whole gallery was a feast for the eyes, but her scanning gaze was drawn to the fantastic jeweled broadsword on display above the mantelpiece.

A low exclamation escaped her. "How . . . marvelous." She moved toward the fireplace and stared up at the gleaming steel blade.

He came to stand by her side, and then looked at her quizzically. "Miss Starling: You are very wise."

She looked at him in surprise. "I am?"

"You have sounded out the most valuable

piece in my entire collection."

"This?" She pointed to the sword. "Even more than the Leonardo?"

"To me, it is."

"Why? Where did you get it?"

When he looked up at it, she stared at his noble profile. "It was handed down to me by my father, and his father before him — and so it has been, for some six hundred years. It belonged to the first Lord Rotherstone. He was a warrior-baron, a knight, at the time of Richard the Lionheart. He took this sword with him to the Holy Land, and with it, slew a hundred of Saladin's Mamluks in the fight to free Jerusalem."

"Really?" she breathed. "This very sword?"

"Yes." He turned again to her with a trace of amusement around the corners of his eyes at her enthusiasm for this bit of family history.

"And now you have it," she echoed.

He nodded, coming closer.

Well, his willingness to join the fray in Bucket Lane certainly made sense now, she thought. He had the battle instinct in his blood.

"Have you ever tried it out?" she asked with a flirtatious look askance, glancing back at the Crusader's sword.

"You really think I go around smiting people, don't you?"

"You didn't answer the question."

"Sorry?" He was staring at her mouth.

He stepped nearer.

She furrowed her brow. "Why is it that when you don't wish to answer a question . . ." Her words trailed off as he laid his hands gently on both sides of her neck at its base, where it met the angle of her shoulders. "My lord —"

"I'm sorry, but I have to do this," he whispered, then he lowered his head and kissed her.

His lips were soft, but the short scruff of his beard was sharp and prickly. It both hurt and startled her; she jerked back automatically, and looked up into his eyes.

He paused, trailing a fingertip gently over her chafed chin. He smiled at her ever so subtly. Then he approached again even more carefully, tilting his head at a wider angle so as not to scrape her. This time he brought no pain, only sweetness, pleasure.

She closed her eyes, slowly exploring the sensations of delight that infused her as his lips played against hers. Growing lightheaded, she rested her hands on his chest to steady herself; vaguely, she gripped the lapels of his silk waistcoat.

"Daphne." He breathed her name, and when she responded with a faint, intoxicated smile, he deepened the enchantment, tasting her with the tip of his tongue, a slow, seductive caress.

She groaned barely audibly, yielding to the coaxing pressure of his lips parting hers. When she opened her mouth uncertainly, he accepted the invitation with smooth and unhesitating ease. Now he was in full control, ruling her senses with the light pressure of his thumbs stroking up the sides of her neck, in time with the mesmerizing glide of his tongue on hers.

He tasted of sugary lemon and French Champagne.

Her head was in a whirl, her heart racing as the Marquess of Rotherstone stole her breath and gave her back his own. The sound of his breathing was deep, its rhythm slowed.

Under his spell of his kiss, she was not sure how or when he had maneuvered her toward the wall nearby, out of the range of vision of any servants who might have happened past the long gallery, shielded, also, from the window and the view of passersby on the street below.

A folded shutter was on one side of her, the ornate frame of some painting on the other, but his kiss and his towering frame filled her world, in front of her, above her, around her. His tongue was in her mouth, teaching her an entirely new way of being in his power, by means of the mindless pleasure he could give her.

At the moment, she was all too happy to submit, even though she had the distant feeling that she was getting in over her head. His kiss was exquisite, paradisiacal, transporting her.

His hand moved gently down the curve of her throat to her heaving chest, his warm fingertips alighting between the lace folds of her neckline. They rested there and then began to stroke, right above the heart they caused to flutter so. Her senses clamored to touch him in return.

Still lost in their kiss, she reached up and molded her hands tentatively against the hard, wide angle of his solid shoulders. He seemed to welcome it. From there, she inched her palms downward over the silk waistcoat that stretched over his chest; she could feel his heart pounding.

Next she explored the strong arms that held her, reveling in the virile power of his iron biceps through his thin white shirtsleeves.

At last, she cupped her hand against his face, marveling at the wonder of its hard planes and angles, his steely jaw, smooth-shaved, and then his square chin with the rougher texture of his short goatee.

He turned his head and kissed her palm. But when he bent lower and began to kiss her neck, Daphne welcomed him, leaning her head back against the gallery's red wall.

With closed eyes, she cradled his head to her, running her fingers through his dark, tousled hair. She melted against him as he kissed her neck without restraint now, the chafing of his beard against her highly sensitized skin bringing a very different effect — not pain, but wild pleasure. She wanted to feel it everywhere, against her skin, her breasts.

Her fingers splayed through his hair in a rougher caress; she gripped his head against her, urging him on, though he needed no coaxing.

He leaned closer against the full length of her body, so warm and strong and exciting, pressing his thigh between her legs — a subtle caress that made her shudder violently.

Indecent thoughts, wanton yearnings gripped her.

Meanwhile, the gently blowing sheers that framed the shuttered windows floated past them and wrapped around them like a whisper of white bedsheets, diffusing the afternoon light.

He shifted against her in the most intoxicating fashion, arousing her to a state of feverish lust. She was weak and shaky, and obviously quite mad, for she would have liked nothing better than to lift her skirts and let him have his wicked way with her at once.

This, observed the last remaining shred of logic in her brain, was clearly why unchaperoned visits were verboten between courting couples.

But Daphne knew deep in her core that she

could never feel this way toward any other man.

He came back up from devouring her neck, hot and hazy-eyed, hair tousled, lips damp and slightly swollen, his face flushed. He was the most beautiful thing she had ever seen, but as he met her aching stare, he just shook his head, a silver-tongued charmer at an utter loss for words.

He didn't have to speak. She could not have agreed with him more. She ran her hands up his chest, adoring him.

He looked into her eyes, then cupped her face between his palms and claimed her mouth again. The unbridled hunger in his kiss set her pulse racing anew; she wanted more.

She arched her body in restless sensuality, pinned deliciously between him and the wall. The instant flames that her sinuous motion aroused in his eyes made her go still, suddenly reminded that she was indeed playing with fire.

"God," he whispered more to himself than to her, "you could wield such power over me." Staring hungrily at her, he came back for more.

"Me?" she asked innocently. "How? Like this?" She wrapped her arms around him and met his searing kiss in reckless abandon.

When she heard his low groan of pleasure it was almost more than she could bear. Her heart was slamming, her body afire with undreamed sensations, her core crying out for a completion she had heard of only once or twice in euphemistic whispers.

Max, she knew, the wicked Marquess of Rotherstone, could teach her everything.

With all his worldly elegance and suave expertise, fairly radiating sex, what better tutor could she hope for to instruct her in every wondrous pleasure that a woman could discover with a man?

But not yet, her swooning conscience reminded her.

Not until she married him — and wasn't that a case of out of the frying pan, into the fire?

All of a sudden, he tore his lips away from hers and stared toward the door, as still as a wolf in a forest hearing some distant sound.

"Someone's coming," he breathed.

"What?" she cried in a hushed tone, still panting with desire.

"Dodsley."

"Oh — !" She shot out of his arms, whirling away from him, and turning her to the distant doorway so the butler would not see the guilt written all over her face, not to mention her immediate, crimson blush. At once, she hurried to tidy her rumpled appearance with shaking hands.

Nearby, Max took a deep breath and did the same.

He cleared his throat and suddenly looked completely nonchalant, just as his old butler hurried into view.

Still wishing she could hide, Daphne was taken aback by his convincing mask of business-as-usual.

"My lord!"

"Yes, what is it?" he clipped out, with only a trace of annoyance in his deep voice.

"My lord, please forgive the interruption. But you have visitors —"

"Visitors?" he bit back angrily. "Dodsley!"

"I crave your pardon, sir! I could not — that is, they say it's very urgent."

His low, infuriated huff made her think he must have some idea who it was.

"Tell the bastards I am not at home," he ordered at the same time his butler said: "The lady refuses to go until she sees you, sir!"

Hearing both their words, Daphne stopped. She looked from Dodsley to his scowling master.

"Lady?" she echoed. Surprise and indignation promptly overrode her embarrassment. Good God, how great of an error had she just made? Was he not the Demon Marquess, after all, leading member of the Inferno Club? To be sure, she had just had a taste of his libertine talents for herself.

Heaven only knew how many female visitors such a man invited into his house on any given day.

She backed away from him with a piercing stare.

At that moment, the echo of light, running footsteps came pounding up the marble stairs. In the next heartbeat, a small boy ran headlong into the room, and came barreling straight toward him.

"Uncle Max!"

CHAPTER 9

"Oh, bloody hell," he uttered under his breath.

"You said a curse!" the small lad shouted as he charged up to Max, stopped short, and craned his neck to stare at him.

Folding his arms across his chest, Max acknowledged the diminutive intruder with no more than a raised eyebrow.

"It's not Their Lordships calling, sir," Dodsley said in a long-suffering tone. "I was trying to say it is Lady Thurloe and the, er, children." Poor Dodsley went hurrying after the boy, who ran off again, tearing through the gallery, hollering like a wild savage. "Young master, I beg you, mind the statues, please!"

Daphne looked on in bewilderment as a lady in a blue carriage dress and an elaborate hat came flouncing into the doorway.

"Why, look! There he is: my infamous brother!"

"Mama, what does 'infamous' mean?"

asked the neat little girl who held the woman's hand, as docile in her manner as the boy was wild.

"Infamous, Flora," the lady replied, leading her daughter into the gallery, "means the sort of man who comes back to London and never even bothers to call on his own sister, who has not seen him in three full years!"

"No, Bea," he replied uncomfortably, "I'm sure it's only been two."

Meanwhile, Dodsley caught one of the Roman amphorae and righted it with a frantic look as the boy went charging past it.

"Infamous," the lady continued, propping one hand grandly on her hip, "means commanding one's butler to tell one's relatives that one is not at home, when one most obviously *is*."

"You mean Uncle Max told a lie, Mama?"

"Papa says he tells loads of 'em!"

"That will do, Timothy. Over here. Right now!"

Daphne watched her in wonder as the lady captured her son by his wrist as he zoomed past.

"As for you, brother," she resumed, securely holding a child's hand in each of her own. "I heard you were at the Edgecombe ball. How strange that I did not see you there! Oh, yes, you scoundrel. I was in attendance!" she informed him reproachfully in answer to his chagrined look. "Of course, I went home

258

early. My Paul does not stay out past eleven."

"I arrived late," he answered, faltering slightly. "Well, I would have looked for you if I had known!" he added with a trace of guilt.

"If you had remembered I exist? Honestly, brother! If we had known you were coming, Paul and I would have stayed to greet you. How long have you been in Town?" she demanded.

"Not very long," he mumbled evasively.

"Well, you can't escape us now, can you? Infamous, I say, dodging us since you arrived!" As she spoke, the little girl released her hand and walked demurely to look at a painting of some horses on the wall.

Daphne was still standing there awkwardly, until the child noticed her and offered a shy smile. She returned it, quite chagrined at her predicament. To think that these children could have walked in on what they had been doing! She wanted to die.

"At any rate," their mother continued in a brisk tone, "we are leaving London for the countryside tomorrow, and we won't be back in Town until the spring, so the least that you can do is acknowledge your niece and nephew before we go. Do you believe how big they're getting, Max? Flora, come away from that — lady."

Her crisp tone and the fact that she had ignored Daphne from the moment she arrived made it obvious what assumptions the woman had already drawn about her brother's female companion of this afternoon. Daphne was mortified.

"Careful, Bea, it isn't how it looks."

"I'm sure." The woman eyed her skeptically.

His face hardened. "Beatrice, Countess of Thurloe, allow me to present the Honorable Miss Daphne Starling." He squared his shoulders and added: "My future wife."

At his bold announcement, Daphne glanced at him in alarm. She was unsettled to hear him stating it as though it were hard fact. To be sure, Lady Thurloe looked equally astonished.

"Max!" she exclaimed in almost breathless tone. "Is this true? This is not one of your pranks?"

"Of course it's not a prank," he said with a scowl. "If it weren't for Daphne, I wouldn't have gone to the Edgecombe ball in the first place."

"But I am amazed!" She took a step closer. "You're getting married and you didn't tell me?"

Oh, dear. This was quickly going from bad to worse. Daphne knew she should speak up and clarify things, but as the cold, hard breeze of sanity returned in a whoosh after the fevered madness of his kiss, it was all too clear that the least scandalous, perhaps the *only* nonscandalous, acceptable excuse for her presence here in Lord Rotherstone's house, alone with him, was the imminent ringing of wedding bells.

The only problem was, she had not yet agreed to the match. Or perhaps she was only fooling herself.

Before she could conjure some alternative credible explanation, Lady Thurloe brushed off her fleeting hurt at her brother's neglect in favor of open rejoicing. "Oh, Max!" She clapped her gloved hands together, fingers clasped. "Miss Starling — Daphne, is it? May I call you Daphne? Oh, but I *thought* I recognized you! Goodness, when I first saw you here, knowing him, I nearly thought — but never mind that! Of course — you are Lord Starling's beautiful daughter whom everyone adores!"

"I-I don't know if that is quite the case, Lady Thurloe," Daphne stammered.

"Call me Beatrice. Oh, my dear — sister! Let me embrace you!" She sailed forward and gave Daphne a polite but enthusiastic hug, and an airy peck on both cheeks. "My dear, dear girl! Oh, Lud, but you will have your work cut out for you." Lady Thurloe laughed as she hugged her. "Promise me you will torment him!"

"I promise." Daphne glowered at Max over his sister's shoulder before the woman released her again.

Lady Thurloe stepped back and paused as she passed a wry but chiding look from Max

261

to Daphne and back again. "Oh, my. So, the two of you in here alone . . . I do declare! Rather naughty, tsk, tsk." She wagged a finger at them with a knowing giggle. "Never fear, my lips are sealed. Flora, Timothy, come over here and meet your future auntie! Isn't she lovely? Oh, this is *too* exciting! My dear brother, I am so happy for you! We've been waiting so long for you to come home and settle down at last!"

While Lady Thurloe gushed on and Max smiled in stoic silence, the children studied her warily, and Daphne cursed herself for ever having agreed to come into this house in the first place.

She had known better, but she hadn't been able to resist him, and now what a perfect pickle she was in.

She maintained a polite smile, but she felt trapped.

Worse, she could hardly think what to do, with her head still spinning after that thrilling brush with passion. Events seemed to be whirling beyond her control, but at the same time, seeing the obviously good-hearted Lady Thurloe's delight over the news of her brother's alleged engagement, Daphne could not bring herself just now to dash the woman's hopes.

It seemed her safest option was to go along with it graciously for the moment, but a panicky feeling was rising in her. Even though she was fairly sure Max had not *planned* his sister's interruption, every tick of the long-case clock nearby somehow attuned her awareness to his cold, calculating will to make her his own.

Dashed if she could not already feel him breathing down her neck in his will to power over her — as much an invasion of her sovereignty as any of Napoleon's incursions across the Rhine.

No, she was not *accusing* him of deliberately arranging for his sister to catch them unchaperoned together; he had appeared as genuinely surprised by the ill-timed visit as she.

But then again, she would not put something like it past him. Was he not the same tricky fellow, after all, who had feigned drunkenness so convincingly in Bucket Lane?

True, he had done it to rescue her, but such deception seemed to come all too naturally to him. Could he really be trusted? Or was he willing to use whatever it took to get what he wanted — his wits, his wealth, his wondrous body?

But why? What in the hell did he think was so special about her, anyway?

But it wasn't about her, and that was the problem. It was all about what Lord Rotherstone wanted and what Lord Rotherstone intended to have.

Why, he thought he could add her to his collection like these paintings and statues, to show her off as Albert had wanted to do, and worse, to breed more Rotherstones for future portraits on his ancestors' wall.

For a fleeting instant, Daphne wanted to kill him.

She felt duped, but was too polite, too well-trained a lady to start the battle now. Not in front of the children or his sister. After all, if Daphne abjured the marriage now, how would she account for her scandalous visit here?

She was between a rock — a stone, no, a Rother-stone — and a hard place.

"Oh, you will love being married," the countess said wistfully. "I know everyone complains of it, but it really is quite nice when you have someone who cares for you."

"Lady Thurloe, if I may impose on your good humor," Daphne spoke up, doing her best to hide her desperation, "we are not, um, really ready to announce our nuptials yet. His Lordship only asked me yesterday."

"His Lordship? Ah, I see. You two are still just getting to know each other. How adorable! I understand completely!" she reassured them, beaming. "I can be discreet until you are ready to tell the world. I wouldn't dare overstep my bounds. After all, my brother does not easily forgive. Be warned of that, Miss Starling."

Daphne nodded in relief, but fortunately, Lady Thurloe didn't stay long. She introduced her children, then took each by the hand, preparing to take their leave.

"Well, brother dear, I'm glad I finally found you at home. Do have a care when you go back out, you lovebirds. All the fashionable fools are still milling about on promenade out there. We wouldn't want any gossip to taint your happy news. Come along, children."

"I'll walk you out," Max said.

"Not necessary, my dear brother. You stay here with your fiancée. Dodsley will show us to the door. I'm sure he will be quite happy to do so."

"Madam," the butler intoned, stepping forward to perform his duty without giving any sign of a reaction to her pointed remark.

The countess paused on her way out, stopping in the doorway to glance back at them. "Max," she said hesitantly, "do please try to keep me apprised of what's going on in your life, won't you? Our parents may be gone, but you are still my brother. You're all that I have left." She turned to Daphne with a warm smile. "And Miss Starling, if I can be of any use at all in helping plan the wedding, do not hesitate to call on me. It would be the delight of my life to be involved!"

"You are altogether kind, my lady. I will write to you, most certainly." Daphne was touched by her kindness.

Lady Thurloe nodded. "Dodsley can give

you my address at our estate in Berkshire. You both are welcome to visit anytime. Congratulations, again!"

"Good-bye!" the children called, waving.

"Good-bye, thank you!" Daphne answered, waving back.

Still, the master of the house just stood there, arms akimbo, his demeanor gone dark and cold and brooding, inexplicably remote. Daphne looked at him after they had gone. *What's the matter with you?* she wondered, but when he eyed her grimly, she decided not to chance it.

"I should go, if you don't mind," she said with guarded restraint. "It's getting late. My father will be wondering where I am."

He dropped his gaze, withdrawing into his own obscure thoughts. "Of course."

Stiffly and self-consciously, they returned downstairs, where the butler gave Daphne back her hat and gloves, and held Lord Rotherstone's coat while he slipped his arms into the sleeves.

A silent walk back out to the cabriolet was followed by a long and uncomfortable ride back to her family's villa in South Kensington.

"I am," he said at length, "deeply sorry about that intrusion."

"Nonsense." Daphne gave him a nervous smile. "Your sister is a lovely woman."

"Yes." He stared between the horse's ears

down the road ahead.

Daphne studied him, wondering what was wrong. She recalled his referring to his gambling father as "cursed," and thought of how he had mentioned having torn down his childhood home and building over it. All those years of travel, and his sister's account of his neglect even after he had returned — and then Lady Thurloe's cryptic warning.

My brother does not easily forgive.

"You keep a distance from your family," she said softly.

Silence.

"Did they wrong you somehow?"

"We are not close. That is all."

He drove a little faster as they rolled along down a shady lane, but the tension pulsating from him began to fray Daphne's nerves.

She wished that he would tell her what was wrong.

He was locked up like a fortress, and she was stuck outside the walls. She did not understand it. Nor did it seem fair.

After all that she had told him about herself, and the things that he had guessed, private things that she had never told anyone — like yesterday, when he probed into her hurt over the terrible loss of Mama — it bothered her that he would seek to know everything about her, and then shut her out when *she* asked for answers, in return.

As she rode along beside him, her resentment of his continued silence grew. If the man desired to be her husband, why was he now acting like a stranger?

She could no longer contain herself. "I cannot think what you could have against Lady Thurloe. She seems very good."

"Oh, that she is, to be sure. And her husband's even more virtuous." He practically spat the word.

His vehemence warned her back. She stared ahead again, her heart pounding. "What are we going to tell her? She thinks we're getting married."

"We are. What?" he demanded when she went silent.

Daphne shook her head, holding on to her tact against the urge to clobber him. "Oh, I don't know. If this is the way you treat the people who care about you, it really doesn't bode well for your future wife."

"That's different."

"Is it? Why do you hate them so much? What did they ever do to you?"

"I don't hate them," he replied. "I just don't give a damn."

"Max," she chided gently. "You're not a very good liar."

This remark made him turn to her with a startled flash in his eyes; but if he had any response, he swallowed it, and drove on without a word.

"I guess I might as well be talking to myself

here," Daphne remarked to the air as she flicked a piece of lint off her glove. "Why won't you tell me what's wrong?"

"Because there *is* nothing wrong."

"So, you ran off to the Continent to escape your family, then. They were more of a threat to you than a war going on everywhere?"

He gave her an impatient look, indeed, a warning look, but he still did not reply. She knew he was getting angry at her, and though he was formidable in the extreme, she was not quite ready to give up yet.

The longer he refused to answer, the angrier she got.

She waited another moment, then steadied her courage for one last try. "Why didn't you go and see your sister when you returned to Town? I mean, for her to have to find out from others that you were at the Edgecombe ball, that must have been hurtful and embarrassing —"

"Do me a favor," he cut her off sharply. "Don't tell me how to treat my sister, and I won't tell you how to deal with your stepmother, agreed?"

She flinched at his harsh tone, but she had caught a fleeting glimpse of turbulent pain beneath his hard, polished veneer.

He sent her a dark glance. "Her brats will get a large inheritance from me. That's all that matters to them, or to anyone else."

"No, it's not. She obviously loves you!"

"You are naïve," he uttered bitterly.

Stung, Daphne stared at him. "At least I am not heartless."

He took a deep breath, and shut her out completely.

For the rest of the ride home, there was nothing more to say. Fortunately, they were almost there. The final minutes seemed to drag. At last, he brought the carriage to a halt before her home. Once more, he set the brake, stepped down, and came round to assist her.

"Here we are." He lifted his hand as before to help her down, but far from the charming persuasion that he had employed to lure her into his Town mansion, his expression now was quite inscrutable.

His eyes, so full of secrets, only mirrored her unanswered questions back to her defiantly, as polished and unyielding as the flat surface of a blade.

She fought with herself to let the matter go. *Fine.* If he did not wish to confide in her, what was that to her?

If that's how he wanted to be, she only wished she wouldn't have let him kiss her or have been foolish enough to be lured into his house, alone with him.

It had been mad of her to jeopardize her reputation further with a man who wanted only a china doll to set up on the mantel, not a wife, not a living, thinking person.

She lowered her gaze in simmering fury, accepted his steadying hand as she picked up the hem of her skirt a bit, and climbed down from his stupid, show-off cabriolet.

Without another word, he walked her to her door.

She sent up a prayer of gratitude that no one from her family came out to pester them. They were probably off having a party over the hope of getting rid of her at last.

Little did they know their celebrations were premature, because there was no way she was marrying this hard, cold, rude, domineering iceberg of a man.

People said that Hell was flames, but they were wrong. This Demon Marquess ruled over an underworld of darkness and cold.

"Must the day be ruined?" he inquired in a mild tone as they neared the graceful entrance of her home. "It was all going so well, I thought."

Unable to hold back, she pivoted sharply to face him. "I want to ask you a question!"

"Another one?" he murmured dryly.

"Yes, and you're not going to like it! But I would appreciate it if you would answer with perfect honesty."

He just looked at her.

"You didn't happen to arrange for your sister to pop by while we were together, did you?"

Angry astonishment flashed in his eyes. "Of

course not." He shook his head at her. "God, you don't trust me at all, do you?"

"You, who would set out to manipulate the whole ton? Dashed right I don't!"

"Daphne."

"How can I trust you if I don't know you, and how can I know you if you won't talk to me?" He dropped his gaze with no response for that, it seemed. She studied him intently. "You are a difficult man, Lord Rotherstone."

"It is a difficult world," he replied, his whole demeanor turned to steel. He had shut her out now as completely as he had his sister.

Was this the sort of marriage he was offering, as well? Sharing her life and her bed with a virtual stranger?

His riches as a substitute for love?

Very well. Daphne nodded in taut anger and a cutting pang of disappointment. "Very well." She turned away, already knowing what she had to do. "Good-bye, Lord Rotherstone."

"Miss Starling — wait."

"What now?" She jerked her elbow out of his light hold.

He searched her face, at a loss. "I'm sorry."

She did not know what to say. "Is this bitter attitude supposed to be endearing?"

"This bitter attitude is simply who I am," he said with a benighted shrug. "Please don't be angry. I told you I'm not perfect. But I'm trying."

"No, you're not, Max."

"Yes, I am! Shall I prove it to you? Done! When I go home, I will, I'll . . ." He cast about for some worthy evidence of his sincerity. "I will shave off my beard!" he declared, actually thinking, it seemed, that she would fall for his charm again. That he could get away with it.

The hopeful, roguish half smile that he offered said it all. But Daphne stared icily at him.

"Don't bother," she replied, then walked back into her house, and let the door bang in his lordly face.

CHAPTER 10

That night, Dresden Bloodwell arrived in London, his new post, replacing Rupert Tavistock. He got settled in his luxurious new quarters, and prepared to get down to work.

On the journey over from France, he had studied the information that Malcolm had given him about Tavistock's various projects and contacts.

Well-versed in the details of his new post by now, he was eager to pick up where Tavistock had left off; however, he had a very different approach to things than his predecessor. Tavistock had been lazy and rather timid.

Dresden did not share these flaws. Nor did he believe in wasting time. He was nothing if not efficient.

That was why Malcolm had specifically entrusted him with an additional task that the leader had purposely concealed from the rest of the Council.

Dresden had orders to find a replacement for their agent in Carlton House, the Prince

Regent's private residence in London.

Carlton House in Pall Mall was always filled with Prinny's various toadies and courtiers, pampered dandies and assorted eccentric bon vivants.

The Prometheans' spy among the Carlton House set had been discovered and dispatched by one of the Order's thrice-damned warriors some months ago.

Now Dresden needed to find or recruit someone new to put in there, someone he could rule through fear or greed or both. The selection was very narrow, however, considering how few men were highborn enough to be worthy of the Regent's royal conviviality.

It would be no small feat, but Dresden was eager for the task. His forte of killing had grown dull long ago.

Now he was armed with a copy of *Debrett's Peerage* on one hand, with its neat listings of every aristocratic male in London; Malcolm had also given him the name of one of their lesser members who could get him into Society.

From there, it would be a simple process of observing different highborn men until he could identify a few possible new recruits.

By and by, he would home in on one by a process of elimination. Finding the right pressure point to apply once he'd picked out his man — that would be the fun part.

He smiled to himself in anticipation as he

glanced out his window at bustling London Town. He intended to show Malcolm that his trust in him had been well-placed.

Soon, there would be changes in the Council.

Later that night alone in her bedchamber, sitting at her vanity, Daphne slowly, hesitantly, picked up the little box that Lord Rotherstone had brought for her yesterday.

Until now she had been afraid to open it. But she supposed she owed the enigmatic marquess the courtesy of at least acknowledging his gift.

As she pulled one end of the ribbon tied around the box, the family cat joined her, leaping up onto her vanity with an agile pounce.

The bow came undone. The cat played with the ribbon, while Daphne's mind churned, filled with thoughts of him.

Going near the Marquess of Rotherstone, she mused, was like standing in front of a deep, stone cave that led down to God-only-knew-where in the earth, some dark, subterranean maze. Where other women might have succumbed to the irresistible pull to climb in and start exploring his darkness, Daphne could feel the palpable danger around him, and ever the rational being, she had the good sense to turn around and walk away as quickly as possible.

And yet . . .

Sliding a fingertip into the edge of the painted pasteboard box, she opened the lid and stole a peek inside.

A swathe of black silk still concealed the gift. She reached in and lifted it out, but when she unwrapped the silk handkerchief, her jaw dropped.

The silk drifted away, sliding down onto her lap. She lifted up an eye-popping sapphire and diamond necklace.

Holding it up to the candlelight, she stared at it in amazement. The luxurious thing glittered like sunlight on the sea, especially the bright blue central stone, round-cut, surrounded by diamond brilliants.

"Oh, for goodness' sake! Who does he think I am, the Queen?" she said under her breath to the cat, laughing a trifle nervously.

The gift was meant to awe her. And in truth, it did. But it also helped to crystallize her suspicions about his true motives for making sure she saw his house today. He thought he could bribe her into compliance by dazzling her with his wealth and power. *Restless, difficult man.* Did he really think that was what mattered in life?

The glitter of the necklace caught the cat's eye. Its dark-tipped ears pricked forward. Daphne held up the necklace and swung it gently before the animal; the furry head followed its teasing motion. While the cat batted at the necklace with one velvet paw, a troubled expression settled over Daphne's face.

There was still the possibility that her father had arranged this match to make up for his losses in the stock market, but if the situation was that serious, then surely, he would have told her so.

Papa kept saying there was no problem, and after the way things had gone today with her would-be husband, she desperately wished to take him at his word. She should probably go and ask her father point-blank, she thought, but the truth was, right now, she did not want to know.

All she wanted was to get out of this match that was beginning to feel like her doom.

Jonathon, she reminded herself halfheartedly. She was marrying Jonathon. Someday. He did not make her heart feel so threatened. It did no good remembering the helpless passion she had felt in Lord Rotherstone's arms when he had kissed her.

What a relief to know she would never be plagued with that sort of thing when she married her childhood friend. It was just as well, for Lord Rotherstone's sensual expertise threatened to sweep away her self-control.

"I am sorry, Lord Rotherstone," she whispered. "I'm afraid you are just too fine for me." With that, she wrapped the excessive necklace back up in the black silk, and put it once more in the box. Her mind made up, she retied the bow, wanting no more truck with the thing — or with the Demon Marquess.

He had volunteered to provide some assistance with the orphanage, but she had enough faith in his honor to believe he would not be so petty as to retaliate at her by refusing to help the children. If he was mean-spirited enough to renege on his offer of charity, then he would thereby prove himself truly no better than Albert, and she would be glad to know she had successfully avoided marrying yet another cad.

With a brooding expression, she went and sat down in her window nook with her portable writing desk on her lap. She sharpened a quill and pricked her finger on it, making sure it was as sharp as she would need to be to deal with him.

Taking out a creamy sheet of linen stationery with her monogram tastefully engraved, she dipped her quill in the indigo ink, and considered how to word her now fourth refusal of a suitor. *Hm . . .*

Maybe she deserved that reputation as a jilt.

The next day, Max hosted Warrington and Falconridge at breakfast after the three had spent the morning at the fencing studio. His friends were in high spirits, but Max was in a strange mood. After the unexpected turn his visit with Daphne had taken yesterday, not even the morning's exertions at combat practice had exorcised his discontent.

Ripples of long-submerged anger had begun breaking the calm surface of his usual cool control. While his friends bantered about nothing in particular, merely glad to have the weight of the world finally lifted off their shoulders, Max found himself brooding on the price they had paid for their involvement in the Order.

Their families had done it to them, and that, he supposed, was the real reason he had been avoiding his sister since he had arrived in Town.

Of course, Bea had had nothing to do with Father's decision to hand him over to the Seeker in exchange for a large sum of gold. Yet, whenever Max looked at his sister, he could not help but see a member of the party that had sold him off like a slave, knowing full well he could be killed. He had been but a child, an innocent.

No wonder he had not wanted to see his sister until he was good and ready. But now that Daphne had uncovered his callous attitude toward Bea — and now that he had seen his coldness toward her through Daphne's eyes — he felt like a miserable cad for his neglect of his closest living kin.

He had been so concerned about his own

scars that he hadn't considered Bea's feelings.

In addition, seeing his little sister all grown up, with children of her own, reminded him anew of all the time he'd lost. He knew the war against the Prometheans had to be fought; but he also understood now how he had been exploited when he was too young to understand what he was getting himself into. The Order might be the side of good in their battle, but they had certainly not hesitated to take advantage of his family's misfortune.

Max did not know what to make of the resentment he felt surfacing toward his old mentor, Virgil. But with his father dead, he had no one else on hand to blame.

He pushed the whole painful tangle of it away, reminding himself again that the war was over. What mattered now was getting on with his life and his future with Daphne . . .

And yet, these leftover thorns stuck in his flesh from all his ordeals had already begun to pose problems between the two of them, like yesterday. Max saw now all too clearly how the Order's requirement of secrecy isolated him and his friends and threatened to keep them from ever truly becoming a part of the world.

Their secrets separated them from the humanity they protected, and had left Max unable to tell Daphne who he really was.

She wanted answers, but her questions had put him adrift, oddly disoriented. His calculating brain was of no use in this realm. Who the hell was he, anyway? He could barely find the solid truth about himself beneath so many years of dissemblance and deception.

Given the shape-shifter he had become, *which* Max was supposed to answer her questions? Which version of him, for which audience? The Grand Tourist? The so-called Demon Marquess?

Or the man beneath it all? Isolated, lonely, though he would not admit it under torture. She would never want *that* Max. No one ever had.

Secrets had a way of slipping out from time to time, and until that moment, Max had managed to hide this one from himself: the real reason he had chosen Daphne.

Gazing into those heaven-blue eyes, he had sensed in her a great capacity for love, and the softness of her heart, based on all he knew about her, made him hope that one day, his own most secret longing might finally be fulfilled. A longing for something he had never known and never thought he could have until he had met her.

It was too threatening. Inwardly, he backed away from it, shocked to grasp in that instant what was really driving him.

The desperate need for love.

But, God, if he could not share himself with

her, he thought in despair, then how would he ever win her heart and the love he craved from her?

"By the way," Jordan spoke up, "are either of you going to that End of Summer Ball next week? The one down in Richmond?"

Max masked his suffering from his friends. The men exchanged a jaded glance.

"Why the hell not," Rohan said wryly. "Stir things up a bit. Maybe Max will introduce us to his future wife."

The other two looked at him expectantly.

Max heaved a rueful sigh. He wanted his friends to meet Daphne, but Lord, these were his fellow Inferno Club hellions, and after yesterday, he was already on shaky ground with her.

Dodsley marched in with his tray before Max could explain. "My lord?"

"Yes?" He turned to him. "What is it?"

"A footman from Miss Starling's residence just delivered this with a note for you, sir. I was asked to see that you got it right away."

Max glanced at Dodsley's silver tray, and his stare homed in on the jewelry box containing his gift to her. The second he saw it, his blood ran cold; his heart began to pound. "Bring it here."

Dodsley did so, advancing into the morning room.

"Isn't that sweet," Rohan drawled. "Where can I get a chit that sends me presents?"

"I don't think she sent it *to* him, War-rington," Jordan said warily, eyeing Max's ashen countenance. "I think it may be some-thing the young lady's . . . sending back."

"Oh, damn," Rohan murmured while Max opened her short note and read it:

Dear Lord Rotherstone,

I thank you again for the honor of your offer, but regretfully, must decline. If you consult your heart, I think you will agree we'd never suit. Our values are too different. But please know I wish you all the best and hope we can be friends.

Respectfully,
The Hon. Miss D. Starling

Friends? He looked up from her letter with flames in his eyes. "Tell the stables to saddle the stallion."

"Is she jilting you now, too?" Rohan asked bluntly.

"Over my dead body." Max rose from his seat in one angry motion and headed for the door. "If you'll excuse me, gentlemen, it ap-pears that I have business to attend to."

"Good luck, Max," Jordan offered.

"Don't need luck," he ground out. "I know just how to handle her, believe me." Slipping the note and the sapphire necklace into his breast pocket, he stalked outside in a cold rage with a vow that she'd *not* get away with this. He refused to be cast off like he was nothing.

Beneath his fury, however, lay an unnerving fear, that if someone as softhearted as Daphne Starling could not be made to care about him, then surely he was always going to be alone. He could not bear it, would not stand for it; he would not be denied. Not after all he'd given, all he'd sacrificed. This was *his* time, and *she* was his reward that he had chosen, the prize he would obtain at any price.

Moments later, he was swinging up onto his towering black stallion, urging him out of the mews, and galloping hell-for-leather toward South Kensington.

It was a blessing to be home alone for once. The whole villa was so marvelously quiet. Penelope had taken the girls shopping in Town, bringing Wilhelmina along to assist. Papa had driven them in and would visit with his gentlemen friends at White's while the ladies shopped.

Curled up on a stone bench on the terrace behind her house overlooking the garden, Daphne balanced her sketch-pad on her lap, her hand moving in long, idle strokes over the page. She was making a charcoal drawing of the birds that congregated around the bird-bath.

With her noisy family gone, there was nothing to hear but the breeze rustling through the yellowed leaves, and the birds chirping as they flittered about the garden. The silence suited her pensive mood, though she was keeping one ear anxiously cocked for the sound of footman William returning from his errand.

Considering the great expense of the sapphire necklace, she had asked him to deliver it personally into the hands of Dodsley, Lord Rotherstone's butler.

The great mystery now was how the Demon Marquess would respond to her rejection. Honestly, though, she thought, after the unpleasantness of their parting yesterday, he was probably going to be relieved.

It should be easy for him to find some other woman who did not mind if he locked himself away behind walls of silence. But *she* did not wish to spend the rest of her life trying to decipher the hidden meanings behind his words or riding out the storms of his inscrutable moods.

And yet, strangely, having sent off her note with the sapphire necklace, she had begun to feel as though she had abandoned him. He didn't know anyone in Town, her heart insisted as softly as the whisper of the wind. People did not understand him. The things they said about him were almost as unfair as Albert's lies about her.

Unpredictable as he was, she knew better than to try to foretell what answer he might send back, if any.

That was why she had not yet told her father that she was refusing Lord Rotherstone's offer.

It seemed prudent to make sure first that it was truly finished between them before she broke the news. After all, if she spoke up too soon before the break was truly decisive, then her father and would-be fiancé might unite against her once more to coerce her into the match.

At that moment, in the quiet, she heard a muffled clatter of hoofbeats approaching around the front of the house, entering the courtyard.

William.

At once, her heart began to pound. She threw her sketch-pad and charcoal pencil aside, jumped to her feet, picked up the hem of her dark green walking gown, and hurried inside, cutting through the house to see what tidings her footman had brought back from Lord Rotherstone.

Hastening through the central corridor, she reached the front door, threw it open, and rushed outside, only to gasp aloud. William was not back yet.

It was the Demon Marquess himself who had arrived, galloping up to the villa astride a powerful black stallion. Instinctual fear darted through her when he sent her an ominous glance, his pale eyes full of fury as he reined in his horse to a stamping, snorting halt.

Daphne gulped as he swung down from the saddle, commanding the horse to stay. The blood drained from her face when she saw him striding toward her with a look of wrath. "Daphne!"

She let out a small cry and fled back into the house. She threw herself against the door to shut it, but before it could close, his black-gauntleted hand was planted on it, one dusty riding boot shoved in the way.

"Don't you dare," he warned. "We are going to talk about this. Let me in."

"What do you think you're doing?" She tried to push against the door. "Go away!"

"Daphne. You cannot keep me out. Move!" When he thrust the door harder, she tried to stay planted, but instead, her soft kid slippers skipped over the hardwood floor.

"Damn you!" she cried, jumping out of the way.

"Such language," he drawled, his eyes glittering with reproach as he stepped over the threshold, looking much too large and darkly threatening in his black clothes, a loose white shirt beneath his jacket.

He wore no neck cloth and appeared as tousled and dangerous as he had that first day in Bucket Lane, when she had first spied him leaving the brothel — with one exception.

He had shaved off the goatee, just as he had promised yesterday in an effort to please her. *How sweet.* Goodness, she could not take her eyes off him as she backed away. He looked simply gorgeous clean-shaved, a few years younger, and ten times more handsome. She refused to admit, however, that his chiseled male perfection had any effect on her.

She was not marrying him, and that was final.

He glanced around, taking in the fact that no one else was home. A glint of wicked intentions passed behind his eyes when he turned to her again. Staring at her in chilly, fierce reproach, he drew off his black riding gauntlets. "That is no way to greet your future husband, my love."

"How dare you barge in here like some sort of robber?"

With a defiant look, he walked over to her, captured her in his arms, and roughly kissed her.

Her heart pounded with wild confusion as he invaded her mouth with his claiming kiss and got her foolish body to react much as it had yesterday in the long gallery. In fact, her burning reaction to him was even worse now, since his shaved chin did not chafe her. But she refused to revel in the sensuous rubbing of his skin against hers.

His smell was that of pure, potent masculinity, and when she planted her hand on his chest to try to push him away, she felt hot bare skin where the V of his shirt fell open slightly. He tried to gather her closer, but with an aching moan, she summoned up her fury and found the strength to push him away.

"Let go of me! You are not," she added, panting, "my future husband."

"Daphne," he chided softly. "You are already mine."

"The devil I am! I belong to no man — and you should not be here." She took another backward step. "As you can see, I am alone."

"Not anymore," he whispered with a lusty stare.

It routed her. Her body trembled. Striving for clarity, she shook her head. "You can show yourself out. My father will be home very soon," she lied as an afterthought.

Forbidding herself to linger for fear of getting caught up in him again, she pivoted with a show of great confidence and retreated into the familiar safety of the parlor on legs that shook beneath her.

To her trepidation, however, with every step, she could already hear the slow, rhythmic striking of his boot heels following her, like a hunter stalking his prey.

When she reached the parlor, she turned around again to face him, folding her arms tightly across her chest. Thankfully, though he joined her, at least Lord Hellfire now saw fit to keep a slightly safer distance. *As if he somehow knew that she did not really want him to leave.*

He eyed her warily as he reached a hand into his pocket. When he took it out again, the glittering strands of the sapphire necklace spilled through his clenched fist.

"Why did you send this back to me?" he demanded, his eyes aglow with cold accusation.

She swallowed hard, lifting her chin a bit. "I saw no way I could accept it. Returning it was obviously the proper thing to do."

"Proper?" he echoed, his lip curling in slight mockery. "Do I look like a man with whom you can play games, my dear Miss Starling?"

"It isn't a game," she replied calmly. "If anyone's playing games here, it's you."

"The hell I am!" he bit back. "I'm not taking this back. It's yours. I don't care what you do with it." He tossed it onto the end table as though it were some cheap trinket. "How dare you send me this, this — dismissal without any sort of explanation? Exactly whom, Miss Starling, do you think you're dealing with?"

Daphne fought the urge to shrink from his show of bluster and forced herself to sound as calm as possible. "I put my explanation in my letter. I believe I said quite plainly that I feel we will not suit."

"Why?" he demanded.

"Because we are too different."

"In what way? Defend your argument. Prove to me you are not just being fickle and vain, as Carew said!"

She inhaled sharply through her nostrils at his goading, for she recognized those charges. "We are too different in our *values*, my lord, as I said plainly in my note."

"How so?"

"How?" She scoffed. "You frequent brothels! You associate with libertines! You treat your own family like strangers, and if you can treat your own sister that way, then I'm sure it would only be a matter of time before I would suffer the same indifference from you, for some unwitting transgression."

"You don't know anything about it."

"I asked! You would not tell me! You ask for my hand, but you don't even want me to know you. What am I to make of a man who claims to appreciate my heart but won't share his own with me?"

Emboldened by his attentive, though angry stare, she forged on.

"Perhaps you can be satisfied with a match based on advantage, but I told you, I need more than that — and I don't mean rank or riches. You must excuse me if I fail to be dazzled by your wealth and power."

"That you are not dazzled only makes me

want you more," he uttered quietly. His stare intensified; he took a step closer. "Come on, Daphne," he urged, his deep voice taut. "What the hell is it going to take?"

"You think I have a price? A bigger neck-lace, a larger house? Is that how you measure everything? Because that's just sad. Or is that merely what you think of me? Does this house look like another brothel to you?" Her voice climbed in pitch and volume with her building anger. "For your information, Lord Rotherstone, I am not for sale — no matter what my father said. But if you conspire with him to find some way to force me into this, then let me warn you in advance that I've learned from Penelope how to make a hus-band's daily life a living hell," she finished with a chilly smile.

He just stared at her. "Well, well, well," he said at length. "It seems I've found myself a little spitfire. The perfect lady, eh? I knew there was more to you than meets the eye." Pacing restlessly across the parlor, he ran a knuckle along the crisp line of his jaw as he sauntered past her.

"Please go," she said, refusing to rise to the bait. "You have my answer."

"No."

"No?" she echoed, furrowing her brow in astonishment. "Will you make me send for the constable?"

He was peering at a picture on the wall,

then he looked askance at her. "Why would you do that?" he murmured. "Are you so afraid of me?"

She narrowed her eyes and lifted her chin a notch. "Of course not."

"I know," he countered softly. "That's another reason I want you, Daphne."

"Stop saying that!"

"It's true."

"Why are you so fixed on me?" she cried. "You don't really want a wife, you want another piece of art for your collection! So, keep looking, by all means! There are plenty of other girls out there who are prettier than I."

"I don't care about their looks any more than you care about my riches. I want *you*," he added, even more decisively as he began prowling toward her.

"For what purpose?" she exclaimed. "Oh, but of course — as a broodmare! Well, if you are so keen to restore your family name, then you should go and find a wife who hasn't already been the target of ton gossip."

"I don't care about any of that anymore." He stepped closer. "I just want you, Daphne."

"Why?" She had to hear him say it, say the words. *Because I love you.* If that was true.

"Because I do," he growled, refusing to say it.

She shook her head at him. "You want to gain me only to hold me at arm's length.

Yesterday I got a taste of how you shut people out. I did not enjoy it, Max."

"Well, I got a taste of something yesterday, too. Something I want more of." He reached for her, but she pulled away.

"You want, you want! Is that all you can care about?"

Unable to get through to him, she saw it was time to resort to her last secret weapon. "I'm sorry, Max. My father should've told you. There is someone else I care for." She willed her face to look convincing. It was true, after all, though it suddenly felt like a lie. "Someone very dear to me, whom I love, and who loves me in return. I cannot marry you," she said, "for another holds my heart."

He studied her for a second, then he began laughing softly. "You are so amusing."

"Wh-what?"

"I take it that you are referring to young Mr. Jonathon White."

Her eyes widened. "You know about him?" she breathed, and then immediately wondered if she had just made a horrible mistake. Dear God! "You will not hurt him?" she cried.

He just looked at her.

"Promise me you won't touch him!"

He gave her an irritated frown. "You probably think I drown puppies in my spare time, as well." He paused. "You don't love him, Daphne."

"I just told you I do! I *do* love Jonathon — dearly!"

"As a brother, yes. A friend. I can live with that."

"And — as a man."

"No." He sent her a heated, knowing smile.

She was flustered as he drew closer. "What do you know of it? Nothing! Why don't you believe me?"

"I have just one question," he murmured softly, staring into her eyes. "Do you want him like you want me?" She quivered when he touched her.

"I always get what I want, my love, eventually," he whispered.

"Oh, don't do that. Please. You mustn't. Oh, Max, no."

"Yes," he breathed as he ran his fingers down the side of her neck.

She swallowed hard and turned away. *I must be strong.* "It isn't going to work."

"No?" Standing behind her, he laid his hands on her waist and kissed her nape beneath her upswept hair. "I have another present for you, Daphne. Since you don't want the necklace . . ."

She shivered, casting about feebly for her ability to resist him. "In the strongest . . . possible terms . . . I must object."

"You go right ahead," he breathed, his warm whisper fraught with wicked seduction. He continued kissing her neck again, teasing her senses into glorious awakening for him. She laid her hands atop his where they rested on her waist, but her power to push him away was fading fast.

When his wandering lips skimmed her earlobe, she was overcome with the need for his kiss. She turned her head and offered him her mouth. He claimed her lips immediately. She moaned at the welcome pleasure of his now clean-shaved face caressing hers. The absence of his scratchy beard made it easier to kiss him with all the passion seething inside her. She lifted her hand and caressed his cheek, savoring the warm, smooth male skin beneath her trembling fingertips.

Slowly, he turned her around to face him. Reveling in his embrace despite her earlier determination not to let this happen, she could not stop herself from feeding on his kisses. At length, however, he stopped her. Ending the kiss, he held her fevered stare as he lowered himself slowly to his knees before her.

Daphne watched him in hazy-eyed silence as he gathered her hands to his lips and began kissing them tenderly, with the utmost care; her palms, each finger, her wrists. When he had lavished these with his attentions, he kissed her midriff through her gown. He grasped her hips gently and continued pressing fervent kisses to her stomach and lower, his hot breath permeating the light cotton layers of her gown and petticoat.

Her heart was slamming in her chest as she wondered with a building sense of thrill what he was about.

She rested her hands on his wide shoulders as he reached down and caressed her legs, again, through her skirts, until he came to her ankles. She shivered eagerly as his fingers played over her anklebones; her eyes flared with rising desire, but she made no effort whatsoever to stop him as his light touch began traveling northward under her skirts. She swallowed hard, but could not have uttered a word of protest if she had wanted to. All she could do was stare helplessly into his eyes, her pulse pounding.

She felt the precise moment that his hands roamed above the tissue-thin layer of her stockings and ventured above her garters, meeting bare skin.

He closed his eyes, visibly savoring the contact.

"Wh-what are you doing?" she breathed at last as he began raising the hem of her skirts.

"I want to please you," he whispered, then bent his head and kissed her thigh. "Let me adore you." He pressed her backward a small space to lean her hips against the sturdy secretaire behind her.

All thoughts beyond this room, this moment, this man soon fled. Forbidden pleasure turned to bliss as he lavished the same scrupulous care on kissing her thighs as he had her neck and hands. She watched him avidly, already aroused to full willingness by the time he parted her legs and drove his openmouthed kiss against her mound.

She melted, moaning, as his tongue stroked and swirled over the tautened bud of her center. Gliding a hand up her leg, he slipped a warm, gentle finger inside her; he deepened his kiss, lapping up the dewy evidence of her desire with a moan of pleasure at the taste.

He was, she realized, as totally aroused as she, lost in his giving; she was so overwhelmed by his intense, inspired passion that she could do nothing but receive.

In that moment, she was his instrument, to do with what he willed. Her body and, more alarmingly, her soul were fully open to him; he could have taken her, and he surely knew it, being a man of the world.

But instead, he used his mouth and hands to beguile her, until suddenly — the delicious tension coiled so tightly in her core broke loose with a vengeance, sending riotous waves of pleasure undulating through her. Her back arched, her hips reached for his kiss; a soft, ragged cry tore from her lips. He lapped at her body in feverish thirst, moaning against her flesh even as the uncontrollable spasms of delight still racked her.

When all her strength had ebbed away, Lord Rotherstone lifted his head. She closed her eyes, still reeling with bewildered bliss; she rested her head weakly on the upper part of the secretaire behind her, and felt him press a damp kiss to her knee.

Enervated, her heart still pounding, she found the power at last to open her eyes. She gazed at him like a woman foxed on some secret wine that only he could give.

He passed his fingers slowly over his lips to dry them, and then he rose, brushing her skirts back down politely, satisfaction in his eyes, discretion in his faint, worldly smile. He leaned down and pressed a lingering kiss to her brow. "You are a feast for all the senses, Daphne."

"Oh, Max," she uttered.

"I will see you at the End of Summer Ball. You owe me a dance and I intend to collect." He laid his fingertip softly over her lips before she could summon up the strength to contradict him. He looked deeply into her eyes, and ran a stray lock of her hair lovingly between his fingers. "No more foolish talk of refusing me," he whispered. "You belong with me. I want you. And I will not be denied."

He was gone after branding her lips with one last, searing kiss, slipping out quietly, leaving her spent and breathless, and even more confused than she had been before.

She closed her eyes for a long moment, trying to regain her wits. When she opened them again, her dazed glance happened upon the sparkling sapphire necklace.

She stared at it with a kind of shock; how had she ended up with it again?

The second she saw it, a cold trickle of anger began to drip its way back into her warm, physical satisfaction.

The sight of it there, glittering in the afternoon light, seemed like a silent reproach for her weakness to his temptation.

She had accused him in so many words of treating her like a harlot, thinking he could buy her at the cost of all the luxury he could bestow. Now he had done this incredible, wanton thing to her, and Daphne was left feeling rather literally like some sort of scarlet woman.

How wicked of her. But what *wouldn't* this man do to get what he wanted?

First, he had tried to tempt her with the chance to share his wealth and power, and when that had failed, he had resorted to an even more powerful weapon: sexual pleasure.

Unfortunately, now that she'd had a taste of this forbidden sweetness, as intoxicating as it was, she realized it was a completely separate thing from what she really craved — an intimacy of the heart with him.

Without a true bond between them, she discovered that such activities could leave a woman with a bad feeling inside, as if she'd had one too many glasses of wine the previous night and acted foolish.

Clearly, with his skill as a lover, he could take her to the heights of desire, but just like his riches, this, too, was no substitute for love.

Surely he knew that. He had merely done this as another means of gaining power over her, she thought. But it wasn't going to work. Her face hardening with her anger at herself and at him, she went and snatched the necklace angrily in her grasp.

She stepped toward the window and peered out in the direction of the drive, but he had already ridden off, leaving the jeweled monstrosity with her intentionally.

As if it was her payment.

So, he refused to take it back? He thought he'd won?

Very well, you blackguard. I've got a better use for it, anyway. She was certainly not going to keep the thing and be forever reminded of him. She knew then what she was going to do with the necklace — and she also made a decision about how to handle him.

At the End of Summer Ball, she would finish this thing between them one way or the other.

He wanted to turn this into a high-stakes game? Very well. He was going to hate her for the public repudiation that she had in mind, but maybe then he'd finally get the message.

This time, she thought grimly, the Demon Marquess had brought it on himself.

CHAPTER 11

Max trusted he had laid her fears to rest. At least that was what he wanted to believe a few days later as his ebony coach rumbled on behind the four black horses, speeding down to nearby Richmond-upon-Thames for the End of Summer Ball. Inside the coach, a jovial spirit reigned as Rohan and Jordan and he passed around a bottle of whisky, imbibing freely ahead of the night's festivities.

His friends were conversing irreverently on which women they might amuse themselves in pursuing tonight, but Max found himself yet again in a state of distraction over Daphne. Lord, what had this girl done to him? He glanced out the carriage window at the splendor of the evening's sunset, unfurled over a wide expanse of countryside.

Dramatic, billowing clouds filled the west, blazing pink and orange on their undersides, lit from below by the September sun slipping over the horizon. The tops and sides of the clouds were smoky lavender, with patches of

303

the fading day's light blue still visible between them. In the east, a full moon rose, wearing a misty gold halo, and the night it gathered round it like a cloak turned from royal blue to dark indigo, spangled with stars.

The trees crowded out the view again as Jordan handed him the bottle. Max accepted it with a wry smile, thought of Daphne again, and took a hearty swig.

Still, the liquor could not chase away the nagging feeling that instead of getting things under control with her in the parlor, maybe he had only made matters worse. Doubt was not the only ailment plaguing him tonight. Along with a high degree of sexual frustration, he was still secretly hurt by her attempt to get rid of him.

He really did not understand her continued resistance.

In what way did she find him lacking? Hell, he had started off barely caring whom he married, but now somehow she had him by the throat.

He had no idea why he was trying so hard, or when he'd become so determined that only she would do. Which was why he was still shocked by her attempted rejection.

He was used to getting what he wanted, and could in all modesty say that women did not usually turn their noses up at him. On those rare occasions when it did occur, he usually just laughed. He never particularly cared.

But this was different somehow. Very, very different. This one got to him because it stirred long-buried fears deep in the core of him that maybe he was not worthy of love.

All Max knew was that it was one thing to be rejected in chameleon mode. That, he did not take personally. But to try, to start, by God, to offer her his real self, and have the inner man rejected, that struck a nerve. What in the hell was it going to take for her to accept him?

When would he ever be enough?

He was already as rich as a king and higher placed in the order of precedence than ninety-nine percent of the population. If that was still not good enough for somebody to find him worthy of love, then he might as well just give up now.

Bloody hell. He viewed his own aching uncertainty and thought himself pathetic. Pathetic like the angry boy who'd been a punching bag for the local bullies, the lonely son who had not mattered enough to his own parents to stop them from selling him off to a secret government agency for gold, even though they'd known he could be killed.

The bottle came around to him again, and Max tried to drown his disgust with another long swig.

Perdition. If this girl could make him hurt

like this before he had even bedded her, then how might she torment him throughout all their coming years as man and wife?

God, if he were anywhere near as shrewd as his comrades in the Order generally thought him, he would wash his hands of her and choose somebody else. Some pretty-headed, agreeable nitwit that he could hold at arm's length in benevolent indifference. Someone who would spend his gold and not dare question how he lived his life.

But despite Miss Starling's aggravating stubbornness, Max could not let go. *You never give up, and you never back down,* Virgil had once said. It was one of the things the Order valued about his nature, but sometimes his kind of stubbornness could be a curse.

Life would've been so much easier if he could just tell Daphne who and what he really was. Instead, there was nothing he could do but wait for her to accept her fate — and hope that, in the meanwhile, his own deepening hunger for her did not drive him into lunacy. He was already feeling a little too close to the edge.

Max noticed then that the carriage had grown silent, the mask of merriment slipping briefly to reveal three of the Order's lost boys, men now, each left to battle private demons of his own.

"Never thought I'd say this," Rohan murmured, taking the bottle back from Max, "but

I am beginning to miss the war."

"I know," Max murmured, "exactly what you mean."

A trace of a bitter smile was Jordan's only answer.

Max let out a taut sigh. "Cheers, lads," he said ironically, and uncorked another bottle.

Unfortunately, he already knew the liquor was not as potent a sedative as that sweet potion he had tasted yesterday, the nectar of her virgin body. Dissolving on his tongue, she had been almost mystically intoxicating. He wished he could've got foxed again tonight on that rare, exquisite wine. She seemed to have medicinal effects on him, as well. But since he had doubtless pushed her far enough, he supposed he could wait . . . until their wedding night.

A breeze as soft as cashmere blew in off the tranquil river, perfecting the night's conditions for the End of Summer Ball. Music floated over the gardens; the colorful lanterns strung up everywhere were already lit in anticipation of the darkness on this night of the equinox.

In hours, summer would concede to autumn, but for now, the countless guests in all their finery strolled the sculpted grounds, chatted with clusters of friends, or sat at the tables and chairs set up beneath the graceful open tent. There, the wine flowed freely, an abundance of delicacies arrayed to tempt the palate.

Meanwhile, inside their hosts' manor house, all the doors to the terrace were flung open; guests had begun crowding into the candlelit ballroom, eager for the dancing to begin. The musicians in the orchestra gave their instruments a final tuning.

Anticipation hung upon the air.

It was to be a grand night, with hundreds in attendance. Daphne had heard that the Regent himself might make an appearance, but her thoughts continuously revolved around one particular guest, who had not yet arrived.

She expected to see Lord Rotherstone at any moment, and the prospect of her dire task tonight had her on edge. It was a good deal more intimidating than her plan a few weeks ago of confronting Albert Carew.

Max had left her house the other day under the impression that he had fixed everything between them and prevented her defection by the things he had done to her. But he was about to find out just how wrong he was.

After their brash encounter in the parlor, she could already sense his control closing around her, enveloping her. It increased her desperation to get out now while she still could.

His superior size, his iron strength, his keen intelligence, his wealth and title, his ability to manipulate her father and Society through his calculating charm — and most of all, his indecent skill at kissing away her protests with overwhelming pleasure — all this made the domineering marquess a powerful foe, indeed.

She could already feel herself slipping into his unyielding grasp, but she still had time and will in her to fight and to keep control of her own destiny. Terrible things could happen, after all, when a person lost control over her own life.

Lady Thurloe had said, *My brother does not easily forgive.* Daphne was counting on that in her scheme to turn Max against her for once and for all. When she answered his inevitable request for a dance in the ballroom tonight with a snub, then maybe then he would finally get the message and leave her in peace.

She did not want to hurt him, just give him enough of a sting to signal that if he was wise, he would give up on his pursuit. He should find somebody else who was content to marry him for his gold and his title.

Daphne wanted more — she wanted him, the person — but he refused to listen. Sharp as he was, he only pretended that he didn't understand.

Unfortunately, word of their drive through Hyde Park together had sparked a fresh wave of gossip that her reputation could really not afford. As Daphne moved through the crowd, going to fetch two glasses of wine for her and Carissa, she noticed several people glancing at her, whispering a bit. She registered an awareness that they were talking about her, but she did not sense any particular hostility behind the glances.

She gave the gossips an unflappable smile and nodded to them politely, then she lifted her chin and walked on, her head held high.

Thank God, the ton knew nothing about their episode in the parlor, nor about those stolen kisses at his house. She hadn't even told Carissa! She had told her friend about the carriage drive, but nothing beyond that. Now she could just imagine how ruined she'd be if Society ever found out the whole story. It was dreadful knowing he could hold those kinds of secrets over her head if he liked.

She wished she could forget that wanton streak he had uncovered in her. It was *so* desperately unladylike, but what could she do? The man turned her into some sort of wild creature. Alas, what was done was done, and now she could only trust in his honor, and hope to God that Lord Rotherstone could keep a secret.

Brushing off a twinge of guilt, she got the wine and carried it back carefully toward where she had last left Carissa. They had split up a few minutes ago in a division of labor; while Daphne fetched the drinks, Carissa had gone to fix a little plate of treats for them to share.

Jonathon had not yet arrived, fashionably late as usual. But it was just as well. She planned on keeping a distance from him tonight for his own safety. No need to test Lord Rotherstone's good nature.

As she made her way through the crowd, she expected at any moment to see Max's gorgeous face by the lanterns' light. Instead, to her distaste, it was Albert Carew who fell into step alongside her.

He was on his way up to the ballroom, but he walked with her a short way. "I heard you were seen taking a drive with Rotherstone last week." His whole demeanor dripped sarcasm.

"What of it?" she replied in annoyance.

"Oh, nothing." He shrugged with his superior air. "There is no accounting for taste." He gave her a cold, scornful smile and walked away.

Daphne clenched her jaw just as petite Carissa came slipping through the crowd, swift and ethereal, moving with elfin haste. Dressed in an enviable gown of pale, seafoam blue, her auburn hair in ringlets, she looked paler than her usual ivory complexion as she rejoined Daphne.

"There you are!"

"What's wrong? Are you all right?"

"God," she uttered. "You'd better give me that."

Daphne immediately handed her a glass of wine. "What's going on? Where are our treats?"

"Never mind that. Bad news." Carissa took a surprisingly large swallow of wine and then steadied herself. "Oh, Daphne — I was over at the refreshments tent, where I just received the shock of my life!"

"What is it?" she asked quickly.

"I hardly know how to tell you what I've just heard —" Carissa winced. "About you."

Me? Daphne stood motionless. She knew that she turned white. She could feel the blood rush from her face. *He wouldn't have told anyone.* A wave of dizziness passed, but her stomach had bunched up in knots.

Good God, if Max had boasted to anyone about the liberties she had let him take — but surely he would not do such a thing. She swallowed hard and braced herself to hear her fate. "Yes?"

Her friend eyed her suspiciously. "I don't know what is going on, but over there just a moment ago, I overheard your stepmother sharing the most shocking confidence with some ladies."

Stepmother? By comparison to what she feared, word of Penelope's meddling would be cause for relief. "What did she say?"

"She was bragging, in fact."

"Indeed?" she asked faintly.

Carissa leaned closer. "She said a *betrothal* is soon to be announced between you and the Marquess of Rotherstone!" she whispered in bewilderment.

"What — ?" Daphne blanched.

"I'm certain that's what I heard her say!"

"Oh, *nooo!*" It was Penelope, after all, who had triggered the whole Albert debacle with her big mouth. "God, I don't believe it. She's done it again?"

"Tell me she is suffering from delusions!" Carissa ordered. "There can be no truth to this fiction, surely?"

"Carissa," Daphne forced out stiffly, "there's something you should know. The truth is —" Daphne licked her lips nervously, for her mouth had gone dry. Then she nodded. "He has offered for me."

Carissa gasped.

"He spoke to my father — and Papa agreed — but I haven't!"

"Oh, I don't believe it!" Carissa clapped a hand briefly over her mouth. Her eyes were round. "The Demon Marquess *proposed* to you?"

"Yes. Well — if you call it that. I mean, his idea of a proposal is *ordering* one to marry him. But whatever he thinks or says, I still said no!"

Confusion furrowed her friend's brow. "But then — why did you go driving with him?"

"Because he charmed me!" she exclaimed in helpless vexation, throwing up her hands. "Oh, you don't understand how wicked he is, how smooth and irresistible! I know now why they call him that. He can tell you black is white and up is down — he gets me so muddled!" She let out a frustrated sigh. "He sweet-talked me into giving him a chance. He said it was only fair. So, I agreed to let him take me out for a drive . . . oh, but he is beautiful, Carissa. He truly is. I wish that he were not."

Carissa's eyes had widened. "You didn't — surely?"

"Hm?" Daphne asked innocently — hoping, anyway, that she still looked somewhat innocent after yesterday.

"You let him *kiss* you?" Carissa demanded in a whisper.

She groaned. "I couldn't help it. He is a devil, I tell you!"

"How was it?" Carissa breathed, wide-eyed.

"Hm." Daphne uttered a sigh of woeful denial to know she would never taste his lips again.

But she was better off that way.

Beyond that, she could not possibly bring herself to admit the full extent of her indiscretion. "After our drive, I declined his offer."

"How did he take it?"

"He didn't listen to me in the least! I said no, but . . . he can be very persuasive." She lifted her eyes toward the now-dark heavens and shook her head. "You have no idea."

Carissa's jaw dropped with an inkling of understanding.

Daphne gripped her arm. "You won't tell anybody, will you?"

"Never, Daphne! Of course not."

"Thank you. It doesn't matter what he says, anyway. My mind's made up. I am telling him tonight that my answer is still no, and that is final. Now that my stepmother's gone and complicated things again — that busybody! — it makes my task tonight even more imperative."

"Well, you had better do something fast," Carissa advised. "You know how quickly such juicy news will travel in the ton. Unfortunately, when you jilt him, this will be a repeat of another recent chapter in your life."

"I know. Blast it, why did she have to tell them?" Daphne fumed. "I'm sure she's been just bursting to reveal it for days!"

Carissa shook her head sympathetically. "She *is* making matters worse. By spreading word of Lord Rotherstone's proposal, your stepmother's making it all the harder for you to back away from this."

"God, she'd do anything to get me out of the house." *Very well, slight change of plans,* Daphne thought. Giving Max the cut direct on the dance floor would just be too scandalous — and too hurtful. She had never wanted to make a fool of him in front of everyone, not when he was already vulnerable to Society's disapproval. "Come on," she said to Carissa.

"What are you going to do?"

"I have to get to him first, before anyone else does. Will you come with me? For moral support?"

"You know I would never desert you."

Daphne gave her a grateful look, then nodded toward the shining ballroom inside the manor house. "Let's go. We've got to go up to the entrance straightaway. I'll have to intercept Lord Rotherstone the moment he arrives, and hopefully head off disaster."

With Carissa by her side, Daphne began walking quickly across the grounds up from the refreshments tent. The night was growing darker by the minute. She ignored the baffling eagerness in her heart at the prospect of seeing him any minute now. It really made no sense.

"I'm surprised to hear you say he's even coming here tonight," Carissa remarked as they strode through a loitering group of young gentlemen who parted like a sea before them, smiling and bowing and trying to draw them into conversation.

Daphne knew she had met them at some point, but couldn't remember any of their names. Nor did she care. Had she ever met another male who had made as powerful an impression on her as Lord Rotherstone? She could not remember any. With a few friendly and noncommittal greetings, the girls pressed on, promptly continuing their private conversation.

"I mean, think of it!" Carissa pointed out. "For years, he barely bothers with the ton, but now he's everywhere — apparently in hopes of seeing you! Oh, Daphne!" She gripped her arm and giggled. "How thrilling for you, honestly! Admit it. It must be a huge feather in your cap to be having such an impact on a rakehell of the first order."

"No, no!" Daphne protested, blushing and trying not to smile. "I have no impact on him at all. Unfortunately, his skull is made of stone. Believe me, I've had no success even getting my refusal through his hard head."

"Maybe he thinks you're just playing hard to get?"

"Well, if there's any chance he has misinterpreted me, I shall take extra pains tonight to disabuse him of the notion. He's not going to like it," she warned. "This could get unpleasant."

Carissa let out a mischievous laugh. "It sounds to me like he is perfectly desperate for you! Come, you can tell me. Aren't you the least bit tempted to accept him?"

Daphne stopped and scowled at her.

"I would be!" Carissa said with a grin. "Marquesses don't grow on trees, you know.

You must admit he is handsome."

Daphne snorted as they sped up the pathway to the terrace. "You don't understand. First of all, he's as highhanded as some Oriental potentate. Secondly, this is all a game to him. He is like a-a terrier with his jaws clamped on what he believes is *his* bone. Well, I am not a bone. I am not a prize. I am a human being."

"Amen."

"Unfortunately, just like Albert, Lord Rotherstone refuses to understand that. *Unlike* Albert, however, he seems prepared to go to much greater lengths to get what he desires. He's been quite ruthless. But all that ends tonight," she concluded grimly. "Penelope has pushed this past the line of all toleration."

"What are you going to do?"

"As soon as he gets here, I am going to tell him that if anyone dares be so bold as to ask him if Penelope's claim is true, he should deny it, and say it's all just a silly rumor."

"What if he won't go along with that?"

"For the sake of his own pride, he had better! Otherwise, I'm afraid the great Lord Rotherstone is going to end up just as embarrassed as dreadful Albert was."

"You are a very disciplined woman," Carissa murmured, eyeing her intently. "I wouldn't be able to do it."

"Egads, not a moment too soon!" Daphne

whispered as soon as they had crossed the terrace, halting at the threshold of the ball-room. "Look!" Carissa turned with a wide-eyed stare in the direction Daphne had nod-ded. "They're here."

Carissa blanched. "God, they're big."

It seemed the Demon Marquess had brought reinforcements with him tonight. Beelzebub and Mephistopheles — good friends of his, no doubt, fellow princes from his kingdom in the netherworld.

The majordomo announced each man as the magnificent trio sauntered in. "His Grace, the Duke of Warrington. My Lord, the Marquess of Rotherstone. My Lord, the Earl of Falconridge."

"Oh, look at them," Carissa whispered in awe as the glittering and formidable men paused for a leisurely perusal of the ballroom before advancing into the room at a wary prowl, as if they knew full well they were venturing more or less into enemy territory.

Every woman in the room appeared riveted by the three, and indeed, they were a breath-taking sight to behold.

The giant Duke of Warrington wore a showy plum coat with black trousers. His long hair was gathered back in a queue, his neck cloth secured by a black pearl cravat pin. He had a star-shaped scar above the corner of his eyebrow.

Lord Falconridge was a creature of sleek

elegance, keen-eyed, quietly smooth-mannered in his demeanor, his sandy hair cropped short; he wore a dark olive tailcoat and ivory trousers.

Between them was Lord Rotherstone, his hair as black as his impeccably tailored coat, which he wore with charcoal-gray trousers, topped off with his usual attitude of bold aplomb.

The ton immediately began to buzz at the scandalous trio's arrival, and the girls began advancing bravely into the ballroom. But the moment Max spotted Daphne, she gulped, for when his stare homed in on her, his pale eyes seemed to gleam with his intimate knowledge of her body.

He gave her a dangerous half smile that sent a feverish tremble through her.

"I fear we are outnumbered," Carissa squeaked, clutching her arm.

"We must not falter." Her heart was pounding, but both girls held their ground as the three Inferno Club hellions strode toward them in a brawny line.

Max's appreciative gaze traveled downward over her white-clad body, with a fond, possessive smile at the pink rose adornments on her gown. As he joined her, he immediately took her gloved hand between his own. "Miss Starling, how perfectly delightful to see you again," he purred. "You look, as always, stunning."

She regarded him uneasily. He gave Carissa a gallant smile, then gestured toward his comrades.

"Allow me to present my friends, Rohan Kilburn, the Duke of Warrington, and Jordan Lennox, the Earl of Falconridge. Gentlemen," he said to them with an air of pride, "this fair goddess is the Honorable Miss Daphne Starling, the one I have been telling you about. And her lovely companion would be . . . Miss Portland, I presume?"

Carissa blinked at the acknowledgment. "Why, yes, my lord. How ever did you know?"

"A lucky guess," he countered smoothly.

"My lord?" Daphne addressed him.

He bowed to her, a hand on his heart. "At your service, my love."

She gave him a warning look in response to his cheeky endearment. "We need to talk."

"Aren't we going to dance? I trust you've saved your first waltz for me. You have a debt of honor on this point, as I recall."

"Never mind that, you rogue." She shrugged off a twinge of guilt for her earlier plan, and noticed Albert Carew at some distance through the crowd. He was watching their whole exchange with a nosy stare. "Would you please come with me, my lord?"

"To the ends of the earth," he declared.

His friends laughed.

Daphne and Carissa exchanged a long-suffering glance.

"I'd be happy with a turn around the gardens if it's not too much trouble," she said. *"Now."*

"Yes, ma'am." He sent his friends a crafty smile that seemed to say, *She wants me.* Daphne ignored it and turned to Their Lordships. "Your Grace, Lord Falconridge — it might be best if you two and Miss Portland would also come along."

"I say, Miss Starling, what exactly do you have in mind?" the blond earl asked with a raffish flash of a smile. The giant duke gave him a wicked look askance, but Carissa eyed both big men warily.

Daphne could only conclude she must be getting used to Max's racy brand of humor; she stifled a huff, pretending not to grasp the innuendo.

Boys, no matter their age, would still be boys.

"Come along, if you don't mind, gentlemen," she said archly. "I must have a private word with your friend."

"Don't get too excited, Jord. I think we're just the cover," the Duke of Warrington said.

He was right. Daphne knew that if they all took a turn around the gardens as a group, her exchange with the marquess might appear slightly less suspicious.

"Well, then. Shall we?" Max offered her his arm, but Daphne stopped herself from taking it.

"Wait — Carissa?"

"Me?"

"Here." She pulled Carissa over to walk with Max. "You go with him. I'll mind these two. Watch what you say to him, too. He's a thoroughgoing slyboots."

"I?"

"Lord Rotherstone," she continued with an insistent smile, "don't you remember I told you I wanted you to meet Carissa?"

"Extraordinary," Max remarked. But he offered his arm to her friend with a look of amusement. Carissa took it with a wry, uncertain smile. "I wonder what is going on."

"Dashed if I know," said the duke.

"Better not question it," Lord Falconridge advised. "I have a feeling the lady knows exactly what she's doing."

"A man of eminent sense," Daphne said in approval. "Gentlemen, if you don't mind?"

Warrington and Falconridge each simultaneously offered her an arm. Daphne took both, and, at last, they all five strolled out in a pack to the moonlight gardens with, what Daphne sincerely hoped, resembled a degree of decorum.

Albert and his two brothers stared after them. Daphne looked over her shoulder at the unpleasant Carew brothers, then she thrust them out of her mind. She had bigger things to worry about as they went out to enjoy the balmy evening.

"Well, Miss Daphne Starling!" Lord Falconridge began. "At last we meet. We have so enjoyed hearing lately how you've been torturing our friend."

"Pardon?" she murmured, cocking an ear to try to hear the conversation going on ahead of her, between Max and Carissa. It went thusly:

"So, Miss Portland, I hear you are something of an amateur spy."

I'm going to kill him.

"You must enlighten me sometime about the techniques you've found effective in this town," Max was saying to Carissa a few steps ahead of them.

"Lord Rotherstone," her friend exclaimed, "are you insinuating that I am a gossip of some kind?"

"Oh, that is such a harsh word!" he denied in a mild tone. "No, you are, as I prefer to call it, a lady of information," he declared. "As it happens, gathering certain intelligence is a hobby that I also find amusing."

If he was setting out to cast his charm on Carissa, too, heaven help the girl, Daphne thought. But meanwhile, she was not faring much better. His two inquisitive friends were not about to pass up this brief opportunity to interview a woman they believed had set her cap at their Inferno Club brother-at-infamy.

"So, Miss Starling, where were you born?"

"And you are how old?"

"Was all your education in the home, or did you also attend a finishing school?"

"Do you speak French? Play piano?"

"Yes, what are your accomplishments?"

"More importantly, what are your thoughts on a gentleman maintaining ties with his old bachelor chums after marriage?" the duke asked pointedly.

"We are not at all in favor of that stale, old, stodgy practice where newlywed wives force their husbands to sever ties with their bachelor friends."

"We knew Max before you did, after all."

"How *do* you gentlemen all know each other?" she countered, just to be spared the interrogation. But then she instantly regretted it when she recalled too late that she already knew the answer.

"Our club," Lord Falconridge answered in a dry tone.

"Oh, yes," Daphne said faintly. "The Inferno Club, is it?"

"I trust you don't object?"

"We're not really as wild as people say," the duke assured her, not very convincingly.

She gave him a dubious look.

"It's true!" the earl agreed. "We just send that rumor round to keep out all the tedious chaps."

"The important thing is you won't banish us from Max's life once you are married, will you?"

Her head was spinning, to think that he had already told them he would marry her, as if it was settled!

What else might he have told these two about their rendezvous together?

"Your concerns are quite unnecessary," she forced out.

"Well, then!" Lord Falconridge declared. "We should all get along quite famously, I daresay."

"Everything all right back there?" Max drawled.

"Switch!" Daphne yelped. As soon as they reached a little grove bounded by sculpted yews and a willow tree that stood at the edge of the water, she fled his friends' inquisition, surging forward to change places with Carissa.

The petite redhead approached her two, tall, smiling escorts with an expression of complete awe and some trepidation.

"What the devil's going on?" Max asked softly as Daphne gladly took his arm. She ached to note how familiar it felt to be with him again. Yet her sole intention this evening was to get it through his head she wasn't marrying him. "Listen to me," she whispered, stopping at the base of the little foot-bridge that arched across the ornamental lake. "The most terrible thing has happened."

His face turned deadly serious with concern. "What's the matter?"

"Penelope has run off at the mouth again and told some people here tonight that you and I are getting married."

"Oh, is that all?" He shrugged it off. "Lord, girl, I thought it was something serious!"

"It is. Max. Please." She looked into his eyes, making sure she had his full attention. The urge to kiss him was very wrongheaded. And very strong. "Max?"

His face sculpted by moonlight, he gave her that irresistible little half smile of his. "Daphne?"

She permitted herself one small, aching touch of his lapel. "It's very important that if anyone here tonight is impertinent enough to ask you if what my stepmother said is true . . ." She paused and regretfully lowered her hand back down to her side. "You must laugh it off, and say it's just a silly rumor."

He furrowed his brow.

"I will say the same," she added, "and hopefully, as long as we're both consistent, we may yet manage to avoid a scandal."

He shook his head with a wary, probing stare. "I don't understand. Why would there be a scandal, and why should we deny it when it's true? I'm ready to tell the world whenever you are, Daphne."

She stared at him for a long, hard moment, saying nothing. She didn't have to.

She could tell as his expression changed that her message was finally getting through.

"No," he whispered.

It took all her strength, but she held fast to her conviction. "As I already told you, I've thought it over carefully and I . . . I still must regretfully decline."

He was shaking his head. "No, I'm not having it."

"Lord Rotherstone — I am perfectly willing to help you gain acceptance in the ton as your friend, without the added lock of marrying you."

"I don't need a friend. I need a wife," he clipped out in sharp rebuke.

The others had stopped their conversation, sensing the tension between the two of them.

From the corner of her eye, Daphne could see their friends watching uneasily, listening, witnessing every excruciating moment. The two lords exchanged uncomfortable glances, but they and Carissa hung back.

Daphne was grateful that her loyal friend refused to abandon her, though, no doubt, Carissa longed to run away from all this as much as she did.

"I thought we resolved this," he said, holding her stare in building anger.

"My feelings are unchanged. I told you my decision. That's why I sent the necklace back, as you recall."

"That's not all that happened that day," he whispered in mounting intensity. "As *you* recall — Miss Starling."

"Nothing's changed. It ends now, my lord."

"It ends when I say it ends!" he erupted in a thunderous tone.

She braced herself, remembering the portraits of all those Rotherstone marquesses, and realizing in that moment that she was attempting to defy several hundred years' worth of autocratic male power, and the lordly blood of privilege that flowed through his veins.

Oh, yes, she was acutely aware just then that his broad-sword-swinging ancestors had been knights who had simply *taken* what they wanted.

Nevertheless, though it must have been unthinkable to him not to get his way, she refused to be intimidated.

She would never respect herself if she cowered before him. "Max," she started calmly — but her calm only seemed to set off his fire.

"I don't understand you!" He leaned toward her, lifting his hands out to his sides. "I have been patient, have I not? I have been fair. Damn it, Daphne! I have laid all that I possess at your feet, and you —" He faltered, changed direction on her. He pulled back and dropped his arms to his sides with a bewildered shrug. "Why are you pretending as if you feel nothing for me? It's obvious you do."

"Well, well, well," a snide voice intruded. "If it isn't the happy couple."

They both looked over angrily. At once, Max bristled ferociously as Albert emerged from the garden greenery a few feet down the path. Daphne rolled her eyes. *Oh, God, were they eavesdropping on our conversation?*

Hands in pockets, the haughty leading dandy ambled toward them with an ugly mocking smile. His two younger brothers followed a step behind, flanking him, as usual.

The Carew brothers were already snickering. As it sank in that they had witnessed her refusing Max's offer of marriage, Daphne felt as though she had been kicked in the chest. Guilt and dread immediately filled her. Max's steely body tensed as the Carew brothers came closer.

Oh, no. Her heart began to pound. "Go away, Albert!" she warned. "You have no business here."

"Oh, but it's just too rich, my dear!" He swaggered closer with a gargoyle smile from ear to ear. "I told you she was trouble, Max. You should have listened to me."

His pale eyes narrowed to slashes of wrathful warning. Albert foolishly kept taunting him. "The mighty Marquess of Rotherstone, laid low by a mere slip of a girl! Oh, how can this be happening? And to you, of all people, Max. For shame! There is no justice in the world. As rich as Croesus and nearly as high in rank as my idiot brother, and still she does not want you. Wonder why!"

They all three laughed.

Max stared at him in icy silence, but Daphne could not bear the way they were mocking him. "What were you doing, Albert, spying on us? You are *so immature!*"

"Ah, but you must grant a man a little moment's gloat, my dear. You might at least afford me that much pleasure."

She shook her head, remembering all too clearly Max's lethal performance in Bucket Lane. "You're being very stupid, Albert. I wouldn't bait him if I were you."

"Spare me your advice, dear lady." Albert halted dangerously close to Max and stood smiling at him insufferably. "I've only come to offer Max my sympathy."

Whether Albert did not realize he was in striking distance, or was emboldened by his brothers' presence, she did not know. But Max had stepped off the footbridge, back onto the grassy banks of the ornamental lake.

Worried by his silence and his look of deepening rage, she glanced over at Warrington and Falconridge. The pair appeared completely nonchalant, keeping an eye on things, but quite unruffled by the opposition.

Indeed, as his friends looked on in cool amusement, Daphne realized they had total faith in his ability to handle all three Carew brothers on his own.

"So, welcome to the club, Max. Daphne Starling's jilted admirers. What of it, Daphne?

Will no man do? Perhaps you would prefer Carissa."

Max stepped toward him.

Albert moved back quickly, laughing, baiting him. "And as for you, my dear Miss Starling," he continued, "before you let this grand new conquest go to your head, it's only fair to tell you the real reason he's been pursuing you. Go on, Max, tell her about our little contest. Now that you've lost, she might as well know the truth."

"What is he talking about?" she murmured.

"He's a liar. Don't listen to him," Max answered barely audibly.

Albert scoffed. "*I'm* a liar? You're the one who's not telling the truth, old boy. Daphne, you daft chit, he doesn't care about you. The only reason your fine Lord Rotherstone ever pursued you in the first place was to try to prove something to *me*. Isn't that right, Max?"

He answered with his fist in Albert's face. One neat blow that dropped him like a stone.

Daphne gasped while the other Carew brothers charged at Max in rage. He slammed his fist into the second man's nose and kicked the third in the stomach, sending him crashing back into the lake.

Albert jumped up, but Max felled him again with a right-left pair of punches to his jaw and middle.

The second brother, Richard, climbed to

his feet, but he took one look at Max's glower and ran.

Daphne also stared at Max, but when he turned to her with guarded, simmering fury in his eyes, she could only shake her head at him in disbelief.

Without another word, shaken by the way his control had snapped, she turned away and walked over the arching bridge, leaving the scene of the fight and heading swiftly for the far side of the garden.

Carissa would be fine with his friends, and for her part, Daphne needed a moment to collect herself. His barbaric display merely confirmed that they were through.

Loud angry footfalls pounded on the wooden planks behind her. "Daphne, wait," Max ordered in a taut tone.

She marched on. "Really, Max! A contest! I should have known! God, you are even worse than him. Let go of me!" she shouted when he took hold of her arm. She pivoted, glaring at him. "I am not marrying you!"

"You cannot believe his lies!"

"I don't know what to believe anymore! If you'd try being open with me instead of manipulating — oh, forget the whole thing, Max! I'm telling my father right now that I am not marrying you."

"I don't think so, Daphne."

"Well, you'd better think again —"

"Your father's broke," he interrupted in a

333

steely tone, "and I've already paid for you."

She gasped, pulling back in astonishment; he stared at her in the darkness, not letting go of her.

"Take your hands off me," she choked out.

Max instantly released her, only then realizing how hard he had been holding on.

Daphne stumbled back from him with a sob. "Stay away from me." Without another word, she spun away and ran.

"Daphne!" he shouted after her.

"Let her go, man!" Lord Falconridge had strode over to his side. "What the hell are you doing? Trying to scare her? Haven't you done enough harm for one night?"

Daphne fled, unable to stop the tears from flowing down her cheeks as she rushed out to the long winding drive where all the waiting carriages were parked.

Hard, cold, ruthless man!

She was not sure what she intended, but she had to get out of here. Blindly searching the long rows of carriages, she tried to find her family's chariot. Footman William, she was sure, would drive her home.

"Daphne! Daphne? Please, wait!" From a distance, she heard Carissa calling to her.

She stopped and waited, wiping tears away, as her friend ran over to her.

"Oh, sweeting! Don't run off. Where are you going?"

"Home. I have to find our carriage."

"Are you all right?"

"I despise him, both of them — Papa and him! I can't believe they did this to me, b-bought and sold me like a sack of flour. I will not stand for it!" she thundered in growing anger now that he was not there to terrify her. "All his ploys to charm me . . . If I never even had a choice, why didn't they just say so? They were only humoring me. Oh, I feel like such a fool." She shook her head. "A contest? And how could he use his fortune to take advantage of Papa?"

"What are you going to do?"

"I don't know. I just want to go home. But wait." She paused. "I can't." Fresh tears surged into her eyes. "They are all against me."

"Oh, how I wish I could help you. I don't know what to do. Perhaps if I spoke to my cousins —"

"No, no." Daphne shook her head firmly, recalling Carissa's own difficult home situation. She wiped away a tear, gathering her strength as best she could. "Thank you for staying with me through all that. I think . . . I might have an idea." Slowly, she began nodding. "Yes. There's only one place left to turn."

Carissa stared at her in question.

She swallowed hard. "I shall throw myself on the mercy of my great-aunt."

Carissa's eyes widened. "You mean . . . ?"

"Yes. The Dowager Dragon. She's my only hope now."

"Oh, my." Carissa looked slightly terrified at the mere mention of the unyielding Dowager Duchess of Anselm.

Daphne nodded more firmly, then she walked on, searching for footman William.

Carissa hurried alongside her.

"I know Her Grace will take me in. As rich as she is, maybe the Dowager Duchess can help to shore up Papa's financial situation. Whatever happens, I know she won't let them force me into this match. I must fly to her." She turned to her friend. "Whatever you do, don't tell them where I've gone — neither Lord Rotherstone nor Papa."

"Never!" Carissa held up her right hand, swearing. "If they come asking for you, I'll make sure that I am not at home to answer them. Look!" She suddenly pointed to another carriage with two white horses just now dashing up the drive, a late arrival. "It's Jonathon!"

"Jono!" She really must be turning into a watering pot, Daphne thought, for the sight of her happy-go-lucky childhood friend brought another wave of tears into her eyes.

Never had she felt more grateful to see him than she was at that moment, when he drove up in his phaeton with a grin and a loud "Cheerio, girls!"

"Jonathon!" Daphne wailed, rushing up to

the side of his halted carriage, crying.

"Oh, my darling dear, whatever is the matter?" he exclaimed. He had hardly set the brake and leaped down from the carriage before Daphne flung herself into his arms and hugged him tightly. "What on earth — ?" he mumbled, returning her embrace uncertainly. "What the devil's wrong?"

"It's a long story," she sobbed out in a woeful tone against his shoulder. "Carissa will tell you all. Jonathon, do you love me?"

" 'Course, I do, old girl."

"Oh — !" She hugged him harder, prepared to ask him right then and there to go ahead and marry her after all these years.

"You're like a sister to me," he added, giving her a fond squeeze about the shoulders.

"A *sister?*" Daphne lifted her tearstained face in irritation and looked up into his guileless blue eyes.

Her heart sank, but it was all too plain that there was nothing between them like the fireworks she had experienced in Max's arms.

It struck her with sudden, overwhelming force just then that it was obscene of her to complain about Max wanting to marry her for the wrong reasons, when she was blithely, blindly prepared to do the exact same thing to dear old hapless Jonathon.

A wave of confusion washed over her. She thought Max was the villain and she the victim, but now . . . ? She pulled back from

Jono's embrace, feeling like a miserable hypo-
crite.

After all, wasn't her foppish chum entitled
to a chance at the same true love that she
claimed to want?

It seemed glaringly obvious now that she
had been prepared to offer Jono no more of
her deepest heart than what Max had offered
her. Maybe less. Indeed, she had wanted to
marry him only because she could control
him.

Control, control, control.

Max would not let her have that. He was
too strong. Was that why she kept running
away from him?

"I say." Jono glanced nervously at Carissa.
"What's with all the waterworks? This is so
unlike her. Here, Star, take my handkerchief
before your snot gets on my coat."

She frowned at him through her tears.
"That's vulgar, Jonathon." But she took it
gratefully and wiped her nose.

"Is she all right?" he asked.

Carissa folded her arms across her chest.
"She will be soon."

"Oh, Jono." With a sniffle, Daphne pulled
back from his brotherly embrace. "I'm so
sorry for how rotten I've been to you," she
forced out, distraught and utterly penitent
for her unwitting selfishness. "I never meant
any harm."

"Right." He furrowed his brow. "I have no

idea what you're talking about. I'm sure all is forgiven."

"You've always been so good to me." She looked at his handkerchief. Case in point. "I really do adore you," she added.

"Oh, I see." His gaze slid to Carissa. "She's been drinking, hasn't she?"

"No," Carissa said wryly. "It's a bit more complicated than that."

"Well, what then?" he exclaimed. "Would one of you ladies explain, by Jove? I am beginning to worry!"

"I'm fine," Daphne said with a sniffle. "Really."

Carissa hesitated, then looked from her to Jonathon and murmured, "She's in love with a man she can't manage."

Daphne turned to her friend in utter shock. "I have eyes, my dear."

"No!" She gazed at the all-knowing Carissa in questioning dread. *"No!"* she cried again, refusing to believe it.

Carissa pressed her lips shut and lowered her gaze discreetly.

"Ah, we're talking about Lord Rotherstone again?" Jono asked without a care.

Daphne turned to him in horror. "You, too?"

"Well, of course." Jono grinned. "You've talked of little else since the bloody Edgecombe ball."

She let out a huge gasp of indignation, her

339

heart pounding with her denial. "That isn't true!"

"Oh, yes, it is," they said in unison.

"No! You both are wrong — wrong, I say! You don't know what you're talking about!" she added.

They just looked at her.

Shaking her head, Daphne turned away, but then the high-perch phaeton in which Jono had just arrived caught her eye. "Jono," she spoke up. "Could I ask you one little, tiny favor?"

He frowned at her in suspicion.

But a few minutes later, Daphne was driving his flashy phaeton homeward, almost as fast as madman Max had gone careening through Hyde Park that day on the afternoon of their infamous drive.

She put that blackguard out of her mind — for the last time.

Marry *him?* Ha! She would rather marry a toad. *In love with the Demon Marquess?*

She scoffed. *Far from it.*

He would see. So would the rest of them!

She would never even *speak* to him again.

CHAPTER 12

Max took a sip of his morning tea as he sat in his study the next day; he stared unseeingly at the Tavistock papers that Virgil had given him to analyze. It was difficult to concentrate, however, because he was fairly sure that all dealings between him and Daphne were over, and that, quite rightly, he was banished from her world.

There was only one thing left to say — *I am sorry.* But he wasn't sure she even wanted to hear that. It might be more respectful at this point, finally, just to leave the girl alone, as she had long been asking him to do.

The worst realization of all, slightly sickening in its impact, though till now it had been invisible to him, was that he had blindly set out to do to Daphne almost the exact same thing that had been done to him when he was a boy. Just as his gambling father had handed him over to the Order for the sake of gold, so Max had sought to acquire Daphne from Lord Starling to fulfill his own plans.

Buy a wife.

He closed his eyes, barely able to believe his own selfish, callous cynicism. Who did he think he was, to impose his will on her?

As badly as he still yearned for her, by the cold light of day, he knew he must give up on this. He had tried every angle he knew, but since she clearly did not want him, he had to let her go.

Yet it made him wonder . . .

If he had been gentler with her heart, more of a lover and less of a spy, might he have had a real chance to win her love?

So much for that.

His churlish display had alienated her. He regretted punching Albert. He had always thought it would bring him great satisfaction to do so, but quite the opposite was true. Letting the bastard goad him into losing his temper just like when they were boys had been no victory.

More like a defeat.

At least the eldest Carew brother, Hayden, the Duke of Holyfield, had enjoyed seeing Alby get a taste of his come-uppance.

Hayden had stopped Max on his way out with a hearty "Well done, Rotherstone! We both know he's had it coming for years."

Very true. Nevertheless, Max knew he had upset Daphne, offended his hosts, and sunk to Albert's level. How could he ever have thought that he deserved her? He let out a

342

sigh, put his pencil down, and rested his forehead in his hand. She was right, he concluded. He was no better than Albert. All the same, he thought, disheartened but as stubborn as ever, if he could not have Daphne, he no longer wanted to marry anyone.

Just then, a loud, angry knock on the front door echoed all the way back to Max's study. He lowered his hand from his brow and lifted his head as Dodsley went past his doorway with sedate strides to answer it. A moment later, Max heard Lord Starling's voice in the entrance hall.

He braced himself.

"Rotherstone! Are you here?" The viscount must have rushed past Dodsley, for he suddenly appeared in the doorway of Max's office, wild-eyed. "Is she here? Is she with you?"

Max furrowed his brow. "No. What is going on?"

"She must be here — my daughter! Tell me the truth, Rotherstone! If she came here last night to be with you —"

"Lord Starling, believe me — what is the matter?"

"Daphne's gone!" he burst out.

"Gone?" The blood drained from Max's face. He got up immediately from his desk and walked around it to the viscount. "Tell me whatever you know."

"This morning we thought she slept in. She

left early last night from the ball, claiming a headache. But when my wife went in to check on her this morning, she was not there! Her bed had not even been slept in!"

"Did she leave a note?"

"No, nothing!"

"Did anyone see anything?"

"The younger girls' governess heard her come in, but she, too, thought Daphne had retired. Not even my footman William knows where they went — he is the twin brother of Daphne's maid. Usually, the twins are inseparable, but this time Daphne took Wilhelmina with her. Not even the maid left word for her brother about where they planned to go."

Max's heart thundered. All of this was his fault. "Sir, did you check with Miss Portland? If she is not with that young lady, at the least, the girl will know where Daphne is."

"No, I came here first. I assumed my daughter stole away here last night to, er, to be with you!"

"With me? Sir, she would never do something like that."

"Oh, for heaven's sake, Rotherstone, I was young once, too," he snapped. "Besides, there is no telling what a young girl in love will do."

"In love?" The words pained him. "Sir, I must be blunt. I am persona non grata with your daughter at the moment. In fact, far from being in love, I am fairly sure she hates me, with good reason." Max lowered his head. "We had a bit of a quarrel last night."

"Ah. Well, then. Perhaps that explains her flight."

"Indeed. My lord, there's something else. I accidentally revealed the, er, financial aspects of our arrangement."

"You did what?" Lord Starling paled with a guilt-stricken look. "I did not want her to know, Rotherstone! I did not want her to worry!"

Or to know about her proud father's financial embarrassment, Max thought. "I realize that, my lord. I am deeply sorry. Whatever happens, know that I am your friend. I don't want anything back from you. I still care for her, and whatever helps you helps her, so . . . so be it." He paused, gathering his will to do the right thing. "As much as I admire her, your daughter does not want me. I can no longer press my suit, as it only appears to infuriate her. I will find her and tell her there is no more need for her to flee or to hide. I know she doesn't want to see me, but I have some expertise in locating people who don't necessarily wish to be found. I will bring your daughter home to you safely."

The poor old gentleman appeared to be in shock over it all. Max quickly pulled over a chair for him. "Do sit down, Lord Starling. Dodsley! Get him something to drink."

"Yes, milord." His butler eyed the shaken

viscount with worry and glided over to pour the man a brandy.

"My poor girl." Lord Starling dabbed at his brow with a handkerchief. "Where can she have gone?"

"Probably to Miss Portland or Jonathon White," Max said. "That would be my guess."

"Oh, she must hate me now," her otherwise doting father moaned. "I really thought that you two would be quite perfect for each other."

"So did I," Max mumbled, but he cleared his throat when Dodsley brought over the drink, and resumed his business-like manner. "You're sure there was no sign of an intruder?" he clarified.

"No, of course not," the viscount said impatiently.

"You checked the grounds, the windows?"

"She took a goodly number of her dresses, Max. The chit's run off, believe me. Now at least I have an inkling why."

Max nodded in relief. "Try not to worry, then. I will find your daughter soon. Do you know where Miss Portland lives?"

He shrugged. "I believe she is the niece of the Earl of Denbury."

"Denbury House stands on the east side of Belgrave Square," Dodsley spoke up.

Lord Starling nodded. "And Jonathon White takes bachelor lodgings at the Althorpe in Piccadilly."

"Then I can be there in no time at all."

"Let me know at once if you hear anything, Max! Send word to my home. Penelope is there. She is beside herself, as well."

Dodsley sent him off with a worried frown. "Godspeed, sir."

Max nodded as he pulled on his coat and paused on his way out the door. "Lord Starling, do not worry. I promise you, I will bring her back with all due haste." Then he went out to saddle his horse and rode off to Denbury House.

A very short while later, he was banging on the door of the stately Town mansion on Belgrave Square.

A butler answered. "May I help you, sir?"

"I am the Marquess of Rotherstone," he clipped out. "I must speak to Miss Carissa Portland immediately."

The butler's eyes widened; Max read the protest in them and rushed to head it off.

"I am afraid this is something of an emergency. Miss Portland's friend, Miss Starling, has gone missing. The girl could be in danger. I am here on Lord Starling's behalf to try to help him find his daughter. Did Miss Starling come here? Please, I must know," he said urgently. "Her family is frantic."

"I-I do not know, my lord," the butler replied, looking slightly rattled at this news. "I did not see Miss Starling here today. But I'm afraid Miss Portland is not at home."

"Not at home?" he challenged.

"Truly! She has gone out with her cousins!"

He narrowed his eyes at him. "Where?"

"Shopping!"

Hiding from me, he thought. So, the little redhead must be in on it. "Do you know where?"

"No, sir, the ladies did not tell me. Bond Street, maybe, the Burlington Arcade. It is difficult to say."

"Very well, when do you expect them back?"

"By teatime, I should think, sir."

"When Miss Portland returns, I would ask you to give her these instructions, from me. Tell her Lord Rotherstone said to send whatever information she may have of Daphne's whereabouts to the Starling home. As Miss Starling's closest friend, she may be the only one who knows where Daphne is. Oh, and do please warn Miss Portland that if I don't hear from her, I will be back to question her myself. Have you got that?"

The butler nodded. "Yes, my lord, indeed."

"Thank you." Max gave the butler a taut nod, then he pivoted and returned to his horse, quickly mounting up again.

Next stop — the fashionable Althorpe.

An inquiry at the small gatehouse that stood guard at the entrance of the elegant, fenced compound revealed which of the

348

many apartments belonged to Jonathon White.

Max pounded on the door; Daphne's first choice of husbands answered quickly, wearing little curler strips of cloth in his hair as he waited for his perfect Grecian curls to dry. The man was quite the dandy.

"Rotherstone?" White frowned. "What are you doing here?"

"Daphne's disappeared," he said bluntly. "If you know where she's gone, you had better tell me now."

"Disappeared?" He paled behind his freckles. "What do you mean?"

"I mean disappeared!" As Max quickly explained what had happened, White began to panic.

"I saw her last night. She was crying. It was awful. So I let her take my carriage. I thought she was just going home!"

"Did she tell you where she was headed?"

"No. Did you ask Carissa?"

"She wasn't home. Damn it, you let her drive off in your carriage while she was crying?"

"Well, don't complain to me, you're the one who made her cry in the first place! Good God, I hope she didn't have an accident on the road on her way home. It was dark, and she's not a terribly experienced driver."

"What kind of carriage?" Max asked.

"A high-perch phaeton," he said uneasily.

You fool, Max thought, staring at him. Those things were made for tipping over if you took a turn too fast.

"It wasn't as if I could say no to her, especially with the tears!"

"Are you going to help me look for her?"

Jonathon blinked. "What, right now?"

Max narrowed his eyes at him. "She wants to marry you, you know. You could show some concern."

He snorted. "For your information, Daphne can take care of herself. Furthermore, I think you know by now that she and I are merely friends."

Max harrumphed and turned to go, but paused. "Can I ask you a question?"

"What is it?"

"You know her better than anyone. Do I have . . . any chance left at all with her?"

"Depends."

"On what?"

"How good are you at groveling?"

Max absorbed this, then gave him a wry look. "If you hear from her, tell her to send word to her father. Old man's distraught."

"I will," Jonathon said. "And if you see her first, tell her I want my blasted carriage back!"

Max waved him off as he strode back to his horse. He considered retracing her route from the location of the ball in Richmond-upon-Thames, but her father had said the younger girls' governess had heard Daphne come home last night. Max decided instead to go back to the Starling villa and see if there was any news of her yet. No matter how angry she was, it seemed unlike her to let her family worry.

As he galloped the stallion along the flat stretches of road toward South Kensington, he was beginning to feel rather frantic with worry for the girl, to say nothing of his guilt to know he was the cause of her running away.

At last, he cantered up to the Starling estate, his horse in need of water. Trying not to wallow too much in remorse — after all, he would need a clear head — he braced himself to go into her house and see if there was any word of her. Perhaps she had come to her senses and returned in the meanwhile. He prayed it was so as Penelope, Lady Starling, answered the door.

She was in a tizzy already, so Max did not bother addressing right now the issue of her prematurely sharing the news of their engagement with Society. The matronly troublemaker had made everything more complicated, but Max put it aside for now as Lady Starling confirmed that her husband and his trusty footman William were not yet back from making more inquiries.

While they were talking, however, a messenger arrived, delivering a note for footman William. Max's heart leaped as Lady Starling announced it was from his twin sister, Wilhelmina.

Max remembered both twins, Daphne's country maid and footman, from his observations that day in Bucket Lane.

Mentally begging footman William's pardon, he took the letter from Penelope, and with her permission, he quickly tore the note open and read it, his heart pounding.

Deer Will,

Tell the fammly not to wurry. We are safe at a inn called the Three Swans on the Great North Rd, where we are sune to meet with a very important personich. Please tell Lord S I am very sorry for this. Since I culd not stop Miss D from going, I thot it best to go along and help her to stay safe. Did not know what else to do. She was vry out of sorts. I better go. Shed be furious if she knew I'd wrote you, but I had to, in hopes that we don't both get sacked.

Yr loyal sister,
W

"Bless you, little Wilhelmina," he murmured in soul-deep relief. "Can't spell, but a heart of gold."

"Oh, my lord," Penelope uttered dramatically, "whatever does she say?"

"Exactly what I needed to know. Clever

lass." He handed her the note. "If you ever *do* see fit to sack these twins, Lady Starling, send them straight to me. The pair are worth their weight in gold." With that, Max was out the door, back up on his horse again, and galloping off toward the Great North Road to bring the errant beauty home.

Daphne felt caged inside her room at the Three Swans Inn. She kept looking out the curtained window for any sign of her great-aunt.

Last night, she had driven this far in Jonathon's phaeton — a hair-raising prospect in itself — but she had been forced to halt when she reached a fork in the road and saw a decision had to be made about which way to go next.

The Dowager Duchess of Anselm owned four estates that lay in four different directions. Daphne had no idea at which one her great-aunt currently tarried. The formidable old woman liked to travel among her lands as harvest time drew near, holding annual audiences with her tenants, settling local quarrels, examining the year's new babies, and keeping a watchful eye on the bringing in of the crops.

Thus, thwarted by practicality, Daphne had had no choice but to stop and send messengers out to each of Her Grace's various homes to find out if the duchess was there.

Now it was just a matter of waiting to hear back. This could take a few days, alas. The waiting was already beginning to fray her nerves.

It did not help that misgivings had begun to plague her. Strange doubts. Her heart felt as hollow as a bell inside her chest. She was still furious at Max at his cold highhandedness. Which made it hard to explain her deepening misery at the prospect of never seeing him again.

She already felt bereft, as if she'd lost a friend.

Striving again to put him out of her mind, she turned her attention back to the more pressing task of figuring out what she would say when she faced the Dowager Dragon.

No doubt there must first be some scolding. Her Grace did not sanction indecorous behavior and was sure to disapprove greatly of her running away.

But she hoped that when she explained the tyranny that was being thrust on her against her will, the grand old dame would unleash her dragon powers on Daphne's behalf.

Beyond that, Daphne thought, Her Grace should be somewhat appeased that at least she had not ventured out totally alone in this madcap adventure. At least she'd had the sense to bring her maid.

Actually, though, she couldn't take credit for that. It was Wilhelmina who had insisted on coming along.

Last night upon arriving at the Starling villa, Daphne had sneaked in to collect her things when a sleepy Wilhelmina had stumbled in as usual to attend her mistress returning from the ball.

Daphne had discovered then that her humble little maid knew her too well for any lie to be successful. In her distraught state, she had finally admitted to Willie that she was fleeing because of Lord Rotherstone; upon failing to talk her out of it, the stout-hearted girl had informed her she was coming with her, bless her heart.

To be sure, it was a great comfort to have a loyal ally near. Her maid's bustling presence lent an air of normalcy to the aftermath of her brash flight. Unfortunately, today, poor Willie seemed even more nervous than she was. Already, the girl had unpacked and refolded Daphne's things twice now just to keep herself busy. Daphne shared her agitation. With every moment, it was growing more difficult to sit still.

"Oh, I can't take this anymore," she declared at length. "I've got to get out of this room."

"Where will you go?" Willie squeaked.

"Just downstairs," Daphne assured her. "Maybe they'll have a London paper."

"I can check for you!"

"It's all right. A walk about will do me good."

Fighting to block thoughts of Max from her mind with every step, Daphne walked down the hotel corridor and made her way downstairs to the busy lobby.

The long-coated guard for one of the stagecoaches was blowing his horn in the final summons to all ticketed passengers to come aboard. Daphne curiously watched the mad scramble of travelers hurrying to settle up with the innkeeper's wife for their supper's bill of fare.

A few moments later, the lobby was empty, its chaos changed to silence; the crowded stagecoach rumbled off from the cobbled yard behind its team of six dusty horses.

Daphne approached the cheerful, bustling landlady of the coaching inn, who was neatening up the benches in the adjoined pub, wiping the tables, and no doubt enjoying the temporary lull that would last only until the next coach came gusting in for a quick respite on its journey.

"Ma'am?"

The landlady looked up with an apple-cheeked smile. "Can I 'elp you, dearie?"

"Has there been any message come for me yet — Miss Starling, in room fourteen?"

"No, miss. Not since the last time ye asked. We'll let you know at once when it arrives."

"Er, thank you." She supposed she had

been a bit persistent. "Have you got the *Post* in yet?"

"That we do." The woman nodded and marched back to the counter in the lobby.

Daphne bought a copy of the famed London paper that was known for having the best Society page. There was sure to be a bit on the End of Summer Ball.

She needed to know but dreaded to see if the gossip writers had caught wind of the rumor Penelope had spread about the supposed impending nuptials between herself and Max. As she sat down and scanned the newspaper, she was relieved to find no mention of it — yet! — nor, for that matter, any gossip of the wild Demon Marquess further darkening his own reputation by punching Albert Carew in the nose. Lowering the paper again, she fought a reluctant smile at the memory.

But her twinge of vengeful pleasure was short-lived when she recalled Albert's claim about the real reason that Max had chosen her to be his future wife. Her faint smile faded. All those lies he had told her about her lovely qualities — and she had believed him!

He had told her he wanted her because she was kind to strangers and cared about the orphans. All that rot. In reality, it all boiled down to yet another man wanting to use her for his own purposes and ignoring the fact that she was a person, with feelings that could be hurt.

She stood up as another wave of restless anger swept her. At least now she knew why Max had not shared his heart with her: Obviously, the marquess did not have one.

Still left with too much time to kill, she decided to go and check on Jono's horses. She was responsible for them, after all, and besides, the equine race always had such a calming effect on a troubled human spirit.

Striding outside, she crossed the shady porch, then walked down the few steps to the cobbled inn yard basking in the afternoon sunshine.

The first day of autumn was fine and breezy, the cloudless skies bright blue. Before going into the stable, she walked to the edge of the inn yard and checked the road for any sign of a liveried messenger sent back from the Dowager Duchess, or perhaps even the magnificent lady herself in her queenly coach.

There was only a twenty-five percent chance that Great-Aunt Anselm was at her Milton Keynes estate, the closest of her properties, and Daphne would not put it past Her Grace to arrive in person if she indeed were there.

Once more, however, the Great North Road was empty.

With a sigh, Daphne shrugged off her impatience and crossed the inn yard to the wide-open doors of the inn's vast livery stables.

As soon as she walked in, she immediately noticed the three bored stable grooms who watched her pass with an admiring interest that she was in no mood for.

Daphne ignored them and strode on into the shadowy dimness of the vast stable. She found the two numbered stalls where Jonathon's pair of white horses had been quartered side by side.

She made sure they had been fed and watered, but as she petted one, she looked over and saw the three grooms sauntering toward her, smiling, staring. They looked a little soft in the head, frankly.

"D'ye need 'elp, miss?"

"No. Thank you. I just thought I'd check on my horses. They seem settled enough," she added in taut courtesy. "That will be all."

To her dismay, they did not leave.

"Are you sure there's nothin' we can do for you, miss? We're 'appy to 'elp such a pr-pr-pretty lady," the lad stuttered.

"No, thank you," she clipped out sternly. "I am fine, I assure you."

"You are that," the toothless one on the end said under his breath.

The others laughed: three witless cousins.

"I beg your pardon?" She gave him an indignant look, her back to the closed stall door.

"Forgive my friend, mum. It's just we don't often see your kind 'round 'ere very much. It's an honor!"

"My kind?" she exclaimed.

"It's all right, we ain't the sort to judge!" They began nodding and laughing eagerly, and Daphne thought if all three of their brains were added together, they might combine to be almost as smart as one of Jono's horses.

"We 'ave a wager, y'see. Bones says you're in the theater, but I says you're one o' the opera dancers, so which is it?"

Daphne's jaw dropped as she grasped their mistaken assumptions about her status. It dawned on her they thought her — not a lady! She snapped her jaw shut quickly.

True, ton debutantes did not usually go off traveling independently in a flashy high-perch phaeton, with only a maid to assist them. Indeed, only one sort of woman was free to do that — the ladybird mistress of a wealthy man.

Some of their scarlet breed were quite notorious celebrities, and Lord knew, they often dressed just as expensively as fine ladies.

Well, no wonder these rubes had been staring at her so slyly! She was mortified by their error, but slightly more disturbing were the lewd grins on their faces, their leering stares.

"I don't think your employer would want you talking to me," she announced, ignoring a fleeting twinge of guilt remembering the sinful things she had allowed Lord Rotherstone to do to her.

Maybe she was not quite scarlet like a real theater woman, but she was certainly not pure white, either, not anymore, thanks to him. She supposed she was an indeterminate shade of pink.

Literally.

Her rosy blush at thoughts of parlors and marquesses' roaming hands must have summoned up a look that the simple grooms took as confirmation of her profession.

Dear God, that brothel-mongering libertine had made a harlot out of her, and somehow these three hayseeds were the first to find her out.

Their smiles widened as they began crowding closer, smelly and dirty and hideously rude.

"Who do you go with? Tell us!"

"You're byoootiful!"

"What is your name? Are you famous?"

"O' course she is. Look at 'er."

"Are you one of the Regent's pretties? Maybe Wellington?"

"No, she's one of Harriet Wilson's sisters, ain't ye, mum? Lass like 'er can have any bloody fool she wants."

"Gentlemen, you really do mistake me." She believed that they were harmless from the moment they'd opened their mouths, but she backed away all the same, more mortified than threatened.

Oh, this was awkward.

"Bet you tread the planks at Drury Lane, right?"

"No, I am actually not an actress, nor a dancer. Nor a singer, I'm afraid —"

"An artist's model!" A gasp escaped one. "You been painted in the naked?"

"Please. I'm just a regular person! Now, as much as I've enjoyed this, I really must go." She kept walking backward toward the stable door, talking calmly, smiling — as if that had worked on the gang members in Bucket Lane.

Why were they following her? They looked like three enchanted thralls, one more of a blockhead than the next.

"It would be best, I think, if you, um, nice lads went back to your duties —"

"Get away from her."

The curt command came from a few feet behind her. Daphne froze; the low, curt tones of that deep, familiar voice seemed to vibrate through her body.

With a gasp, she whirled around and saw Max striding into the stable at a smart pace, his black greatcoat flowing out behind him. His face was etched with tension, his pale green eyes as hard as marble.

Beyond him, through the distant, wide-open stable door, she could see his black stallion being handled by another groom out in the courtyard.

"Max!" she burst out in shock. "What are you doing here?"

The three grooms who had been pestering her took one look at him and fled.

This seemed to her an eminently sensible idea as well, as he marched toward her, drawing off his black riding gauntlets.

"Hullo, Daphne," he clipped out. "I've come to take you home."

CHAPTER 13

"Oh, no, you don't!" Jolted out of her shock to see him, Daphne turned and fled, her heart pounding. She had no idea how he had tracked her down, but intimately familiar by now with his relentless ways and implacable will, she dared not let him take control again.

"Daphne, come back!"

She ignored him, gritting her teeth at the order.

"Don't run from me." His footsteps came on faster behind her.

She focused on lengthening her lead before him, hurrying down the stable aisle in the opposite direction.

He followed at a quick, undaunted march. "Would you please just stop and talk to me?"

"We've got nothing to say to each other, my lord."

"At least tell me if you are all right!"

"Of course I am!" she shot back over her shoulder as she sped on. "Do you think I'm too helpless to take care of myself without you? I'm fine!"

"Well, your father's not. He's sick with worry."

"Humph," she replied. "He deserves it."

"Don't blame him. Blame me."

"I blame you both!" In her haste to stay out of Max's reach, she almost stepped on a barn cat that raced across her path. She shot a scowling glance over her shoulder. He was gaining on her. "Leave me alone!"

"No. I didn't spend all day searching for you just to let you dash off again."

"How did you know I was here?"

"That's not important."

"It was Willie, wasn't it? She was acting too suspicious by half this morning. I had a feeling she might've ratted me out! I take it she wrote home?"

"Daphne, the girl was scared to death — for her livelihood, and for both your safety. We all were. How could you run off like this?"

"Oh, did your merchandise escape?" she taunted as she hurried past a groom leading a spotted horse out toward the courtyard. "Don't worry. You will get your money back once I've spoken to my great-aunt."

"I don't want anything back from anyone. Damn it, would you stand still and talk to me?"

"I have nothing further to say to you."

He let out a low sigh and stopped following her.

Daphne's heart was pounding. Reaching what she thought was an intersection at the end of the aisle, she swerved to the left, but promptly found herself trapped in a dead end: The aisle ended with the tack room. She would have to retrace her steps, but Max was on the move again; she could hear his footsteps and, with a glance behind, saw him coming through some of the stall bars.

She quickly discarded the hope of rushing past him, knowing he would catch her in his arms. She warded off a memory of what a pleasant place that was to be. She glanced around, but it appeared her only escape route was the ladder up to the hayloft. She dashed over to it, stepped onto the first rung, and began climbing.

"Daphne, what are you doing?" he asked in a long-suffering tone. "Come down from there."

"Let go of me!" she shouted as he grasped her by the waist a second later.

He started to pluck her off the ladder, but she clung to the rails with a scowl, shoving him off with a firm, controlled donkey kick to his middle — not enough to hurt him — after all, she knew firsthand that his beautiful abdomen was carved from stone. Just enough to make him lose his grip.

The second he let go, she scrambled up the ladder, escaping into the loft.

At once, she knocked the ladder down so

he could not follow. The nearest horses let out angry whinnies, spooked in their stalls as the ladder clattered onto the stable floor. Max cursed, jumping out of the way as it fell.

Ha.

Daphne immediately glanced around for another way down. If she could make it back down to the ground and run across the courtyard into the hotel, then the landlord and his wife would surely help her keep the handsome fiend at bay.

At the very least, she could lock herself in her room until he gave up and went home. With a twinge of guilt, she decided to make sure she hadn't brained him with the falling ladder.

Heart pounding, she peered over the edge of the hayloft, then gasped to see he was alive and well, running to reach the next ladder down the aisle before she could use it to get down.

"Blast!" She bolted forward to try to beat him to it, but he was faster and won their race.

She stopped in her tracks as he vaulted up off the ladder into the hayloft with her, several feet ahead.

With a gleam in his eyes, Max knocked the other ladder down just as she had.

Her jaw dropped.

Now neither of them had any means of escape!

"Oh, brilliant, Rotherstone! Now how are we going to get down?" she exclaimed.

"We're not," he replied. "Not until we've settled this."

"Would you two stop throwing ladders down?" one of the stable boys shouted. "You're scaring the horses!"

"Give us a minute, lads!" His Lordship called back. "There's a guinea in it for each of you if you leave those ladders down until I ask for them. My lady friend and I have got a small disagreement to work out."

"There you go, throwing your gold around again," she taunted, for a guinea was probably equal to at least a fortnight's pay for them.

But she clenched her jaw and glared at Max when she heard the grooms' low-toned conclusions as they murmured among themselves. "Knew she was some rich man's ladybird."

Max raised an eyebrow. "That will be all, gentlemen. Leave us alone for a while, will you?"

"Yes, sir!" they called back eagerly.

"Have at it," one of them jested in a lower tone, rousing crude laughter out of his mates.

Daphne shook her head at Max, while below, the grooms scattered to allow them privacy.

It seemed pointless to protest this or to demand that one of the boys prop the ladder back up so she could get down, for the brooding look on Max's chiseled face told her he would hunt her to the ends of the earth until he was satisfied.

It seemed her only option was to face her demon now.

He stalked toward her, tall, formidably muscular, all dressed in black, the strewn hay crackling under his leather boots. He stared at her intensely, the hard lines of his jaw and cheekbones softened slightly by the golden haze of dusty sunlight that angled into the loft from the rectangular opening cut into the front of the barn, where hay could be thrown down to the courtyard below.

"All I ask, Miss Starling, is that you take one moment and listen to me."

"I'm rather sure I heard enough last night," she replied as she folded her arms across her chest. "And don't even try to sweet-talk me out of how I feel! I have a right to be angry. If you staked your oversized ego on conquering me, whose fault is that? Certainly not mine. Now you're embarrassed in front of the ton? It's all your own doing. You behaved last night like a wild beast, you know."

"I know," he conceded through gritted teeth. "That is why I'm here. To tell you that I am sorry."

His apology took her off guard; she raised an eyebrow.

He heaved a sigh and halted his advance,

holding her briefly in a tortured stare. "I hate myself for hurting you."

She eyed him warily. "You're sorry."

"Yes."

"Why should I believe you?" she countered, remaining on her guard, resisting mightily her weakness for him. "You'd say anything to get your way. You've already proved that. How do I know this isn't just your latest strategy?"

"It's the truth!" he ground out, then dropped his stare. "I am sorry. More than you will ever know. Do you think I don't know what I've done, what I've ruined for both of us?"

Her heart quaked and her soul was beginning to hurt at the forlorn air around him, but she strove not to get drawn in again. "Very well." She swallowed hard, lifted her chin. "I will accept your apology if that's what it takes to make you go away."

"Thank you," he replied, lifting his head again. "But I'm afraid I am not leaving here without you."

"What?"

"I promised your father I'd find you and bring you home safely."

"Oh, did you, indeed?" she cried, a flush of renewed anger heating her cheeks. "The two of you, what a pair! Well, you can both go to the devil, because I'm not going anywhere with you, Lord Rotherstone. I'm not marrying you, and you will never have the right to tell me what to do!"

"Oh, Lord," he muttered under his breath. He gave her a look of mingled pain and dry, defeated humor, and went and sat down wearily on a hay bale.

She stood trembling in high dudgeon, her nostrils flared.

"If you would listen, I'm trying to tell you there is no further need for you to run away, Miss Starling. You can quit this misadventure, and we can all go home."

"Why is that?"

He looked at her sharply. "I'm done chasing you." Then he lowered his head. "You win, Daphne. I have withdrawn my suit. I spoke to your father. We are going to work out his monetary problems — I'm sure it can easily be remedied — but the point is, you're not involved anymore. I came personally to tell you so. Rest assured I am not here to capture you or win your hand. I'm only here out of concern for you, and because I promised your family I would find you and bring you home safely. After all," he muttered, "it was my fault that you fled."

It took her a long moment to absorb this revelation.

"So," she said slowly, "you don't want to marry me anymore?"

Though this was exactly what she had wanted last night when she had broken off their arranged betrothal, now that he had finally agreed to it, she felt a startling sense of disequilibrium.

"It's not a matter of what I want," he said with a world-weary sigh.

"Oh, right," she answered skeptically, "I almost forgot. What you wanted in all this was never *me* in the first place, was it? I was merely the tool of your petty revenge on Albert."

"You can believe that if you want to."

"I see now why you couldn't tell me the real reason you were pursuing me. All those pretty lies about why you had chosen me, out of all the girls in London, to be your marchioness." She shook her head and fought the lump that rose in her throat. "I feel so stupid, Max, because, you know, I almost believed you."

"And so you should!" He rose, anger flashing across his countenance. "Every reason I gave for my admiration of you was true."

"Mm."

"You're going to believe Albert's words instead?" he demanded. "A man who's been going around telling lies about you? You think he even knows what he's talking about when it comes to how I feel?"

"You did not deny it." Tears rushed into her eyes. "When he said there was a contest between you two regarding me, all you said in answer was 'I can explain.' That's as good as a confirmation! Well, it makes sense to me!" she pursued at his look of frustration. "Your proposal came out of the blue from the start. Your main reasons for choosing me were cold and utilitarian and all about your own needs and desires, how I could be of use to you, and then when I saw how you shut me out the same way you did your sister —"

"What do you even care at this point?" he interrupted angrily. He ran his fingers through his dark hair as though striving for patience. "You were already in the middle of throwing me out of your life when Carew interrupted last night. I still don't understand why. I thought everything was going fine between us!"

"Oh, you cannot truly believe that what you did to me in the parlor really settled anything!" she whispered with a blush at the recollection of his mouth all over her body.

He just looked at her, at a loss, and dropped his hands back down to his sides.

She shook her head, then pressed her fingertips to her brow, striving for patience. "Max — honestly. You would have fared much better with me from the start if you had tried being open, rather than all these tactics, all these games that you like playing with my mind!"

"I don't play games —"

"Oh, yes, you do!" she thundered. "From the first time I saw you in Bucket Lane, you were working a ruse over those ruffians, pretending to be drunk —"

"To save *your* arse, my love!"

"Everything has to have an air of mystery. I can't take it anymore!" she cried. "I have no idea how or what you feel for me, aside from lust! Why can't you just be straightforward with me so I can be certain of where I stand with you? *Max.*" She reached out and cupped his face in her palm with frustrated affection in spite of herself. "I have always been inclined to like you." *That was putting it mildly.* "But I never dared let my feelings run away with me, because I never fully felt that I could trust you."

"You *can* trust me," he whispered, laying his hand over hers where it still cradled his cheek. "I would do anything for you, Daphne."

"Except risk exposing your heart," she replied. "Now I know why. Because your motives for pursuing me in the first place had more to do with Albert than with me."

"God, give me patience!" He pulled away from her and turned around, keeping his back to her for a moment.

Daphne stared at him, noting the angry set of his wide shoulders.

"Very well," he growled after a moment. "You want the truth? I admit it." He turned around slowly and met her stare in bristling wariness. "It's true that my need for heirs started my search for a bride, and my family's bad reputation forced me to seek some well-favored, highbred, Society debutante — creatures, who, as a rule, frankly, bore me to tears. When I first found out there was a suitable girl named Daphne Starling who had jilted my boyhood foe, I admit, I thought it might be . . . amusing to needle him a bit by indulging in, perhaps, a small flirtation with her. But, God, Daphne," he whispered. "Then I saw you."

She quivered at the intensity in his passionate gaze, and warned herself against the first signs of her weakening. When he looked at her like that, her knees went a bit wobbly.

He shook his head. "Everything changed from the first moment I laid eyes on you. It changed — in me. The more I learned about you . . . you shook me to the core."

"Do not say that," she warned him barely audibly, clinging by a thread to her resolve to despise him. "It's too late. I don't believe you. I know the lies you tell."

"I swear to you by St. Michael, I'm telling the truth."

She was frightened of getting drawn in again by his magnetic charm, and yet the whole loft resonated with the urgent sincerity of his words.

"I'm not just referring to your beauty," he added with a pointed look. "I've known beautiful women before, but they were not like you. Nobody is. None of them could ever make me trust them."

"You trust me?"

"I told you so the first day I came to your house."

"Then why is it so hard for you to be more open with me?"

"I don't know," he said softly, shaking his head. "It's just the way I've always been. All I know is you came and found me at the Edgecombe ball and you were the only person who cared if I left or stayed. You spoke to me and I found you . . . enchanting." He stared at her, then lowered his gaze. "I had to leave that night, it's true, but from that moment forward, I knew you were the woman for me. And every time we've been together since, my certainty of that has only grown stronger." He paused. "I am not in the habit, Daphne, of wearing my heart on my sleeve, if you'll pardon me. If the reasons I have given for wanting you have not rung true, as you say, that's probably because what I feel for you scares the hell out of me."

She did her best to absorb his words in wonder. "You, scared?" she murmured, still in doubt. He never seemed afraid of anything.

He nodded slowly. "I've been trying to give myself sane, logical reasons for this . . . obsession you've cast over me. Trying to tell myself it's just a simple, practical match, for the sake of producing heirs. Nothing to be alarmed about. But that's not the truth of how I feel."

"How do you feel, Max?" she prompted in a soft tone.

For a long moment, he considered, as though peering gingerly into himself. "Lost. Daphne . . . this is not an easy feeling for a man who always knows exactly where he's going."

She felt tears beginning to sting the backs of her eyelids. She wanted to take him into her arms. He was such an expert at so many things, and so hopeless when it came to affairs of the heart. Clearly, he needed her.

"I've never experienced anything like this, and I've experienced a lot of things, believe me. But never this. Never . . . anything like you. You're the first thing on my mind when I wake up in the morning and the last thought in my head before I fall asleep. Don't misunderstand me, the lost feeling isn't all misery," he amended. "There is also, when I'm with you, a wonderful joy. If I fought for you too hard, Daphne, it's only because I didn't want to lose this, or lose you. I've never had this before, you see. You've opened up new doors in me that . . . Oh, God, I sound absolutely ridiculous." He shut his eyes and turned away. "Would you just shoot me now and be done with it, please?"

"I don't want to shoot you." The tears she had been fighting now rose to blur her vision. "And I don't think you sound ridiculous at all." She sat down weakly on a nearby hay bale since her legs felt too shaky to hold her up much longer.

"Well." Max opened his eyes and stood with his hands propped on his waist, his head down. "For some reason," he said in a low and heavy tone, "I thought you were feeling the same way. But then last night, you told me we were through. I did not understand. I still don't." His shoulders lifted in a weary shrug. "I don't know what else to do or say to win you. I've tried everything I know, and obviously, nothing's worked. Last night, when I saw I was really losing you, I guess I lost control."

"Well, Max, yes, but I saw how Albert kept trying to provoke you," she offered cautiously. "We both know you could have done a great deal worse to all three of the Carew brothers, if you had wanted to."

He shrugged, avoiding her gaze. "I promised you once that I'd never permit any man to insult you in my presence, which he did. All the same, I should have dealt with him later, not in front of you. Eh, enough of all this," he declared, as though waving off the dangerous emotions that filled the air between them. "I am not making excuses. You were right to be rid of me, and that's the end of it. I just wanted to say, mainly, that I am sorry for all the different ways I've tried . . . to pressure you into doing what I want. What matters is what you want." He took a deep breath and forged on bravely. "Whatever you decide for me, I will accept. If you just want a friend, that is what I'll be. If you never want to speak to me again, I'll stay away. If all you want is an attack dog to deal with any fool who might ever bother you, just let me know. I will respect your wishes no matter what you choose. Your happiness, Miss Starling, is my only remaining concern."

Daphne could feel herself losing the battle not to cry. Her lips were quivering, and the tears now crowded into her eyes. It was time for one last, excruciating admission. She was frightened to say it, but let the chips fall where they may.

"Max, all I ever really wanted was to marry somebody who loves me for me. Is that so much to ask?"

"Not at all!" He was right in front of her in the next heartbeat, dropping to his knees before the hay bale where she sat. He took both her hands and stared earnestly into her eyes. "You still *can.*"

"Max." She lowered her head. A pair of her tears fell on their joined hands.

He rested his forehead against hers and was silent for a moment, as though gathering his courage, in turn. "Daphne?"

"Yes?" She held her breath as she waited for him to speak.

"If I loved you for you," he whispered, "would you love me for me? Not for my title, not for my gold. Knowing full well that I sometimes act like an evil bastard. Could you love someone like that?"

"Oh, Max," she choked out, "I already do."

He pulled back a small space to stare into her eyes with a stunned look. "You do?"

She nodded emphatically, stifling a sob. "That's why I tried to end our match last night."

He furrowed his brow. "I'm sorry, you tried to end our match because you love me?"

"Yes, that's what has been so impossible for me in all this! Don't you see? The way you were shutting me out — I didn't want my love to go unrequited! What else could I do but pull away while I still had the strength? I didn't want to consign myself to a living hell of loving someone I could never reach. I wanted my love to be returned in equal measure."

"It is. It is," he whispered as he cupped her face between his hands and wiped her tears away with his thumbs. He leaned closer and pressed a fervent kiss to her brow.

"You say that now," she cautioned when he pulled back, "but what about tomorrow? You can be so hard to read, and when you shut down like you did after your sister's visit, how can I possibly know what you're feeling? If I don't know what you're feeling, especially toward me, then how can I trust myself to you the way a commitment like marriage will require me to? A wife is expected to hand over control of her life to her husband, and how can I do that, let alone give you my heart, if I don't even really know you?"

He gazed into her eyes, visibly hanging on every word.

"Max, if I give all of myself to you in marriage, then I want all of you in return. Maybe that's more than most women dare to expect in this world, but I don't want to risk a dark future of your domination, with me under your thumb, and you a distant stranger. Society is full of those kinds of marriages —"

"Good God, if that's how you think your life would be married to me, no wonder you kept saying no! My darling angel, that is not an accurate picture," he chided softly.

"No?"

"It need not be. Daphne. Please listen." He brought her hand to his lips as he held her gaze, kissed her fingers, and continued. "I don't want to control or dominate you in any way. Who cares if that's the way the rest of Society lives? We don't have to follow their rules. My life is proof of that, if nothing else. We can find a way that best suits us."

"You mean . . . an unconventional sort of marriage?"

"A love match," he whispered with a tender gaze. "We'll make our own country and you will be the queen."

"Oh, Max." Gazing into his eyes, she

adored the spirit in the man. It was just the sort of thing that he would say.

"I don't want to dominate you, sweeting. I just want your love." He shook his head. "God, I never wanted to admit that."

"Why?"

"No one has ever loved me," he said very quietly, hesitantly. "That's part of why I am not, as you say, very open. I suppose I thought the less you knew of me, the better my chances of winning you."

"Oh, Max!" she exclaimed in tender reproach. "My dear, you are so wrong."

He pressed closer, torment in his eyes. "Tell me what you want me to do. I'd do anything to have you in my life. Can we start over? If you'd give me another chance, I would spend every day finding ways to make you happy."

Overwhelmed, she captured his face between her hands and kissed him wholeheartedly. He responded with a soft moan, molding his hands against her waist.

At first he was tentative, letting her set the pace, but she was suddenly on fire for him. Clutching and caressing him, she drew him closer. He wrapped his arms around her, until their bodies were firmly pressed together.

She draped one arm around his neck and ran her fingers through his hair as she returned his kisses. They were slow and deep, a waking dream. The sumptuous slide of his mouth on hers stoked her need for more. She ran her hands down his muscled back. She wanted him so badly. A touch was all it took to coax him down on top of her, a rustle of hay as she lay back; and then he eased atop her, sliding his forearm under her head to cradle it.

Her blood throbbed as she gazed up into his eyes. *Make love to me.*

"You intoxicate me," he breathed, forcing himself to pause.

"Oh, Max." Though the thin layer of hay over the wood planks of the loft floor did not provide much of a bed, still, she gloried in the dense weight of him atop her. But then she saw the troubled look that had passed across his brow. "What is it, my love?"

"Perhaps you would be better off without me." His voice sounded so perfectly lonely. "I've been so selfish, but maybe you'd —"

"Do not be absurd!" She laid her finger on his lips to silence him. "You said this would be my decision."

He stared into her eyes, realizing she was talking about their future — and right now.

"I love you," she whispered. "And I'm ready, Max."

Sheer passion rushed into his face.

At once, his lips swooped down onto hers, and he kissed her with wild abandon. Longing to give herself to him right here and now, before she lost her nerve, Daphne returned his amorous frenzy ounce for ounce. She was so caught up in consuming his kisses and reveling in the warmth of his hand on her breast that when she heard the rumbling wheels of another stagecoach arriving in the inn yard, she paid it no mind.

Until about two minutes later.

For, as it turned out, it was not a stagecoach at all that had arrived. The scramble of liveried servants below and the great commotion that followed heralded the arrival of a very important personage, indeed.

At first, the voices from below could not penetrate their little secret world of carnal rapture in the hayloft, nor interrupt the fierce debate that she gathered her Demon Marquess was having with himself, over whether he ought to grant her wishes and deflower her now, or wait for a slightly more decorous situation for them to make love for the first time. She reached down and touched him boldly in a place that certified her preference on the matter.

But at that moment, the voice of the Dowager Dragon thundered through the air. "I am here for my niece, Miss Daphne Starling! Fetch the gel at once and tell her I am here."

Daphne gasped, lying stock-still beneath Lord Rotherstone.

"Shite," he breathed, as they both looked toward the little doorway at the end of the loft.

"What is the meaning of this? I dropped

everything to come in answer to what I was told was an emergency. We were on the road all night. Now where is my niece?"

Wilhelmina's voice followed. "Beggin' your pardon, Duchess Anselm, Miss Daphne went into the stable a while ago."

"Um, if you mean the young lady with the blond hair," one of the grooms spoke up, "she's in the hayloft. And, er, I don't think she wishes to be disturbed, milady."

"In the hayloft? I say. Daphne Starling! Are you up there? Show yourself at once!"

She and Max looked at each other, wide-eyed.

"Well, then," he remarked. He got off her and she sat up, but from their flushed cheeks, rumpled clothes, and the bits of hay in their hair, it was fairly obvious what they had been doing.

Daphne let out a forceful exhalation, trying to catch her breath. She looked to Max for his usual cool leadership in a crisis. "What do we do?"

"It's your choice," he answered meaning-fully.

She absorbed this for a long, thoughtful moment. Then she smiled at him with grate-ful understanding, and kissed him on the nose.

Bracing herself, she stood, and walked over to the rectangular opening, poking her head out into the sunshine.

"Hullo, Great-Aunt Anselm! Up here!"

The Dowager Dragon lifted her head, her gray hair wound in a tight bun. Her severe face registered astonishment. "Jove's nightgown, Daphne Starling! Come down from there before you fall and break your head."

It *was* a steep drop down.

"Will someone bring the ladder?" Daphne called.

Her formidable aunt stood beside her magnificent carriage with an array of liveried footmen to attend her.

Willie was shading her eyes, staring up at Daphne in perplexity.

Daphne glanced over her shoulder back into the loft and then held out her hand to Max.

"What are you doing up there, anyway?" her great-aunt demanded while all her servants suddenly appeared to be fighting laughter. "I say! Who is that man you have with you?" the dowager cried as Max came over to stand beside her in the little doorway.

The two of them exchanged a glance. Daphne smiled at him, and then looked back down at her mighty kinswoman.

"Aunt Anselm," she announced, "this is my fiancé!" She suddenly wanted to shout it from the rooftops, laughing, despite her great-aunt's appalled look to find her in such a state.

Max had colored slightly, but it seemed

they both wore a bit of a glow.

"Well, I should certainly hope so!" her great-aunt replied, drawing herself up with a grand look that affirmed Her Grace would not countenance any other outcome now.

It was settled, then. The two of them were headed for the altar.

"Well, come down from there and do the introductions!" the old duchess commanded, already betraying a show of warmth beneath her stern manner.

"Yes, ma'am!" Daphne took Max's hand as they both left the window. As soon as they ducked out of sight, she kissed him again. He wrapped his arms around her.

"Thank you," he whispered in her ear. "I won't ever make you regret this."

"I know." She closed her eyes in a state of amazed elation. This all might be madness, but she refused to let him escape her embrace. "From now on, I will place my trust in you."

"And I you, my darling." There was a bang behind them as one of the grooms propped the ladder back up where it belonged. "Your aunt," Max murmured. "She seems like a force to be reckoned with."

"Oh, she is," Daphne answered with a grin. "But don't worry, no female stands a chance against your charm, as you well know."

"We'd better go. Uh, Daphne —" He started laughing, for with her arms wrapped tightly around his neck, she could not stop hugging him.

Now that he had caught her, she never wanted to let him go.

CHAPTER 14

London seemed familiar.

Drake knew the names of streets and landmarks and could not remember how he knew them. Though his memory was still badly damaged, he was getting stronger.

They had arrived a few days ago after their hard journey from Bavaria, settling into the sumptuous Pulteney Hotel where James kept apartments.

On their first morning there over breakfast, James had handed Drake a copy of the *Post* and asked him to read the newspaper through each day, pointing out any names that seemed familiar. Drake had agreed to this willingly.

He only wished he knew his own.

When a few days passed without any real progress, James approached him in the evening with a broad smile. "My boy. I have a special present for you tonight. Come along."

"Where are you taking me?" he asked quickly, his haunted eyes burning with alarm.

He was still scarred by fear after his ordeal at the torturers' hands.

"Don't worry, Drake. You've been locked up for a long time. We think you could do with some . . . pleasant company," James said in a delicate tone as he herded him out into the city's lamp-lit darkness.

"What do you mean?"

Talon flashed a wolfish smile. "We're going to get you a girl."

"What for?" Drake uttered.

Talon laughed. "You've even forgotten what to do with a woman? Eh, don't worry, it'll all come back to you." With that, he pushed him into James's carriage.

A moment later, they were under way. Drake cast James a worried glance, but his aged protector merely gave him an encouraging nod.

Before long, they arrived at the Royal Opera House at the Haymarket. The driver brought James's coach to a halt outside the grand theater, where elegantly dressed aficionados of the art were promenading in with small groups of friends or in pairs.

"Wait here," James commanded as he got out of the carriage. "I will find our friend a suitable companion for the evening. Talon, mind you, keep the curtain drawn."

James did not want passersby getting a look at Drake. Agents of the Order could be anywhere.

That was also why he had been careful to keep their captive confined either to the carriage or to his rooms in the Pulteney Hotel since their arrival.

He did not want the Council's enemies getting to Drake before James even knew for certain who he was.

Though James had grown somewhat fond of his docile prisoner, he was running out of patience with Drake's inability to remember his full name. Talon, of course, had never entirely swallowed Drake's claim of memory loss. But fortunately, James had devised another means of trying to uncover their captured agent's real identity.

What he needed, James mused as he scanned the people gathering outside the theater, was someone with a vested interest in knowing who all the powerful men in London were. A disinterested third party, with a talent for discretion.

Namely, one of London's leading courtesans.

His stare homed in on a voluptuous demimondaine in an elaborate teased blond wig and a scarlet dress with a plunging décolleté that nearly gave the world a fine preview of her nipples. Diamonds dripping from her neck, she wore a mink stole thrown across her shoulders, and was smoking a thin cigarillo as she played with the affections of three young lordlings down from Oxford, probably for the Michaelmas break.

James strolled over to the courtesan and interrupted her sport. Like all of her breed, she knew the smell of real power and abandoned the boys to take his offered arm, never mind that he was old and frail.

"What can I do for you tonight, sir?" she asked, tapping his cheek with her folded silken fan in brazen coquetry.

"Are those real diamonds?" he asked in amusement.

She flicked the ashes off her cheroot and said, "I earned 'em."

He let out an urbane chuckle, but removed the thing from her fingers and cast it onto the pavement, waving away the smoke. "I wonder if I could prevail on you to spend a couple of hours with my young friend. He's in the carriage. May I introduce you?"

She paused, eyeing him and then his waiting carriage warily. Lord, these ladies of the demimonde had the instincts of an alley cat, he thought.

"No one is going to hurt you," James murmured. "My friend, you see, he was badly injured in the war. He has not been with a woman in a long time."

"Ah." A wistful frown of what James quite believed was genuine sympathy came over her painted face. A good-hearted whore, it would seem. "Did he lose a limb, poor boy? Wife can't take it? Cruel."

"No, no. It was a head wound, I'm afraid. He's been — confused ever since. I think the pleasure of your company would do him a world of good."

"Of course it would!"

"May I introduce you?"

"Well, there is the small matter of my fee."

He slipped a small purse of gold into her hand discreetly. "Be kind to him. He's been through a lot."

"I understand completely, grandfather. Lead on."

"You are cheeky, aren't you?"

"It's in my blood," she said.

James opened the carriage door for her, but she peered cautiously into the dark carriage to make sure the situation was all right before stepping up into it.

"Hullo, love. May I join ye? I hear somebody needs some cheerin' up in here — oh, my God!" she suddenly shouted, staring at Drake. "Westie!"

Drake gave her a blank stare.

"Westie, is it really you! God's bones, I cannot believe it!" With a joyous squeal, she flung her arms around him, barely noticing his tense recoil. "Oh, darlin,' what did that horrid Boney do to you? I didn't even know you was in the army! But now you're back! Oh, Westie, love, thank God you are alive."

"Westie?" Talon drawled.

The courtesan shot him a pointed look over

her shoulder. "For the Earl of Westwood, of course."

"Ah," James said, slowly smiling. He had been holding his breath, but now it seemed they had their answer.

Drake began shaking his head. "That can't be right. I have never heard that name before. I have no idea who this woman is."

"Westie, love, it's me, your own Gingercat!" She looked at James in bewilderment. "He doesn't know who he is?"

"Afraid not," James replied.

"I am sorry, madam," Drake forced out, his head down, his body bristling.

"Oh, poor dear, it's all right. You must've been through a terrible ordeal. But believe me, we spent many a merry night in our revelries." She planted a kiss on his cheek that left a rouge imprint of her lips there.

Drake wiped it off with an agitated look. "Please take her away. I don't want her, James."

"I'll take her," Talon muttered, smiling.

The woman glanced over her shoulder at him with a frown.

"You know, my dear," James said, "it might help to speed his recovery if you could provide us with any further information that you might have about him. Who his friends might be, for instance. If you could give us their names, we could deliver Lord Westwood to them so they could care for him."

"I thought you were his friends," she countered with another flash of cagey distrust in her eyes.

"Well, we are, of course, but there must be others. Mates of his?"

She shook her head, as though beginning to sense that something wasn't quite right. "If you don't want to look after him, let him come with me. He needs a woman's care."

"I don't think he's ready for that."

"Well, I'm just a whore, old man," she concluded, giving James a cheeky shrug. "What do you want to know, what positions he likes? He used to come to the brothel and join in the drinking and songs, among other things. That's the wild Westie I used to know. Not this invalid," she added with an indifferent glance, as though deliberately trying to distance herself.

Perhaps she sensed the danger she was in.

James stared at her. "Very well. In that case, you may go," he finally dismissed her, though he suspected she was bluffing.

Good riddance, said her eyes. She handed him back the little purse of gold he had given her.

"Keep it," James invited her.

"I don't want it. Even a whore's got her pride, milord." She hopped out of the carriage and slammed the door behind her.

"I don't trust her," Talon said after a moment as the courtesan rejoined her Oxford lordlings in the square.

James watched the three young men encircle her.

"There you are, Ginger-cat!"

"You nearly broke our hearts!"

"Hang the opera. Let's go to the pub!"

She glanced back warily over her shoulder at James's carriage as she and her admirers strolled off to pursue their night's pleasures elsewhere.

Talon looked at James. "Shall I go after her?"

"No." He shook his head. "We got what we needed for now. If we want her again, she shouldn't be hard to find. 'Ginger-cat' is not exactly inconspicuous." He rapped on the carriage to signal his driver, and a moment later, they were under way.

Drake, meanwhile, had no idea why it had mattered so much to him that the painted woman go free. He kept his head down and said nothing as they rode back to the Pulteney Hotel in silence.

All the while, he kept turning over in his mind the name that she had called him. The Earl of Westwood. That was he? The name did not even ring a bell.

When they reached the Pulteney, James locked him in his room for the night. Drake sighed. He had been expecting that.

Out in the sitting room, James gave Talon his new orders in a low tone. "Now that we know he is the Earl of Westwood, I want you to find his family's home and get one of our spies into the household, probably as a servant. Once they are in the house, I want them to search for any clues about his past involvement in the Order. Also, have them report back on any pertinent activity that comes up."

"Understood. Do you also want me to call on Dresden Bloodwell? He should be in London by now. I believe Malcolm gave you the address."

"Yes, I have it here." He unlocked his portable writing desk and took out a slip of paper with Dresden's location on it. He handed it to Talon. "Drive past and have a look, but don't approach him by yourself. Give him a wide berth. The man is, after all, a murderous lunatic. We'll call on him together soon and make sure he is keeping his mischief to a minimum. While you take care of that, I have a meeting tomorrow at Newgate."

"What, at the jail?" Talon asked in surprise.

"Yes, several months ago I received a communiqué from one of Tavistock's underlings, a warden at Newgate. He told of a convict locked up there who was clamoring to see Tavistock. O'Banyon is the prisoner's name. He claims to have information about where the lost treasure tomb of the Alche mist can be found."

Talon stared at him in astonishment. "Truly?"

James shrugged. "We shall see. Since Tavistock is no longer with us, the unfortunate Mr. O'Banyon will have to make do with me. I shall hear him out tomorrow and see for myself if he has any credibility. Considering where he is presently, I have my doubts."

"The lost treasure tomb of the Alchemist . . ." Talon murmured. "Wouldn't that be something if it turned out to be real? If one of the missing scrolls could actually be found?"

"It could hold the key to unimaginable power," James replied in a low tone. *Just the thing to help me overthrow Malcolm.*

Talon shrugged. "I guess we can only take O'Banyon's words with a grain of salt, though. What's he in Newgate for, anyway?"

"According to the warden, O'Banyon is a thief and a mutineer. He claims that he was the first mate on a privateer ship, but the court brought piracy charges against him."

Talon snorted. "No doubt this blackguard would say anything if he thinks you can help him escape the hangman's noose."

"No doubt," James agreed, but his eyes glowed at the mere possibility of getting his hands on one of the lost scrolls containing undreamed-of secrets discovered by the earliest Prometheans, including their greatest occult master, the Renaissance-era alchemist known as Valerian.

"Well, if we're both going to be gone tomorrow, who's going to mind the ape?" Talon asked.

James gave him a wry look. "If you're referring to the Earl of Westwood, I shall have my driver and a couple of other men on hand to stand guard."

Talon nodded. "I'd better check on him, anyway. He's too quiet in there." He marched across the suite and unlocked their captive's door, thrusting his head rudely into the room. "What are you doing?" he demanded.

Drake was lying on his bed reading the newspaper, as ordered. He just looked at Talon.

Talon huffed and shut the door again, locking it.

Go to hell, Drake thought. There was no love lost between him and the eye-patch bastard.

When the door closed again, Drake returned his gaze to the Society column and stared once more at the detailed wedding announcement of one of Society's apparently elite couples.

It was to be held right here in London, and it was scheduled for tomorrow morning.

The bride's name was unknown to him. But Drake kept staring at the groom's name with an inexplicable certainty that he knew this man, this marquess.

An idea was forming in his head.

He did not tell James that he had recognized the name. Perhaps he would. But first, desperate for any solid answers, Drake felt compelled to sneak away to this wedding tomorrow and get a look at the groom's face if he could manage it somehow. The name sounded so familiar . . .

Rotherstone.

The great day had come at last.

The morning glowed with golden promise, but behind her veil, Daphne's face was pale with nervousness as she rode with her family in her father's rarely used state coach, festooned with flowers for the occasion, and drawn by four horses wearing white plumes on their heads.

She was eager to marry Max, but not without a trace of fear, for once this day was done, there was no turning back. The thought had her gripping her bouquet so tightly she nearly crushed the flowers' delicate stems.

Her heart pounded in time with the bells' joyous caroling as the Starling family's coach rolled to a halt before St. George's in Hanover Square.

The pillars of Mayfair's most fashionable church were adorned with ribbonlike swirls of pale cloth. Large urns of flowers flanked the white carpet that had been laid down from the pavement into the church's wide-open entrance.

Inside, Daphne glimpsed a throng of people she knew, garbed in their finest attire. She swallowed hard. Last-minute fears surged and dove in her again like leaping dolphins as she contemplated all the unknowns of her future life with a man they called the Demon Marquess.

With her heart in her throat, she got out of the carriage with her father's steadying hand. They had made up their differences weeks ago, of course. Wilhelmina quickly followed, helping to maneuver her billowing skirts.

The music rose to a crescendo — then silence.

Papa gave her a bolstering smile and walked her into the church; they prepared themselves for their entrance processional while Penelope and the girls, in purple and pink, hurried to take their seats.

The music started up anew; the congregation rose.

Letting Papa watch for the preacher's signal to come forward, Daphne scanned the crowded church with her pulse throbbing. She spotted Max's sister, Lady Thurloe, and her children and husband. The countess had had a hand in the planning for today.

She also took note of his friends, the Duke of Warrington and Lord Falconridge, standing with a giant, grizzled Scottish laird in full Highland regalia.

Lord, who is that imposing fellow? she thought, then her gaze traveled on until she spotted her great-aunt Anselm seated in the first pew at the front of the church.

Jonathon was close by, and when their eyes met, he grinned and sent her a boyish wave. She smiled fondly at him, put at ease a bit by his clownish humor, but she had never been more sure that she had made the right decision.

Carissa stood nearby with her haughty cousins. The petite redhead gave Daphne a firm nod of encouragement, which, in turn, thrust Daphne's attention back to the task at hand.

As Max stepped into view at the front of the church, just where he should be, any last misgivings evaporated like the morning dew. The sight of him swelled her heart with renewed certainty.

He stared at her from across the church, waiting for her by the altar, looking like a dream of Prince Charming, in a dark blue morning coat. This he wore over a silver waistcoat and cream-colored breeches with formal white stockings and black shoes. His gloves were also white; he had a white flower bud boutonniere.

Papa's light nudge jarred her from her staring with the signal to move ahead. Gathering herself, she glided forward with all the refined grace she had made it her mission to learn from an early age, in an effort to make her mother's spirit proud.

With each slow, smooth step she took down the aisle of the simple, crowded church, she kept her stare on Max.

As she neared him, her heart began to soar. Very well, then, so she was marrying the Demon Marquess, and once she spoke those vows, she would never look back.

There was a splendid radiance about his dark male beauty this morning, his glowing scrubbed skin clean-shaved, his black hair combed back and tamed neatly with a light coating of pomade. She could not take her eyes off him. Joining him, she let her father pass her on to this man without any further argument, her gaze fixed on him, while her soul exulted. Being near him was pure heaven.

No one has ever loved me, he had said that day in the hayloft. The words still made her heart clench.

I will, she thought. In that moment, she made up her mind irrevocably. *I am going to love you, and give you everything I've got,* she told him with her heartfelt gaze.

He searched her face through her translucent bridal veil, a subtle question in his eyes, a curious flicker on his brow as he offered her his hand.

Instead, she took his arm and moved even closer to him. *I hope you're ready, Max, my love. You asked for it.*

The music drew to a close. He slanted her another mystified, slightly suspicious glance from the corner of his eye. Daphne smiled at him in anticipation, then they both turned their attention to the balding reverend, who looked up from his open prayer book.

Pushing his round spectacles back up onto his nose, the vicar beamed at them, and at the congregation, in turn.

"Dearly beloved," he began, "we are gathered here today . . ."

He was married. Just like that, it was done.

A couple of hours later, at the reception, Max could still barely believe he had finally achieved his goal and won his chosen lady.

She had put up quite the battle royal, as he had told his friends, but after all his meticulous planning, he had learned beyond any doubt that the heart of a woman was a force of nature no man could control.

If there had been any doubt of that, her kiss at the climax of the ceremony had removed it.

When the preacher had told Max he was free to kiss his bride, he had lifted her veil and lowered his head to claim her lips, only to have her throw her arms around him and kiss him passionately.

He had not been expecting that — and neither had Society. Several people in the

404

church had laughed, but she paid them no mind, planting a wedding kiss on his lips that soon had the whole congregation cheering and applauding them. A loud wolf whistle from the back of the church had come from Rohan, but even Max had felt a little sheepish by the time his bride had got through with him.

It seemed he'd found himself a Demon Marchioness.

Delighted, and already anticipating tonight, they proceeded on to Almack's, which her father had let for the day for the reception. Musicians played; greetings and gifts from the crème de la crème of London Society streamed in; wine and liquor flowed, some of the best to be had in the world. Tables loaded with food were laid out, and eventually, together, they made a wish and cut into the fanciful white tower of a wedding cake from Gunter's.

It was all a bit of a blur.

Still, Max found it rather odd that he should have been married only a couple of hours, and already was beginning to feel like more of a member of the world.

At length, he was summoned outside for a celebratory cigar with his father-in-law and the set of older gentlemen who made up Lord Starling's circle of friends.

To keep the cloud of smoke from drifting indoors and annoying the ladies, they congregated in the alley between Almack's and the livery stable next door.

While Max was smoking, grinning at the old married men's ribbing about how he must at least appear to comply with all his new wife's orders, he noticed a hackney coach go driving by very slowly out on King Street, perpendicular to the narrow alley where the men were loitering.

At first, he thought nothing of it. There were any number of onlookers who might want to get a glimpse of an aristocratic wedding, especially one that was not hidden away in some distant country house.

Word of their pending nuptial date had run in the Society columns, and the journalists who made their living tattling on the lives of the ton would no doubt be lurking to see what they could see.

But then, as the hackney rolled past the intersection with the alley, in plain view, Max saw the passenger inside. Behind the looped-back swath of dingy curtain, a face appeared. A face he knew at once.

Max froze.

The man's stare met his own for a fleeting second with dark, intense eyes.

Max stood motionless, barely able to believe his senses. *A ghost? Hallucination?*

He saw the face of a fallen brother. The coach passed, picking up speed. For a second, Max just stood there in utter shock.

Drake.

In the next instant, he threw aside his cigar without a word of explanation to his father-in-law or anyone else.

He ran out of the alley, turned left, and began chasing the hackney coach up King Street.

"Rotherstone, I say!" he heard Lord Starling exclaim. Max did not look back.

Having picked up its pace, the coach was already turning left onto busy St. James's Street a good stone's throw ahead.

Max ran faster, questioning his own sanity but somehow refusing to doubt. He knew what he'd seen, and dear God, if Drake was alive . . .

He could not even think about the implications right now. He had to know for sure. Hope and ominous questions swirled in his mind. He dashed past pedestrians milling around the various shops. Chasing the coach down St. James's Street in the direction of Piccadilly, he fought the unsubtle urge to call out his friend's name to try to get him to stop.

If it was indeed Drake and he was alive, he would have stopped already if everything was all right. If he had wanted to be found. *Dear God, had Drake gone rogue?*

Maybe he was mistaken. Maybe it wasn't he at all. Max thrust a growing sense of dread out of his mind and pushed himself to run harder, though the slippery soles of his formal shoes were not helping matters. He'd be lucky if he did not land on his arse. The bustling traffic had checked the coach's pace, but still, on foot, Max was no match for the two horses drawing the vehicle.

When it turned the corner ahead, he lost visual contact for about two minutes, but, chest heaving, he soon arrived on the corner with Piccadilly. He looked to the left, the direction he had seen the hackney turn, but quickly lost it in the sea of nondescript black carriages trundling back and forth on the grand avenue.

Damn it!

Other carriages were parked along both sides of Piccadilly, waiting to pick up passengers going to and from the row of fashionable shops and clubs and coffeehouses.

Max scanned the pavements in both directions in case Drake had slipped out of the hackney and continued on foot.

He focused on the male pedestrians, but it was difficult to tell since nearly all of them wore hats, their faces shaded by the brims of top hats, round hats, beaver hats, or military bicorns. Beginning to feel stymied, Max spotted one of the hackneys in the row of parked carriages and thought the horses similarly colored to those of the coach he had been chasing, one a ragged chestnut, the other a slightly darker liver brown. *That could be it.*

Max raced toward it, ignoring the stares of passersby. He supposed he looked like a fool running around the streets of London dressed in some of the most formal clothes he owned. What would Society say about a groom running like hell from his own wedding reception, and for that matter, what would Daphne think?

He could not deal with that now. If Drake was alive and had gone rogue on them, he had much more serious problems than the disapproval of the Patronesses of Almack's. He rushed down the street to the parked carriage, and threw the door open without warning.

It was empty. If Drake was there a moment ago, he had vanished like a puff of smoke.

"Can I 'elp you, sir?" the hackney driver asked from up on his box. "Need a ride?"

"Where did that man go? Your passenger!"

The driver shook his head and gave Max an indifferent shrug. *Don't know, don't care.*

"Stay there, I need to talk to you!" Max ordered him, but he was fairly sure he was on the right path. Quickly checking the shops right near the place where the hackney had pulled over, he looked into several of the merchants' open doors. A milliner's, a confectioner's, a candle maker's, a linen draper's. *No.* But when he glanced into the crowded sundries shop, staring past the aisles down to the far end of the long, narrow space, he caught the briefest glimpse of a man in black disappearing through the back exit.

Max sprinted after him, ignoring the shopkeeper's " 'Hoy! Where are you going?"

Max went tearing out the back door and bolted into the garden.

There was no one there. A high brick wall girded the shopkeeper's kitchen garden. The family probably lived above the shop. Max swept the area with a baleful glance and listened for any sound. *Nothing.* He could not see him or hear him, but he felt him very near.

"Drake!" he bellowed all of a sudden. "Show yourself!"

Instead of his brother agent, the shopkeeper came storming out the back door after him at that moment. " 'Hoy! Trespasser! What do you think you're doing? You can't come back here!"

"Did you see a man run through here?"

"Aside from you?" the beefy, aproned merchant demanded, hands on hips. *Bloody aristocrats,* his pugnacious glower seemed to say.

"Sorry," Max muttered, but he walked away from the man all the same and climbed up onto the wall.

"I'm going to call for the constable if you don't get off my property. You got no right to be here."

"Fine." Max jumped down on the other side and continued the hunt, just as Warrington and Falconridge rushed into the merchant's garden.

"Max!"

"Who the hell are you?" the merchant cried angrily.

"Sorry, we're trying to find our friend."

"He went that way."

"What, over the wall?"

"I'm right here," Max called back in disgust, finding no sign of Drake. He climbed back over the shopkeeper's wall and rejoined his friends.

"The three of you move along or I'm sending for the constable. I don't want your money!" he retorted when Warrington tried to offer him a fiver for his pains.

"What the hell is going on?" Jordan murmured.

They left the shop.

"I saw Drake."

"What?"

Max glanced grimly at them as they put some distance between themselves and the indignant shopkeeper, who was still standing in his shop doorway making sure they were not coming back.

"Here?"

"Alive?"

"I could swear it was he."

"You must be mistaken."

"It can't be!"

"I know. After all, if Drake were alive, why

411

wouldn't he make himself known to us? But I'm telling you, I know what I saw. I chased him as far as here, then he got away."

"We'll look for him. Which way did he go?"

"He disappeared! Just the way we've all been taught to do," Max added grimly. "At this point —" He glanced around, then shook his head. "He could be anywhere."

"Well, if Drake is alive, then we've bloody well got to find him. Fast."

"I know. I don't understand it." Max shook his head, bewildered. "Am I seeing things?"

"Couldn't have been a trick of the mind, could it? Nostalgia, a remembrance of old friends?" Jordan suggested.

"Or his ghost?" Rohan added.

They just looked at him.

"I grew up in a haunted castle, boys. If you've never had a ghost try to push you down the stairs, you've never lived."

"Not helpful, Rohan," Jordan said, then rested a brotherly hand on Max's shoulder. "Maybe it was just the guilt that you made it back and he didn't. I know we have all felt our share of that. And now you've got this lovely girl, this wonderful new life ahead of you —"

"I'm not seeing things, Jordan." Max dragged his hand through his hair. "At least — I don't think I am."

"Listen, let us worry about this," Rohan murmured. "We'll look for Drake, ghost or man. You've got better things to do."

"Make sure you talk to the hackney driver," he said. "I don't think he really knew anything, but he would have seen him and could describe him and where he picked him up. Whatever you can find out."

Jordan nodded, but then his two friends exchanged a hesitant glance.

"I think we'd better tell him," Rohan said to Jordan in a low voice.

"Tell me what?" Something in the duke's tone made Max's blood run cold foreknowingly.

"Jordan spotted Dresden Bloodwell at the End of Summer Ball."

"Dresden Bloodwell . . . the assassin? What the hell is he doing in London?"

"No idea."

"Where did you see him?"

"Inside the house. He must've come in with one of the guests. He was leaning on the wall in the ballroom and seemed to be taking stock of things. I was in the middle of dancing with some woman, and by the time I got away from her, he had disappeared."

"Why the hell didn't you tell me?" Max snarled.

"You were already gone. It was after you left, after that whole debacle with Carew."

"That was weeks ago!"

"We've been working on it ourselves. Don't worry. Come on, man, we did not want to ruin this time for you. You've been madly in love and preparing for your wedding," Rohan said. "And for that matter, you had better get back to it. You caused quite a stir with your disappearing act."

"Bloody hell, what am I going to tell them?"

"You saw a cutpurse rob an old lady and took matters in your own hands," Jordan informed him matter-of-factly. "Now, go and get your hero's glory. Don't worry. We'll back you up."

"Right." Max shook his head with an angry sigh and a deep uneasiness in his soul. "That's just perfect," he muttered under his breath. "My first bloody day as a married man and I've already got to lie to her."

It did not bode well.

He knew me.

Drake's heart was still pounding as he slipped back into the Pulteney Hotel, stealing back up to the balcony by which he had climbed down. He had to get back before James returned from his errand. He'd been told that Talon would not return for a few days, thankfully, but he did not know where the eye-patch man had gone.

It had been strange to be free out in the world, but Drake had become disoriented. He could see no good reason why he should go back to his captors, except that something deep inside him told him that he should.

414

Maybe he had truly come to believe the Prometheans when they said they were his friends. All Drake knew was that out in the world, especially after that frightening chase, he did not feel secure in this strange city without James. He needed the benevolent structure given him by his aged protector.

So, he fixed his sights on sneaking back *into* the Pulteney Hotel. His body seemed to know what it was doing, even if his brain did not. It seemed to have a plan. Maybe his reasons for returning were something else entirely.

Maybe that lost continent submerged within him knew exactly what he was doing. Drake could not say.

But deep in his bones, he knew better than to tell James what he had done. At least not yet, not until he figured out if Rotherstone was friend or foe.

He was still at a loss to explain where the ability to evade capture like that had come from. To be sure, he had not expected to be seen, but when Rotherstone started chasing him, his escape reactions had come without forethought, as if by instinct.

It left him wondering how he had managed to get caught in Bavaria. *Why could he not remember?* He was feeling rattled again as he slipped back into the window of the room he'd been assigned.

With shaking hands, he poured himself a

drink of water from the pitcher, then sat down on his bed, trying to catch his breath. He steadied his shaking hands and clung to this single shred of recognition for all he was worth.

Rotherstone knew him. The painted woman last night had known him, too — Ginger. And now he had managed to escape and to get back in again undetected. These were all promising signs. He let out a quiet exhalation as his trembling finally eased.

Maybe, just maybe, there was hope for him.

CHAPTER 15

The long day had ended, and Daphne sat before the mirrored vanity, brushing her hair until it gleamed. Free at last of stockings and stays, all she wore under her blue satin dressing gown was a white linen shift. It felt wonderful to relax after the strain of having to be the center of attention for so many hours.

With each soothing stroke of her brush, she enjoyed the wink of the candlelight on the gold band on her finger.

She tried to ignore her nervous awareness that Max would be joining her at any moment for their first night in what would be *their* bedchamber. Of course, it would take some time to get used to her new life, as well as her new home. She had to keep reminding herself that she was now the lady of his opulent Town palace, with its splendid portrait gallery and ornate dining room and all the rest.

It was so much bigger and grander and

more formal than Papa's cozy villa that it made her feel as if she should be on her best behavior. Even here in the large, imposing bedchamber, the feeble glow of the candelabra could not penetrate the shadowed heights of the fifteen-foot ceiling.

Such a large house ought to have been chilly, too, but the fire burning in the hearth had made the sprawling chamber rather toasty, and considering that she would soon be asked to remove all her clothes, she supposed she ought to be grateful for that. Tomorrow they would set out for his estate, but tonight . . .

Acutely aware of the large canopied bed a few feet away, she reached for another swallow of wine and continued trying to talk herself out of another attack of virginal nerves.

Obviously, their first night together was going to produce some anxiety, since she really did not know what she was in for beyond the basic facts. But she had made up her mind to enter into this marriage wholeheartedly, and besides, she was sure her chivalrous husband would do all in his power to make it as easy as possible on her.

She wondered if she would conceive on their very first night together — but this was such an overwhelming prospect that she turned her attention humorously to the thought of her bridegroom dashing out of their wedding reception and through the streets of London to chase a cutpurse.

Ever the hero, she thought, smiling into the mirror with pride in him. He couldn't seem to help himself when it came to his courageous brand of gallantry. It was, she mused, one of his more adorable qualities.

She heard the door click from her seat on the other end of the immense, dimly lit chamber. She turned around and steadied herself against a frisson of awareness as the door creaked open, and Max stepped into the room.

He smiled at her as he closed the door behind him. She smiled back, still gripping her hairbrush. Her heart beat faster as he crossed the room, gazing at her in open admiration. "There's my treasure," he greeted her in a low, fond, husky murmur.

She blushed at his flattering stare and lowered her head as he came to stand beside her.

"Are you really mine?" he whispered, running a knuckle gently over the now-gleaming gold of her hair.

She lifted her head and gazed into his eyes, nodding. "You know I am."

He bent and pressed a worshipful kiss to her lips. "I am the luckiest of men."

Her mouth curved under his. She reached for his hand as he straightened up again. Letting her hand rest between both of his, he held her gaze warmly for a long moment.

Daphne's heart glowed in the silence with him.

"How are you?" he asked softly.

"Good! Happy."

"Good," he whispered.

"You?"

"Happy," he echoed with measured caution, as though tasting the word warily, letting her lead him into it.

She raised an eyebrow. "You're not sure?"

"I'm not used to this."

She held on to his hand a little more tightly. "You will be before long."

"So, we're married then," he said in a mildly businesslike tone.

"That we are," she answered with a grin. "Imagine that! You got your way."

He frowned with a crestfallen look. "Don't say that. It must be mutual, Daphne."

"I'm only teasing. Of course it is. Still, what hope did I ever have with the likes of you chasing me? But I do wonder one thing."

"What's that?"

She stood up from the vanity and slid her arms around his neck. "Now that you've caught me, Rotherstone, what are you going to do with me?"

He let out a low laugh full of gusto, lowered his head, and kissed her hungrily. When the fire popped loudly in the hearth, she betrayed her nervousness with her slight, startled jump at the sound.

Max ended the kiss and gave her a compassionate little frown, realizing she was having a case of the nerves.

"There, there, sweeting. There's no reason to be so much on edge. Come here. Sit with me." He led her over to the Moroccan leather armchair, sat down, and held out his hand in invitation.

She smiled sheepishly at him and accepted, arranging herself across his lap, her body perpendicular to his. She smoothed the skirts of her shift and her dressing gown, then draped her arms loosely around his neck.

"There now, isn't this cozy?" he teased, tucking her bare feet gently under his thigh to keep them warm.

She smiled, grateful for his efforts to put her at ease. He held her gaze for a long moment with a mystified look. "You seem different," he said all of a sudden.

"I do?"

"Yes. You've got, I don't know . . . a twinkle in your eyes. Ever since the wedding ceremony. That kiss you gave me. *Whew.*"

She grinned. "Did you like it?"

"Darling, if I'd liked it any better, I'd have ravished you on the altar and got us both struck by lightning. So? Confess. What is the cause of this devilish twinkle?"

"You are." She let out a dreamy sigh and caressed his face for a moment, but then

recalled the small weight upon her conscience. She didn't want any remaining
secrets between them before she gave herself
to him for the first time. "Max?"

"Yes."

"I have — a confession to make."

"Oh, dear. Go on."

"Do you promise you won't get angry?"

"Absolutely. It is our wedding day. What is
the matter, darling?"

She lowered her gaze. "I pawned the sapphire necklace for the orphanage." Wincing,
she looked up at him from beneath her lashes
to gauge his reaction. "You know that building I wanted to buy to house the children?
That boarding school for sale?"

He had raised an eyebrow. "Yes?"

"Unfortunately, my hopes of doing good
then hit a snag."

He regarded her intently, but true to his
word, did not look angry. "What sort of snag,
my dear? The sum was not enough?"

"No, the money was sufficient to cover the
cost when I added it to the donations that we
had already accrued."

"What then? Did someone else already buy
it?"

"No." She could not disguise her resentment. "They would not sell me the building
because I am a woman."

"Ah." He raised both eyebrows. "Well, my
dear Lady Rotherstone," he replied. "We'll

just have to see about that." He kissed her nose and started laughing softly. "You nearly had me worried for a second."

"You are not cross I sold the necklace? We weren't getting along too well when I did it. If we had been —"

"Enough. That I am lucky enough to have married a woman who thinks not of herself but would turn around and spend the proceeds of a gift on a bunch of ragged children . . . you are an angel, Daphne. I can't believe you're mine."

She hugged him. "Thank you for understanding."

"Do you want another necklace?"

"No. I'd rather have beds and a new set of clothes for all the children."

"Done," he whispered. "It will be my wedding gift."

"Oh, Max."

"Actually, Daphne, if we're going to be baring our souls here, there's something that I need to tell you, too."

She furrowed her brow, determined to take his secret, whatever it was, as well as he had taken hers. When he looked at her for a moment, she read a glimmer of mischief in his eyes. "What is it, you rogue?" she murmured, studying him in suspicion.

"You know that day in Bucket Lane, how you saw me coming out of the, er, brothel?"

She nodded, trying to hide her distaste for

that nasty establishment.

"I wasn't there for the reason you think," he informed her. "As a matter of fact, I was only there to have a look at you."

"What?"

"As God is my witness . . ." He proceeded to tell her the whole astonishing story of how he had ordered his man-of-business to start researching a list of possible brides for him before he had even returned to England from abroad.

He had her laughing and exclaiming in wonder at his absurd account, and she didn't think she would've believed him at all, except that he then got up and produced the letter, handing it over for her to read.

"Hypatia Glendale? This is my competition? Oh, I'm problematical, am I?"

"Very," he agreed.

She laughed heartily at it, because, after all, what else could she do? She was not about to get angry at him on their wedding night.

In truth, she was delighted to hear that he had not been in that bordello to exploit the women there, but instead to spy on her.

Of course, it was odd. But she accepted his explanation of why he had done it.

"You've gone about in Society long enough to know that the second a bachelor nobleman shows the slightest interest in any young lady, the gossips immediately began running amok."

"Still," she chided, shaking her head despite her laughter, "I cannot believe you listed all these traits as your requirements! Breeding, beauty, dowry, temperament, what else?"

"Reputation."

"Pshaw! Your poor solicitor! It's a wonder he found even one girl who could live up to this list of standards, let alone five. Honestly, Rotherstone, I cannot believe you practically ordered me out of a catalogue like a-a farming implement!" He laughed merrily at her reproach. "Oh, you deserve all the trouble I gave you, every jot!"

"All I know is I'm very happy with my choice."

"You really are too much." Still laughing, she captured his face between her hands and kissed him. "I have a feeling you are going to make my life very interesting."

"I'll try."

"Well, I'm glad you told me," she said as she sat down on his lap again and tossed Oliver Smith's letter aside. "I realize you've got a long way to go with learning to be more direct, my love, but this is a definite step in the right direction. I'm proud of you."

"Thanks for not throttling me."

"Well, I haven't had my way with you yet! Maybe after. Max?"

He gave her a smoldering smile. "Yes, Daphne?"

She gazed earnestly into his eyes. "I'm going to be an excellent wife to you."

"I have no doubt of that."

"No, I really mean it. I fought this for a long time, but now . . . it's full sail ahead," she whispered, toying with the single button on the neckline of his shirt.

"Sounds good to me."

Smiling, she leaned closer and pressed another kiss to his lips, closing her eyes with a soft chuckle. "Hypatia Glendale, indeed. You're mine now, all mine. Your lips. Your nose, your eyes, your cheeks . . ." She kissed each part, in turn. "Your chin, all of you. Your neck . . . What's this?" she exclaimed all of a sudden, halting and staring at the pale scar on the side of his neck beneath his ear.

"Oh, that? That's nothing," he said. "Just where some unfortunate fellow tried to kill me."

"*Kill* you?" she cried. "What for?"

"Fun and profit, in the main. Tried to rob me, too. Rome, it was. Don't worry, it was long ago."

"Darling, you could've been killed!"

"No, Fate had better things in mind for me, my pretty lady. Namely, you. Don't worry! I was faster." He pulled her close and kissed away her astonishment.

She forgot about the scar, clutching breathlessly at his shirt. "Max?"

"Yes, my bride?"

"You really don't need this anymore, do you?"

She saw the flash of startled delight in his eyes. He stared at her in fascination. "You're right." He nodded vaguely and quickly pulled his shirt off over his head.

"Mm, lovely." Cuddling on his lap, she rested her head against his bare shoulder and amused herself with walking her fingers up his splendid chest.

But then, all of a sudden, once more, her strolling fingers stopped. "Max," she said firmly.

"Yes, love?" he answered, his deep voice gone slightly scratchy with desire. It seemed her playfulness was having a curious effect on him.

"Max," she said, "there is another scar here. On your chest."

"There is?"

"Max!"

"Did the robber stab you here, too?"

"Uh, that was from another fellow."

"Somebody *else* tried to kill you?"

"It wasn't my fault."

"You really have to learn how to get along with others, darling! Honestly. Do people often try to kill you?"

"Only now and then. Ah, you need not fear for me, my love. Don't you know I'm descended from warlords and Crusaders?" he reminded her sardonically. "Even a few

427

Knights Templar thrown into the mix."

She looked askance at him, but thrilled to that small endearment: *my love.* She tucked it away like a treasure inside her heart and dared to hope she was making real progress with him at last. She gave his second scar a kiss. "Someday you'll have to tell me all about it."

"I don't think I will," he murmured, skimming his smiling lips along her neck even as he tightened his embrace. "It is a very nasty business."

"Well," she conceded with a sensuous sigh, enjoying his warm nibbling at her earlobe, "you do have a penchant for getting into trouble. Are there any other scars that I should know about? Being as I am your wife and all."

"Why don't you keep looking and find out for yourself?" he breathed by her ear.

"You really are wicked, you know."

"Not past redemption, surely?"

"I didn't say I thought it was a flaw."

He let out a low laugh and slid his arms around her waist, kissing her in earnest. Daphne reveled in the satin glide of his tongue against hers and caressed him everywhere, caught up in his intoxicating taste.

She sensed, heard, breathed in the quickening of his breath as her fingers inched over his bare skin, savoring the sculpted hardness of his abdomen, upward to the muscled swells of his chest.

She curled her hands in lustful awe over his powerful shoulders, and then raked her nails in teasing lightness down his enormous biceps. Meanwhile, he had slid his clever fingers under the edge of her satin dressing gown, slowly pushing it down off her shoulders.

He tore his lips away from hers and let his kiss now follow where his hands glided. Daphne moaned softly as he nibbled her bare shoulder, but when his lips moved up the curve of her neck, his hand roamed down to cup her breast through the thin cloth of her chemise.

She tilted her head back as his thumb began teasing her nipple to burning erectness. Leaving her breast temporarily, he grasped her hips and shifted her up onto her knees astride his lap. This brought her breasts right up to his face. Immediately, he returned to lavishing them with his attentions. Her dressing gown was now hanging about her elbows, but she was still dressed in her linen chemise.

Kneeling on the fabric, she grew impatient to be rid of it, but there was such pleasure in straddling him, feeling the heat and the hardness of him between the juncture of her thighs.

Her breasts strained against the linen restraint of her garment, but Max did his best to work around it, kissing her chest where the scoop neck of her chemise left her skin bare, and teasing her breasts into aching response through the fine paper-thin cloth.

Raking her fingers through his thick dark hair, she moved against him in a subtle rhythm; her body sought a closer fit with his. She didn't think they were going to find it on this chair, but, God, he was driving her mad.

Her restless blood clamored for a deeper fulfillment.

As he gripped her hips and helped her grind against him, she suddenly couldn't take it anymore. God, she had burned for this man from the first moment she had laid eyes on him, looking like sex incarnate coming out of that brothel.

She wanted to know tonight exactly what her libertine could do.

With sweet, carnal memories of his mouth between her legs, she captured his chin and drew his rapt kisses away from her breasts. "Max," she whispered breathlessly. "I need — a drink of wine." With a vixenish stare, she climbed off his lap and stood up a trifle unsteadily.

She let her blue satin dressing gown fall to the floor with an idle shrug. He watched her with an avid, wolflike stare as she turned away, going to steady her nerves with a final swallow of wine. Before she reached the vanity where she had left her cup, she felt him watching her and glanced back at him over her shoulder. There was a look on his face almost of pain as he stared at her.

She paused and turned around. "What is it?"

"Your shift is quite transparent when you stand before the fire."

"Oh?" She glanced down at herself, blushing slightly. "Well, then. I don't suppose I need it anymore." With a surge of brazen daring, she sent him a sultry smile and lifted the chemise off over her head.

She heard his whispery groan as she shook out her hair and dropped the filmy garment on the floor. Standing in place for a moment, she let him look, then casually turned away and walked over to retrieve her wine.

In the mirror of the vanity, she could see his stare devouring her nude body. She was not sure what had gotten into her. Only that she wanted him.

The one thing she was beginning to understand was that these physical pleasures gave her a way to reach him more deeply. When he was engrossed with her in the giving and receiving of amorous bliss, he forgot about keeping his guard up; the mask he wore came down.

Even now, his desire seemed to reach out to her from across the room like a stream of powerful heat.

She turned and watched him watching her, drank the last swallow of her wine, and then, instead of going back to him, walked slowly over to the bed.

His stare intensified, but he held himself back as if with a leash. She drew the covers back and climbed into his bed. "Mm." As she slid down between the silky cream-colored sheets, she was enveloped in luxurious warmth from the coal-filled bed warmer already spreading its heat.

Reclining on the pillows piled against the headboard, she crooked her finger at him. "Come here, husband."

He rose and went to her. She held his stare, leaning back on her elbows. The look on his face was that of a man who had got what he wanted and knew that, at last, the long-relished time had come to enjoy his prize.

He had been holding himself back for the sake of her sensibilities, she thought, but she hoped he saw now that if he wanted, he should take.

And he definitely wanted.

With his gaze locked on hers, he reached the bed and slowly joined her, moving on all fours atop her. Daphne quivered, waiting for his kiss in the darkness. She tilted her head back, offering her lips.

He swooped down and claimed them as though he could not withstand another second of denial. He consumed her mouth, her breath, her soul, in ravenous need, one hand cupping her head, the other reaching down to free himself from his breeches.

Daphne was swept away as she returned his kisses, running her hands up and down his silken sides. She helped him push his breeches down past his hips, unbearable excitement rising in her. He lay between her legs.

She was acutely aware of the softness of her quivering stomach against his hard, chiseled abdomen, her satiny breasts against his muscled chest. Their mouths were joined as their bodies soon would be, her fingers twined behind his neck.

He reached down to stroke her gently and moaned to find her core already soaked with her readiness for him.

"I need you," he panted.

In response, she drew him closer into her embrace. The next thing she knew, she felt him slowly, carefully entering her. Her heart thundered as he mounted her, but behind her closed eyes, she was wild with yearning for him.

His fevered panting rasped against her cheek as he overwhelmed her maiden barrier. Her hands tensed atop his shoulders, but she did not cry out.

He dragged his lips across her brow in a savage remnant of a kiss; having fully invaded, he now stopped. Already in full penetration of her, he could go no farther, could only wait for her virginal body to accept the depth of his taking, the width of his grand incursion.

She barely dared breathe.

"Good girl, good girl," he panted, soothing her ever so seductively.

Daphne willed her body to open completely to him. It was pleasure. It was pain. It was sheer intoxication. The pain passed, trickling away by the second while a floodtide of desire rose anew and engulfed them both.

He began to move, awakening her with a blissful friction of their bodies. The undulant waves of his taking built toward a crescendo of resounding power. She wrapped her legs around his hips, gifting him with a surrender that only seemed to take him higher.

"Oh, God, Daphne." They both were shaking with frantic need. His iron arms clenched around her waist as he claimed her in a frenzied, driving consummation. She thrashed beneath him, wanting all he had to give, letting him unleash his storm. The cries of wrenching pleasure that escaped her filled the room as he ravished her.

Sweet heaven, this was how she wanted him, all his cool control stripped away, ravenous, aye, desperate for her, not hiding behind his clever wordplay, his sardonic humor, his quicksilver mind.

There was no hiding for either of them in a moment like this. She did not even mind that he was slightly rough with her, because in this moment, he was so raw and utterly real. The darkness that he tried to hide, the depths in him that he would never give voice to, all were revealed in every touch, every kiss, every thrust as he claimed her for his own. His body gave expression to what his silver tongue refused to share.

They reached their climax in furious unison, writhing, burning, locked in a searing kiss, her hips lifting to meet each slamming stroke from him. He stopped as he, too, was overcome, throwing his head back, his arms rigid around her. He arched his spine, buried to the hilt inside her passage. Reality pulsated with pleasure like a racing heartbeat.

Their ecstasy blotted out the world; his low groan as he filled her with another powerful spurt of his seed harkened to her out among the cosmos, where her mind, as ravished as her body, had been floating briefly.

Time had been suspended . . .

Then he sighed, such a sound, deep, soulful, from his core. "Oh, Daphne," he breathed. He pressed a shaken kiss warmly to her lips.

"Max." She wrapped her leaden arms around him as he laid his head down on the pillow just above her shoulder.

She turned her face at length to look into his eyes. There was nothing more to say; it was the closest she had ever felt to him. No words required.

She touched his hair wearily, and smiled as he closed his eyes with a look of total bliss. She went on caressing him until he fell asleep, yet she was still haunted by the words he had confided in that stable.

No one has ever loved me.

Gazing sweetly at him in the silence, she kissed his brow. *My love, there is a first time for everything.*

CHAPTER 16

"Wake up, sleepyhead," Max whispered in her ear the next morning.

Daphne shifted luxuriously beside him. "It's early."

"There's something we need to take care of before we leave Town."

She rolled onto her back and gazed at him. "What is it?"

He just smiled. "Come with me."

Thus began their orphanage project, in which Daphne and he assembled a team of helpers and accomplished what amounted to a month's worth of work in roughly a week.

First Max summoned Oliver Smith, Esquire, along with the property agent for the boarding school. They all drove out to Islington so His Lordship could personally inspect the premises.

Finding it all in reasonably good order, with only a few repairs needed, Max took the property agent aside to negotiate the deal. This was quickly accomplished, but before the children could move in, a considerable number of preparations had to be completed.

While Daphne was responsible for listing *what* the children needed, he put himself in charge of the *how.*

He quickly marshaled up an army of resources to help get the boarding school ready for the orphans. First he recruited his butler Dodsley, at the head of his entire domestic staff, to clean the boarding school from tip to stern.

Second, since the orphans' caretakers had long been overwhelmed, Max hunted down and rehired a number of the kindly spinsters who had worked there when it was a school.

Daphne summoned the older boys and girls who had been apprenticed out or hired all over London to come and work for a day helping to get the place ready.

Papa and his gentlemen friends spent a day watching footman William and one of Max's coachmen fix up the two old wagons and the governess cart that they had contributed for the cause. Lord Falconridge donated an enormous sum to stock the orphanage's pantry with long-term stores of food. He also pitched in for a slew of books and chalks and slates for the classroom. At the same time, the Duke of Warrington pitched in with a delivery of coal stores sufficient to warm the orphanage all the way through to next summer.

Jono and Carissa went around to all the toy shops in London and coaxed the toymakers into handing over some of their wares for the children to play with, hoops and balls and pull toys, dolls and stuffed animals.

Oliver Smith was given the task of making arrangements with a shop full of seamstresses and another team of cobblers to outfit the children with their new clothes and shoes.

It occurred to Daphne that Penelope had the perfect talents to help organize all the activity on move-in day. Since the location no longer entailed the dangerous environs of Bucket Lane, her stepmother agreed to help, too, and even brought Sarah and Anna to come and assist.

Penelope herself took charge of stocking the medicinal cabinet with plenty of herbal remedies and potions for warding off the children's sniffles. Even Albert Carew's elder brother, Hayden, the Duke of Holyfield, made a contribution before heading off on his holiday in France with his expectant wife, to enjoy the pleasures of Paris before the birth of their first child.

By move-in day, everything was ready. The new caretakers were in place, all smiles at the prospect of their charges' arrival. A receiving line of seamstresses and cobblers waited at the orphanage to measure all the children for their new sets of clothes and shoes. Penelope bustled around making sure everything was in order and quite reveling in her newfound role.

At last, the fixed-up, newly painted wagons rolled into Bucket Lane to transport the children to their new home. Small faces peered out of every grimy window as their makeshift army of concerned citizens arrived: Daphne and Max, the two Willies, Oliver Smith, Dodsley. Warrington and Falconridge had also come along to keep the local ruffians at bay.

Before long, they left Bucket Lane behind forever, and as the wagons full of cheering orphans arrived at their new home, Daphne's eyes filled with tears at all the joyous hubbub. There were children running about everywhere, never having been set loose in a country meadow before. The seamstresses were hard-pressed to still each wriggly toddler long enough to be measured.

The little girls were immediately crowding around the huge gentle draft horses, petting them, and the boys were chasing one another around the fenced-in garden.

At length, however, their energies flagging, the children were herded into their new home, going single-file into the doorway over which hung a placard that read: *The Emma, Lady Starling, Home for Orphans.*

It had been Max's idea to dedicate the place to Daphne's mother. Watching him all week, she thought him extraordinary, but what surprised her the most was his natural way with the children. In fact, Daphne thought, he seemed to have surprised himself. When one giggling two-year-old escaped the old cobbler who had been trying to measure her tiny feet, Max dashed off after the escaping urchin and swept her up into his arms.

The toddler hung down, trailing her arms limply, and laughing her head off as he carried her back snugly to the shoemaker. He also befriended Jemmy, the thirteen-year-old who had run away from two apprenticeships that Daphne had managed to arrange for him in the past.

The lad was so much in awe of Max that he agreed to come with them to Worcestershire, where there were any number of openings for him in the many projects her husband had under way.

By teatime, watching the children finally begin to settle into their new home, Max put his arm around Daphne and pressed a kiss to her head. "How could I have failed to understand you?" he whispered as she wiped away a sentimental tear at the sight of her mission accomplished. "To think I gave you sapphires? There are no jewels perfect enough to add one iota to your beauty."

She turned and hugged him tightly. "Thank you — for all of this."

"I was glad to do it." He was silent for a moment, remembering the pain of lack during his own childhood, she suspected. "I think, in all, they're going to do quite well here."

"Yes, indeed. Between Oliver Smith and my stepmother, I sincerely doubt that any detail shall ever fall between the cracks." She tilted her head back and gazed lovingly at him. *"Now,"* she added, "we can go to Worcestershire."

And so they did.

They took the Oxford Road out of London the next day, passed the dreaming spires of the university town, and pressed on westward through Cheltenham, where he pointed out the elegant new terraces with an array of shops as fine as any in London, and the spas like those in Bath, where one could take the medicinal waters.

From there, they proceeded north to the capital of his county. He showed her the medieval grandeur of Worcester Cathedral and the open Market Hall that had sheltered trade of all kinds since the Renaissance.

Daphne was eager to see her new home, however, so they did not linger in the big town, but headed into the surrounding countryside.

October in the Midlands offered green rolling panoramas in the rain-soaked pastures, and tree lines painted with all the patchwork colors of the autumn.

Berries adorned the hedgerows, attracting

large flocks of rooks, while partridges, wood-cocks, and wild turkeys pecked among the stubble corn. The wild fowl, in turn, drew the hunters. They saw the rosy-cheeked huntsmen trudging through the fields with their fowling pieces at the ready and their bird dogs bounding along with them, ready to retrieve any feathered game that the hunters brought down for their supper tables.

Quaint villages along the way were blocked out with rows of stone cottages, roofs either of gray slate tiles or of traditional cozy thatch-ing. Here and there stood a timber-framed house of Tudor origins, tidily maintained since Shakespeare's day.

To while away the time on their long jour-ney, Max discussed with her a little about his investments in the local textile mills, potter-ies producing high-quality ceramics, as well as his shares in a few canals and an ironworks farther up the Gorge. He also owned the land on which a great wool merchant raised his herds of sheep, which in turn produced wool for the textile mills.

Hearing him speak so ably and authorita-tively on matters that other males of the aristocracy would consider hideously beneath them helped her to understand another reason that, perhaps, the ton had viewed him as an outsider.

But for her part, she respected his initiative and was intrigued by his affection for the

ordinary people, whom he called the back-
bone of England. He nodded to some peasants picking apples in a distant orchard as
they drove, others plowing the soil to get the
fields ready for the sowing of the winter
wheat.

The countryside hummed with all the
activities of another year drawing to a close.
Beekeepers taking in the honey, a shepherd
boy minding his flock. A rustic, red corn mill
sat alongside the river, its huge round stone
grinding flour, powered by the busily turning
waterwheel that dipped again and again endlessly into the water's placid but relentless
current.

"We're almost there," Max said, nodding
ahead as the driver turned his traveling
chariot off the country road, through a pair
of giant, wrought-iron gates.

A long drive lined with large, graceful beech
trees led up to a house of giant proportions.

A perfectly uniformed staff streamed out of
the princely entrance of the house and rushed
into formation to welcome their lord and his
new lady home. Footmen in powdered wigs
were clad in dark red livery coats and black
breeches; the maids wore black dresses with
neat white aprons and caps.

When the chariot halted, Max handed her
down and presented her with her new home.
He announced her to the staff, introduced a
few key members, and then led her into the

black and white marble entrance hall.

It was mainly white, with occasional black diamonds in the floor and large black greenery urns, a stunning formal contrast of creamy walls with scalloped niche alcoves, each housing a life-sized statue of black bronze.

The dazzling entrance hall set the tone for the whole house, she soon found out: painted ceilings, colorful patterned rugs, fine furniture, and porcelain on display. She saw the same Maltese white cross displayed in the family chapel, along with the ceremonial shield and helm of the first Baron Rotherstone, whose broadsword was on display in the Town house.

Then Max led her out onto the terrace that overlooked the extraordinary formal gardens. The sweeping expanses and precise lines of the exquisitely manicured formal gardens awed her. Conical topiaries flanked the graveled walks. Triangular parterres were packed with colorful masses of autumn marigolds and phloxes, Michaelmas daisies and China asters.

Beyond that lay a sprawling park bounded, in turn, by woodlands crisscrossed, he said, with pleasant walking paths.

Max stood with her and explained that it was a working estate with three villages, twelve farms, two churches, three schools, two pubs each brewing its own varieties of celebrated ale, and one market. The dowager cottage, he added, had been converted into a pension house for wounded veterans returning from the war against Napoleon.

The crops had been harvested, but the pastures were filled with the estate's prize cattle, plump sheep, and the dozens of horses that populated the Rotherstone stables. He explained that he fostered friendly competition between his farms to produce the best livestock.

The whole estate, she thought, was a gleaming jewel of excellence in the English countryside.

The fact that Max had been absent so much of the time made it even more remarkable how well everything ran, from his lands, to his investments, to casting his absentee votes in the House of Lords even while he was off traveling the Continent, expanding his business ventures and collecting works of art.

At least now it made sense to her how he had prepared his so-called bride list. It seemed nothing was lost on the man. No detail was too small to escape his notice.

She was beginning to think this new husband of hers was altogether remarkable. But in light of all this, the one thing that made less and less sense to her was his wicked reputation. None of this fit with the usual devil-may-care neglect of a libertine.

They went back inside, and she walked around agog at all she saw. She could not have imagined it, and even now that she was looking at the Rotherstone holdings, it had never sunk into her brain before now they would be like rulers of a tiny kingdom, or that she would be living almost like a princess, just as Papa had claimed when he had first unveiled the arranged match.

In the dining room, Max showed her the formal chimneypiece with a bare spot above the mantel that awaited, he declared, *her* official portrait.

"My picture, there? But, my lord, any guests we have will think me terribly immodest."

"No, they will think you terribly beautiful, and me, rightfully proud to have snared such a prize. Come."

As their tour of the house continued, they came to the drawing room that had a gleaming pianoforte in front of a bank of windows overlooking a beautiful farm view of the horses in the meadows. Daphne gazed wistfully at the graceful instrument.

"Another pianoforte," she remarked. She had seen one in the morning room as well.

"I told you, I'm an avid listener." Max gestured to it. "Why don't you give it a try?"

"But I don't play."

"That's not what your father told me." He cast her a knowing smile and walked away.

"Let me show you the upper floors."

"I am certain I shall get lost in here," she remarked, her head spinning after the dizzying ascent up the cantilevered staircase that seemed to float, weightless, in the air. "How many bedrooms does the house have?"

"Thirty bedchambers, my lady," said the taciturn head butler, Mr. Chatters.

She flicked a devilish look in her husband's direction, and whispered to him, "That should keep us busy for a while."

"You haven't even seen the gardens yet," he answered just as softly, a lecherous gleam in his eyes.

"Are you sure no one can see us?" she panted a while later as their garden stroll took a naughty detour.

"They can't, nor would they dare to try."

With an admitted ulterior motive, Max had brought her to the far end of the pleasure grounds, into a garden room bounded on all sides by ten-foot boxwoods, and shaded by an ornamental pear tree.

The main attraction of the private garden room was the low-walled goldfish pond with its little center fountain.

When she bent forward to peer down at the well-fed koi swimming about beneath the lily pads that floated on the surface, Max had eyed the beckoning curve of her derriere and found his lovely bride beyond tempting.

He had laid his coat down on the ground for her to kneel on; she had braced her hands against the sun-warmed stone wall around the fountain as he had lowered himself onto his knees behind her.

"I want you . . . just like this." He breathed his words softly in her ear. "I want to make love to you with the sunshine on your face. Your body one with mine."

Drowning deliciously in the golden silk of her hair, he lifted her skirts and took her from behind. Facing forward straddling his lap, she moved with him, enjoying the ride as he took her with a leisured thoroughness. His hands on her waist guided her motions. With a honeyed moan, she rested her head back against his shoulder, draping her arm languidly around his neck.

High above them, a hawk circled in the blue sky.

Max nibbled her earlobe, but as she let him have his way with her, he found himself growing ever more crazed with his passion for her.

His hands ran up and down her body through her clothing. Needing to feel her skin, he reached under her skirts and grasped the creamy thighs draped over his, her lithe muscles working as she balanced on her knees, her hips lifting up and down, riding him into a lather.

He uttered an epithet of helpless need at the pleasure she stoked in him with her willing innocence. He stroked the fine curls between her legs and caressed her clitoris ever so lightly while he kissed her earlobe. He felt her surging response as his fingers played against her mound, and her wet core clenched him like a sweet, silken glove.

When she moaned aloud with pleasure, he quickly muffled her noise with a hand over her mouth. "Shh," he whispered in her ear.

She obeyed; indeed, the light restraint seemed to arouse her all the more. The sleek, wet grip of her fiery core quivered against his throbbing cock. The lower moan that escaped her from behind his hand begged him for release.

Max gripped her shoulder as he impaled her with slow, relentless strokes, plunging into her, until her soft groans of pleasure frayed the last of his control. He bent her forward, reveling in wild lust as he took her in total, claiming possession. Never had he had it like this before, with this white-hot intensity, never fully sated; the more she surrendered, the deeper he craved, as if she had tapped a well of desperate need in him so long ignored, a thirst that only she could quench. The moment she reached her climax, he surrendered to his own shattering orgasm. It swept through him like a firestorm, each profound pulsation emptying him into her. She was everything.

A fragment of a thought trailed through his

dazzled mind: He wondered with a shiver how Lord Starling had ever survived the death of his first wife. If he had felt anything like the near-obsession Max felt for Daphne, by all rights, he should have lost his mind.

"Oh, Max." She stayed where she was on his lap, just savoring the feel of his still-swollen member inside her. Reaching up, she dragged her hand wearily through his hair in a dreamy caress.

He loved her touch. He turned his face and kissed her wrist as she petted his head. He never wanted to leave her body.

"I can't believe I ever fought you on this," she whispered. "You have every right to say you told me so. You never doubted," she whispered to him, her tone tender and confiding. "It took me longer to see it, but now I know that I was made for you. You were right. A thousand times, you were right from the start and I was wrong."

"My darling Daphne," he answered barely audibly, "I only hope that one day I might actually deserve you."

"Oh!" she murmured, a chiding sound of softhearted protest at his words. But with her very yielding, she conquered yet another hardened fortress in his heretofore impregnable heart.

As October wore on, the weeks that passed were a heady time of making their plans for

451

the future, meeting all the people around her new home, and becoming familiar with all the aspects of her new life as Lady Rotherstone.

There were social calls to be made to her new neighbors, many thank-you notes to be written to all her wedding guests back in Town, and a harvest home to plan for the whole estate, with three days of work off for everyone.

She was soon considered a local authority on all things concerning London and the fashions. Back in Town, she knew, Parliament would have reopened for the autumn session, with the more intimate social occasions of the Little Season under way.

Among the local gentry, meanwhile, there was talk of the annual assizes, the county judges making their rounds to hear any new criminal cases or other disputes that had arisen.

An invitation arrived for a hunt ball in November, but each day proved that her friends' information had indeed been wrong. Country life was not at all dull. All around the estate was a hum of activity, some new thing to see and learn about. The estate's mill was busily churning out several types of flours, grinding down the corn and rye and wheat; the distillery fires crackled away, producing an array of potent libations. Daphne watched the workwomen simmering down the ripened fruits of summer with large amounts of sugar to ferment them — cherries, raspberries, currants. Each was boiled down to a thick, sweet syrup to be used in creating different flavors of brandy and wine.

The kitchen staff was on a mighty campaign of pickling and preserves; the field hands hung the new hay in the barn to dry; the gardeners were trimming back the faded perennials and planting more spring bulbs; the stable managers pampered the broodmares already expecting next spring's foals.

Meanwhile, to Max's amusement but Daphne's dismay, the house was so vast that she kept getting lost, until one day, she walked into the central staircase hall and found a waist-high fingerpost sign that her cheeky husband had made for her. It had thick, painted arrows pointing in various directions: *Drawing Room, Music Room, Dining Room,* and so on.

Numerous servants peeked to see her reaction as she stood laughing at the prank and blushing with embarrassment, calling for her husband, whom she knew at first glance was behind it. "Where is that scoundrel?"

"I solved your little problem for you," he replied as he sauntered out of the library with a grin.

"You!" She chased him, and he ran with a devilish laugh. He hid from her, for, after all, it was an excellent house for playing hide-

and-seek. She stalked him into one of the upstairs bedchambers, and when she finally found him, he seduced her.

It became a bit of a game for them, but there were many other activities afoot. While Max went out for a leisurely bit of shooting, she corresponded with her family, who would be coming to stay with them at Christmas.

She was particularly keen for her two young stepsisters to get a taste of country life.

She wrote to Carissa, too, recounting with some humor the whole process of being measured for her court robes of crimson velvet with miniver trim, as well as for the dainty coronet that was now being made for her, with the silver balls and strawberry leaves of her new rank.

After all, as Max had said, with "Farmer" George in such ill health, likely to pop off at any moment, she would need the full regalia of her new rank for the Regent's coronation, whenever God saw fit to summon their poor mad king to his reward.

Attendance on that day in the proper traditional attire would, of course, be mandatory for the entire aristocracy. Max being Max, he insisted on being prepared well in advance for the inevitable occasion.

He had also made arrangements with the famous portrait artist Sir Thomas Lawrence, who was now scheduled to come early next year and stay with them until he painted her for posterity. When her portrait was done, it would hang above the mantelpiece in the dining room, and in time, she supposed, be added to the gallery of her husband's illustrious family ancestors.

With every day that passed, she felt prouder to have joined his august line. She knew, of course, that his father and grandfather had both been intemperate men with an unhealthy attachment to the cards and the dice.

But whatever people might think of her so-called Demon Marquess back in London, here in the country, Daphne saw all around her, it was a drastically different story.

Perhaps here in the countryside they did not know he was a leading member of the Inferno Club. Or perhaps here he was more at ease and could be himself. All she knew was people for miles around loved him and held her husband in the highest regard.

All of which brought new questions to her mind. The mystery of him only seemed to deepen, and the more she loved him day by day, the more determined she was to eventually solve it.

As October turned to November, she still felt she had not quite figured him out. If she dwelled on it too much, it worried her, in truth.

She knew she had a whole lifetime to grow into a fuller understanding of him. No doubt in a few years' time, they'd be finishing each other's sentences. But for now, as happy as they were together, she felt as if she kept running up against an invisible barrier inside him. As if he was happy to welcome her into his heart — but only up to a point.

She had no idea what lay behind the gates of his hidden self. She only knew she did not like being kept out. It made her all the more uneasy, because she might already be carrying his child; it was too soon to say.

At any rate, having made all their social calls on the surrounding neighbors, it was time to extend the hospitality of their home to the local Quality, in turn. Daphne planned her first dinner party as a married woman, to be held in early December. She began consulting meticulously with the man-chef of the house on their menu before sending out her invitations.

While visiting the chef's domain in the kitchens, she noticed that the whole time they were discussing the best foods in season for the grand event, Wilhelmina and the young chef could not stop staring at each other. She hid her smile. It seemed a bit of an attachment might be forming.

Some mistresses might have been angry, but Daphne was glad. Now that she knew what love was like herself, she wanted everybody to experience it, too, especially a young woman as good-hearted as her loyal maid. The chef seemed like a solid young man, and after all, a woman who married a chef would never starve.

A few days later, when Daphne caught Willie savoring a special little vanilla cake that the handsome young chef had lovingly made just for her, she teased her about it, and Willie shyly confessed to their newly blossoming friendship.

Both twins, in fact, had received a warm welcome at the estate; country folk at heart themselves, they both fit in with ease. Certainly, Daphne had noticed that footman William spent much of his days being followed around by giggling maids.

As for the young orphan boy, Jemmy, he was making new friends and gradually beginning to lose his Bucket Lane attitude.

Daphne had him hard at work with the other servants on the frosty December day of the dinner party.

Several hours before the guests were due to start arriving, she was dashing about the house making sure that all preparations were moving along smoothly. Passing through the entrance hall, she saw their butler paying their country postman and realized the mail had just been delivered. Max had already taken it and was just now opening a letter he had received.

Daphne hurried over to him. "Any last-minute cancellations from our guests?"

"No!" he said cheerfully. "But this arrived

for you from London. Another novel from Miss Portland," he added as he handed her the latest thick letter from Carissa.

Daphne took it with a frisson of happiness, but put it in the pocket of her apron. "I'll save it for later. Too much to do right now."

"Too busy even for me?" he asked in a wicked murmur, leaning closer.

She blushed. "I'm afraid so, Lord Rotherstone." She slid her hand up his shoulder. "You can wait until after the party, can't you?"

"If I must," he purred as he trailed a smoldering stare over her.

"I see you got something from London, too." She stood on her tiptoes, peeking at the letter he had already opened. "Oh, dear. The old fierce Highlander again."

"He's keeping me apprised of any new broodmares of particular quality arriving at Tattersall's," he replied. "I had told him I'm interested in expanding our stock. Man knows his horseflesh."

Glancing at Virgil's short letter, she scanned a terse description of a black Arabian mare with four white feet, costing a full two hundred pounds. She eyed Max dubiously.

"Are you going to buy her?"

"Maybe. I think I will go write back to him and tell him to make an offer on my behalf."

"I see. So, you trust him with your money?" she asked dryly.

"Darling, I would trust him with my life." He bent and kissed her cheek, then marched off across the entrance hall to go and write his answer.

"Maybe when you answer him, you could ask him why he doesn't like me," Daphne remarked as he walked away.

"Doesn't like you?" Max exclaimed, glancing back and pausing at the bottom of the stairs. "Nonsense."

"He glowered at me at our wedding."

He laughed. "That's just his face, Daphne. He couldn't have been happier to see me married off, especially to such a 'fine young filly.' "

She snorted.

He flashed a grin at her, then jogged up the stairs to escape, she suspected, the controlled chaos of the party preparations.

Daphne watched him with a vague uneasiness until he had disappeared into the upper floor. She could not quite put her finger on it, but she had learned to read her husband well enough to detect the subtle change that came over him whenever he received a communiqué from that taciturn old Scot.

Doing her best to shrug off her inexplicable misgivings, she decided to take a moment from her party preparations just to steal a quick peek at her new letter from Carissa.

She still had a hundred things to do to get ready, but both girls missed each other deeply. Daphne felt guilty, as though she had abandoned her, for she knew Carissa was having a hard time of it, left in London to deal with her obnoxious cousins without Daphne as an ally.

While the servants carried more chairs and a large floral arrangement into the dining room, Daphne got out of the way to read her letter, wishing Carissa could have been at the party tonight. It would have made it so much more fun, plus, her friend's presence would have helped to calm her nerves over her first occasion of playing Max's high-ranking hostess. She still sometimes felt that she had no idea of how a marchioness was supposed to act.

At any rate, she vowed to read only the first page of Carissa's letter, but she quickly saw that her friend had written in such a distressed state that she raced through the whole thing. With Daphne gone, Carissa's cousins had begun tormenting her with renewed vigor; worse, Carissa's newfound acquaintance with the scandalous Warrington and Falconridge had given the jealous harpies an easy source of new material. Their taunting and innuendos, Daphne could well imagine, would have jeopardized any girl's reputation.

Dire worry had gripped her by the time she got to the end. At once, she knew that either she had to invite Carissa to come to the estate for a holiday or return to London herself long enough to rescue her friend.

Distracted by her concern over Carissa, she desired a moment in Max's company to soothe her anxiousness and put her mind at ease. Hurrying upstairs to ask what he thought of the situation, quickly giving a few more directions to her staff along the way, she no longer needed the fingerpost sign to find the master suite.

Out of habit, she went in by the second door, which opened into her side of the master suite. The his-and-hers double bed-chambers were connected by a little mirrored passageway with a closet and a hidden jewelry safe on one side, and a decadent Roman-style bath on the other, quite the miracle of modern innovation, with its marble columns framing the large nickel-plated tub, and already heated running water almost constantly available from the spigot.

It was extraordinarily quiet in their joined chambers.

She furrowed her brow and walked toward Max's room, wondering if he had not come up here, after all.

But then all of a sudden, she caught a whiff of what she could have sworn was brimstone, with a hint of vinegar, emanating from his end of their suite.

She paused, grimacing. The harsh, pungent odor made her eyes water. Already reaching her end of the little passageway, she started to ask what he was doing, then saw his reflection in the mirror, and stopped, staring in fleeting confusion.

Without going any farther, she could see him sitting on the edge of the bed, using a tiny eyedropper to place a few drops of some solution on the letter he had received from Virgil.

Daphne went no farther but held her breath, watching silently as Max replaced the eyedropper into a little vial of some solution, which she gathered was the source of that hideous smell. She felt a chilly draft and realized he had opened a window in his bedchamber to help disperse its unpleasant fumes.

Then he blew on the moistened letter, as if to dry the droplets he had placed on the sheet of paper. Her heart began to pound as he reread the letter with a new intensity, as though perceiving information previously hidden. *Invisible ink?* she thought in utter shock.

What on earth is going on?

If this were not astonishing enough, Daphne's eyes widened in deepening incredulity when she saw his hiding place. There was a small decorative niche in the wall by his bed, which usually held a vase. At the moment, it was a gaping hole in the wall.

Satisfied with his letter from London, Max now took it, along with the vial of mysterious liquid, and placed the items inside some sort of hollow hidden inside the wall. Sliding the little curved part of the niche back down, he clicked it into place, put the vase back where it belonged, then went and shut the window. She glimpsed his troubled expression as he passed by her line of sight.

Daphne quickly backed away from the passage between their bedchambers as something warned her not to let him see her there. She was in a state of shock.

What do I do? What on earth is he hiding from me?

With a houseful of guests expected in a few hours and several dozen things still left to do, she realized she did not have the wherewithal to confront him right now. She did not want to start a fight just ahead of the local gentry arriving for her first effort as a married hostess.

She did not want all her neighbors coming in at the tail end of their first marital row, especially one that was sure to be apocalyptic in proportions. She shook her head, trembling with fury as she heard him leave his chamber by the matching door on the other side of the suite.

Leaning against the wall for a moment to try to collect her wits, she felt sick to her stomach to have confirmation of something she had sensed, but could never quite put her finger on — that Max was being less than open with her, as usual.

She felt like such a dupe! Living with him, waking, sleeping, eating, bathing with him, spending day and night together, and it had taken her a blasted month to catch on that there was a whole other side of her husband of which she had no inkling yet.

His betrayal of her trust felt like a stab in her heart. She had given him her all, and in return, he was making a mockery of her faith in him. A tremor of fury and fear rippled through her. What sort of dark business was he up to that he had to be so secretive? It must be bad — why else would he choose to conceal it?

Panic threatened to rise with her sudden sense of having no control whatsoever over her life, indeed, quite the opposite, of being entirely under *his* control, but she tamped it down, clinging to the strength that anger gave her instead.

A horse at bloody Tattersall's? God, she wanted to hit him, shake that air of cool control right out of him, that liar. She looked around the corner of the passageway, wondering if she should go in there at once, rip open that hiding place, and find out what was going on.

She paused, listening as hard as she could for any sound of him returning. Instead, she did hear someone coming, but it couldn't be Max. The footsteps were too light and swift.

Just then, there was a light knock at her bed-chamber door, which already stood ajar.

"Yes?" she forced out.

A maid peeked in. "My lady, Chef Joseph asked if you would like to come down and give your opinion on the almond soup."

God, she could barely force herself to focus on the dinner party preparations now, but somehow, she managed a nod. Pushing away from the wall, she put Carissa's letter back in her pocket and followed the maid back down to the kitchens, brooding on her next move all the way.

It might be nothing, she tried to tell herself. As he was her lord and husband, was it not his male prerogative to withhold important information that was not considered part of a woman's domain?

But everything in her recoiled from her attempt to wave it off. She knew in her bones it was something big, and probably something deeply wicked, considering the lengths he had gone to, to keep her in the dark.

Resentment burned through her, all the sharper when she recalled how thoroughly he had investigated *her* before deciding to pursue her. To be sure, he had made a point of finding out everything he possibly could about her before deciding if she was right for him. In return, he had given her secrecy and deception. She shook her head to herself.

You lying, two-faced fiend.

Well, obviously, there was no point in confronting Max with his lies until she could find out for herself what exactly he was hiding. She couldn't believe he had done this to her, but why waste her breath asking for answers or demanding explanations?

Slick as he was, the Demon Marquess would merely lie again unless she had hard evidence to put in front of him. That smooth devil could talk his way out of anything. But this time, he had pushed her too far.

She was growing wise to him. If he liked underhanded dealings, he would get just that.

It was far more intelligent, she decided, to wait for an opportune moment to look inside that little hiding place herself. She dreaded to ponder what she might find, but for now, she decided not to breathe a word or show any sign that she had finally caught on until she got a chance to see for herself exactly what was going on.

CHAPTER 17

Virgil had been scant on details, but apparently there had been another sighting of Drake.

As his team's Link, Max had received fresh orders to get to the Westwood estate without delay and finesse whatever information he could out of Lady Westwood, Drake's dear old mama.

His particular goal was to find out if the countess had received any communication from her supposedly dead son. It was feasible, after all, that Drake would want to spare his heartbroken mother any further mourning, considering he was alive.

Beyond that, Max knew very little. He would simply have to see what he might find when he got there. It wasn't more than a three-hour drive in the direction of London.

In the meanwhile, he would have to come up with some credible story to give his wife to explain his upcoming departure. All through their dinner party, Max let his calculating mind brew on how to proceed, even as he played the gracious host.

Being rather skilled at compartmentalizing different areas of his life, he was able to put tomorrow's mission aside for the moment — just as he had put aside his endless sense of guilt over lying to his beloved since their wedding day. He ignored it all with a will, focusing his attention on the dinner party. He knew how much a success tonight meant to Daphne.

So far, it was all going smoothly.

As for Lady Rotherstone, Max thought she looked more gorgeous than ever tonight. He had never seen her wear red before, and the effect was stunning.

Now that she was a married woman, she seemed to enjoy experimenting with the bold colors that were generally considered inappropriate for debutantes.

Clad in a rose-red gown of taffeta with simple lines and short puffed sleeves, she wore her bright blond hair pinned up in a sleek and elegant coif, her frosty beauty at odds with her fiery gown.

She had a pearl choker around her neck and a rare touch of rouge on her lips as if to keep her pale complexion from being overwhelmed by the crimson she wore.

It was a dramatic and sophisticated look, and it made him want her in a new and urgent way. Max had thought her beautiful before, of course, wholesome and innocent, with her sunshine loveliness, but she seemed different tonight, like a young woman fully coming into her own as she adjusted to her new place in the world as his marchioness.

She displayed an expert charm with their guests, but showed a little less of her usual endearing warmth, in favor of a touch more confident authority.

The room resounded with conversation and laughter, and glowed with the brilliance of the candelabras. Everyone seemed to be enjoying themselves, and in all, Max thought she had done a magnificent job with every detail of their dinner party.

The lavish courses were perfection, from the almond soup, pigeon pie, broiled salmon, leg of lamb, and plum pudding, just to name a few, to the roasted lobsters, oyster loafs, savory pheasant, and stewed pears.

The sweet course was delightful, especially the fanciful "hedgehog" on display in the middle of the table, with its blanched almond bristles. The carefully sculpted animal creation was spun from a concoction of egg whites, sugar, butter, and cream, Daphne explained to them all.

Its eyes and nose were made from little pieces of black licorice, and she thought their Chef Joseph a genius for his art. The guests regretted cutting into the hedgehog in order to eat it, but eagerness to taste it outweighed their guilt at destroying it, and sure enough, it turned out to be delicious.

Meanwhile, a colorful array of fruits and nuts, apricot puffs, biscuits, custards, and three different types of cheese-cakes were passed round. At last, the ladies repaired to the drawing room for tea while the men remained at table to enjoy their port and sherry.

Max, however, was eager to rejoin Daphne. Separated by their respective places at the head and foot of a dining table that seemed nearly as long as a cricket pitch, he was missing his lady's company and feeling deprived of her conversation.

He refused to dwell too much on his guilt over the latest lie he'd have to tell her tomorrow. He knew his duty for the Order, and the trip would not take long.

He had to admit he had still not quite figured out how to handle the complexities of his double life from an emotional standpoint. His blood ran cold whenever he tried to imagine how Daphne would react if she were to hear the truth of his life story at this late date.

But even if Virgil would have permitted it, how could he come out with such revelations now, when he was already in it so deeply with her? He had only just barely convinced her to marry him in the first place.

If he told her the truth, she might regret

ever agreeing to this, and then he risked losing her love. And if that happened, obviously, he would die. Or at least, to be sure, he would not want to live.

It was better, cleaner all around if she never knew, he thought, but the inner battle was tearing him apart.

He did his best to put the whole thing out of his mind. It was too late now to start telling her what he should have said months ago, but was neither then nor now at liberty to share.

With a deepening uneasiness gnawing at him, he told himself he would just have to be careful to keep the two main strands of his life from becoming tangled.

He could do this. He had lived this way for years, had he not? An expert liar, he had never had any trouble separating the truth of his inner self as an agent of the Order from his external mask as the drunken Grand Tourist.

Yet for the first time in his career, Max found himself beginning to resent his duty. Deeply.

It wasn't fair to have to live this way. And worse, in his gut, he was beginning to fear that he could be either a true husband or a solid agent, but not both.

He could not see himself ever shirking his duty for the Order. It was too deeply ingrained in him. Which meant that it was only a matter of time before his marriage, the newer claim on him, ran into serious trouble.

Maybe he shouldn't have hounded her so relentlessly to marry him, he thought. Maybe he should've spared her all this and chosen some other woman he could not love. Then again, he could not imagine his life without his darling Daphne. She was the most important person in the world to him. God, he would drive himself mad with all this. Best not to dwell on it. He had no choice but to lie, and besides, he did not want her dragged into all the Order's intrigue.

With a slight prompting, at last he managed to shepherd his male guests into the drawing room to rejoin their ladies. Before long, the whole company removed into the music room, where the ladies each began to entertain them, in turn, with their various musical talents.

Recalling what his father-in-law had told him about Daphne's love of playing the pianoforte with her mother years ago, he went out on a limb to suggest in front of all their guests that she take a turn and play for them.

She stared at him for a long moment, and then bowed her head like the model wife. "As you wish, my lord," she murmured, but as she brushed past him on her way to the instrument, he thought he detected a hint of frost in her blue eyes.

She opened the hinged lid of the piano seat

and took out some printed music, which she duly leaned above the keyboard. Taking her place at the pianoforte, she tentatively touched a few keys, as though becoming re-acquainted with a long-lost friend.

With a deep breath, she began to play.

It was a simple, soulful piece full of expression; Max recognized it as a pianoforte arrangement of a famous piece by Albinoni.

The haunting adagio filled the chamber with its sorrowful beauty, slow, but building in passion to a vaguely ominous crescendo.

Max furrowed his brow. What a bizarre choice for a dinner party, he mused. Maybe it was the only piece she knew. But, surely, after all the pains she had taken to create a pleasant atmosphere for their guests, this music changed the mood, to say the least.

It did not take Max long to realize this could be some sort of message. To him.

He stared at his wife as she played, feeling as though, in a way, he was seeing her for the first time.

Not in a thousand years could he have guessed at the depth of the feeling bottled up inside her. And it began to dawn on him that for all his careful research beforehand, there were perhaps still parts of Daphne he did not know.

Either he had finally asked the right question by requesting that she play, or she was merely ready now to share this part of herself, for reasons of her own.

The adagio and her unimagined passion in the playing left them all agog. After about eight minutes, her performance came to its resonating end.

The guests were silent for a few seconds, carried away in reverie, then Max began applauding for her as he held her in his stare, and everyone else followed suit.

"Oh, I say!"

"Quite affecting," the guests exclaimed.

With her music ended, she looked up slowly from the piano as though she had just come through an ordeal. She met Max's gaze, and as the others continued to applaud and praise her unheralded talent, he walked over to her, offering his hand to help her rise.

On one hand, he was bursting with husbandly pride in her talent, but on the other, he was wondering what the hell was going on.

"You are full of surprises, my lady," he murmured as he assisted her up from the piano seat. "Any other secrets I should know about?"

"Not from me, my lord. And you?" She did not wait for his answer, but released his hand and glided away, returning to her guests like the perfect hostess.

Max was flummoxed.

It was curious that he could read strangers, but only now began to see that his beloved was just a few degrees shy of ignoring him.

Had he done something wrong? Perhaps she was merely concentrating on their guests. He had no doubt this night had been a nerve-racking experience for her. He knew it had been weeks in preparation.

Still, the revelation of her soulful performance put him in mind of one of the trap-doors inside Dante House — the turning bookcase in the drawing room, which could only be opened by playing a precise series of notes on the dusty old harpsichord in the middle of the room.

She stood a few feet away charming the local vicar and his wife. Max studied her with renewed fascination, though perhaps he should have been worried. All he knew was that the longer she kept him at arm's length, the more everything in him clamored for her.

She seemed to have erected some kind of invisible barrier between them, and though Max knew he had no room whatsoever to complain, he was not at all used to this, and did not like it.

For the briefest instant, he wondered if there was any chance she had seen something she ought not to see. Might she have stumbled across some stray detail of his role in the Order?

Oh, but that was impossible. He knew he had grown very comfortable with her, true, which Virgil had warned him to be wary of, but he was too experienced an agent to have done something careless.

He could not imagine that he had blown his cover with his own wife. It had to be something else. Whatever the cause of her almost imperceptible alteration in her demeanor, he wanted his usual Daphne back.

Immediately.

"Your father told me you used to love music, but I had no idea you could play so beautifully," he said when they were in their room several hours later, taking off their formal clothes after the last guests had gone.

It was two hours after midnight.

"I am glad I can still surprise you, my lord." She was sitting at her vanity, drawing off her long satin gloves, while he walked in from his adjoining chamber, untying his cravat.

Tugging it loose, he went over to her side and gazed down at her for a moment. "Daphne, are you all right?"

"Yes, why?"

"You seem . . . distracted," he said warily as he moved behind her and took over the task of helping her unlatch the clasp of her necklace.

She dropped her gaze, holding up her hair so it would not catch on the strand of pearls. Max studied her in the mirror while he waited for her answer.

"Actually," she said at length, "I'm worried about Carissa."

"Carissa?" He frowned as he put the unfastened necklace in her hand. He had forgotten about her friend's letter. "Why? Is something wrong?"

"Her cousins are being unkind again. I am thinking of going to London to give her some moral support. You wouldn't mind, would you, darling?"

Max thought he detected a sharp undertone in her cool-toned question. "It's rather late in the year for London. Why not just invite her here?"

"I can go to London if I want to. It's not as though I am your prisoner here, am I?" She sent him an unflappable smile, but he read a different story in her blue eyes.

He gave her a chiding frown, concealing his deepening awareness of her tension. "Of course you're not my prisoner, darling. Are you getting bored of country life? Or maybe you're just getting bored of me."

She eyed him askance, then set her earrings aside with a shrug. "Now that the dinner party's done, I don't know what I shall do with myself."

Behind her, Max leaned forward, bracing his hands on either side of her against her cherrywood vanity. "If you really want to go back to Town to see your friends, my love, I will take you there myself, if that would make you happy. However, you'll have to wait a few days until I get back."

"From where?" She looked at him in surprise in the mirror, clearly unsatisfied with his answer.

"I have to go up the Gorge to pay a visit to the ironworks. I think I told you I own a controlling share of the company."

"Controlling, yes," she murmured.

"Now that the war is over, there's not much call for cannons. The men who run the factory want to show me some ideas for what can be manufactured there instead."

"I see."

"It won't take more than a couple of days. I'll be there and back before you even miss me. When I return, then we can go to London."

She stared at him in the reflection. "Why don't I come with you?"

"To an ironworks? And you think you're bored here?"

"I didn't say that I was bored."

He held his easy smile in place by dint of will. "You will be if you come with me." He backed away and began unbuttoning his waistcoat.

"I don't think so. I've never seen an iron factory."

"It is a dangerous place, Daphne, full of roaring fires and noxious fumes. If you are with child, especially, it's best that you not breathe that tainted air."

She dropped her gaze once more, as though

she saw no point in even arguing with him. He was relieved, because of course he had no plans of visiting the ironworks.

"Very well, my lord. If that is your will."

"Do you know what I think?" he murmured, returning to her after a moment. "I think you have been putting too much pressure on yourself of late. It's over now." He kissed her head. "You can finally relax. You did splendidly. A man couldn't ask for a better wife. Even if he were to order her out of a catalogue."

She succumbed to a reluctant trace of a smile.

It seemed to warm the room — and Max's heart.

"There she is," he whispered. "I know how to cheer you up. Shall I draw us both a nice hot bath?"

She sighed and looked away. "I don't know."

"Maybe not a bath, then. I think I know what you need." He slipped his finger into the back of her gown, sliding it along her shoulder blade. "A good, thorough loving."

Her blue eyes flicked to his in the mirror as he began to rub her lovely white shoulders, bared for his touch by the sweeping neckline of her gown.

The ironworks, eh? Daphne had her doubts, to say the least. The man had no idea that she despised him at the moment. Yet, it was the strangest thing. For, even so, his touch still aroused her instantly.

Oh, the devil. He had always had a talent for stirring her blood, even when she knew she should not want him. She refused to let the sigh that rose escape her when he bent and kissed her neck, ever so enticingly.

She almost offered up some dreary excuse — that she was too tired or she had a headache — but then she suddenly recalled how deeply her husband always slept after they made love.

What a wicked notion came into her mind just then. *Dared she?* Daphne went very still. As his slow, nibbling kisses moved to her earlobe, she thought abruptly of their battle over the sapphire necklace several weeks ago, and the extreme techniques he had employed to gain — he thought — her compliance.

That day he had shown up at her father's house, he had overwhelmed her in the parlor, refusing to go away until he had conquered her senses in a flood of mindless pleasure.

Well, my darling, two can play that game. She closed her eyes, enjoying his sensual kisses. So far tonight, she had taken great satisfaction in knowing she had thrown her lord off balance with her music.

She had taken herself off guard, as well, but if he was going to throw down the gauntlet to her like that in front of their guests, she was not about to answer like a coward.

Seeing him look so surprised and slightly uneasy with her stormy playing had been a marvelous victory, well worth the risk she had taken of making a fool of herself, playing for guests when she was years out of practice. But it had gone well.

Indeed, what an exquisite joy it was to know that, for once, she had rattled his supreme self-control.

Maybe she should continue in that vein, she mused, for his suave kisses traveling down her nape told her in no uncertain terms that her husband was still under the false impression that he was the one in control here, as usual.

We'll see.

It was time to turn the tables on the Demon Marquess, and beat him at his own game.

"I want you," he whispered, raising goose bumps of thrill on her skin.

She gave him a sultry smile in the mirror and said, "I want you, too."

When Daphne rose and turned to him, the devilish gleam in her blue eyes made Max wonder if she was spending too much time with him. Maybe he was rather a bad influence on her, he mused as Lady Rotherstone laid her hand on his chest and began backing him toward the armchair.

He went willingly; holding his stare, she pushed him down into it.

Max awaited her pleasure, his heart pounding. Her unusual mood added to the excitement, for him. She was unpredictable tonight, as though they were tapping into some new side of Daphne he had not been privy to before.

Maybe it had something to do with her playing the music, but clearly something had unleashed the woman's passion to a degree he had not seen before.

With that, she opened the placket of his trousers and lowered herself to her knees. She took him in hand and stroked him urgently, but Max was breathless when she lowered her head and took him into her mouth. Her moist, rouged lips cradled his cock; her tongue laved his length and played against his tip.

The restrained modest frill on the cuff of his shirtsleeve trailed over her golden hair as he petted her head, watching avidly. He caressed the beautiful face making love to his member.

After a moment, quite transported, he laid his head back with an anguished groan of pleasure, relishing her ministrations. With each determined squeeze of her hand and silken stroke of her mouth, she drove him ever closer to the edge. His legs tensed. When he was on the brink of climax, she halted, cruelly.

She looked up with wet lips and glittering

eyes. "Get in my bed," she whispered. "Take off your clothes."

He gave her a hazy-eyed stare, but he liked these orders very much. True, they shocked him a bit coming from his good lady wife. Still, what sane man would question it?

He smiled warily at her and did as he was told.

Maybe she finally felt safe enough to flex her sexual power with him; of course, if Max did not know better, he would have guessed she was as angry as hell about something. But then again, if she was angry, why was she all over him this way? She was not a calculating female.

Women.

He did not want to question it. He liked this hot intensity from her. As much as he loved his darling Daphne, this harder, more intoxicating version of her seemed to answer something deep within his soul. A need he had never shared because he just assumed a man couldn't ask that sort of thing from his wife.

From a mistress, maybe. But Max did not want anyone else ever again.

She sat back and watched him strip off his clothes and walk, buck naked, to her bed. As he lay back, she rose and came toward him, idly taking the ivory combs out of her hair, loosely shaking out her golden tresses. She did not remove her gown, but climbed onto the bed in a delicate rustle of taffeta. The fire's glow slid over the rich fabric with a fluid sheen, like dancing fire.

"Tonight," she said as she moved toward him on the mattress on all fours, "I'm going to use you for my pleasure, Rotherstone. I just thought you should know."

"Go right ahead." As naked as the day he was born, he lay back on his elbows in a pose of invitation, his proud erection standing up tall in full salute at the lady's approach. He was quite ready and willing to be used as she saw fit.

She fluffed her skirts across his waiting body as she moved her thigh across his hips and straddled him.

God, in that red dress, she looked like one of Satan's minions, expert in seduction. Perhaps she had come to enslave him, Max thought. This was one temptation against which he knew he did not stand a chance.

He was trembling with anticipation for her as she leaned down slowly to kiss him. Reaching down between their bodies, she took his cock in hand, and with a frank lust equal to his own, guided him into her body, letting him stroke the source of her craving with the part of him made to satisfy it.

She moaned as his extraordinary size tonight proved just how much he liked this brazen side of her.

Once she had him deep inside her, she sat

up and began to ride him. Watching the fierce pleasure on her face, Max wondered how he was going to last, especially after her attentions in the chair.

She rode him faster, baring her teeth, tossing her head and taking him in earnest now, just as she said she would. Max clutched her thighs; she braced her hands on his ribs, arching her back, having her way with him completely.

Overwhelmed with a crazed, sudden desperation for her breasts, he leaned up and fumbled with her bodice, got angry at it two seconds later, and tore the fabric open with a growl. He ripped away her stays, and as her plump young breasts bounced out to greet him, he feasted on her nipples like a starved man. *"Mmm."*

She went still, reveling in his hands and his mouth all over her creamy bosoms. She clutched his head against her body, her erect nipples straining for his tongue.

Quavering groans escaped her, pure pleasure as he raked the taut bud gently with his teeth. "Oh, Max." She pressed him back down onto the bed a moment later with a stare full of wild hunger.

And she then proceeded to drive him completely out of his mind, touching herself as she resumed his helpless ravishment. Max could feel his control coming apart at the seams like a ship rocked on stormy seas. She was kissing, teething his stubbly jaw with a feminine snarl of pleasure.

No longer able to resist her, Max let out a low shout and lost control. The ferocity of her passion swept over him as she joined him in the extreme hinterlands of sweaty, heaving pleasure. Their bodies remained joined as she clasped him between her silken legs, milking him for every last ounce of satisfaction.

For a long moment, Max was incapable of speech.

He could not believe his little bride possessed such power, but she had fucked him into a blissful stupor. Now he was enervated, completely at her mercy, in her thrall.

She separated their bodies gingerly and left the bed. She went, he supposed, to change out of her ruined dress. He pulled the coverlet over his body, feeling almost too lazy to move; he watched her for a moment with a heavy-lidded gaze, a drugged smile on his lips as she let fall her ruined gown and crossed naked to the closet to get her banyan robe.

But his sweet Demon Marchioness had her way with him tonight. Before long, he had fallen into a spent and dreamless sleep.

Daphne stared at him for a moment longer while he slept. God, he was beautiful.

The bastard.

She had never seduced anyone before, but she thought it had gone well. She had experienced a wild, savage lust tonight, the likes of which she had never known.

Perhaps she felt a little dirty for what she had done, but she did not regret it. Indeed, she had enjoyed herself immensely, as had he, and after all, one had to fight fire with fire.

He would sleep now, deeply, just as he always did after they made love. This, in turn, would give her a brief window of opportunity to find out what her man was hiding.

Regrettable, she thought, that she had to resort to this. Maybe it wasn't much of a war if he didn't even realize they were fighting. But when dealing with such a powerful foe as the Marquess of Rotherstone, she had to take whatever advantage she could steal.

Anyway, if he did not like what she had done tonight, he only had himself to thank. He was the one who had given her the idea.

Completely satisfied and a trifle sore between her legs, she waited one more moment until she was sure he was fast asleep, then she left her room silently, still dressed in her blue banyan robe. Carrying a single candle in a pewter holder, she crept down the dark passageway and into Max's chamber.

She sincerely doubted there was any urgent business at the ironworks, so now he had her wondering what else he might have lied about. The cutpurse at their wedding? The true reason for the enmity between him and the Carew brothers? The Inferno Club? His travels?

His love for her?

Tears filled her eyes at this last, new area of doubt, but she shook her head. Whatever lies he had told, she could not believe he did not care for her.

On the other hand, if he returned her feelings as he claimed, then how could he deceive her?

If he really loved her, why wouldn't he tell her the truth? Was it that awful?

She barely dared imagine what she'd find as she closed his chamber door behind her with the smallest sound, and braced herself to face whatever secrets he was hiding.

Maybe she'd regret this once she learned the truth, but she had to find out what was going on.

Her mind raced with dread at what she might discover. Nefarious business dealings? An illegitimate child hidden away somewhere? Some dark personal revenge?

At least she was fairly confident it had nothing to do with any other woman, for why, then, would Virgil be involved? But if she was wrong — if he was keeping a mistress somewhere — Daphne vowed there would be hell to pay.

She crossed his dark chamber to the little niche with the vase displayed. She moved the vase away and set it on his bed. Then she held her candle closer and felt around inside the niche. She tried to push the curved back of it upward, the way she had seen it open earlier, but she could not get it to budge.

After a moment, she recalled the spring-loaded mechanism of the equally deceptive jewelry safe built seamlessly into the closet. She gave the alcove a small, sudden shove with her fingertips, and drew in her breath at the sound of a small click inside the wall.

It worked. Now she found she was able to slide the back of the alcove upward, so the whole back rolled up into the hollow part of the wall. *Ingenious,* she thought.

With the back of the alcove out of the way, the small shelf part where the vase had stood could be pulled out like a drawer.

Her heart pounding, she glanced over her shoulder to make sure the small noises she had made had not disturbed him. From the other chamber, all was still.

Fear pulsed through her now that the moment of truth was at hand. Shoring up her courage, she thrust her hand into the small, dark hiding place in bold determination to see what she would see.

She pulled out the vial of solution that had stunk up the room earlier. She put it aside and kept it away from the candle, aware it might be flammable. A second brave reach into the dark hole produced a little inkpot, but why hide ink? she thought. Ah, unless it was the type used for invisible writing.

Next she pulled out a small pistol. Well, that was self-explanatory, though she was surprised he kept a loaded weapon in his bedroom. She put it aside with a worried look.

Her next reach into the little cubbyhole yielded a strange pasteboard disk about the size of her hand. It had block letters all around the edges, a second pasteboard circle fixed atop the first by a single brass tack.

She examined it and found that the top disk could be turned, so that the letters lined up in any combination. She had no idea what it was. Reaching into the hiding place again, she felt a small metal object.

When she brought it forth into the candle-light, it proved to be a man's ring wrought of chunky gold. She held the ring up closer to the candle to examine the image it bore. Oh, this was too bizarre.

The design on the seal of the ring matched the white Maltese cross that she had seen in his ancestors' portraits, and which was hanging in their family chapel.

God, what have I got myself into? There were still no clear answers. All she had at this point was the crushing confirmation of her worst fears, that he was lying to her. She did not understand. If you loved someone, if you had any respect for them at all, you did not deal them false.

Brushing away a tear, she reached one last time into the now almost empty hiding place; finally, on the bottom, she felt paper. Drymouthed with uneasiness, she slowly took out Virgil's letter.

The paper was stiff and still stank faintly from the now-dried solution Max had applied to it earlier today. She unfolded the single crease with the hairs on the back of her neck standing on end.

The white space below Virgil's short description of the black Arabian mare for sale at Tattersall's was now filled in with a set of instructions for her husband.

She stared in shocked confusion at the few short lines.

First: Who did this Highlander think he was, to be giving orders to a more powerful and higher-ranking peer like Max?

Second: Who was Drake?

And third and most importantly: What did they want with dear old Lady Westwood?

As active as she had always been in Society, Daphne was well acquainted with the widowed countess, a dear, sad, fluttery old thing, the helpless damsel type.

They belonged to the same church, and Daphne had seen her there each week for years, all dressed in her widow's black. She had always thought Lady Westwood rather an odd duck; she always seemed to be a nervous wreck, and also slightly paranoid. *Probably how I am going to end up, too, if I have to endure a lifetime of these intrigues.*

None of it made any sense. Her first reaction was confusion, but glancing toward her chamber where he slept on peacefully, she felt her anger returning with a vengeance.

Who was he? What did it mean? Did she even know him at all?

Turning her attention once more to the letter, she had half a mind to go and wake the blackguard up and demand that he tell her what was really going on.

But how naïve could she be? He would only lie again. If he had taken such pains to conceal this mystery from her, what made her think that now he would magically oblige her and simply start explaining?

No, she realized. He was going to have to be forced into it. She shook her head in seething anger, but she already knew what she was going to do. It seemed it was *her* turn now to investigate him, just as he had done to her for several weeks before they had even met.

The sense of burning betrayal at his secrecy made her soul ache, but nothing would stop her now from finding out exactly who he was, this man she had married, and what sort of mischief he was up to.

She saw no other choice, because this was not the marriage that she had agreed to. In the hayloft of the Three Swans Inn, she had asked Max to be open with her, and had taken him at his word when he said he would. Yet despite his promise, he had persisted in deception.

He had broken the terms of the understanding they had reached, never mind that she had finally accepted his offer of marriage precisely *because* she had thought they would be on equal terms.

This wasn't equal. He had turned her into a patsy.

All this time, while she had been holding him in the very center of her heart, giving him all the love she had to give and holding nothing back, he had been carefully concealing himself from her. As usual.

God, she felt so stupid. For a few moments, she struggled against tears of hurt and dread.

All she knew was that she was done listening to his lies. She narrowed her eyes in rage. Since it was clear he wasn't going to tell her the truth, she had no choice but to investigate him for herself. *Let's see how* you *like it.*

She threw Virgil's letter onto his bed and stalked off to her closet to get dressed. It would be light in a few hours. *You want to play games with me, husband? Very well.*

I'm not the pretty-headed idiot you take me for.

Max awoke later than usual the next morning with a stretch and a yawn and a feeling of pure, well-serviced bliss lingering in his body.

His lovely seductress was already awake, apparently, going about her day. He was in bed alone, and judging by the light, he guessed it was about nine o'clock. He wanted breakfast, but he lingered in contentment, hoping that any moment, he would see her smiling face coming in to greet him.

Surely after a night like that she would have slept off her strange mood and returned to her usual amiability, back to her adorable self.

"Daph?" Maybe she was bathing in the tub between their rooms or in the closet picking out her clothes. "Sweet, are you here?"

No answer.

Max sighed, dragged his hand through his hair, and decided to go down to breakfast. She was probably already there, though he did not like this business of waking up alone.

He had grown used to sleeping with her in his arms, and it was very unusual for her to slip out without waking him.

He found it odd.

With a wry glance at his clothes strewn around her chamber, not to mention her red taffeta gown lying in a heap where she had discarded it, he walked naked from her bed into the mirrored passageway that joined their chambers, eyed his scruffy jaw in need of a shave, scratched his chest; he glanced into the bathing room, and then the closet, making sure she was not there.

When he proceeded on into his chamber,

however, he suddenly froze in horror at the threshold of the room.

What he saw stopped his heart for a second, knocked the air out of his lungs.

All of his spy-related items from his secret hiding place were strewn across his bed. The vase was cast aside; the alcove niche stood open, exposed for all the world to see.

With his heart in his throat, he turned and saw the mirror over his dressing table. Through the reflection of his own stunned, ashen face, he read the one-word message that she had written there for him in angry red rouge.

LIAR.

CHAPTER 18

"It is so kind of you to call on me, Miss Starling — pardon — I mean, Lady Rotherstone," the frail old Countess of Westwood corrected herself with a fond smile.

Daphne sat with her in her stately drawing room, waiting for the servant to bring the tea. "Well, you know, I was passing by and admiring the house from afar, and when one of your local peasants told me it was Westwood Manor, I could not pass up the chance to come and pay my respects."

"Such a thoughtful gel."

"It really is a beautiful home. Thank you for showing it to me," she offered. "The grounds are lovely, too."

"Rather stark now, with all the leaves fallen," the old woman conceded with a sigh as she gazed out the window overlooking the terrace. "Oh, I was going to ask you — how is your dear great-aunt Anselm these days?"

Daphne smiled and began chatting warmly about the latest news from the Dowager

Dragon, but her thoughts strayed back to Max. She was keeping one eye on the mantel clock.

Though she had a comfortable lead on him, she had no doubt he'd be arriving soon, and he was not going to be happy. She could not wait to see his face when he arrived and saw that for once, she had outfoxed him.

Oh, she was going to relish his wrath.

At least this time she had not dragged the two Willies into her mischief. Now that Max was technically their employer, she did not want to risk him giving them the sack just to punish her for running off again.

At the carriage house at their estate, she had discovered her husband owned a high-perch phaeton similar to Jono's. Since she had gained a good deal of experience driving this type of vehicle, she had asked the grooms to ready it for her, and had driven off "to take the morning air," leaving no one on the staff with any real idea of where she was going. Her husband, she trusted, was canny enough to figure it out for himself.

At any rate, the crisp, late-autumn day was perfect for a country drive; she had set out knowing the general route of how to get here, but whenever she needed more specific directions to Westwood Manor, she simply stopped and asked.

"Ah," said Lady Westwood, "here is John with the tea."

The tall, liveried footman carried in their tea service on a silver tray and carefully set it down on the dainty table between them.

He gave Lady Westwood a somber bow. "Will there be anything else, madam?"

"Yes, would you move the fire screen, John? The room is a bit drafty. And fetch my pillow for my back."

"Yes, milady." He strode over to the embroidered fire screen and removed it so the heat could more easily reach the old woman. Then he brought her pillow from the other reading chair by the window and arranged it almost tenderly behind her.

Daphne had noticed since she had arrived that this tall, strapping male servant looked after the countess as attentively as if she were his own aged mother. He barely let her out of his sight. It was very touching.

During her tour of the house, footman John had been ever at the ready to assist Lady Westwood, who walked with a cane and had some difficulty getting around on account of her arthritis.

Seeing her move so stiffly, Daphne had hated putting the old woman through the tour, but Lady Westwood had clearly been delighted to have a young visitor, and with an air of great pride, had taken Daphne on a friendly tour of her very formal stately home, with all its exquisite furnishings and fine art.

This exercise would not have been possible

if not for the solicitous aid of footman John, shadowing the countess, assisting her up and down the stairs, getting doors for her as she required, providing quick physical support, a steadying hand, or a strong arm for his frail mistress to lean on.

"That will be all, John."

"Yes, milady." He bowed when she dismissed him, and withdrew into the distant doorway of the room for the next time he was needed — which, by the look of things, was probably soon.

Noticing Lady Westwood rubbing her hands with a frown, Daphne leaned forward. "Would you prefer me to pour out, my lady?"

"Oh, my dear, if you would not mind doing the honors. My joints do not appreciate this cold." She let another dismal sigh. "Ah, but I'm afraid it will only get worse. Winter will be here before you know it. And the snow." She made a face as Daphne poured the tea into their cups.

"Well, at least you have no trouble with your domestics," she remarked. "Your fellow there seems to do a fine job looking after you."

"You mean footman John? Yes, well, he is merely taking pains to be kind to me in the hopes that when I pop off, I may leave him a few extra pounds." She let out a baleful sigh. "It is shrewd of him, for I doubt that I shall last into the spring."

"My lady, do not say such a thing."

"Ah, well, it is true. But you're right. He is much better than his predecessor was, especially for only having been in his post a few weeks. That last blackguard ran off as soon as he had collected his pay. Can you imagine such a thing? Dashed off without a word after years of service."

"Really."

"Peter." She nodded. "He never was much use. John is a vast improvement, though he never smiles."

"Even so, he is not bad to look at," Daphne teased in a softer tone.

Lady Westwood laughed abruptly, jarred out of her misery for a moment. "That he is, I'll grant you! A handsome face is never an impediment in this world, whether it belongs to a servant or a prince."

The two women laughed conspiratorially. But as Daphne handed a cup of tea to Lady Westwood, she glanced discreetly at the portrait above the mantel.

"Speaking of handsome faces, may I ask who that gentleman is in the picture?"

"Ah." Her bony shoulders dropped. Her momentary laughter faded. "That is my Drake. My son."

"He is very handsome."

"Was, my dear. He has gone to be with the Lord."

"Oh — I am so sorry!"

"Yes, those are his ashes in the urn."

"Please forgive me! I did not know."

"It's all right." Lady Westwood lowered her head.

Daphne was, however, immediately confused. Virgil's letter to Max had mentioned this Drake, but the Highlander had written that someone had seen him — alive.

"When did he die?" she asked softly.

"Nearly a year ago."

"Was he . . . may I ask . . . in the war?"

"No, no, my Drake never bothered with politics. There were those who considered him a rakehell, my dear, and honestly, they were not far off the mark." She flinched and rested her tea on her lap. "I am sorry to say he spent most of his time chasing pleasure. He died abroad. I told him not to go. But he could never stay in one place. Oh, it's all been so dreadful. Now the two different branches of the family are wrangling over who will get the title. At least I shall be allowed to live on here until the lawyers can determine which of my nephews has the greater claim."

"I am so sorry for your loss." Daphne reached over and rested her hand on the lady's thin forearm. "It must be unbearable for you, going through all this. I had no idea."

"I pray you will never know the grief of losing a child, my dear, or watching your darling son go astray. But I fear, alas, it is a common plague."

Daphne felt a chill steal across her heart. "Is there anything I can do for you?" she asked softly.

The old woman gave her a wan smile. "You already have, just by visiting me. I should have liked my Drake to meet a girl like you. Unfortunately, he wasted his time on unmentionable women and died before he ever fell in love."

She smiled sadly at Lady Westwood's words, and leaned back again in her chair. But at least now she was beginning to see a possible reason why Virgil would want Max to come here and check on Lady Westwood. With all the time that Max had spent on the Continent, maybe he had known Drake over there. Daphne did not have the slightest notion what was going on, but she sincerely hoped for Lady Westwood's sake that the woman's rakehell son might still be alive.

"Lady Westwood, do you think . . . your son might have been acquainted with my husband?"

The countess turned to her intently. "Yes, my dear, I'm rather sure he was."

At that moment, Daphne felt someone watching her. She looked over slowly and saw footman John's cold stare fixed on her. Goodness, this protective servant did not seem to like her asking questions that might upset his fragile mistress.

A flash of motion through the picture

window caught her eye just then. Looking over, she spotted Max astride his galloping horse, charging up the long drive.

"Well, it appears my husband has finally found me," she remarked in an airy tone. "He is so protective. I had a feeling he might come looking for me."

"Newlyweds." Lady Westwood smiled.

"If you'll pardon me for a moment, I shall go out and greet him, and assure him I'm all right so he won't come in here scowling like a surly bear."

She chuckled. "As you wish, Lady Rotherstone."

Daphne set her tea down and left the drawing room, going out the front door. *This should be interesting,* she thought, and she braced herself for a storm.

Striding past the great pillars of the façade, she slowly descended the stairs of the front portico as Max rode up to the house, dressed all in black as he had been that day in Bucket Lane.

He was bareheaded, his dark hair tousled, his cheeks ruddy from wind and sun; his pale eyes glittered with anger as he shot a fierce stare her way, pulled the blowing horse to a halt, and swung down from the saddle.

One of Lady Westwood's stable boys dashed out to take his horse. Max didn't even look at the lad. His gaze was locked on her.

As he stalked toward Daphne, she quivered

half with a spurt of apprehension about his reaction, and half with relief that he had cared enough to come.

Absently, she noticed in wifely fashion that he had left the house without a shave. He must have raced out as soon as he had seen her little message on his mirror. She took a small degree of satisfaction in that. But with that dark scruff roughening his jaw, he looked even tougher and more dangerous than usual; instead of being afraid of him, though, her mind was flooded with images of their wild coupling last night.

As he approached her, she was filled with a disturbing surge of lust for him, despite her anger and hurt and her general desire to throttle the man.

"Hullo, darling," he said coldly.

Daphne smiled at him, with an aloof lift of her chin as he bent and kissed her cheek, reproach shooting from his eyes.

"Fancy seeing you here."

"Lady Westwood goes to my church back in Town," she replied. "Did you know that?"

"Well, my Society girl, you do know everyone, don't you?" he answered as they stared at each other.

"Everyone but you, my lord. So it would seem."

He flinched but showed no signs of backing down. "You should not be here."

"Why? What is going on around here?"

"Be quiet," he ordered in a harsh whisper as the butler opened the door for them.

"Be quiet?" she retorted in an outraged yet equally soft tone. "How dare you say such a thing to me? May I remind you, you are in no position to be giving me orders!"

"I am your husband! And as for you," he whispered angrily as he took her elbow and steered her back inside, "you are in so far over your head right now, you have no idea what you're dealing with. If you blow this investigation for me, you could endanger all of England, so I suggest you keep your eyes open and your mouth shut. Follow my lead; remain calm, whatever happens; and we will settle this later between ourselves."

"Well, I don't see how one frail old lady can be such a terrible threat to the realm," she hissed under her breath as they walked back into the house.

"I'm warning you," he answered in a low, pleasant sing-song just as they strolled past footman John and returned to the drawing room.

"Lady Westwood," Max greeted the countess, turning on that damnable Rotherstone charm.

Daphne introduced her husband to their hostess.

"Please forgive my appearance!" Max said with a dazzling roguish grin as he brushed off a stray bit of dust from the road. "When my wife did not return from her drive after a couple of hours, I became worried and set out to find her."

"Oh, I told you I'd be quite safe. He thinks I'm a ninny-head."

"Not at all, my darling!" He kissed her hand and smiled again at their hostess. "It is a husband's duty to worry. Dashing off on your merry way. It will not do, my dear. It will not do a'tall."

Lady Westwood chuckled at their exchange, unaware of the powerful currents of tension that passed between them.

"As I was telling Her Ladyship," Daphne said, "I was simply driving by and could not resist coming in to visit."

Max sent her a small frown askance, and the impatient look in his eyes told her just what he thought of her cover story to the old woman.

Of course, she was not the accomplished liar that he was. She gave him an artificial smile in return.

"In any case, I hope we're not intruding," he said to the countess. "It's just like my wife, the social butterfly, to seek out any opportunity for a cup of scandal broth." He nodded amiably toward the tea service.

"For shame, my lord, we have not been gossiping at all. Certainly not about you," Daphne assured him pointedly.

"I was just beginning to bore your dear

young lady with my tales of Drake."

"Bore me? Nonsense!" Daphne said.

"Drake?" Max echoed innocently.

Daphne eyed him askance.

"My son," said Lady Westwood. "I was under the impression that you knew him."

Max paused. "I cannot recall," he answered in a friendly tone, and shrugged.

"There's his portrait," Daphne said, her suspicions rising. "Does he not look familiar?"

"Well, I might have gone to school with him," Max said slowly. "But the person I'd remember would have been just a boy. Do you have a picture of him when he was younger?"

Lady Westwood lit up. "Oh, yes! Would you like to see one?"

"Very much, ma'am. Do not trouble yourself, my lady," he said quickly when she started to get up. He took note of her stiff movements and shook his head. "Point me to where it is, and I shall bring it to you."

"Oh, but it's all the way upstairs in his old room."

Max flashed his most disarming smile. "Which door?"

"First door on the right at the top of the stairs. But I'll send John —"

"No need." He nodded with a warm smile. "I'll be back in a trice."

Daphne was fascinated. What on earth was

he about?

His explanation seemed simple enough, but in light of Virgil's letter, she grasped that Max wanted to get into Drake's chamber, God only knew why.

Well. She supposed that the best way to eventually get answers out of him was to assist.

She endeavored to entertain Lady Westwood while he was gone. But perhaps she should have been more concerned with footman John.

The liveried servant was standing in the doorway with a bristling posture and a bit of a scowl in the direction Max had gone.

"How dear he is," Lady Westwood was cooing about the perplexing, infuriating, unknown quantity called Lord Rotherstone.

"Occasionally," she conceded. "I see your footman is as protective as my husband." She nodded toward footman John, who also heard her words.

Lady Westwood smiled.

"You needn't look so concerned, John," Daphne spoke up wryly. "To the best of my knowledge, my husband is not a thief."

Just a liar.

To her surprise, however, footman John showed no sign of humor at her idle jest.

He returned her smile with an icy stare, then he left the doorway and went after Max.

Very well, he could admit it. He could throttle his wife for being here, but Daphne's friendly visit to the lonely old lady seemed a good deal less suspicious than if he had simply arrived here himself, as planned.

It figured she knew Lady Westwood. The blasted woman seemed to know everyone in England. His main concern had been for her safety, but the moment he had seen her standing quite unharmed out on the portico, his thoughts had moved to his second gravest worry — her current and understandable fury at him.

The two disparate halves of his life had begun to collide and crumple into each other, and he had no idea what he ought to do.

No, he thought. *Correction.* He knew exactly what he ought to do. The problem was, it could cost him everything.

Stealing up to the top of the staircase, Max had found Drake's apartment within Westwood Manor, and was quickly and methodically searching them for anything useful. There was a sitting room, a bedchamber, and a dressing room.

It was possible Drake on his last visit home might have left some telltale sign of whatever sort of leads he had been following at the time of his disappearance.

As Max moved through the apartment searching high and low for clues, he continued to battle with himself over how much, if anything, to reveal to Daphne.

Telling her about the Order would change the whole picture for her, and he did not assume she would be pleased with what she saw. It might only make things worse. Maybe she'd be better off not knowing the burden that lay so heavily on the family that she had married into. He didn't dare imagine how she might react when he told her that one day, they might have to hand their own son over to some future recruiter, as he had been handed over to Virgil twenty years ago.

Closer to hand, telling Daphne about the Order also meant placing the security of their whole secret web in her hands. Every new inductee into their world of deception became another risk to all of them.

Trusting the woman he loved with his own life was not too difficult. But if he revealed the Order to her, that meant placing Rohan and Jordan and Virgil's lives in her hands, as well — and through them, all the other agents in the field. They were trained to keep secrets. They'd had it beaten into them. But she was not. Any Promethean could then take her and extract by means of fear and threat and pain whatever information Max had entrusted to her.

With one weak link in the chain, the whole

cause could be lost. Oh, God, he couldn't possibly tell her. His closest friends, the only friends he really had, might hate him for it.

But then again, if he did not reveal the truth of who he really was, he was going to lose his marriage, and the heart of the only woman he had ever loved.

He was holding on to hope like the last strand of a fraying lifeline that she might just let him off the hook. Maybe she would accept not knowing the full truth, like an ordinary wife. But Max knew full well that that was not the sort of marriage Daphne had agreed to in the hayloft of the Three Swans Inn.

He had won her hand at last by promising that they could make their own country, set their own rules, and he had promised to be open with her, as much as possible.

Agonized over what to do, he put the whole tangled matter into a little mental box for the moment, and forged on with the mission at hand.

The question, however, about how much of the truth past generations of Order agents told their wives about their activities made Max wonder if old Lady Westwood had any inkling about the real reasons that Drake had sailed off to the Continent.

His own mother had been told next to nothing. It was customary to keep the women out of it.

God, he was so angry at himself for his carelessness, letting her catch wind of his double life in the first place. How could he be so stupid?

It was so unlike him — almost as if some small, ornery part of him had *wanted* to get caught. *Disturbing thought.* It was almost as if he had undermined himself on purpose, against all logic, so that his darling Daphne could finally know him completely, and their love could be whole . . .

Just then, Max sensed a presence outside the door to Drake's apartment, which he had closed.

He went motionless, then he glanced at the bottom of the door. Through the faint daylight coming in under the seam, he could make out the shadow of two feet.

Somebody was listening to his movements inside the apartment. When the door swung open abruptly a moment later, as if to take him off guard, Max was already alerted to the fact that he was not alone.

The large footman from downstairs gave him a bow of cursory respect, but the belligerent glare behind the man's eyes revealed his disapproval. "Can I help you, sir?"

"Ah, yes, excellent." Max assumed a breezy tone, but the footman did not look happy about his snooping. "Lady Westwood asked me to fetch some . . . . childhood portrait of her son. Can't seem to find it."

The footman stepped toward the bookshelf and plucked down a miniature painting in a gilded frame.

Max feigned a sheepish smile. "Ah — of course. Right in front of my eyes."

"Anything else, my lord?" the servant intoned without a hint of impertinence.

"No, no. Er, thank you for your assistance."

The footman remained planted in place, making it clear he was not leaving until Max did.

He was eyeing Max's pockets as though studying him to see if he had taken anything from the room.

Max was well aware that his behavior must seem a tad bizarre. Since he could not think of any fresh excuses off the top of his head to account for his snooping through the belongings of Lady Westwood's supposedly dead son, he fixed a haughty smile on his face and exited the room, the little boyhood portrait of his fellow agent in hand.

Damn, where could Drake have hidden any final clues he might have left behind before his capture?

The irritating footman shadowed him all the way back to the drawing room, where Max politely handed Lady Westwood the portrait of her son.

She took it and trailed her gnarled hand lovingly over it. "We had this made of him before he went away to school."

"A very handsome boy," Daphne remarked.

"He took after his father. So, did you know my Drake, Lord Rotherstone?"

"Yes, I believe we once engaged in a rather brutal round of fisticuffs at school." Max smiled.

Lady Westwood laughed. "That sounds like him. Over what manner of disagreement, do you recall?"

"Some minor point of honor, I believe, though the details have escaped me. It was long ago." Max noticed the footman still eyeing him suspiciously from the threshold of the room. "Ahem. I almost didn't find it, but your man there was good enough to point it out."

"Footman John," Daphne informed him.

"Indeed, I was just telling your wife how this fellow has become quite indispensable to me, though he's only been here two months. I hardly know how I ever got on without him."

"Two months." Roughly the same time period as their wedding, the day Max had seen Drake. Max's stare homed in on the man. "Is that so?" he murmured.

Footman John, seemingly in spite of himself, returned his stare the way no common servant ordinarily would dare.

"Where were you in service before this?" Max inquired, moving toward him, putting the two women behind him.

"I worked for a family near Cambridge, my lord."

"By what name?"

"Lamb."

"I see. Lady Westwood, what prompted you to hire this fellow? Perhaps a sudden unexpected vacancy on your staff?"

"Why, yes, my lord. How ever did you know?"

Max narrowed his eyes, not taking his stare off the man. "A lucky . . . guess."

Without warning, footman John suddenly bolted.

Already expecting this, Max flew into action, charging after the footman — or rather, the Promethean spy.

Daphne's jaw dropped as her husband tore out of the room hot on the footman's trail.

"Good heavens!" Lady Westwood uttered some distance behind her as Daphne rushed out into the corridor to see where they had gone.

"Stay back!" Max barked at her over his shoulder — an order also meant for the other servants, who also came rushing onto the scene in a flurry of anxious activity.

Footman John went barreling out a back entrance, and Max was right behind him.

Daphne rushed back into the drawing room, and crossed to the large picture window just as footman John raced across the raised terrace.

He vaulted over the low stone balustrade as Max appeared mere steps behind him.

Dropping down to the flat green below, John had taken only two or three paces when Max leaped off the same stone balustrade and tackled him onto the ground.

The men rolled to the grassy area just below her window, exchanged several crushing punches before climbing to their feet, circling like lions.

Daphne gasped as footman John suddenly produced a knife. Lord, she might be angry at her husband, but she did not want to see him stabbed before her eyes.

John swung the knife savagely at Max, who ducked aside, lunged for the man's arm, and used the force of John's own attack to throw him facedown onto the ground.

Before he could get up, Max was behind him. He swept out his pistol and thrust it against the back of the man's head, roaring at him not to move.

Daphne tore herself away from the window and ran outside without a word to Lady Westwood, who sat there, pale with shock.

As she rushed out the back door that Max had used, she found that the rest of the male servants had poured out onto the terrace, and seemed close to rioting over the violence that had broken out.

"Everybody, please remain calm!" Max was

ordering them. "The situation is in hand! You, go get some rope to bind him."

"What's he done?" another footman demanded.

"This man is a fugitive," Max declared to the rest of the servants. "He took this post under false pretenses. I'd wager my best horse that his predecessor on your staff lies somewhere on these grounds in a shallow grave."

"He lies!" footman John yelled from the ground.

"Stay down and keep your hands behind your head!"

"Peter? He's murdered Peter?" the servants murmured among themselves.

"Why would he do that?" the plump housekeeper cried.

"He is involved in Lord Westwood's disappearance," Max declared. "I'm taking him into custody. Now, would you bring me that rope."

"Do as he says!" Daphne ordered with a sharp look.

A groom from Her Ladyship's stables brought Max a three-foot lead rope in short order. "Will this do?"

He nodded and took it. "Daphne?"

"Yes, my lord?"

"Come here."

Heart pounding, she went over to him. "Keep the gun on him. If I say shoot him, you bloody well shoot him. Can you do that?"

She looked at him in shock, then glanced back down at the man who had tried to stab her husband, and nodded.

Max handed her the pistol. She kept it trained on the footman with both hands while her husband quickly tied John's wrists behind his back with a wicked knot that would likely have impressed Horatio Nelson himself.

"Your husband is mad, Lady Rotherstone. I beg you, call him off!"

"Don't you dare speak to her."

"I have no idea what this is about!" he insisted.

"Oh, really?" Max backed Daphne off a couple of steps with a curt nod. Then he hauled the servant to his feet.

Daphne kept the pistol pointed at John, her pulse throbbing in her ears.

Max jerked the footman around to face him. He laid hold of the man's lapels and, without warning, ripped open the top few buttons of his livery coat, exposing the region of his heart. Daphne caught a glimpse of a round mark on the footman's chest, either a brand or some sort of tattoo.

A look of disgust came over Max's face. "Footman, eh? An odd career for one who bears the *Non Serviam*."

Footman John spit on Max in answer.

Daphne's eyes widened, but Max refused to be baited.

Giving his prisoner a cold, mocking smile,

he merely took out his handkerchief and wiped the spittle off his coat. "You may want to mind your manners from this point onward," he advised. "Where you're going, such pranks are frowned upon."

"Is that what the Order has sunk to?" the footman asked with a sneer. "Sending in their women as distractions? You're all a lot of cowards."

"At least we don't hold old ladies hostage in their own homes," he answered softly. Then Max glanced at the others. "The rest of you, go back to work! Check on Lady Westwood! You must guard her yourselves until I can arrange for Her Ladyship's protection."

"Guard her? My lord, is our mistress in danger?" the bewildered under-butler asked.

"Just be on your guard, and don't let any more strangers into the house."

The countess herself joined them just then, leaning on her cane. "Lord Rotherstone, what is the meaning of this?"

"Ma'am, His Lordship says footman John killed footman Peter to get his job, and might've had something to do with Lord Westwood's disappearance!" the under-butler relayed to her.

Daphne hurried to steady Lady Westwood, but rather than looking overwhelmed, the old countess seemed able to make more sense of this than she could.

She squared her bony shoulders as she

leaned on her cane. "Do whatever Lord Rotherstone says!" she ordered her staff. "Obey him — for my sake."

Well, at least one woman here trusted him, Daphne thought in confusion.

Max nodded to Lady Westwood in gratitude. Having secured the prisoner, he made some of the male servants watch footman John so that he could take a moment to speak to Drake's mother.

A short while later, the three of them had returned to the drawing room, where the tea had grown cold.

"Lady Westwood, I apologize for what happened here today. But you must not give up hope," Max said as she took her seat again. "We have reason to believe Drake could still be alive."

"Alive?" the old woman breathed.

"Max!" Daphne uttered.

The countess gripped the arms of her chair. "Oh, God, I knew it in my heart." She glanced toward the mantel. "I knew those ashes couldn't be his. I just knew it, somewhere, somehow, that my son was still alive."

"Well, your mothering instincts may prove as correct as your memory did. You were right when you said I knew your son. I knew him very well. We were like brothers when we were young. The fact is, I believe I caught a glimpse of Drake myself in London about six weeks ago."

Both women marveled.

"We don't know why he refuses to make contact with the Order," Max continued with a taut expression. "We assume he's in some sort of danger, but our goal is to find out who has him, and get him back safely. Do you understand what I am telling you?"

"Yes," she whispered. "Oh, yes."

"I don't!" Daphne broke in, glaring at him.

He ignored her, for Lady Westwood's eyes had filled with tears. "Oh, if my son could be alive, Lord Rotherstone . . . What would you or Virgil have me do? Anything!"

"If Drake makes any effort to contact you, send for me first before you answer him, lest it prove to be a trap," Max instructed. "You must write to me at this address." He went over to her secretaire, helped himself to a sheet of paper, and jotted down a few lines. "My contact at this location will make sure I get your message within twenty-four hours. Give no answer until you hear from me first. Will you do that?"

"Yes, yes." She took the paper, read it, then looked up at him in confusion. "A hat shop?"

He gave her a rueful smile. "A busy shop helps conceal our comings and goings."

"May I talk to you?" Daphne finally interrupted when their exchange seemed about at an end.

Max looked over warily at her, then nodded. She walked into the next room, a dim and empty music room. He followed. She sincerely wanted to shake him, but when she turned to him, she could not escape her most pressing emotion: worry.

"What is going on? What is this Order you're talking about?"

He stared at her.

"Were you hurt at all in that fight?"

"I'm fine."

Daphne shook her head, confounded. "Who is Drake, why did the footman attack you, and how could you get an old woman's hopes up before you know for sure if her son is alive?"

"I'm as sure as I *can* be at this point, and it looks to me like hope is all she's got left to live for. Didn't you see the shrine in there — the urn, the portrait? Those are not his ashes in that vase."

"How do you know?"

"Never mind that. I have to get to London. If the people who planted footman John into Westwood Manor make another move against the countess, she needs to be aware of what she's dealing with."

"Unlike me?" Her swift riposte appeared to take him off guard. "Do you intend to keep me in the dark, husband?"

He lowered his head, pausing. "Do I have a choice?"

"Not if you still want the same kind of future between us."

He looked up angrily again. "Is that a threat? Of what? Divorce?"

Daphne's eyes filled with tears. "How are we supposed to have any kind of life together if you don't tell me what is going on?"

He grasped her forearm pleadingly. "You have got to *trust* me. Daphne, please."

"How can I?" she cried, shaking off his touch. "I don't even know you! How dare you ask for my trust when you are up to your eyes in deception!"

"You don't understand — I have a duty!"

"One that apparently matters to you more than I do!" she yelled in his face as tears flooded her eyes.

"No!" He grasped her arms. "Daphne, you are the most important thing to me in this world. I am trying to protect you by keeping you out of all this! You've got to believe me. Please," he whispered.

She pulled free of his hold. "No. We're past that, Max. I'm sorry. You can't have it both ways. I've come too far with you to have the door slammed in my face. I will not accept this. At this moment, I have no idea who you really are. I can't take it. You're my husband and you're acting like a stranger. I'm trying to love you, but you need to decide. You can either have it like you did last night with me," she told him slowly, meaningfully, reminding him with a potent stare of the seduction, "or you can go back to being essentially alone.

The choice is yours."

"Ruthless," he whispered, shaking his head as he stared at her. "You have learned well, my lady."

"I was taught by the best," she answered. "So, what is it going to be?"

He stared at her for a long moment; Daphne refused to back down. He had to know the love they shared was hanging by a thread. It was in his hands.

At last, he gave her a grim and barely perceptible nod. "Very well. You'll be safer with me, anyway. Let's just hope we both don't soon regret it."

"What are you going to do with him?"

"We're taking him to London."

"What for?"

"The usual, Daphne. So we can beat the hell out of him until he breaks down and tells us what he knows — in this case, who has Drake." He sent her a sharp look. "Aren't you glad you asked, Little Miss Curious?"

CHAPTER 19

"Don't speak in front of the prisoner unless it's absolutely necessary," Max ordered her at the start of their very long — and quiet — ride to London.

They had swapped carriages with Lady Westwood temporarily, leaving the phaeton Daphne had driven there in exchange for the countess's closed coach, the better to conceal and contain the enemy agent Max had captured.

Lady Westwood had also lent them the services of her trusted head coachman, who had been twenty years in her employment, unlike footman John. The latter now sat bound and gagged and blindfolded next to Max; Daphne sat across from the two men on the opposite seat.

Max and she spent most of the long ride just gazing warily at each other. The three of them rode in silence for hours, reaching London as daylight waned.

Daphne was not sure what instructions

Max had given the driver, but he took them down to a lonely quay a stone's throw from the Strand. There they stopped and transferred from the carriage into a little waiting rowboat.

"Sit in the front," Max ordered her.

Then the burly coachman got down from his box and helped to shepherd the bound captive into the bobbing wherry. Max shoved footman John down in the middle of the boat and covered him over with a tarp.

"Stay still." Max sat down in the back of the boat and nodded to Daphne with a hard look. "Hold on."

Then he shoved off from the quay with an oar, leaving the coachman watching after them on the dock.

Daphne's heart pounded as they drifted downstream and began to zoom faster down the Thames. The cold breeze from their motion blew her hair behind her. Holding on tightly to the boat's wooden edges, she glanced back and saw Max's face fixed with grim resolve.

He plowed the oars into the waves, slowing the wherry about a half mile downstream. Within another hundred yards, he guided them up to the back of one of the old riverside buildings. They glided under a low brick arch, and then came to a heavy wooden river gate.

The boat bobbed as Max maneuvered closer to a weathered rope that hung down with a weight tied to it. Meanwhile, footman John groaned in protest from underneath the tarp. He sounded a bit seasick. Daphne cast a worried look over her shoulder, but Max opted to ignore the man's suffering with stony indifference.

He pulled on the rope in a distinct series of tugs. It dawned on Daphne that it was some sort of bellpull signaling to someone inside to open the gate.

The response came swiftly. There was a loud noise that gave her a jolt, a bang and a creak, and with that, the wooden river gate began to rise before them like a portcullis, dripping Thames water.

Max rowed under it quickly, advancing into a dark, cavernous area ahead underneath the building. The river gate began to close behind them a moment later. Daphne looked all around her in wonder.

What is this place?

No longer controlled by the current, still waters swirled all around them as Max rowed on, until, in short order, they glided up to a small stone dock lit by a single burning torch.

"Where are we?" she started to ask, but the second she spoke, the dark, hollow space was filled with savage barking. With a clank of chain, a huge black dog charged out of the shadows barking its head off, snarling, baring its teeth like some cousin of Cerberus, the three-headed dog of Hades.

Max shouted at the black beast in a foreign language, and it suddenly stopped. He spoke to it again, and its whole demeanor changed.

Daphne stared, wide-eyed, as the dog shook itself and began wagging its tail, jumping eagerly toward Max. Her heart was still pounding with fright, though the beast was now wagging its tail and sitting tamely, as ordered.

Max gave her another firm, steadying look. "Stay here while I see to him. Don't go anywhere. Don't move."

Daphne looked uneasily at the dog with no intention of crossing that thing's path. "Don't worry, I won't."

Max pulled the tarp off footman John. "Get up." He untied the man's blindfold so he could see where to step without falling into the water, but he kept his hands tied.

Daphne did her best to be helpful, reaching out to steady the boat against the dock as the two men got off the boat. The dog bristled and stared at the male stranger with a low snarl, but at another order from Max, the beast lay down on its stomach and began panting.

Max marched footman John across the small dock and up a stone tunnel that had been dug beneath the house, or whatever it was above them. With gooseflesh on her arms, she stared into the darkness in the direction they had gone. She still had no clear notion of what in heaven's name was going on. She was doing her best to keep her terror at bay, but she was beginning to wonder, truly, what manner of man she had married.

The dog's ears pricked up at a loud metallic bang from deeper into the darkness. Daphne swallowed hard, but a moment later, Max reappeared, all in black, emerging from the shadows. The torchlight sculpted his angular face.

He gave the dog an order, pointing to the wall. It got up and trotted back to where he had told it to go. Then he came to the edge of the dock and reached down to her, holding out his hand.

She took it warily and climbed out of the boat.

"What have you done with the footman?" she asked with an uneasy glance around.

"He's in a holding cell. Come on." When he started once more up the limestone tunnel, she had no choice but to follow him into the darkness.

"What is this place?" she whispered.

"You are in, or rather under, Dante House."

"Dante House," she murmured as the tunnel ended in a sparse stone chamber with a rough-hewn wooden table, a colorful floor mosaic of St. Michael the Archangel as in the stained-glass window, and a white Maltese cross suspended on a chain from the living rock. It matched the one in the Rotherstone portraits, the family chapel, and the signet ring she had found.

She turned to him all of a sudden. "The Inferno Club?"

"Yes."

"Max —"

"You'll get the answers you seek, Daphne, but first I must speak to Virgil." He walked away from her, crossing the dim, clammy chamber. "Can you climb?" He laid his hand on a ladder that ascended into a dark chute.

She nodded, and stepped onto the first rung.

With Max a few rungs below her, they climbed to the pitch-black top of the ladder. From what little light there was, Daphne could just make out an oval opening, a sort of doorway. Max told her to get off the ladder and go through it. Groping around nervously in the dark, she managed to find her way. She stepped off the ladder, through the opening, into a narrow, lightless passageway.

When Max joined her, he took her hand. "Follow me."

Daphne did so gladly, staying close to him. He led her through some sort of blind maze, but at last, he opened one more hidden door, and she breathed a sigh of relief. A moment later, they emerged from what proved to be a closet in some bedchamber.

Max pulled the hidden door shut behind

them, and then closed the closet door. He cast her a glance. "This way."

They left the bedchamber, squinting a little from the change from pitch-black into daylight, though even this was fading fast. They proceeded to walk down the corridor, and then down the carved staircase of the gaudiest house interior that Daphne had ever seen.

Dante House seemed deliberately fashioned in bad taste, or perhaps by a drunken architect: florid, feverish, dizzying in its ornate rococo style, as though someone had set out to create a place that was intended to disorient the visitor.

"What do you think?" Max asked, eyeing her askance.

"It's horrid," she replied.

"That is the idea. Here. You can wait in the parlor. Oh, hullo," he said as he looked into the room.

The parlor was already occupied.

"Hullo, yourself!" A highly made-up woman jumped up from the chaise longue where she had been reclining and fanning herself in a pose of utter boredom. She was dressed in a gaudy style that perfectly matched the house. "Am I allowed out yet?"

"Huh?"

"Can I go?"

Max snapped his fingers. "I'm sorry, I can't remember your name."

"It's Ginger!"

"Ah, of course. Ginger-cat! What are you doing here in the middle of the day?" he asked in an amiable tone.

"Your mad Highlander is making me stay here!" she said with a huge roll of her kohl-lined eyes. "He will not let me leave. Says it's for me own safety. He's been holdin' me here against my will for days, ever since I came and told him I'd seen Westie."

"Oh, it was you who saw Drake?"

"Aye! He was in a carriage with two other blokes. He were not himself a'tall. Oh, I tried to get him to come with me, but he didn't even remember who I was! So, anyway, that's all I know. I told your Scotsman that, but he still won't let me out of 'ere. A girl's got to make a livin'!"

"Well, my dear, if Virgil says you have to stay, you'd better make yourself comfortable." He looked at Daphne in amusement. "Why don't you two girls amuse yourselves with a nice little chat? I won't be long."

"Max!"

"I'll be back, Daphne. Cool your heels."

"How do you like that?" Ginger declared, putting a sympathetic arm around her shoulders. "Aw, honey, are they keeping you locked up here, too?"

"Um, no. Well, I hope not. I came in with my husband."

"Husband?" Ginger exclaimed. "Oh, *very* nice! Damn me, you landed Rotherstone?

Well done, my girl."

At her colorful language, it dawned on Daphne that she was in the presence of a demirep.

Oh, dear. She instantly thought of the Dowager Dragon. This was not at all approved company for a lady of the ton.

On the other hand, leave it to Max to deposit her into the company of a brothel woman. Blast the man. He was testing her. Again.

Ha, she thought. "I say — Ginger, is it?"

"Yes, love. And you are?"

"Daphne. You haven't ever . . . entertained my old man, have you?" She raised a curious eyebrow at the woman.

"Oh, no. Not with 'im, regrettably. But that Warrington —" She gave Daphne a broad wink. "I know why they call 'im the Beast. Lud, that lovely brute can leave a girl right sore with the way he goes at it."

Daphne's eyes shot open wide; Ginger let out a peal of hearty laughter, as though she had shocked "the fine lady" on purpose.

But as the harlot laughed aloud, Daphne slowly joined her, giving vent to her nervous tension after the day's wild events. Their shared laughter filled the room. For when Daphne thought of how she had behaved last night with Max, it struck her with an oddly liberating glee that, for all her earlier disapproval of the breed, maybe she and this brazen scarlet woman had a thing or two in common, after all.

Taut with apprehension over what his old mentor was going to say about his bringing Daphne into the Inferno Club, Max walked down the corridor looking for Virgil, but when he found him, he realized at once that the Scot already knew. He must have either seen her or heard them both come in.

Max spotted the aging Highland warrior in the dining room. He was pouring himself a large draught of whisky. Warily, Max stepped into the dining room with its florid murals.

Virgil did not look at him. He took another swallow of liquor and then he shook his head. "You've done a very foolish thing, Max. How could you bring her here?"

Max went toward him cautiously. "You can trust her, Virgil. I wouldn't have risked it if I had any doubts."

He snorted. "Trust a woman."

"She is my wife. She deserves to know what she's in for. She can handle it."

He shook his head. "You're a damned fool. You've put all our lives in jeopardy, and hers. You shouldn't have dragged her into this."

"I had no choice," he said wearily. "She found one of my key hiding places at home."

Virgil slammed down his cup. "I knew you would grow careless as a result of this — sentimentality!"

"Sentimentality?" Max stared at him with anger flooding his veins. "I love her, man."

"If you really loved her, you would take her home and tell her to forget all that she's seen!"

"It is too late for that."

"You had no right to do this, Max."

"No, Virgil, *you* have no right to ask me to lie to the woman I love for the rest of my life! What more do you want from me? I gave you twenty years of my life. You can go to hell if you don't like it. Damn you, and damn all of this. What I wouldn't give to wash my hands of it!"

"Oh, the sacrifice is too hard for you?" the old Highlander mocked him. "You boast of twenty years? Well, I've given nigh forty, you ungrateful whelp." Virgil shook his shaggy head, and then paused for a long moment. "Her blood is on your hands now if they ever get to her — and if they break her, so is all of ours."

Max closed his eyes and lowered his head. "I'm not going to let anything happen to her. Ever."

"That's what I said, too, a very long time ago, but somehow my lady is no longer with us." Virgil fell silent abruptly and turned away.

Max knew the story. He stared at his old mentor's back. "Virgil, I know your brother Malcolm took your woman from you, but that —"

"Silence!" he thundered, whipping around to glare at Max. "Do not speak of her to me!"

Jordan walked in just as Max lowered his gaze, Virgil's bellow still echoing on the air.

Max braced himself before he glanced over to gauge his friend's reaction to his having brought Daphne into their secret lair. "Good day, Lord Falconridge. The queue for those wanting to run me through starts over there." He pointed at Virgil.

Jordan gave him a wry look, but shook his head with a degree of worry in his eyes. "I trust your assessment of the matter, Max. If you say she can be trusted, that's good enough for me."

Max nodded slowly, staring at him. "Thanks, Jord."

"How much have you told her?"

"Nothing yet. There was a spy planted inside Westwood Manor when I got there. Daphne saw me catch the Promethean. She saw the Initiate's brand when I confirmed his status. Other than that, nothing."

"Keep it to a minimum, eh? For all our sakes."

Max dropped his gaze. "I only want to tell her who I am."

Rohan suddenly appeared in the doorway, bracing his hands on the lintel. "Hate to break up the tea party, boys, but things just got a bit more interesting."

"What is it?" Max asked quickly.

"A firestorm of gossip out there, that's what. The news just broke all over London that your unassuming neighbor, the Duke of Holyfield, and his pregnant duchess are both dead. They died in France."

"What?" Max pressed away from the sideboard where he had been leaning.

"It happened two days ago, in what they're calling a boating accident," Rohan supplied in response to their astonished looks. He pushed away from the doorway and walked into the room. "Seems the couple hired a small vessel to take them cruising on the Loire River to view all the chateaux. The boat sank. The couple drowned."

"In the Loire?" Max echoed. "That's in Malcolm's back garden, isn't it?"

Virgil bristled at the mention of his hated brother.

"How do you drown in the bloody Loire?" Jordan asked. "It's a gentle river."

"Maybe they had help."

Max shook his head, saddened and frankly stunned by the news. "Who would want to murder harmless Hayden Carew? Albert's the one who stands to gain, but even I know he's not that ambitious. As a younger son, he's got a fine income, a trust fund, and no responsibilities."

"He also has no real power," Rohan said.

"Isn't an accident ever just an accident?" Max asked wearily. "I mean, look at Hayden, a meek little fellow. I could easily believe he could drown in the Loire, especially if he was more concerned about trying to rescue his pregnant wife."

"What about the boat's crew? Did they 'drown,' too?" Jordan asked.

"Haven't heard yet." Rohan shook his head. "I just think it sounds incredibly suspicious."

"I agree. Maybe it's got something to do with Dresden Bloodwell's recent appearance in London."

"But why? What would killing the Duke of Holyfield and his wife accomplish, other than elevating Albert Carew to the dukedom?"

Rohan shrugged impassively. "Maybe they've got plans for him. You have to admit, it is kind of funny, Max. Your old boyhood nemesis now outranks you."

"That's just perfect," he muttered. "Daphne will be sorry she did not marry him. Where was Albert when this boating accident took place across the Channel? Do we know?"

"He was right here in London. According to the gossips, he wept copiously when he heard the news and had to be helped home."

"Oh, very touching," Max muttered.

"I say we watch him," Jordan advised.

"Definitely."

"Jordan, you'll be in charge of watching Carew," Virgil said. "I'll deal with the captive Max brought in. Rohan, you stay on the Dresden Bloodwell matter."

"Actually, old boy, that could be a problem," Warrington said. "Afraid I must take a small reprieve to put down some serious trouble brewing back at home in Cornwall. I am sorry. It cannot be helped."

"What's going on?" Max asked.

"You know those local smugglers that I allow to operate on my lands? They supply me with useful information from the ports and the criminal underworld. On occasion, they've run covert messages for me, in exchange for my turning a blind eye to their activities. Well, they know I have certain rules, limits to what I am willing to ignore. On the whole, they've kept things within reason, but now they've crossed the line. The Coast Guard office contacted me and said that in my absence, the smugglers have resorted to their old sport of causing shipwrecks and picking up whatever booty floats ashore."

"Oh, that *is* serious," Jordan murmured. "What do they do, use lights to simulate a lighthouse, yes? And lure the ships onto the rocks?"

"Exactly. I hear they've been having a grand old time while I've been gone. If I don't get down there and restore order, several of my local men are going to be arrested and probably sent to the hangman — which they might bloody well deserve — but would put an end to a very useful source of information that ought not go to waste."

Virgil nodded. "Not to mention that any highly public arrests like that could also bring unwanted attention our way. Handle it as quietly as you can before the Coast Guard moves on them."

"I will. They're not bad fellows, really. It's just that with the war's end, the black market these seaside bandits have thrived on has dried up. So now it looks like they've resorted to considerably more nefarious behavior."

"Need any help with it?" Max asked.

"Hell, no." Rohan grinned. "They're more terrified of their local Beast than they are of the Coast Guard, I assure you."

"As well they should be, Beast," Jordan replied with a sardonic look.

"So, anyway, since I have to go and handle this, can you get someone else to keep hunting Dresden?" the duke asked Virgil.

"I'll do it," Max said grimly.

"*You* want to go after Dresden?" Virgil countered skeptically, but Jordan interrupted.

"Listen, if you think about it, what's the point of hunting Dresden Bloodwell in his lair? Let's just wait for him to come out again in Society the way he did once before, and then take it from there."

"Wait for him to strike?"

Jordan shrugged. "Under the circumstances, not knowing Drake's status, I don't see how it helps *us* to risk drawing attention to ourselves right now unnecessarily."

"He's got a point," Rohan agreed. "Our main advantage is that we know who he is and he does not know who we are."

"Very well," Virgil said, nodding. "We'll put every pair of eyes we have to watch for Blood-well, and once he's seen, we'll make sure to track the bastard."

"Maybe we can work out some kind of a trap," Max said.

"Maybe so, but we're going to need more of our men to work on this with us," Jordan said.

Virgil nodded. "Beauchamp's team should be returning soon."

"Were they able to find out anything about this Rupert Tavistock?" Max asked.

"Yes, in fact, they did. Some of my agents still do as I ask them," the Highlander said sharply.

"Virgil."

"Tavistock is dead," the Seeker grumbled.

"And all the money he transferred into the Promethean accounts?"

"Gone. Malcolm's hidden it."

"Can't say I'm surprised," Max murmured. Then he told his friends what had happened at Westwood Manor, and learned in exchange what the demirep, Ginger, had said about her encounter with Drake.

Max listened keenly as they told him how Ginger had seen Drake in a carriage with two other men outside the Royal Opera House.

The older of the two men had told Ginger that Drake had suffered a head wound and, to her, Drake had seemed out of sorts, not at all himself.

He had not recognized her, though, for that matter, even Max had forgotten her name a short while ago.

But the two men she had seen him with fit the description of James Falkirk, an elite member of the Council, and his longtime assistant, the one-eyed operative known as Talon.

Max took all this in with a frown. "If James Falkirk has Drake, then why are we still alive? If Drake intended to reveal our identities, the Prometheans would've attacked us by now, especially with the Council's favorite assassin Bloodwell in Town to organize the job. Falkirk need only extract our names from Drake and then hand over that information to Dresden."

"God, I can't imagine what he's been through," Jordan murmured, staring at the floor.

"Maybe it's like the harlot said. Maybe he really can't remember us. Had Drake's mother heard from him?"

"No."

"Maybe he doesn't remember her, either."

"Maybe he doesn't even remember himself," Virgil said quietly while they were still pondering it.

"Well, the Prometheans certainly know who Drake is, otherwise, they wouldn't have known to plant a spy in his family's home."

"We need to send some proper guards to Westwood Manor," Max added, concerned about the old Lady Westwood's safety. "One advantage we can claim is that the Prometheans don't know I got their man. Maybe the so-called footman I dragged in today will be able to confirm if it's Falkirk who has Drake, and where they're holding him."

Jordan shook his head with an agonized look over their brother's well-being. "God, we have to help him."

"Before they break him," Rohan murmured.

"What if they already have? If he turns against us, we are in serious trouble."

"He won't," Max and Virgil declared simultaneously.

Then they all fell silent.

"And so it all begins again," Rohan murmured at length.

"God, I hope not," Jordan whispered. "For if they really do have Drake, all of our lives are in his hands. Including Daphne's," he added, glancing at Max.

"I should get back to her." He paused, warding off an icy chill to know that she now shared the danger. "You know, I just want to say that I did not want to bring her here. I tried to keep her out of it, for all our sakes, and hers, but when you're married . . . There were just too many lies."

"I think we all understand, Max." Rohan gave him a subdued nod, which Max returned with a look of gratitude.

"Very well, then, here's the plan," Virgil said gruffly. "Max, you watch Albert Carew. That makes more sense, since you've known the family longest. I'll deal with the spy from Westwood Manor and press on with finding Drake. Jordan, you stay on the watch for Dresden Bloodwell in Society as you suggested, and Warrington, you deal with your smugglers, and get back to Town as soon as you can."

"Done," Max said.

The others nodded, as well.

Max let out a low sigh of relief to have it all sorted out, and went to collect Daphne from the parlor where he had left her. With all other business attended to, the hour of his reckoning had come.

He was going to take her down to the Pit. Into the heart of their darkness.

CHAPTER 20

Daphne was waiting patiently in the parlor when Max returned. He beckoned to her to come with him; she got up and followed, noting that his expression was still grim and a touch apprehensive.

Without a word, he led her into a torrid red drawing room, and walked over to the harpsichord. He played a few specific notes on the instrument, and to her amazement, a full-length bookcase against the wall rotated open, revealing another dark, secret passageway.

"Come on."

She followed him into the lightless maze once more, and they made their way back to the same ladder by which they had ascended.

Max went first this time to help her if her footing slipped. After climbing back down the ladder, she found herself once more in the mysterious stone chamber underneath Dante House.

"You can sit down if you want to." He

gestured toward the rough-hewn wooden table. "Would you like a drink?" Without waiting for her answer, he poured her a glass of red wine from the dusty bottle on the table.

Daphne accepted it wordlessly; maybe he thought she was going to need it. He looked at her for a long moment.

"Do you remember when you asked me about Albert saying I disappeared when we were boys?"

She nodded slowly.

"The school that I was sent to is, indeed, in Scotland, but it is not an ordinary academy."

She stared at him, holding her breath. Max searched her eyes.

"I belong to a hereditary order of chivalry named after St. Michael the Archangel." He pointed to the floor mosaic. "You know his role, I am sure — God's warrior angel who cast Satan down from Heaven with his fiery sword. The castle in Scotland is, in fact, the Order's headquarters, and that's where I was sent, to fulfill an oath made by the first Lord Rotherstone."

"The original owner of that broadsword in your gallery?" she murmured.

He nodded. "This duty was passed down through my family to me. Not all my prede-cessors were called upon to serve — the threat varies over the centuries, and many have escaped it altogether — but I could not.

"When I was thirteen, Virgil came to our

estate and made arrangements with my father for me to be handed over to the Order and taken away to Scotland to begin my training as an agent for them. That's where I met Rohan and Jordan — and Drake, among others. This whole Inferno Club is merely a false front."

He lowered his gaze, his angular face sculpted by the candle's glow. "The Order's motto is taken from the book of Hebrews: *'He makes His angels winds, and His servants flames of fire.'* The Order is named after St. Michael, for like him, we are dedicated to battling a pernicious evil. Struggling to rid the world of it, though there seems to be no end in sight."

"What is this evil?" she breathed.

"The Promethean Council. A secret society of very powerful men, bent on enslaving humanity. Their lust for power never changes, only the names do. They've infiltrated every government on earth . . . but all this has been going for six hundred years."

She shook her head in wonder.

"The struggle dates back to the late twelfth century," he continued. "Long ago, the first Lord Rotherstone, along with my friends' medieval ancestors, joined King Richard the Lionheart in the Holy Land on a quest to free Jerusalem from the armies of Saladin.

"This was the Third Crusade, and since it was unsuccessful, if you recall your history lessons, the even bloodier Fourth Crusade was launched a few years later. Our ancestors remained in the Holy Land for that one, too."

"I see," she whispered, and took a drink of her wine.

Max gazed at her. "The story goes that, one day, King Richard sent out a scouting party of about twenty knights to determine the enemy's location. A sandstorm began forming in the desert, so the knights took shelter with their horses in a cavern that they noticed amid the rocks. They began searching around inside the caves to see if there was any source of water there for their horses to drink, but instead, they came across some ancient clay jars.

"When they looked inside these jars, the Crusaders found that they contained a mysterious set of scrolls. One of the knights — Falconridge's ancestor, it was — was an accomplished scholar who had spent some years of prayer and study in a monastery. So, with his greater learning, he was able to make some sense of what was written on the scrolls.

"The scrolls were already a couple hundred years old when the Crusaders found them — apocrypha written in Syriac, from about A.D. 900. The first thing the scholar-knight recognized was that the scroll announced itself as one of a few existing copies of an older document, whose original had been burned in the great fire that destroyed the ancient Library of Alexandria."

Daphne marveled at the tale. "What did these scrolls contain?"

"Something very dark. A sort of unholy bible for a strange cult of mixed origins, dedicated to Prometheus. Its founding tale sprang out of an Old Testament story, concerning the great Bible patriarch Joseph. You know, the one who was sold off into slavery in Egypt by his brothers?"

"Oh, yes," she said. "The brothers were jealous that their father had given Joseph the coat of many colors, while they had no such token of his favor."

"Just so," Max replied. "As I'm sure you will recall, Joseph did fairly well for himself in Egypt in spite of his brothers' treachery. By correctly interpreting Pharaoh's dream, he saved Egypt from a terrible famine.

"Now, the lesser-known part of that story is that Pharaoh wanted to reward Joseph for his service to the kingdom, so the grateful Pharaoh arranged an advantageous marriage as his reward. Joseph was given the beautiful Aseneth for his bride. Aseneth was the semi-royal daughter of the Egyptian high priest of Heliopolis.

"The two were married," he continued, "Hebrew and Egyptian, and from those beginnings, a cult took root, mixing the sacred mysteries of the Jewish Kabbalah with the divination and the rites of the Egyptian high priests. The earliest practitioners of this Joseph-and-Aseneth cult had a particular interest in the Egyptian practices aimed at preparing the soul for immortality, the very purpose for which her people had built the Pyramids in which to bury their god-kings. But it did not end there.

"As this occult sect spread, they constantly incorporated new beliefs and rituals, seeking supernatural abilities, such as those that were said to belong to the Magi, like the three wise men who showed up at Bethlehem. It seemed the earliest Prometheans would try anything in their search for occult powers.

"Ancient Greek beliefs were also absorbed, the use of oracles like the one at Delphi, for example. There were also darker practices, the occasional human sacrifice. That one, they supposedly picked up at Crete, the home of the Minotaur."

"How dreadful." She shuddered in the clammy darkness of the stone chamber. She could almost imagine the bullheaded monster emerging from one of those stone-carved tunnels.

"Dreadful, yes, to us or to any sane person. But not to them. The Prometheans savor bloodshed, and they're not afraid to die because they don't believe that is the end. Essentially, they believe they are above death, and that by their black magic, the processes of death and regeneration can be brought under their control.

"As a result, not surprisingly, it was the Greek myth of Prometheus that inspired the name they have come to be known by."

"Prometheus, who stole fire from the gods," she echoed.

"Yes. Like him, they see themselves as mankind's savior, bringing light into the world."

"But wait." She furrowed her brow. "I thought bringing light into the world was supposed to be Jesus' job."

"Not to them, indeed. Did you know the name of Lucifer means Light-bearer?"

She stared at him in amazement. "Are you telling me they have actual black magic?"

"All I know is *they* believe it's real. So much so that they're willing to kill for it. They chose the Titan, Prometheus, as their icon because in spite of his horrible torment, what with the eagle coming each night to eat out his liver, each day he awoke anew, whole and unscathed.

"In itself, that might have been harmless. But unfortunately, the whole point of their longed-for immortality is to slowly bring all of mankind under their control. I'm sure you know who Jesus called the 'master of this world.' "

"Satan."

"That is their true god," he said, nodding grimly. "Of course, they don't openly admit that. They prefer to pretend that they are working for the 'good' of humanity. That if mankind has to have the 'true illumination' rammed down its throat by force, then so be it. But first, to the conclusion of our story about the Crusaders and their temptation in the desert."

"Yes, what happened to them?"

"By the time the sandstorm was over, the knights' reaction to the scrolls was split. Half of them thought the scrolls vile and unholy, and the work of the Devil. After all, these were medieval men. They immediately wanted to burn the scrolls — cast them into the Inferno, if you will.

"The other group had a very different idea. They saw this ancient 'magic' as perhaps dangerous, but still useful information. Some of them wanted to bring the scrolls to King Richard and use the black magic they contained as a possible secret weapon that might allow them to defeat Saladin and his ferocious Mamluk armies. The Crusade was going badly, after all, and considering that the goal was to free Jerusalem, a noble cause, the ends, in their view, justified the means."

"Always dangerous thinking," she murmured.

"Indeed. The knights' argument soon grew heated. Their whole party quickly turned to chaos, and being medieval warriors, it wasn't long before violence broke out. One of the men was struck down. Seeing they had murdered one of their own, the knights in favor of trying out the magic escaped with some of the scrolls. They knew they could not go back to King Richard without dire consequences for killing one of their comrades."

He paused. "At least the evildoers did not get away with all of the scrolls. In the fray, the knights who remained true were able to keep a number of the documents out of their hands. But from these murderous beginnings, turning knight against knight and friend against friend, the poisonous effects of these ancient writings were very clear.

"To the best of our knowledge, the others eventually approached King Richard's court astrologer to see if His Majesty might want to try using the scrolls' black magic against Saladin after all. According to the legend, our Christian warrior-king did not dare attempt to dabble in such stuff. At least," Max added slowly, "not at first.

"But after the Third Crusade failed, after His Majesty had emptied England's coffers to pay for his war, some say Richard allowed the court astrologer to have at it when the Fourth Crusade came round.

"It is rumored that the use of the scrolls resulted not just in the victories of the Fourth Crusade, but also in the fact that that whole campaign was hideously bloody, with battles and sieges that were considered wholesale slaughters, even by medieval standards. Whether the magic is real or not, the evil of these scrolls seems to have that effect on men."

Daphne stared at him in awe.

"Eventually, the Crusaders who had embraced these dark ancient writings returned to Europe, bringing their newfound cult back with them like the Plague." Max shook his head. "They did not care how far they went or how twisted they became. All they cared about was using their newfound creed to gain power.

"Of course, the Church quickly pronounced their beliefs heretical, so they had to take their rituals underground. It was then, too, that the Order of St. Michael was established to root them out.

"With the Pope's blessing, King Richard established our Order to hunt down this cult, destroy the scrolls, and bring this evil to an end. My ancestor, the first Baron Rotherstone, and Warrington's and Falconridge's, all took the blood oath swearing not just themselves but their descendants to the fight.

"Unfortunately, our enemies have proved as determined to persist as we have been in seeking to thwart them. Once this evil took hold, they have never stopped working to achieve their aims."

"What exactly are their aims?" she asked in

an ominous tone.

"Originally, the Prometheans claimed that, having seen the bloodshed in the Holy Land and throughout their barbarous Europe of the Dark Ages, their main desire was to use the occult secrets in the scrolls to end all future wars, by establishing one vast kingdom that would stretch across the entire world. They painted themselves as benevolent when in fact they were anything but. For years, they claimed that what they were trying to establish was nothing less than the kingdom of Heaven on earth."

"But Jesus said the kingdom of Heaven is already at hand," Daphne murmured. "And it has nothing to do with worldly power."

"Exactly. It was a lie. And before long, even the Prometheans themselves gave up this pretense. Their quest was for raw, naked power, and it continues to this day."

He lowered his head. "Everything I've told you about my life, traveling in Europe, international investments, collecting art — all of that is only the surface truth. The real reason for my travels, indeed, the whole soul and substance of my life till I met you, was in this duty on my lineage, to persist continuously to topple them.

"In recent years, they had grown powerful. Certain members of their cabal had wormed their way into high positions around Napoleon, as well as in other European courts.

Given Napoleon's genius and the extent of the empire he established, they thought they could use him to finally bring about their vision of one seat of power to rule the earth. They got very close."

"Oh, God."

"You asked me once how I ended up at the Battle of Waterloo," he said. "The real answer is that I received a message from Jordan warning me that the Prometheans had sent an assassin after the Duke of Wellington. They had managed to get a spy into his headquarters like the one you and I unmasked at Westwood Manor. They had already planned in advance that if things went badly for Napoleon at Waterloo, our General Wellington was to be shot on the field. This would have thrown the allies into chaos long enough to let Napoleon regroup.

"My mission was to identify and destroy the enemy agent they had planted in Wellington's headquarters, and that is exactly what I went to Waterloo to accomplish."

"You killed the would-be assassin?" she whispered.

"Yes," he replied in cool, unflinching calm. "The mask of the libertine nobleman was merely a device I employed to ward off the suspicions of both the enemy and everyone else. The charade allowed me to travel about freely on my various missions. Only the men here, my fellow agents, my brothers, have known who I really am. It is very important to me now, Daphne, that you also know."

"Oh, Max." She got up from the table and went around it to hug him.

He caught her up hard in his arms. "Sweeting." He closed his eyes and pressed a kiss to her forehead. "God, after Waterloo, I truly thought all this was over, that, at least, we had held them off for another fifty years," he whispered. "If there had been any doubt in my mind, I would never have started down this path of marriage. Not for all the world would I have brought you into danger. But now that you are in it, I can only think it is safer for you to know the nature of the threat we face.

"I will teach you. All right?" He pulled back slightly and took her face between his hands, staring passionately into her eyes. His own had darkened a shade with his troubled intensity. "I will teach you how to keep yourself safe, so that even when I am not there . . . Oh, I could never let anything happen to you.

"But above all, Daphne, now you must share in our pact of secrecy, no matter what. You can tell no one. Not Carissa, not Jonathon, not even your father. You must carry this as I have, and understand that it now separates you from the rest of the world, as it has separated all of us."

"Oh, Max. As long as I am not separated

from you."

He pulled her close again.

"Darling, I had no idea you were part of something reaching back across the centuries. I'm glad you told me. I can't imagine what would have become of our love if you had not shared this with me. It's too huge and important to have let it stand between us for the rest of our lives." She paused, trying to wrap her mind around all he had told her. "And now you say one of your agents is missing. Drake?"

"Yes."

"Lady Westwood's son," she murmured.

"The rest of his team was killed," Max said. "We thought Drake was dead, too. That would have been awful enough. But then . . . I saw him on our wedding day."

She looked at him in surprise.

"I was outside with your father having a smoke. He went riding past in a blasted hackney coach. I thought I'd seen a ghost. It was almost as if he came looking for me. The notice of our wedding was in all the papers. But he did not stop." Max shook his head. "And that bodes very ill."

"So, that was the 'cutpurse' you chased."

He nodded slowly. "You cannot know how much I hated lying to you — on our wedding day, of all days."

She gazed sadly at him.

"I was not able to catch him." He shrugged.

"I wasn't even sure if my mind was not playing tricks on me. But then that woman upstairs, Ginger, she saw him, too. She's been to a few of our parties, so she knows the lads. She waited awhile out of fear, but she finally came and told Virgil. That's when Virgil wrote to me with instructions to call on Lady Westwood."

"So, her son really is out there somewhere, alive?"

"Yes, probably being held captive, not unlike *our* prisoner, John the footman. If Drake gives our names to whoever's holding him, then it's only a matter of time before they come looking for us."

"What shall we do, Max?"

He looked at her for a long moment. "Stick together," he said softly. "You stay alert and aware, but I will tell you if there comes a point where you should be afraid. Until then, I promise you, we are all right." He shook his head, staring wistfully into her eyes. "I did not want to tell you all these things. I didn't want you to have to live in fear. We generally leave the women out of it as a rule."

"Well," she said slowly, "you and I agreed to make our own rules. But, Max, I want you to know you can trust me. No one, no matter how horrible, could ever induce me to betray you, or to reveal the things that you've entrusted to me. Not if it cost me my life."

He gazed at her longingly. "I love you,

Daphne."

"I love you, too." As he held her again, Daphne nestled in his arms, until all of a sudden, a thought came into her mind that made her blood run cold. "Max?" She pulled back suddenly, paling. "Does this mean someday they will come to take away *our* son?"

He flinched, but he did not deny it.

She pulled away from him, stricken. "How could you not tell me this before?"

"Forgive me," he whispered. He put his head down.

Daphne moved back to the table, leaning against it to steady herself against this terrible future possibility. She was silent for a long moment. "You finish this, Max. Do whatever you have to do. You and the Scotsman and Warrington, Falconridge, whoever else it takes. End this battle for once and for all, so our sons won't have to."

"I will do all in my power to make it so." He came up tentatively behind her and slipped his arms around her waist.

Her heart in a tumult of emotion, she turned around and returned his embrace, burying her face against his chest for a moment. She willed herself to hold on to her courage, pressing her eyes closed. "I believe in you," she whispered fiercely. "And I will support you in this however I can. I love you, Max."

"That's all I need to hear." He hugged her

harder, his impassioned whisper strained with feeling. "Virgil thinks the cause itself is enough to inspire us, but I'd give so much more to fight for you than for humanity at large. You are everything to me, Daphne."

As twin tears spilled from her eyes, he bent his head and kissed her.

"Thank you, my lord," she breathed against his lips. "Thank you for what you've done. Keeping people safe, and they don't even know it." She caressed him in reverent adoration. "They have no idea of your sacrifice."

"If you know, that's enough for me." He rested his forehead against hers, closing his eyes. "I never wanted to keep secrets from you, Daphne."

She took his face between her hands. "It doesn't matter anymore. What matters is that we are in accord now, and at last, you've let me see you — the man I truly love. Finally now I understand you, where you've been, and what's been driving you. I love you, Max. I do. I always will."

"Daphne." He tilted his head and kissed her in stormy tenderness.

With the truth out in the open at last and the shadows between them cleared away, she was suddenly dying to have him inside her. She wanted nothing but to be one with him completely. She caressed his shoulders and held him in possessive passion, kissing him hungrily; his male instincts quickly got the message. He set her up on the edge of the table and continued kissing her. She arched as he cupped her breasts.

"Max?"

"Mmm?"

"What if we had a daughter?" she murmured between kisses. "Would the Order also claim her?"

"No. Though, on second thought, maybe they should. Because if our daughter took after her mother, she'd probably be even more dangerous than our son."

"Me, dangerous?" Daphne replied with an innocent glance.

Max paused, a lazy smile curving his lips as they lingered against hers. "Damned right, my love. Did I mention how much I liked you last night?"

She laughed softly and pulled back to give him a vixenish smile. "I rather liked me, too. Of course, I was furious at you," she added.

"You can get angry at me like that anytime," he purred before burying his lips against her neck.

"Well, now I think it's time that we made up," she replied, trailing her fingers down his chest.

"Couldn't agree with you more. God, you drive me to distraction."

"Take me."

She sat on the end of the long wooden table; he stood between her thighs. They were still fully clothed, but he lifted her skirts and moved closer; she reached down and freed him from his trousers.

A moment later, her heart racing, she drew in her breath in sensuous welcome as he entered her. He groaned aloud.

The blissful relief of their bodies joined once more in love swept over her senses. A throaty moan of pleasure escaped her as he rocked her slowly, with dark tenderness, savoring their union.

The flickering torchlight played over the uneven stone walls of the Pit. As the pleasure of his loving ravishment overcame her senses, she lay back slowly on the table, offering herself as a gift to his hunger.

He leaned down and thrust more deeply into her, aroused to new heights by her willing yielding. She wrapped her legs around him, hooking her heels behind his hips.

The intoxicating passion of his wild, claiming kisses half suffocated her with dizzying pleasure. She raked her fingers through his tousled hair until she had to gasp for breath; she ended the kiss, panting, while her hands ran hungrily all over him, claiming every inch of him for her own.

"I love you," she breathed against his scruffy cheek as she gave herself to him, no longer in blind faith, but knowing fully who and what he was, and loving him all the more for the nobleness she had always sensed in him, but only now, finally, had proved.

Max rested his elbows on either side of her head on the coarse wooden table and gazed for a long moment, wistfully, into her eyes.

He was amazed to find himself finally known, truly loved, and accepted. "I love you, Daphne," he whispered as he captured a strand of her hair and rubbed it longingly against his face. "You're so much more than I ever dreamed I could have. Please don't ever leave me again. You've run away twice from me now. I don't think I could take a third time. If you do go, you know I'm only going to follow you."

"I'm not going anywhere, love. You have me now, forever."

He moaned softly against her neck in ecstasy at her words. Finally, he knew the meaning of home.

He might not have all the answers, and perhaps the war against the evil they were duty-bound to fight must yet go on. But at last, for him, there was a kind of peace.

After all his years of solitary wandering, ever on the hunt, a stranger in a strange land, at least he was no longer alone. He had her now, and they were one, in spirit as in flesh, made whole again, as though each had found the missing pieces of themselves inside each other. She gave new purpose to his strength; he gave shelter to her caring heart.

Max held her close as he loved her, whispering his devotion in her ear.

If all his years of wandering had taught him one thing, it was that the heart was its own place, its own country — and for him, she was its queen.

There was nowhere else he'd rather be than right here in the arms of the woman he trusted and loved, his mate, his wife, his angel.

Together they could share in their own secret heaven, even as the storms outside them raged.

EPILOGUE

A fortnight later

"I'm so glad you're back in Town," Carissa said as Daphne and she strolled through the brilliant ballroom together just like they used to.

"Well, I'm just happy to see that your cousins are behaving themselves again."

"Yes, it's remarkable how they suddenly turned around," Carissa said dryly. "I must admit, I so enjoyed seeing them bowing and scraping to you, Marchioness."

Daphne chuckled. "Maybe I can find a marquess for you, too, my dear. Of course, there is always the new bachelor Duke of Holyfield." Daphne gave her a subtle nod at Albert Carew, who was leaning by one of the columns in the ballroom, looking as malcontent as ever.

Albert seemed very different since his brother's death, the dandy's flamboyant colors replaced by the somber black of his mourning.

When he saw Daphne, he sent her a sneering imitation of a smile and turned away. Daphne shrugged off her former suitor's unpleasantness and nudged Carissa.

"So, do you want to visit the orphans with me before we all leave for Worcestershire? We're going to let the children decorate the whole place for Christmas."

"I wouldn't dream of missing it."

"Max bought a used pianoforte for the children, too, did I tell you? We are going to sing some carols, and I think I may even give some of the older girls their first music lesson."

"I still can't believe how well you play."

"I do love it. I wish I hadn't left off it all those years. It hurt too much before. It was always something I shared with Mama."

"Well, you certainly haven't lost your touch. Oh, look, there is your husband. Oh, dear." Carissa frowned. "Why is he off in that quiet alcove talking to another lady?"

Daphne followed Carissa's glance, then smiled. "That's his sister, Lady Thurloe."

"Shall we join them?"

She shook her head, warmed to see her husband finally reaching out to his devoted sister. "Better to leave them in peace for now. They have a lot to say to each other."

"There's a message I've needed to pass along to you for a long time, Max, from our father.

Something he said on his deathbed that he wanted you to know."

Max stared into his sister's eyes. After seeing how painful Drake's absence was for Lady Westwood, he had begun to realize that his own family might have suffered similarly with him gone. So, cautiously, he had sought out Beatrice. He figured he was as ready to hear what she had to say as he ever would be.

"Max, you have no idea how proud of you Daddy really was," she said. "I was with him for several days leading up to the end. We talked a lot. You see, I was angry at you for not being there when he was dying. I felt you had abandoned us for your quest for riches or your search for pleasure. But Daddy didn't want me to be angry at you. He swore me to secrecy and then, on his deathbed, told me the real reason you were always gone. He told me how noble it was, what you were doing, and he made me promise never to give up on you. Don't worry, I never told anyone. Not even my Paul. Our father swore me to secrecy, and I have honored that."

"Good."

"Max, even more importantly, when I asked him if he had any regrets, he said there was only one. He said his biggest regret was not letting himself be closer to you," she said softly. "He said you were the best son any man could have, but he never really showed his love because he knew they'd come to take you away. He knew he'd have to give you up. The weaker your ties to us, the less painful it would be for you when the time came for you to go."

He closed his eyes for a moment.

"You also need to know how ashamed Daddy was of the money the Order gave us to put our affairs in line. But he accepted it for Mama's sake and mine. As hard as that was for his Rotherstone pride, what was even worse for him was knowing that he had no way to protect you from this burden on our lineage. He felt impotent to do anything about it, and I believe that is one of the main reasons he drank."

Max nodded grimly. He could believe it. Until now, he had not been quite able to put himself in his father's shoes. But as the prospective father of a future agent of the Order, he could now easily empathize with how his father must have felt to have to let Virgil take him. It must have been even worse for his father, Max thought, because at least he had the training and the wherewithal to fight back so that, God willing, *his* son one day could be spared.

"You may remember that Daddy's drinking got worse after you left. He withdrew deeper and deeper into himself. Only I, in all my adorable childhood glory back then, was able to charm him back out of his depression on occasion. But at least he no longer gambled. He told me the powers-that-be at the Order had established those terms with him. If he ever broke their terms and gambled again, he was told he would never see you again. They would not even have allowed you to come home on those brief breaks from school that you sometimes got."

Max stared at her, stunned. "He quit gambling for me?"

She nodded. "He loved you, Max. Some people don't show it very well, and I'm not making excuses for him, but our sire had a good heart under it all." She paused. "I can't even imagine all you've been through, or how it must have felt for you as a boy, dragged off to be turned into a warrior, and to know your family had received gold in return. You must have thought they sold you. And maybe they did, I don't know. I don't think that your Highlander friend gave our parents much choice. But I want you to know that your sacrifice was not in vain."

"What do you mean?" he forced out, barely able to speak past the lump in his throat.

"When I turned seventeen, the money we had received paid for my Season, where I met my Paul, the love of my life. And in turn, we now have our two beautiful children, whom we utterly adore, and hopefully several more to come. My big brother, you gave me the chance to find happiness, and, at least, now I get the chance to thank you."

She shook her head. "Dear heaven, if you had not done it, if you had not gone with the Order — if they had not given us the money, and we had stayed poor — I never could've had a Season, or met my husband. I would've had to stay in the country in Worcestershire, and probably would've ended up marrying one of our neighbor boys, the Carew brothers!"

He furrowed his brow as he saw the truth of her words.

"Due to my rank, I probably would've married the eldest, Hayden. Don't you see? That wife of his, who drowned with him in France — if it weren't for you, big brother, that could have been me."

Max drew in his breath, stunned by this revelation.

Beatrice hugged him, and this time, Max hugged her back, gathering her more tightly after a moment. His mind was reeling as the same past he'd always looked at one way assumed a whole new, different shape.

He had always interpreted his father's distant attitude as disappointment, disapproval. He saw now that was not necessarily the case. "Thank you for telling me all this. It really changes the picture for me."

"You thought nobody cared."

He nodded silently.

She shook her head and gave him a misty-eyed smile.

"Well." She sniffled, bringing her emotions under control. "At least I don't have to worry about you as much anymore, now that you've married Daphne." Beatrice glanced toward the ballroom. "She's probably wondering where you've run off to."

Max spotted his beautiful lady, who was looking over at them with obvious curiosity about what they were discussing. He would have to share this with her later. He sent her a smile from across the room when she gave him a little flirtatious wave. "Yes," he murmured, "it does appear I'm wanted."

The words were casual on the face of it, but the truth of them resonated into the depths of his soul.

"Ah! Go to her." Bea let him go with a doting pat on his cheek. "Your pesky sister's done monopolizing you for now." She turned and waved to Daphne.

"Pesky. I suppose you are that." Max laughed softly, gave his sister a peck on the forehead, and said he'd see her later.

Then he went to rejoin his lovely mate.

Dressed in royal blue, Daphne held out her hand to him as he approached her, the light from her eyes washing over him with an adoring gaze.

He took her outstretched hand, but instead of pulling her closer, he suddenly paused, taking note of the music that was starting.

She let out a wordless exclamation as he suddenly bent and kissed her knuckles with a Continental flourish of a bow. "My lady!" he declared in a formal tone. "As I recall, you have *long* owed me a dance."

A radiant smile burst across her face. He could see the thrill that came over her at his nearness, and he knew so well now that he was loved.

"A debt I will pay gladly, my lord," she declared with equal enthusiasm.

The smiling, ever-watchful ton cleared a path for them as he escorted his lady to the dance floor, her delicate gloved fingers resting on his palm.

His other hand, lightly fisted, was poised behind his back in formal fashion. Her chin was high, her step graceful, the slender curves of her body molded by her flowing gown.

The rest of Society didn't even bother to join them, but stood back and watched as the orchestra introduced a waltz.

In the center of the gleaming dance floor, Daphne curtsied to her partner: Max bowed.

With a twinkle of adoring love in her blue eyes, she rested her dainty right hand on his left shoulder. Max set his left hand on her waist. Staring into her eyes, he stretched out his right hand, opening his palm, much as he had opened his heart.

She ran a small caress across his waiting palm as she joined her hand with his, the wonderful familiarity, the simple homecoming of her touch sending a frisson of passion through his body.

The bright, graceful music washed over them, and they began to dance.

Daphne gazed at him tenderly as the music swept them away, turning and gliding under the twinkling chandeliers; he could only stare into her eyes, until he had lost all awareness of the world watching them. There was only she, the utter joy of his life, his true love.

As he whisked her smoothly around the ballroom in their timeless waltz, he knew they both agreed their dance, at last, had been well worth the wait.

Oh, they make me sick, thought Albert Carew.

At least he now outranked Rotherstone, but somehow, even his newly gained dukedom was cold comfort compared to the irritating happiness on their two faces.

I'm getting out of here.

As he walked out of the ballroom with his nose in the air, as usual, he enjoyed the bowing and scraping that was now his due, and yet, in truth, it was already growing rather stale.

He went home, but a few seconds after he walked into his dimly lit library to pour himself a brandy, he suddenly felt a presence.

He whirled around and spotted the outline of a man sitting idly, with his feet up, on Albert's desk.

"You!"

"Hullo, Your Grace."

Albert's heart instantly began to pound. The stranger had approached him once before only briefly, months ago, at the End of Summer Ball. "H-how did you get in here?"

"Enjoying your new title?"

"What are you doing here?"

"Oh, don't be naïve." The silhouette moved, lean and deadly. The man brought his feet back down onto the floor and rose from the chair.

Albert swallowed hard. "What do you want?"

"Merely your cooperation, as we discussed." A wolfish smile flashed in the darkness.

"I have no idea what you are referring to."

"Don't pretend not to know my meaning, or what I've done for you. It's time to pay the piper, my fine fellow."

Dresden Bloodwell walked out of the shadows.

Albert backed away. His heart was thudding in his chest. "I never asked you to kill my brother!"

"Don't waste my time," the stranger mocked him. "You knew exactly what I intended to do, and as I recall, you uttered not one word of protest. So be quiet. Don't forget, Your Grace, you still have three younger brothers. I'm happy to keep going through the lot of you, until I get to one who will finally cooperate. Now, I suggest that if you wish to keep your miserable life and your nice new dukedom, you sit down, shut up, and do exactly as you're told."

He reached out without warning and clutched him by the throat. Albert whimpered, trying to dislodge the unrelenting hand.

Inches from his face, the killer stared into Albert's eyes. Bloodwell's own were as black as doom, and as deep as a bottomless well.

"You listen to me. I elevated you to this post for a reason. I own you now. And that's the way it is — Your Grace. Forget that at your own cost." With this, he shoved Albert down into the nearby leather club chair and proceeded to explain.

"What do you want from me?" Albert whispered, his whole body shaking.

"It's very simple," Dresden replied as he tugged his sleeve back neatly into place. "You bragged when I first met you that you are an acquaintance of the Regent. It's time for you to strengthen that friendship. Now that you are a duke, you should have no trouble working your way into the Carlton House set . . ."

Outside his door in the Pulteney Hotel, Drake could hear James and Talon engaged in a none-too-friendly conversation with the convict they had gotten out of Newgate.

O'Banyon was his name. Some sort of privateer.

"It's done now," O'Banyon was saying. "The girl has been secured."

"You got her?" Talon asked urgently.

"Aye. It was not difficult."

"So, where is she? You were supposed to bring her here," James said in a tone of indignation.

"Aye, I thought of that," O'Banyon answered with a note of impudence in his rough voice. "But then it dawned on me. Once you gentl'men get the girl, you don't have much need for me, now, do you? I weren't about to take any chance o' you sendin' me back to prison once I served my purpose."

"What have you done with her?" James demanded.

"I told you, she's secured."

"You've brought in help, without our authorization?"

"No worries! Just some of my old mates from my seafarin' days. We're going to do this my way."

"How dare you!"

"Listen to me, old man."

Drake tensed behind the door, wanting to go to James's aid if O'Banyon was threatening him.

"You don't seem to realize that you need me," the cut-throat convict said. "Especially when her father comes back in from the sea

577

to pay her ransom. You may think you're a bad fellow, Eye-Patch, but you've never dealt with the likes o' Captain Fox. Why do you think he had his little girl livin' in seclusion? You steal a pirate's treasure, that is bad enough," O'Banyon warned. "You kidnap his daughter, and there'll be hell to pay. Trust me, I'm the only one who has a clue how to handle her papa, and he's the one who knows where the Alchemist's tomb is."

"So, what do you suggest we do, then, hm?" James inquired, sounding like he was losing patience.

"We wait, mainly. Just like we have to do at sea. It'll be awhile before the message reaches her father, and more time still for the old Sea Fox to get back to England. Not to mention the fact that the Coast Guard will be wantin' to arrest him the moment he sets foot on English soil. In the meantime, I, for one, intend to go enjoy me freedom."

Through the crack in the door, Drake saw Talon grab the grubby O'Banyon by the shirt. "You think you can succeed in double-crossing us?"

"Take your hands off me, Eye-Patch. To get to the Alchemist's treasure, you need Captain Fox; and to bring in Captain Fox, you need his pretty daughter. And to get your hands on the girl, you need me, seein' as I'm the only one who knows where the lovely lass is stowed at the moment."

James nodded to Talon.

He, in turn, released O'Banyon angrily.

"I wouldn't agitate Mr. Talon if I were you, O'Banyon. He's killed men for much less, I can assure you."

"Well, so have I, old fellow. Believe me. So have I."

"At least tell me that Miss Fox is safe. She is of no worth as a hostage if she's dead."

"Aye, safe enough. Young Miss Kate ain't too comfortable, I warrant, but she ain't in any danger."

"You trust whoever's holding her, then?"

O'Banyon grinned. "Frankly, gov, I don't trust nobody."

The girl sat huddled and shivering on a cold stone floor, sightless behind the black blindfold tied around her head. Her hands were also tied, her wrists bound before her, resting on her bent knees.

Kate refused to cry, forcing herself to focus her available senses on whatever she could glean. Heavy tromping footfalls paced above her. Rough voices, mainly male. Busy warehouse. People shuffling boxes or crates around upstairs. What were they? Not ordinary merchants.

Smugglers?

The hint of salt that hung on the cold air took her memory back to ages and ages ago, the rocking masts against the azure sky. Her father's bold grin as he made a little bo'sun out of her, telling her the orders to shout to the crew in her high-pitched, child's voice. *Trim the topsail, you lazy buggers! Steady as she goes!*

Suddenly, she heard a door creak up at the top of the wooden stairs above the clammy cellar where her captors had deposited her. Someone was coming. Kate sat very still, listening for all she was worth.

She had heard them talking before, but now their voices sounded unexpectedly agitated.

"I don't give a damn what O'Banyon said! If the duke's on his way home, that changes everything!"

"What are we goin' to do?"

"I don't know, but we got to get rid of her before Warrington gets back!"

"What do you mean, get rid of her? Do we kill her? Let her go?"

Kate drew in her breath, listening keenly. *Quite a choice.* She could barely hear above the pounding of her heart.

There was a silence.

"I don't know," one of the smugglers answered. He seemed to be the one in charge. "We could tell O'Banyon the lass got away."

"But the money!"

"Who would you rather cross, O'Banyon or the Beast?"

Beast? she thought in rising panic.

"Well, that's no contest."

"Tell me about it!"

"I wish we'd had more warning that His Grace was comin' home."

"He was bound to come eventually. He owns this bloody place for miles around."

"What are we goin' to do with her once he gets here? That oversized devil's already goin' to roast us alive for the shipwreck last month. If he hears that now we been party to a kidnappin' . . ."

"Aye," the first said grimly. "Well . . . maybe there's a way we can kill two birds with one stone."

"What do you mean?"

"If O'Banyon wants the lass, let *him* deal with the Duke of Warrington."

"You mean . . . hand the girl over to the Beast?"

"Aye! Like a little present. You know, a little welcome-home package from us and the boys, eh?"

"Aye, that's brilliant! Then maybe he won't bash our heads in quite so much!"

"That's what I'm sayin'! She's pretty enough for 'im. You know how he is with the ladies. A welcome-home gift like her ought to take some of the hammer out of his wrath."

"Right, and playin' with her, at least that'll keep him preoccupied for a night or two while we wrap up our business."

"It might work."

"Ye hear that, girlie? Handful o' trouble,

you are," the leader said, no doubt still swollen and sore in the groin where she had kicked him upon her arrival. "See how far it gets you with the Beast! You try givin' him your sass, and you're goin' to wish you was back down 'ere in this cellar."

"Aw, don't cry, lass," the other mocked her. "There's worse things than becomin' the Beast's concubine. 'Course, I can't think of any right now . . ."

Her head reeled as the smugglers' coarse laughter echoed all around her in the darkness. Her whole body was shivering with dread.

I'm not afraid, Kate thought over and over again. *I'm not afraid . . .*

The employees of Thorndike Press hope you have enjoyed this Large Print book. All our Thorndike, Wheeler, and Kennebec Large Print titles are designed for easy reading, and all our books are made to last. Other Thorndike Press Large Print books are available at your library, through selected bookstores, or directly from us.

For information about titles, please call:

(800) 223-1244

or visit our Web site at:

http://gale.cengage.com/thorndike

To share your comments, please write:

Publisher
Thorndike Press
295 Kennedy Memorial Drive
Waterville, ME 04901